Jill Mansell worked for many years at the Burden
Neurological Hospital, Bristol, and now writes full-
time. Amongst her many *Sunday Times* bestsellers
are NADIA KNOWS BEST, FALLING FOR YOU,
THE ONE YOU REALLY WANT and MAKING
YOUR MIND UP; a full list of her books appears
on page ii.

Also by Jill Mansell and available from Headline Review

Thinking Of You
Making Your Mind Up
The One You Really Want
Falling For You
Nadia Knows Best
Good At Games
Millie's Fling
Head Over Heels
Miranda's Big Mistake
Mixed Doubles
Perfect Timing
Fast Friends
Solo
Kiss
Sheer Mischief
Open House
Two's Company

Jill Mansell

staying at
daisy's

headline
review

First published in 2002 by
HEADLINE PUBLISHING GROUP

First published in paperback in 2002 by
HEADLINE PUBLISHING GROUP

This edition published in paperback in 2007
by HEADLINE REVIEW
An imprint of HEADLINE PUBLISHING GROUP

6

ISBN 978 0 7472 6487 3 (A format)
ISBN 978 0 7553 3260 1 (B format)

Typeset in Times by Palimpsest Book Production Limited,
Grangemouth, Stirlingshire

Printed and bound in the UK by
CPI Mackays, Chatham ME5 8TD

Headline's policy is to use papers that are natural, renewable and
recyclable products and made from wood grown in
sustainable forests. The logging and manufacturing processes
are expected to conform to the environmental
regulations of the country of origin.

HEADLINE PUBLISHING GROUP
A division of Hachette Livre UK Ltd
338 Euston Road
LONDON NW1 3BH

www.reviewbooks.co.uk
www.hodderheadline.com

For Mum and Dad
With all my love

Huge and grateful thanks to Marie-Louise Pecorelli, marketing manager of the fabulous Manor House hotel at Castle Combe, Wilts, for all her help in explaining to me how a hotel is run. Needless to say, the fictional characters in this novel aren't nearly so efficient . . .

Chapter 1

In the absence of a gavel, Hector MacLean seized a heavy glass ashtray and rattled it against the mahogany-topped bar.

'Ladies and gentlemen, your attention please. Quiet at the back there, you Aussie riffraff. I feel the need to propose a toast. Over here, darling, over here.' Beckoning Daisy towards him, he slung an arm round her waist. 'And now would you all raise your glasses . . . to my beautiful daughter.'

'To your beautiful daughter,' chorused everyone in the room, causing Daisy to roll her eyes.

Honestly, did he have to be quite so embarrassing?

'You missed a bit out,' she told him. 'What you actually meant to say was "To my beautiful, intelligent and staggeringly hard-working daughter, without whom this hotel would crumble and go out of business within a week."'

'All that. Absolutely. Goes without saying.' Hector gestured expansively with his tumbler of Glenmorangie. 'Everyone here already knows that. Just as they know you're also stubborn, bossy and incredibly lacking in modesty. But I'm still proud of you. Considering all you ever did at school was smoke and play truant, and your mother and I never thought you'd amount to anything, you've turned out pretty well. And now, for my next toast, I'd like you all to raise your glasses once more to dear old Dennis.'

1

'Dear old Dennis,' they all bellowed back at him, even those guests who hadn't the foggiest idea who Dennis was. That was the thing about Hector MacLean, his enthusiasm and *joie de vivre* was infectious.

As usual, Daisy marvelled, and in no time at all, a quiet gathering for a few drinks had turned into an impromptu, rip-roaring party. It wouldn't be long now before her father called for his accordion and got the dancing underway. The fact that they were all supposed to be taking advantage of these few relatively peaceful days – the Christmas guests having departed and the New Year's Eve ones yet to arrive – was of no consequence to Hector. The fact that it was December the twenty-eighth was, as far as he was concerned, a good enough reason to celebrate. Why take it easy when you could be having fun?

Daisy, glad that her spritzer was nine-tenths soda water, eased herself onto a bar stool while her father greeted a couple of late arrivals as though they were his dearest friends.

'At last! How marvellous! Listen, we're in danger of having a bit of a knees-up – either of you two handy with a piano?'

One of the Australians materialised at Daisy's side as she was busily lining her empty stomach with cashews and roasted almonds. Not ideal, but better than nothing.

'Your dad's a character. When this place was recommended to us, we thought Jeez, some old country house hotel full of la-di-da tweedy women and pompous old colonel types, *no way*. But our friends promised us it wasn't like that here, and they were right. This place is great.'

'You may change your mind,' said Daisy, 'when my father gets his bagpipes out.'

'You're kidding!' The Australian's face lit up. 'He actually plays the bagpipes?'

'No. He just thinks he can. If you know what's good for you,' Daisy whispered, 'you'll persuade him to stick with the accordion.'

He laughed, even though she hadn't been joking.

'And who's this other guy we just drank to, dear old Dennis? Is he someone else who works here?'

'Ah well. Dennis is our benefactor. Without him,' Daisy explained, 'we wouldn't have this hotel.'

'You mean he owns it?'

Behind the bar, Rocky casually flipped a tumbler into the air and caught it. No one was currently drinking cocktails but he did it anyway. Grinning at Daisy, he began to whistle a catchy tune.

'You probably know Dennis,' Daisy told the Australian. Tilting her head in Rocky's direction she added, 'If you recognise that song, you definitely know him.'

Standing next to the Australian, Tara Donovan joined in the whistling. The Australian frowned. 'It's that kid's thing, yeah? Dennis the Dashing Dachshund? I'm sorry, you've lost me.'

Unable to help themselves – they'd started so they'd finish – Rocky and Tara whistled and jiggled their way through to the end of the song.

'My father may not have been blessed with many brilliant ideas in his lifetime,' Daisy said fondly, 'but twenty-five years ago he had an excellent one. He came up with Dennis.'

'You're kidding! Are you serious? That's incredible!' The Australian slapped his knee in delight. 'I used to buy those books for my kids.'

Rocky was well away now, tap-dancing behind the bar and singing under his breath, 'My name is Den-nis, the dashing dachshund', because Dennis danced like Fred Astaire and Rocky liked to show off the fact that he had been to stage school.

Actually, Daisy amended, he just liked to show off. Then again, it was why she had hired him in the first place.

'Dad used to make up stories for me when I was small,' Daisy told the enthralled Australian, 'about this effeminate dachshund. But I didn't know what he looked like so Dad started drawing pictures of him. I took the pictures into school, told the stories to my friends and the next thing we knew, all the mothers were asking where they could get hold of these Dennis books their kids kept pestering them for. So Dad sent his stories off to a publisher and they snapped them up. Then a TV company got involved and Dennis fever took off – soft toys, games, pyjamas, the whole merchandising malarkey. All from one dear little idea. Dad sold the rights five years ago and bought this place,' Daisy concluded. 'So you see, we owe everything to Dennis.'

'I used to have a Dennis the Dachshund duvet cover,' Rocky put in cheerfully. 'And Dennis slippers with ears on them that waggled when you walked.'

'I had Dennis everything.' Daisy groaned and pulled a face. 'By the time I was nine it was embarrassing. All I cared about then was Adam Ant.'

One of the late arrivals was being persuaded to go and fetch his harmonica; he might not be able to play the piano but, Hector assured him, a mouth organ would do just as well.

'I love this place,' exclaimed the Australian. 'I must go and talk to your dad.'

'Are you all right?' Rocky leaned across the bar and lowered his voice as the man moved away. 'You look a bit . . . knackered.'

'Me? I'm fine!' Daisy realised he'd caught her off guard for a moment. What was the difference between putting on a brave front and telling a great big bare-faced lie? 'Of course I'm fine, why wouldn't I be?'

4

Rocky shrugged, reached for the silver tongs and lobbed a couple of ice cubes into a tumbler.

'Thought you might be missing Steven. When's he back?'

'New Year's Eve.' Scooping up another handful of nuts, Daisy gave him a bright smile. Rocky wasn't wild about Steven, she knew that, and he might even have an inkling about the events of the previous week, but there was no way in the world she was going to blurt out the whole story. She hadn't told a soul. Not Tara, not even her own father. For now, she just had to carry on as if nothing was wrong.

'Because if you're feeling a bit lonely, I know just the thing to cheer you up.' Rocky waggled a playful eyebrow as he said it, flashing her his naughtiest Robbie Williams smirk. 'I'm young, single and available. Not to mention totally irresistible.'

Rocky was twenty-three, with a wicked smile and a peroxide crop. His favourite band was Oasis, which meant she could never fancy him in a million years.

'It's really kind of you to offer.' Solemnly, Daisy patted his hand. 'But you're five years younger than me. You think Liam Gallagher's a cool bloke.' She frowned, pretending to think for a moment. 'Oh yes, I knew there was something else. And I'm married.'

'You don't know what you're missing. I'm at my sexual peak.'

'I'm still married.' God help me.

Rocky said, 'Is that all that's stopping you? I'm sure we can sort something out.' Privately, he didn't think much of marriage if what Daisy and Steven shared was a shining example. Daisy might be pretending everything was great, but you only had to see the two of them together to guess there were problems. The chief one being the fact that Steven Standish was a prize prat.

'What are you two talking about?' Tara shimmied up to them

5

in search of more wine. Drinking and partying was so much more fun than being a chambermaid, she couldn't imagine why she wasn't allowed to do it for a living. She'd make such a great It girl, if only she could have been christened Tinker Tonker-Parkinson. Fate was truly unfair.

'Sex,' Daisy announced with a wink. 'And the fact that poor old Rocky here isn't getting any.'

'I didn't say that. I didn't say I wasn't getting any,' protested Rocky, who wasn't. 'I just offered Daisy the opportunity of a lifetime and she's *pretending* not to be interested, going all prim on me, making out she doesn't want to upset her husband.'

'We've got a visitor.' Tara nudged Daisy, drawing her attention to the police car moving slowly up the drive. Turning back to Rocky she said, 'Opportunity of a lifetime? *You?* Oh dear, what a shame, now you'll have to be arrested. The big scary policeman's going to charge you with deception and fraud.'

'On the other hand,' Rocky jeered, 'they could be here to arrest you for thinking you're funny when you're not.'

This was typical of the way Rocky and Tara carried on.

'They can't have come to complain about Dad's bagpipes.' Daisy was indignant. 'He hasn't even got them out yet.'

The panda car drew to a halt at the top of the drive. Through the French windows they watched Barry Foster, their local policeman, haul himself out and mutter a few words into his walkie-talkie. As he slammed the driver's door shut and moved towards the entrance to the hotel, Daisy slid off her high stool. 'I just hope he hasn't come to arrest any of our guests.'

'Unless it's that one.' Tara grimaced in the direction of the Geordie who only thought he could play the mouth organ.

'Oh well, obviously,' said Daisy with a grin. 'He's welcome to take Mr Harmonica.'

*   *   *

In Daisy's office, Barry Foster pulled out a handkerchief and surreptitiously wiped his perspiring palms. Being the bearer of bad news was the thing he hated most about his job.

The green and gold wallpapered walls of the office appeared to be moving in and out. Daisy blinked slowly in an effort to get them to stay still.

'Look, it must be some kind of mistake.' She paused, licking dry lips. 'Steven isn't even *in* Bristol. He's up in Glasgow, visiting his grandfather. He's not due back until New Year's Eve.'

Barry gave her a sympathetic look. He knew and liked Daisy. Knew Steven too.

'I'm sorry, love. It was Steven's car. His driving licence was in his wallet . . . would you like a glass of water?'

'No thanks.' Daisy shook her head, aware of her heart pounding in her chest. The accident had happened on Siston Common, according to Barry. Less than ten miles away. Steven's BMW had skidded on a patch of ice and smashed into a wall. But Barry was still looking uncomfortable, as if there was something else he hadn't quite plucked up the courage to tell her yet.

Unless . . .

'Oh God.' Daisy swallowed hard. 'Is he dead?'

'No, no,' Barry said hurriedly. 'No, love, he's not dead. It's serious, like I said. Condition critical. But he's still alive, I promise you that.'

Critical. With a head injury. Deeply unconscious.

'So why are you . . . ?' Nodding at his hands, Daisy mimicked the agitated handkerchief-crushing movements. None of this made sense; Steven had phoned her last night from Glasgow and moaned about the weather up there. He had talked about buying tickets to see Glasgow Rangers play at home tomorrow. He was arranging for a plumber to come to his grandfather's house to fix the broken thermostat on the boiler.

And no, he hadn't told his grandfather about the other thing. Poor old fellow, he was eighty-three, didn't he already have enough to cope with?

'Daisy, I'm really sorry. Steven wasn't alone in the car when it crashed.'

'What?' For a split second she thought he meant Steven had had his grandfather with him.

But no, of course he hadn't meant that. The reason for the hand-wringing abruptly became clear, zooming into focus like a Nikon.

'Go on,' Daisy prompted. It was like the end of a crime thriller, suddenly realising who the murderer was.

'He . . . um . . . had a girl with him.' Barry clearly wasn't happy; in fact, he was the one who looked as if he could do with a stiff drink.

Daisy frowned. 'You mean a girlfriend-type girl?'

'Ah, well . . . looks that way, yes.'

'And is she unconscious too?'

'No. No, love. She was lucky. Escaped with minor injuries.'

Is this really happening? *To me?*

Daisy discovered she'd been twirling a long strand of hair round her index finger so tightly the end of her finger had gone blue. Beyond the closed office door she heard a burst of laughter drifting through from the bar, and the sound of an accordion being revved up.

She really should tell Hector what was going on, but it was all so complicated. How could she explain something like this when she was still so confused herself?

'They're having a party.' Daisy gestured – fairly unnecessarily – in the direction of the bar. 'I don't want to spoil it for everyone else. My car's parked behind the hotel.'

'You don't want to drive, love.' Barry's chins wobbled as he shook his head. 'I can take you to the hospital.'

'No need. I'm OK.' Daisy wondered if she should be crying. The walls of the office had stopped going in and out, which was something to be grateful for. Somewhat shakily, she stood up. 'I'll be fine.'

Chapter 2

Fifteen minutes down the motorway was all it took to reach Frenchay Hospital on the outskirts of Bristol. For the first time in years Daisy drove without music blasting from the stereo to sing along to. Nor, when she parked the car in the tree-lined avenue next to the wards, did she reach automatically into her bag to re-do her lipstick in the rear-view mirror.

It was three forty-five. The sky was darkening from ash-grey to charcoal and lights were flickering on in the various buildings that made up the hospital. Daisy followed a sign pointing the way to the intensive care unit. Staff and visitors were walking around as if nothing had happened. A small girl let out a shriek of outrage as she dropped her bag of Jellytots on the path outside the WRVS shop.

How *could* Steven have been seeing someone else?

The doctor was incredibly kind. He explained the functions of the various types of machinery that surrounded Steven's bed. This was the ventilator, which was taking care of his breathing. This smaller one was the ECG machine, monitoring his heartbeat. That clip on his finger was a pulse oximeter, the intravenous line enabled them to administer the various medications he needed and the drip was supplying him with fluids.

The intensive care unit was ultra-bright. Everything was white apart from the staff uniforms, which were pale blue. Feeling ludicrously out of place in her red velvet shirt, black leather skirt and black patent high heels, Daisy tried hard to concentrate on what the doctor was telling her. She felt it was vital to understand everything he said, as if this were an A level she absolutely mustn't fail.

Except it appeared to be an A level in a language she'd never learned. She was able to hear the words but they were making no sense. Apart from the bit about Steven's condition being critical.

The doctor's beeper went off.

'Here, why don't you sit down.' Pulling a moulded plastic chair up to the bed, the doctor steered her towards it. 'Hold his hand. Talk to him. You can stay as long as you like. I'll be back later, OK?'

He shot off to deal with the next crisis, leaving Daisy alone with Steven. Well, not really alone. Fifteen feet away, a couple of nurses were keeping a discreet eye on her.

She sat down on the unforgiving plastic chair and held Steven's hand, as instructed.

He was looking ridiculously healthy. A narrow white sheet covered his groin, otherwise he was naked. Tanned and muscular and obviously a fit chap, proud of his physique and deservedly so. All those hours in the gym had paid off. This was the body of a man in peak condition. He didn't look injured at all.

Daisy blinked, pulled herself together. What was it she was meant to be doing now? Oh yes, talking to him.

But what was she supposed to say? Not 'You lying cheating fucking *bastard*', that was for sure. Oh no, that definitely wasn't the kind of thing the doctor would have had in mind.

After twenty minutes Daisy rose to leave.

'You go and wait in the relatives' room,' urged the kindly

nurse who was checking Steven's blood pressure, 'and I'll bring you a nice cup of tea.'

Daisy wondered why people always said that. It might be a truly horrible cup of tea but they'd still call it *nice*.

'It's OK, I'm fine. Just going outside for a bit, for some fresh air.'

'Right, love, you do that. Is there anyone else you'd like us to contact?'

'No thanks.' Smiling briefly, to make up for her uncharitable thought about the tea, Daisy indicated her bag. 'I've got my phone with me. I'll go and do that now.'

In the echoey sloping corridor outside the entrance to the ward, she had to leap out of the way as a porter whizzed passed with a boy in a wheelchair. A girl in jeans and a navy Puffa jacket was studying the noticeboard intently. The fluorescent lights flickered overhead, accentuating her pallor. Daisy hesitated, struck by the fact that the girl had glanced at her then abruptly, almost guiltily, turned away.

Taking her phone out of her bag, Daisy punched out a series of numbers and said, 'Hi, it's me. I'm leaving the hospital now. I'll be home by five.'

Less than a minute after pushing through the doors marked EXIT, Daisy slid back into the corridor. The girl in the Puffa was no longer loitering by the noticeboard.

Peering through the glass porthole of the outer entrance to the intensive care unit, Daisy saw her standing by the second door, the one that led into the ward itself.

She was being spoken to by the kindly nurse, and sobbing as if her heart would break.

Feeling absurdly jealous, Daisy realised that the nurse was being just as nice to Puffa girl as she'd been to her, only instead of offering a nice cup of tea she was handing her a tissue.

There was a bandage, Daisy now saw, round the Puffa girl's left wrist.

Leaning against the outer door so that it opened just a fraction, Daisy heard the nurse saying in a warm, soothing voice, 'I'm so sorry, love, but you can't go in. It's relatives only.'

The girl was distraught. If she hadn't been crying, she'd be pretty, Daisy automatically noted. Then again – and maybe it was inappropriate under the circumstances, but she still couldn't help thinking it – the girl might be pretty, but not as pretty as *her*.

Daisy eased the pressure on the door, allowing it to close once more. Now she really did need some fresh air. It was also about time she actually rang Hector, rather than just pretending to ring Hector. He'd be wondering where she'd got to by now.

Steven's condition deteriorated during the night. By eleven o'clock the next morning, dry-mouthed and light-headed from lack of sleep, Daisy found herself being led from the unit and ushered into the bad news office. You could tell it was the bad news office, it contained comfortable chairs.

The consultant, who was in his fifties and wearing a crumpled checked shirt under his immaculate white coat, said, 'Mrs Standish, I'm sorry. We've carried out the second set of tests and they confirm what we feared. Your husband sustained an extremely severe head injury. There are no signs of brain function.'

Oh God.

Oh God.

'Right.' Daisy nodded and gazed out of the window. It was raining hard outside. 'So, basically, he's already dead.'

'I'm afraid so.'

There was a box of tissues on the desk in front of her. For the tears, of course. Daisy, embarrassed by her inability to cry, said, 'Well, thank you for everything you've done.'

The consultant cleared his throat. 'There is one other thing I'd like to discuss with you, as Steven's next of kin. The opportunity to allow others the chance of life.' He rested his long fingers on a form and slid it across the desk towards her. 'I don't know if you and your husband ever discussed the issue of organ donation, but in our experience it can be of great comfort to the family in years to come, knowing that—'

'You want to use Steven's organs for transplant?' Astonished, Daisy's eyebrows shot up. 'What, even though he has cancer? Wouldn't that be risky for whoever got them?'

The consultant frowned. 'Cancer? I'm sorry, I'm not with you.'

'His cancer. I assumed it was all in there.' Daisy nodded at the hospital notes, lying open on the desk. 'He said he'd seen one of the doctors here . . . well, I thought it was this hospital. Unless he went private.'

The consultant's frown deepened. 'Just give me a couple of minutes.'

Daisy waited alone in the bad news room and watched the rain rattling against the windows. Since she couldn't begin to gather her thoughts, she concentrated instead on counting the raindrops as they slid down the glass.

The consultant duly returned several minutes later.

'I've spoken to Steven's GP. She hasn't seen your husband for over two years, and he couldn't be referred to a hospital – any hospital – without a GP referral. I think we can safely assume there's been some kind of misunderstanding here,' he concluded gently. 'Your husband doesn't have cancer.'

Daisy found the nurse she was looking for, stacking away metal kidney dishes in the sluice room.

'The consultant's told me about Steven,' Daisy announced, and the kindly nurse put down the dishes at once.

'Oh, my dear, I'm so sorry. Would you like me to make you a nice cup of tea?'

'No thanks.'

'And you're being so brave.'

Privately, Daisy thought it more likely that the nurses on the unit thought she was downright weird.

'I wanted to ask you about the girl who was here yesterday afternoon. The one who was in the car with Steven when he had the accident.'

The nurse flushed slightly. Which confirmed it.

'The thing is,' Daisy went on, 'I heard you telling her she couldn't see him, because she wasn't a relative. But under the circumstances . . . well, it wouldn't hurt, would it? You could let her in for a few minutes while I stay out of the way.'

The nurse, her fair skin the colour of strawberry Angel Delight, said, 'She isn't here, love. I told her to go home.'

Daisy gave her a long look. 'But I bet she gave you her phone number.'

From the expression on the nurse's face, it was clear that the girl had. Well, it was only natural.

'Ring her up,' said Daisy. 'I don't know who she is, and I don't want to meet her. But if she's Steven's girlfriend, at least she deserves the chance to say goodbye.'

Chapter 3

One Year Later

'Daisy, can you be around this afternoon? The Cross-Dressers are arriving at four to discuss the menus for the wedding reception.'

Tara Donovan, who worked as a chambermaid at the hotel, suppressed a smile. Her own parents were dead now, but her father had been the quiet, pipe and slippers type. It must be fun to have someone like Hector as a dad.

Daisy gave her father a 'behave yourself' look. His loud voice and stupendous lack of tact were going to get him into big trouble one day.

'Fine, but you have to stop calling them that.'

'Darling, I know, but they deserve it. These people are starting to get on my nerves,' Hector declared. 'Why can't they just decide on a menu and stick with the bloody thing? For the life of me I can't imagine why anyone would want to invite a vegan to a wedding in the first place.'

This time Tara and Daisy exchanged glances, and Daisy heaved a sigh. Discretion wasn't Hector's forte. Luckily there were no guests currently within earshot. Reaching across the

16

reception desk for her pile of unopened mail, Daisy said, 'Dad, I'll deal with them. We'll charge double for vegans. And they aren't the Cross-Dressers or the Cross-Pollinators *or* the Hot Cross Buns, OK? They're the Cross-Calverts and you're jolly well going to be nice to them.'

Tara, who was vacuuming the staircase, promptly dropped her nozzle.

'Who?' Her heart thumping, she switched off the machine and anchored it with her foot before it could tumble down the stairs and kill someone. Maybe she'd misheard. 'What did you say their name was?'

'Mr and Mrs Cross-Your-Heart-Bra,' Hector replied gravely. 'And she needs a good-sized one, I can tell you. Sturdy straps, reinforced elastic, all that palaver.' Hector wasn't much of a one for political correctness either.

'My father, the dinosaur.' Daisy rolled her eyes. 'Funny how he's never remarried.'

Tara tried again. 'Did you say Cross-Calvert?'

'That's right.' Daisy was nodding absently, her attention on the letter she had just opened.

'Dominic Cross-Calvert?' This time she heard her voice as if the words hadn't come from her own mouth.

'Dominic, that's it, that's the fellow.' Intrigued, Hector straightened up. 'Know him, do you?'

'I do.' Idiotically, Tara realised that she sounded as if she were making her wedding vows. That was what you said, wasn't it, when you promised to cherish your husband for richer or poorer, in sickness and in health, until death did you part? Or was it 'I will'? Never having made that particular pledge, she wasn't actually sure. Men thought she was pretty and a great laugh, and they were especially fond of her oversized chest, but none of them had ever offered to marry her.

'Ha! Look at your face,' Hector exclaimed. 'He's one of your exes, isn't he? Some long-lost soul from your sordid past. Come on then, you can tell us. Who dumped who?'

As loftily as she could manage, Tara announced, 'I do not have a sordid past.' Which was, obviously, a big lie. Worse still, Hector knew it.

'Which means he dumped you.' Hector was triumphant. 'My darling, I'm riveted. Right, that's it, put that silly vacuum cleaner away and come and tell us all about it.'

She wavered. 'I'm supposed to finish the stairs.'

This was both the good and the bad thing about Hector. His irreverent approach to owning and running a hotel meant he was wonderful to work for. On the other hand, the job still had to be done. On the *other* other hand, she *was* longing to find out more about Dominic.

Hector gestured dismissively at the staircase. 'Bugger the cleaning, let's have a drink! Daisy, are you coming to hear this?'

Daisy was engrossed in the contents of her letter. She wasn't listening. Honestly, and she called herself a friend.

Tara said, 'When's he getting married?'

'Two weeks' time. January the tenth. Ninety-six guests, three wheat allergies, two lactose intolerants, seventeen vegetarians, and,' Hector's lip curled in disgust, 'a vegan.'

'And this girl he's . . . um, marrying?' Tara did her level best to sound casual.

Hector, not fooled for a moment, spoilt it all by throwing back his head and roaring with laughter. 'Her name's Annabel. Big girl, like I said. You and Daisy together could squeeze into her wedding dress.'

Tara was well enough acquainted with Hector's tendency towards exaggeration to guess that this meant Annabel was probably a curvy size fourteen. A *voluptuous* size fourteen.

'Yes, but is she pretty?' Not that she could imagine for a moment Dominic marrying someone who wasn't. Far too infra dig.

Hector clapped an arm round Tara's shoulders as he led her through to the bar. 'My darling, she's not a patch on you.'

'Walking in a winter wonderland,' went the song in Daisy's head as she made her way down the hotel's drive. It had been playing on the radio when she'd woken up this morning and had stuck in her mind ever since, which was no hardship because it was a song she loved, so Christmassy and jaunty it couldn't fail to lift the spirits. If there could have been real snow to go with it, that would have made it better still, but you couldn't have everything. And frost was beautiful too, Daisy thought loyally. Particularly when the sun was out, as it was now, and everything sparkled like one of those glittery snowstorm things you picked up and shook.

Even without snow, the hotel was looking gorgeous. Having reached the end of the drive, Daisy hopped over the honey-coloured Cotswold stone wall to her right and took the short cut through to the churchyard. There was nobody else about as she headed for Steven's grave.

Mervyn Tucker, whose wife was buried next to Steven, had left behind the aluminium bucket he used to water the plants on her plot. Borrowing it, Daisy sat down and pulled the envelope from the depths of her dark blue velvet coat. It wasn't the most comfortable of buckets, but she preferred to sit. It seemed friendlier, somehow.

'Hi, it's me. I've got some news for you.' As she spoke, it occurred to Daisy that anyone watching her now would think she'd gone mad. Perched on an upended tin bucket reading a letter to a pile of earth. Still, what did it matter? She was alone in the churchyard. Nobody could see or hear her. And this was a letter Steven should know about.

Blowing on her fingers to defrost them, her breath visible in the icy air, Daisy unfolded the first of the two sheets of paper contained in the envelope.

'Right, well. This letter arrived today, from someone called Barney. You gave him one of your kidneys and the operation was a complete success. Imagine that! He's twenty-five years old and you saved his life. Here, I'll read it to you. It starts with "Dear Friend", because he doesn't know my name. He had to give this letter to his transplant co-ordinator and she's forwarded it to me – they have to do it this way, apparently, for security reasons. Anyway, he says: "Dear Friend, I hope you don't mind me writing to you. I can't imagine how difficult it must have been, to make the decision you did at such a terrible time. But I so wanted to thank you for giving me a new life. Any words I choose will be inadequate – thank you has to be the understatement of the year. What else can I say? You are a wonderful person – I'm sure your husband was too – and I just hope that reading this letter will help in some small way as you begin to come to terms with your bereavement. You truly deserve to be happy again. I will always be grateful to you. If you feel able to write back, via my co-ordinator, I would love to hear from you. If not, I will of course understand. Thank you again, and my very best wishes, Barney."'

Silence.

Having finished reading aloud, Daisy brushed a strand of hair from her eyes and rested her hand on Steven's white marble gravestone.

'There, that's it. Isn't that a fantastic letter? One year ago today, you died and gave Barney his life back. You finally did

something decent. And he sounds so sweet, don't you think? I'll definitely have to write back and thank him. I wonder how long it took him to think of what to say – oh, and he's got nice handwriting too. Black ink on good quality cream paper, and no spelling mistakes. I'm so glad he didn't do it on a word processor, that wouldn't have been the same at all, I never—'

Daisy abruptly broke off, sensing movement at the periphery of her vision. Someone in a bright red jacket was standing by the lych gate, over to her left. Realising that she'd been spotted, but keen nevertheless not to be thought of as a complete nutcase, Daisy stayed where she was and kept quiet.

The raised metal rim round the base of the bucket was starting to dig into her bottom. She resisted the urge to wriggle in case she toppled off it.

Finally, because the person beside the lych gate wasn't moving, Daisy turned her head and gazed directly at them. When she realised who it was, she nearly toppled off her bucket anyway.

Then again, it was the anniversary of Steven's death. Maybe she shouldn't be that surprised.

Recovering rapidly, Daisy called out, 'It's OK, you can come over.'

Puffa jacket – only this time she wasn't wearing a Puffa – hesitated, then began to thread her way between the gravestones. The frosted grass crunched beneath her flat leather boots. She wore a scarlet fleece, white jeans, a bright green woolly scarf and blue knitted gloves. In her arms she carried a small cellophane-wrapped bunch of white roses.

Warily approaching Daisy, she said, 'Look, sorry about this. I could go away and come back later, when—'

'Don't worry, I've pretty much finished here anyway. You can have my seat if you like.' Easing her bottom off the bucket

– ouch – Daisy stood up and gestured for the girl to take her place. Deeply curious, she smiled briefly and said, 'I recognise you from the hospital. I'm Daisy.'

'I know.' The girl's nose and cheeks were pink with cold, and she was looking uncomfortable. Ha, thought Daisy, wait until you try sitting on that bucket.

'My name's Mel,' she said at last.

Daisy wondered whether they should be shaking hands, but hers were warming up nicely inside her coat pockets. Besides, the girl didn't look as if she much wanted to.

'OK, look, I suppose this could count as one of those tricky social situations, but it really doesn't have to be.' Now that the girl was here, Daisy was curious to know more about her. 'I'm sure Steven told you our marriage was pretty much on the rocks. Well, pretty much doesn't come into it, to be honest. Absolutely on the rocks, more like.' She was doing her best to be friendly, but it didn't seem to be having much effect.

'I know that.' Mel began unwrapping the stiff, crackling cellophane from the bunch of roses. 'He wanted a divorce and you refused.'

Confused, Daisy stared at the girl's bent head.

'What?'

'He wanted to leave you,' Mel repeated. 'But you wouldn't let him go.'

'Oh no, I'm sorry, but that is wrong. Wrong, wrong, *wrong*.' Abruptly, Daisy discovered that Steven still possessed the ability to astound her. 'I was desperate for a divorce! I told him it was all over between us the week before Christmas. That was when he told me he had cancer.'

'*Cancer?*' It was Mel's turn to look stunned. 'Oh God, I didn't know he had cancer!'

'Yes, well. He didn't. He was lying. It was his way of

blackmailing me into staying with him.' Daisy forced herself to stay calm. 'And do you know what? I fell for it. I thought I couldn't abandon him to cope with something like that on his own.' She paused, remembering the moment in the bad news office. 'Except it wasn't even true.'

'I don't believe you.' Mel was winter-white, her hands trembling. 'He wouldn't do that. You're making it up.'

'Trust me. If I was going to make up a story like that, I'd have come up with something more original,' Daisy shot back. 'It's such a cliché! Remember *EastEnders*, Angie doing it to Dirty Den? You see, that was the thing about Steven. He was a con artist. He told me that his only chance of recovery was some new form of treatment in America. He said it cost twenty thousand pounds and asked me to lend him the money – which, basically, meant *give* him the money, because Steven didn't have any left of his own. Who knows what he planned to do with it,' Daisy concluded with a shrug. 'Run off to America with you, probably. And come back six months later, miraculously cured.'

Was she being cruel, telling Mel this? More to the point, did Mel believe her now?

The creamy-white roses lay across the grave, unwrapped and untouched.

Mel said slowly, 'I don't know what to think any more.' There were tears in her grey eyes.

'Oh please, I'm sorry, I didn't mean to upset you,' Daisy blurted out. 'But you have to know what Steven was really like. I hadn't any idea he was having an affair, but our marriage was over anyway.'

'What I don't understand,' Mel said slowly, 'is why he would lie to me. We loved each other. We wanted to be together more than anything. If you were happy to get a divorce, why would he want to stay with you?'

Daisy, who had long ago figured this one out, simply gestured over the churchyard wall. In the valley, with the river snaking around the perimeter of the landscaped gardens, the hotel nestled seductively, bathed in winter sunlight, and looking as if it had been liberally dusted with castor sugar. The twenty-foot high Norwegian spruce by the entrance was garlanded with silver lights. The Manor House itself, parts of which dated back to the fifteenth century, was like something out of a Ralph Lauren ad. The other week a reviewer in one of the Sunday papers had hailed it as one of the most glorious hotels in Britain. He'd also mentioned that it was owned by one of the most flamboyant characters in the business and had gone on to describe Hector as Basil Fawlty with attitude, which would probably put off zillions of potential clients, but you couldn't win them all.

'Look at it,' Daisy said simply. 'This is why Steven wanted to stay with me. He enjoyed the lifestyle too much.' She didn't add that Steven had never been much of a one for slumming it. Or for working his fingers to the bone.

'The trouble is,' Mel frowned, 'you can say anything you like about him now and he can't answer back.'

'Oh, come on, think it through! If Steven had really wanted to leave me, why didn't he?' Impatiently, Daisy swept back her long dark hair. 'I couldn't stop him, could I? He was an adult. It wasn't as if I could tie him up and shove him in the cellar!'

Unexpectedly, Mel said, 'Would you have given him the twenty thousand pounds?'

Daisy shrugged. 'I suppose so. He was still my husband. I could hardly say, gosh, cancer, how horrid, but I'm sorry I can't actually spare the cash right now, I'd really set my heart on a new car.'

Mel, her gaze unwavering, said, 'Did you love him?'

Considering they were virtual strangers, thought Daisy, they were having an astonishingly frank conversation.

She shook her head. 'Not at the end, no.'

'So why are you here, visiting his grave?' Mel's tone was faintly challenging. 'I saw you talking to him just now.'

Daisy's fingers brushed against the letter in her pocket. But first she had a few more questions of her own.

'I'll tell you in a minute. Did *you* love Steven?'

Mel shot her a pitying look. 'Of course I did. Otherwise why would I be here now? And I brought him some flowers.' Her grey eyes glittered as she added pointedly, 'Which is more than you've ever done.'

'Ever done? So you've been here before?' It was on the tip of Daisy's tongue to say 'Do you come here often?'

'I visit every week. It's allowed,' Mel retorted with a flash of defiance. 'You can't stop me.'

'I didn't say I was going to stop you.' Heavens, she was touchy! 'In a weird way, it's nice to know he has a visitor. How old are you?' Swiftly, Daisy changed the subject. See? I can ask personal questions too.

'Twenty-six,' Mel said stiffly.

Hmm, older than she looked, then. With that schoolgirl fringe and neat little mouth, Daisy had guessed twenty-one or -two.

'So you were twenty-five when you got involved with somebody else's husband. No qualms about that?'

Mel's hands were as red as her nose as she clumsily began to arrange the roses in the stone vase. The frost from the grass was melting into the knees of her white jeans.

'I felt sorry for him. He said he was trapped in a loveless marriage – which was *true* – and that you were, well . . .'

'Let me guess. The bitch from hell?' That figured, thought Daisy. She could picture it clearly in her mind, nobody could lie or charm their way through life more convincingly than Steven. 'Actually, I'm not. I'm really nice. Not that I'd expect you to believe that, but I am.'

Mel looked up. 'You did do one nice thing. Telling the nurse at the hospital to let me into the intensive care unit. That meant so much to me. I couldn't believe you'd done that.'

Daisy smiled briefly. 'Ah well, there you go. Like I said, I'm actually a fantastically lovely person.'

Mel, too tense to smile back, said, 'That was something else Steven told me, that you were full of yourself. Hardly the shrinking violet type, he said.'

'Shrinking violets can't run hotels. Speaking of which, I should be getting back.' Checking her watch, and at the same time noticing Mel check it out – yes, it was a Cartier and no, it wasn't a fake – Daisy said, 'Before I go, there's something you might like to see.'

Mel took the envelope and shook out the two sheets of paper. Her fingers clearly numb with cold, she unfolded them and began to read, first the explanatory letter from the co-ordinator, then the one from Barney.

She only read the first few lines of the second letter. Not bothering to carry on to the end, she stuffed them back into the envelope and thrust the whole lot into Daisy's hand.

'Doesn't it help?' Daisy frowned, taken aback. This wasn't the reaction she'd been expecting.

'Why would it?'

'But I think it's brilliant! That's why I had to come and tell Steven. He did a good thing. Thanks to him, this boy's got his life back.'

'But he's a complete stranger.' As she spoke, angry tears

sprang into Mel's eyes. 'I don't care about him. I'd rather Steven was still alive. I want *him* to have his life back, not some boy I don't even know.'

Chapter 4

Tara, nudging the door open with her bottom and backing into Room 12 with her arms full of fresh towels, nearly jumped out of her skin when she realised she wasn't alone. The current occupiers having just taken off in their helicopter, she had, naturally enough, expected the room to be empty.

'Oh, it's you! Good grief, what are you *doing*?' Dumping the towels onto the four-poster, Tara veered across to the windows where Daisy, kneeling up on the window seat, was peering through a pair of binoculars. 'Not birdwatching!' Tara let out a wail of dismay. 'Please don't tell me you've taken up birdwatching, that is *such* a nerdy thing to do. You'll have to go around in one of those hideous green anoraky things and start wearing a woolly bobble hat and I'm telling you now, you'll *never* get a boyfriend—'

'I'm not birdwatching, I'm spying on someone,' Daisy interrupted her diatribe.

'Oh well, that's all right then, that's an excellent hobby.' Tara nodded in approval. 'Who is it?'

'Ooh, nobody special. Just the girl who was having an affair with Steven before he died.'

'*What?*'

'*Ouch.*' Daisy yelped as the strap of the binoculars abruptly tightened round her neck. Sensing that strangulation could seriously

28

damage her health, she disentangled herself and passed them over to Tara. 'Over there in the churchyard. Red jacket, dark hair.'

'Got her.' Tara pressed the binoculars against the glass, gazing avidly at the girl who was kneeling next to Steven's grave. 'But how do you know for sure she's the girlfriend?'

'I've just been over there, talking to her. We got a few things sorted out.' Daisy heaved a sigh. 'Steven told her almost as many lies as he told me.'

Blimey. 'Lying never works. You always end up getting caught out,' Tara said sadly. 'Like I was telling your dad earlier, that's just how me and Dominic broke up.'

Her mind evidently elsewhere, Daisy said, 'Dominic? Dominic who?'

'Dominic Cross-Calvert, you twit.'

Daisy looked astonished. 'Cross-Calvert? But that's the name of the chap who's getting married here in two weeks' time. Are you telling me you used to go out with him?'

Tara tut-tutted and tilted her head sympathetically to one side. 'Honestly, I worry about you sometimes. I told you that this morning.'

'Did you? Oh well, never mind. If it's going to be awkward, we'll just re-jig your shifts. You don't have to see him.' As she said it, Daisy was watching Mel leave Steven's grave and make her way slowly out of the tree-lined churchyard.

'Don't be daft.' Tara was indignant. 'It was no big thing. I'm fine about Dominic.'

'So you promise you won't be doing anything embarrassing, like leaping up in the middle of the ceremony and yelling, "Yes, yes, *I* know a reason why he can't get married!" Because if you did do that,' Daisy shook her head in sorrowful fashion, 'I'm afraid I'd have to sack you, then chop you up into little pieces and feed you to Bert Connelly's dogs.'

Yuk. Bert Connelly, one of the hotel's handymen, kept a small pack of snarling, ravenous pit bulls.

'I'm not going to do anything,' Tara protested. 'Just say hi, that's all. Crikey, I haven't even thought about Dominic for months. He was never that important. Life goes on. If he's getting married, I'm happy for him. And I promise not to do anything embarrassing.'

Daisy nodded, relieved. She could see that Tara was telling the truth.

'Actually, they're coming down this afternoon. Maybe you could hang around after your shift and say hello, get it out of the way before the wedding.'

'I thought of that, and I'd have loved to,' Tara said honestly, 'but I've got a hair appointment at four, and it's my last chance before Zoe goes off on maternity leave.' This was also true. Zoe, the only hairdresser in the world she trusted with her hair, had thoughtlessly gone and got herself knocked up. This afternoon she had to cut and highlight Tara's spiky blonde hair thoroughly enough to see her through the next four months, while she herself *selfishly* gave birth and lazed around at home looking after a small baby. Honestly, hairdressers could be so inconsiderate. Didn't they realise the psychological harm they were inflicting on their loyal clients? Couldn't they just remember to take their Pills?

'I can't miss my appointment,' said Tara, feeling like a heroin addict being asked to give up her next fix.

'Don't panic. I just thought it might be easier to see him this afternoon. I don't want you getting upset on the day of the wedding.'

'Honestly, you've got this *so* out of proportion,' Tara complained. 'I'm not the tiniest bit in love with Dominic Cross-Calvert. He means nothing to me.'

'OK, OK.' Realising she'd overdone it, Daisy waved her arms in surrender. 'So long as you're sure.'

On the morning of the wedding, it rained. Not just normal rain, either. It was bucketing down.

When the bride-to-be arrived with her mother and sister at ten thirty, Daisy greeted them in reception and led them upstairs to their suite.

'I know we're early,' gushed Annabel, who was plump, blonde and china-doll pretty, 'but we wanted to allow plenty of time to get down here, and I've been up since five o'clock anyway, all of a flutter. Dominic thinks I'm mad, he says I'm a hopeless case, but how can I not be excited?' Panting slightly as she followed Daisy up the staircase, she declared with pride, 'It's the morning of my wedding, the most important day of my life!'

The suite's sitting room had been specially prepared for them with welcoming bowls of flowers and champagne on ice. A fire was crackling away in the grate.

'Of course it's important,' said Daisy. 'And I bet you any money he's as excited as you are. Men just like to pretend they aren't, it's one of those blokey things they do. What time's he going to be arriving?'

The wedding ceremony itself was due to take place at three o'clock. Annabel had plenty of time in which to titivate and get herself ready.

'Oh, two-ish. His best man's driving him down here. But Dominic mustn't see me, don't forget – it's bad luck for the groom to see the bride before the wedding! Still, I expect they'll stay downstairs in the bar. Another of those good old male traditions.' Annabel rolled her eyes in good-natured resignation, then broke into an uncontrollable grin. 'I still can't believe this is actually happening to me, I think I must be the luckiest girl in the world. How about you, are you married?'

'Me? Nooo.' Brightly, Daisy shook her head. This was one of those questions she preferred to veer away from.

'What? How can you never have been married?' Annabel looked shocked. 'You're so beautiful you could have any man you want!'

Oh dear, nothing worse than shattering a girl's illusions hours before her nuptials. No blushing bride-to-be wants to be reminded that some men might trick you into thinking they're the answer to a single girl's prayers but that deep down they're all cheating lying warthogs.

'Well, I tried it once,' Daisy said super-casually, 'but it didn't work out. Oh wow, that is *fabulous*.' Diverting attention from her own unfortunate brush with matrimony, she exclaimed over the wedding gown Annabel's mother was lovingly unzipping from its case. 'What a dress . . . look at that *beading*.'

'Every single bead sewn on by hand,' Annabel twinkled as her mother blushed with pride. 'Mummy made the dress for me. Isn't it just fantastic? She's been working on it for months.'

'Gorgeous,' Daisy agreed, though quite so much beading and intricate white-on-white embroidery wasn't really her thing. 'Well, I'd better leave you to settle in. I'll have a pot of coffee sent up, and you can just buzz down to reception if there's anything else you need.'

'Thanks.' Annabel plonked herself joyfully on the end of the bed, almost squashing the elaborate make-up kit her sister had just unpacked. 'Oops, clumsy me! Jeannie's doing my hair first, then my nails, then my face . . . just as well, the way my hands are shaking!'

'I'll see you later,' Daisy told them as she moved to the door. 'Have fun.'

*   *   *

It wasn't as if Tara was desperate to impress Dominic. Then again, it was only natural to aim to be looking your best when you bumped into an old boyfriend you haven't seen for years. No one in their right mind wanted their ex to scuttle off breathing a sigh of relief and thinking phew, a narrow escape there.

Tara shuddered at the prospect. Hopefully, Dominic wouldn't think that. Today she had applied her make-up with a lot more care and attention to detail than usual. Her hair, by sheer chance, was looking great. And just for that smidgen of added confidence she was wearing her pushy-uppy, ultra-padded peacock-blue bra.

It was a shame, of course, about the outfit, but these things couldn't be helped, and at least it was plain navy. Tara knew that as far as chambermaids' uniforms went, she could have done a lot worse.

Oh God, that was the other bit she wasn't looking forward to. When she had known Dominic, she'd been an aspiring actress. An aspiring actress with dreams and, um, aspirations. Was he going to laugh his head off when he discovered what she was doing for a living now? Worse still, would he sneer?

Tara, on her knees in Room 4, scrubbing energetically at what looked like a squelched-in bit of chewing gum on the carpet, briefly entertained the idea of pretending to Dominic that she was here undercover, secretly researching the job of a chambermaid for some high-budget drama series commissioned by ITV. That sounded a bit more impressive.

Oh, stop it, thought Tara with a burst of impatience, what am I *doing*? I'm a chambermaid and that's nothing to be ashamed of. We can't all be Kate Winslet. This is Dominic's wedding day, for crying out loud. He isn't going to care what I do for a living and I don't give two hoots what he thinks of me anyway.

Tara heard the waiters downstairs shouting instructions to each other across the dining room as they organised the tables according to the seating plan. Checking her watch, she saw that it was one thirty. Dominic would be here soon. And Annabel, his prospective bride, had already spent three hours primping and preparing herself for the ceremony.

Glad that nobody was around to read her mind, Tara leaned back on her heels and recalled how she had once spent hours lovingly practising her signature, should she end up marrying Dominic. Tara Cross-Calvert had sounded *so* much more actressy and upmarket than plain old bog standard Tara Donovan. To be honest, she'd probably been more taken with the surname than she had been with Dominic himself.

And now, in less than three hours, somebody else would be able to call herself Mrs Cross-Calvert and write her glamorous new signature with a flourish.

It occurred to Tara that, with her luck, she'd more than likely end up marrying someone with a surname like Grimshaw or Winkle or Puke.

The sound of a car on the gravelled drive outside had an electrifying effect, but it was only one of the other guests, an American currently in possession of the loudest wife known to man. A wife, Tara belatedly recalled, who had asked her to replace the firm pillows in their room with soft ones. If she didn't want her eardrums shattered, she'd better deal with that now.

Ho hum. Who said chambermaiding wasn't a glamorous life?

Chapter 5

'Oof,' gasped Tara, turning a corner and colliding head on with a figure coming in the opposite direction. Happily, thanks to the fact that her arms had been full of squashy goosedown pillows, it was a painless – even bouncy – collision. 'I'm really sorry, are you OK?'

Bending down to retrieve the scattered pillows and simultaneously getting her first proper look at her bump-ee, she caught her breath. Because, there was no getting away from it, he was truly, madly and *deeply* gorgeous. Dark, glossy hair, even darker eyes with a glint of laughter in them, and the kind of unseasonal tan that had left his mouth a shade paler than his skin. When he smiled, his teeth were as white as his polo shirt. He had a lean, hard, broad-shouldered body to die for. He was also familiar, although Tara couldn't immediately place him. He certainly wasn't one of the hotel guests.

'I'll live.' Grinning down at her as she clumsily gathered up the pillows, he added, 'I like your bra.'

Tara blushed furiously. She couldn't help it. Glancing down, she discovered that the top button of her navy overall had popped undone, leaving the v-shaped neckline gaping dramatically. From his elevated position this stunning dark-eyed man could probably see not only her bra but all the way down to her navel.

Hastily sucking in her stomach just in case, Tara fumbled with the button and refastened it. But as well as blushing, she was aware of biting her lip in an effort not to smirk because, to be honest, it wasn't every day you had your bra admired by someone quite so pulse-racingly gorgeous.

And it *had* been nice of him to say he liked it. Tara was both flattered and pleased, seeing as the thing had cost her thirty-eight pounds fifty. Such a beautiful bra deserved to be appreciated.

'Come on, up you get.' Holding out a hand, he hauled her efficiently to her feet. 'No injuries that might need looking at?'

Tara felt her skin begin to prickle with pleasurable delight.

'I'm fine.' Grinning broadly now, she thought how brilliant it would be if he were a guest who had just booked into the hotel for a month. 'But you've got . . . excuse me . . .'

'What?' His eyebrows rocketed in mock alarm as Tara reached out towards the front of his jeans.

'Sorry. There you go.' Having retrieved the small curly feather, Tara waved it at him. 'It was on your trousers. Must have escaped from one of the pillows.'

Lucky feather!

'Phew. For a second there I wondered what you were about to do.' He smiled as he said it, revealing wicked dimples. Behind her, Tara was vaguely aware of a door opening and clicking shut. Realising that another guest had just emerged from the Gents and would be needing to squeeze past them in the narrow corridor, she automatically clutched the pillows to her chest and moved to one side.

The next moment a stunned male voice gasped, 'I don't believe it. *Tara?*'

She turned and there he was. Dominic, looking exactly as she remembered. Except maybe more poleaxed.

'Hello, Dominic. Getting married at last, I hear. Congratulations.' She'd been practising these lines for days, needless to say, but the great thing about being an actress was you could rehearse endlessly and still make it come out sounding spontaneous and completely natural. Even failed actresses could manage that.

Pleased with herself, Tara flashed Dominic a breezy smile. Then, because it seemed rude not to, she planted a brief kiss on his cheek.

'Hang on. I don't understand.' Dominic was shaking his head, still in shock. 'What are you doing here?'

Determined not to be ashamed, Tara raised her chin and said, 'Working. I'm a chambermaid now.' She nearly managed to pull it off, to make it sound as though it couldn't matter less that she was no longer in the business, but the faint wobble in her voice let her down. Oh yes, this is me, these days I earn my living picking other people's chewing gum out of carpets.

Dominic was incredulous. 'What happened to the . . . other stuff?'

'The acting, you mean?' Praying her voice wouldn't betray her a second time, Tara shrugged nonchalantly. 'I gave it up. Too competitive. Well, maybe I just wasn't good enough. Anyway, it was time to get out of London. Aunt Maggie invited me to stay down here with her – she's got a gorgeous little cottage in the village – and I've been here ever since. Not what you'd call a glitzy career, but we have a laugh.' As she rattled on, Tara turned to include the Feather man in the conversation in case he might be feeling left out, but he was no longer there. Silently, he had slipped away.

Oh well, never mind, she was bound to bump into him again before long.

And in the meantime . . .

'I just don't believe this. I just do not believe this is happening.' Dominic slowly shook his head.

I say, steady on.

'I know, it's been a while, hasn't it?' Tara hadn't expected him to react quite so dramatically. He was staring at her as if she'd suddenly turned into Madonna or someone. The colour had drained from his face. As he reached for her hand she realised that he was trembling.

'God, Tara, this isn't fair. I'm supposed to be getting married in two hours' time.'

'What?' Tara laughed at his slip of the tongue. 'You're not *supposed* to be getting married, you twit! You *are* getting married.'

Dominic's tone grew urgent. 'I'm sorry but you don't know what this means to me. You have no idea.' He lowered his voice still further as another guest passed them in the corridor. 'Tara, we have to talk.'

Tara, her heart starting to thump, clutched the pillows tighter to her chest.

'Dom, I can't. I'm busy. And you have to get yourself ready for the wedding.'

'Come to my room.' He pulled a key from his jeans pocket. Tara stared at it in disbelief. 'Are you mad? Of course I'm not coming to your room! What would it look like if anyone saw us?'

'Tara, this is important. If you won't talk to me, I'll cancel the wedding. And then it'll be all your fault.' He was smiling his familiar lopsided smile as he said it. Tara's heart went *twaannggg* as she remembered how he had always been able to make her laugh.

'Just five minutes,' Dominic persisted, his straight fair hair flopping into his eyes.

38

'I've got to take these to Room Six.' Helplessly, she indicated the pillows.

'Great idea. We'll talk in there.'

'We will not!' Thinking fast, instinctively aware that any bedroom anywhere was a bad idea, Tara said, 'Let me just take these up. I'll be back in two minutes.'

'I've waited this long.' Dominic gave her another one of those heart-melting smiles. 'I don't suppose another couple of minutes will hurt.'

Upstairs, Tara shook the pillows into fresh pillowcases and tried to figure out why Dominic had reacted the way he had. What was the big deal? Crikey, it wasn't as if she'd ended their relationship and Dominic had spent the last two years pining like a dog. He was the one who had finished with her.

Downstairs, she found him waiting in exactly the same place in the corridor, pretending to admire a painting on the wall. Ahead of them, the reception area was buzzing with preparations for the wedding, the finishing touches were being put to the flower arrangements.

The clatter of cutlery being laid out drifted through from the dining room. Reversing back down the corridor and taking a couple of left turns with Dominic in tow, Tara opened one of the side doors leading outside and murmured, 'There's a summerhouse next to the pool. We won't be disturbed there.'

'We certainly won't.' Dominic peered up at the leaden sky. 'Nobody else in their right mind would be mad enough to go out in this.'

It was raining harder than ever. Really hammering down now.

'You're going to get wet,' Tara warned.

'You don't say.' His bright eyes narrowed with amusement. 'Never mind, you're worth it.'

But *why*? Tara wanted to yell. Why, why, why am I suddenly worth it?

Oh well, only one way to find out.

'OK.' Closing the door behind them, she gasped as the first icy blast of rain hurled itself at her like gravel. 'See the roof of the summerhouse over there? One, two, three . . . *go*.'

'Th-this is the w-w-worst idea I ever h-had,' Tara stammered through frantically chattering teeth, forty seconds later. The summerhouse might be a discreet place to talk but it was also concrete-floored and colder than being trapped in a deep-freeze.

'Don't worry, I'll warm you up.' Dominic's arms were round her before she had a chance to protest, and Tara was unable to summon the willpower to move away. The heat of his body was gorgeous, better than any electric blanket. And he was rubbing her arms and back in a brisk, circulation-boosting kind of way.

'Right,' said Tara, when she was able to speak again without risking biting through her tongue. 'So are you going to tell me what this is all about?' Glancing at her watch she added, 'Bearing in mind that your future wife is probably, at this very moment, climbing into her wedding dress.'

'Look at you.' Ignoring the question, Dominic slowly trailed a finger down one side of her face. 'You haven't changed a bit. Not on the outside, at least.'

'I haven't changed on the inside,' Tara protested. 'I'm exactly the same.'

'Wrong. You only think that. But you have changed,' he told her. 'More than you know.'

A wooden bench ran along the back wall of the summerhouse. As they sat down together, Tara shivered and warned, 'Say it quickly then, whatever it is. Five minutes and I'm going back inside.' Despite pretending to be stern, she was bursting with curiosity. It was *such* a thrill, discovering that you'd had more of an effect on someone than you'd ever imagined.

'I loved you,' Dominic said simply. 'You were my dream girl. You were funny and beautiful and the best fun in the world.'

Not to mention fab in bed, thought Tara, don't forget that bit.

Aloud she said, with just a *hint* of sarcasm, 'If I was that much fun, seems a bit strange that you decided to chuck me.'

'Can't you guess why I did that? Can you really not work it out?' Dominic shook his head sadly. 'You were perfect in almost every way. But the one thing I couldn't cope with was the one thing you cared about more than anything else in the world.'

Tara boggled. Good grief, was he seriously saying he couldn't cope with her addiction to toffee pecan ice cream?

'Your so-called career,' Dominic went on. 'You were obsessed with it. Nothing else mattered. Your whole life revolved around this crazy dream that you were going to make it big one day and you just couldn't see what it was doing to you. Every Thursday you'd buy *The Stage* and read it from cover to cover. Then there were the endless auditions that never came to anything. So you started doing the tacky stuff, convinced that it didn't matter, it was better than nothing and you might still get your big break. You actually managed to convince yourself that some hotshot producer might spot a topless photo of you and decide that you were the girl he needed to star in his next Hollywood blockbuster.'

Tara, her skin prickling with embarrassment, said indignantly, 'But everyone has to go through that! The whole thing about acting is you *do* have to struggle before you get noticed. Madonna went through it. And Geri Halliwell. God, even Joanna Lumley did it.' She knew he'd always had a soft spot for Joanna Lumley.

41

'Maybe they did. But I couldn't handle seeing you do that to yourself. It made me feel . . . well, a bit sick, to be honest. And then I heard through a friend of a friend that you'd gone along to audition for a job in a lap-dancing club and I knew I couldn't handle it any more. I loved you, but I didn't want a girlfriend who was a lap-dancer. And when I asked you about the work, you told me it was waitressing. That was the last straw. I had to end our relationship.'

Tara was astounded. OK, she'd lied to him and been caught out, but she hadn't realised he'd felt this strongly about her whole career.

'But you never even gave me a clue! If you hated me doing it so much, why didn't you tell me? For crying out loud, Dominic, I didn't have any idea!'

He shrugged. 'I know you didn't. That's because you were obsessed. Acting was more important to you than anything or anyone else. It was the love of your life. There was no point asking you to give it up because, well, you just wouldn't have done it. You were like an alcoholic refusing to believe you had a problem. I just decided to get out while I still could. It hurt like hell, but I realised I didn't have any choice. It was a no-win situation. I couldn't stop you doing what you wanted to do.'

Tara shivered, her sodden uniform cold and clammy against her skin. No doubt Dominic had envisaged her ending up as some bloated, silicone-pumped old hag starring in soft porn movies. The really shaming thing was, it could so nearly have happened. She'd been there, teetering right at the top of that scary slippery slope. All it would have taken was one tiny push.

She had, thank God, come to her senses in the nick of time. Realising what she was on the verge of doing, she'd stepped back.

'That's all in the past now,' Tara said slowly. 'I faced up to the fact that I'd been kidding myself. I was never going to make it as an actress. So I gave it all up and moved down here. Does that make you feel better?' she added with a wry smile. 'Knowing you were right all along?'

Dominic roughly raked back his hair, his expression strained. 'Tara, listen to me. Don't you understand, don't you see what this means? You were perfect in every *other* way. The only thing that came between us was your acting. And now you aren't doing it any more. Which makes you . . .'

'Perfect?' quipped Tara.

But Dominic wasn't laughing. There was anguish in his eyes as he uttered, 'God, yes, *yes*,' and made his lunge.

Caught off guard by the unexpectedness of the onslaught, Tara toppled backwards along the wooden bench. Dominic's arms were all over her like tentacles, his body pressing against hers as he groaned and kissed her passionately on the mouth. To stop herself falling off the bench, Tara was forced to hang on to him. She let out a muffled *wmpphh* of surprise and grabbed his shoulders, dimly aware that one of her knees was trapped between his legs. Dominic's warm tongue had snaked its way into her mouth and he was kissing her so hard she could barely breathe. His wet hair was flopping into her eyes, she could feel his heart thump-thumping against her chest and the smell of his aftershave was—

'*Stop it, stop it, stop it!*' shrieked a female voice as the door of the summerhouse crashed open so hard it almost flew off its hinges. '*For God's sake, let him go!*'

Chapter 6

Every nerve-ending in Tara's body went *zzinnggg* with the need to leap six feet in the air, but Dominic was on top of her and she was unable to leap anywhere. His weight pinned her to the narrow slatted bench. He lay there, not moving a muscle either, rather like a two-year-old thinking that if he closes his eyes, keeps still and pretends hard enough not to be there, he won't be spotted.

It didn't work. Moments later, Dominic was seized none too gently by the shoulders and yanked off the bench. Tara, flushed and mortified, jack-knifed into a sitting position and pulled her rucked-up uniform back down over her thighs.

God, this was awful, just awful.

'You filthy disgusting little tart!' bellowed a furious-looking girl in a peach satin bridesmaid's dress. 'What the bloody hell do you think you're doing to my sister's fiancé? How *dare* you!'

Horrified, Tara stammered, 'B-but it's not what you th-think . . . it wasn't *like* that . . .' and stared wildly at Dominic, waiting for him to leap to her defence.

But Dominic, pale and tight-lipped, was shaking his head in sorrowful fashion. 'Jeannie, don't blow your top. She didn't mean to get carried away. I tried to stop her . . . the thing is, we knew each other years ago. She was just a bit overwhelmed to see me again.'

At this jaw-dropping, outright lie, Tara yelped, 'Oh, excuse me, are you serious? You were the one who kissed me!'

'You brought him out here,' Jeannie blazed. 'I looked out of our bathroom window and saw you leading the way. I thought it seemed a bit odd, that's why I left it for a few minutes, but when you didn't come back I came downstairs and followed the path from the back of the hotel. I couldn't imagine where you'd gone, until I came round the corner and saw this place with all the windows steamed up. And surprise, surprise, here you were.' She gestured in disgust at Tara, as if she were covered in sores. 'My God, you are beyond belief, you really are. Trying to seduce a man who's getting married in an hour and a half. I mean, do you have any idea what this is going to do to my sister?'

'Jeannie, Jeannie, you can't do that,' Dominic said hurriedly. 'You mustn't tell Annabel, you just *can't*.'

Tara, in deep shock, wailed, 'I wasn't trying to seduce him! I swear to you, I didn't even want him to kiss me!'

'Stop it, Tara.' Dominic's tone was pitying. 'You're only making things worse for yourself.'

'But I wouldn't *do* anything like that,' she protested to Jeannie. 'I'm not that sort of person.'

Jeannie's upper lip curled with disdain and her gaze dropped from Tara's anguished face to her cleavage. Tara suddenly realised that in addition to her ruffled-up hair and smudged lipstick, the top button of her navy uniform had popped undone. Again.

God, it certainly picked its moments.

With heavy sarcasm Jeannie said, 'Oh no, of course you aren't. Don't tell me, you're actually a nun.'

'Oh please, you have to believe me, I swear to God I didn't do anything wrong, it was him, not me!'

Daisy, perched on the edge of her desk, was so angry she could barely speak. Tara was pacing agitatedly around the office, her eyes red-rimmed, her movements jerky and her hair sticking up like a parakeet's. She may only have known Tara for three years but they had become close friends in that time and although she might be many things, Tara wasn't dishonest. Daisy knew all about the less salubrious aspects of her past. If anything, Tara was too naive and too trusting for her own good. She certainly didn't lie.

'Look, sit down, of course I believe you.' Tara's frantic pacing was beginning to make Daisy feel dizzy. 'But we have to figure out some way to sort this out. Annabel's upstairs refusing to come out of her room. She's insisting the wedding's off. Bloody hell, why couldn't that deranged sister of hers have kept her big mouth shut? If she's so convinced you're the one to blame for all this, why did she even have to tell Annabel what she'd seen? If Dominic's innocent, why does Annabel want to cancel the wedding? God, who's *that*?' she sighed as a knock came at the door. 'Please don't let it be Jerry Springer.'

Or the bride's mother, thought Tara fearfully. Or a troupe of furious relatives all snarling like Rottweilers and baying for blood.

Daisy opened the door and Tara almost fainted with relief. It was the Feather man, the one she had bumped into in the corridor outside the Gents, the one who had smiled and teased and flirted with her so deliciously earlier. And now it looked as if he was something to do with the wedding, which could only be good news. He would be bound to take her side.

Daisy, who was more *au fait* with rugby than Tara, recognised him immediately.

'I'm Dev Tyzack.' Briefly, he shook Daisy's hand before shooting a cool glance in Tara's direction. 'I was meant to be the best man at this wedding. Right, we officially have a fiasco on our hands and it needs sorting out. I assume you have already sacked Mata Hari here.'

'Would it help if I told you I had?' said Daisy.

His dark eyes flickered over her. 'It would be a start.'

'Really?' She slid down from the desk. 'Well, I haven't. Tara told me what happened and I believe her. Your friend Dominic appears to be the one at fault here.'

'Oh, come on, you aren't serious, I saw her in action myself,' Dev Tyzack shot back. 'She tried it on with me, for God's sake, literally *seconds* before she clapped eyes on Dominic. She made all the running, I can tell you. This girl is no shrinking violet. Dominic came here today to get married and she knew that. I've spoken to Dominic and he's told me everything. She dragged him out to that summerhouse and—'

'I did not!' Tara shrieked. 'I didn't drag him *anywhere*. He was desperate to talk to me about something and I just thought the summerhouse would be the best place to go because I didn't want anyone seeing us together and getting the wrong idea!'

Dev Tyzack drawled, 'And didn't that work well.'

'Would you mind not talking to a member of my staff like that?' Daisy was having to force herself to keep her temper.

'You mean you'd like me to be *really* honest?' he flashed back.

'This isn't *fair*.' Tara's voice shot up another couple of octaves. 'I didn't do anything wrong! It was Dominic, not me. He told me how much he'd loved me and said I was perfect and then he just *launched* himself at me on that bench. I had no idea he was going to kiss me . . . I didn't *want* him to kiss me . . .'

'But I gather you did manage to show him your bra.' Dev Tyzack feigned surprise. 'The very same one you revealed to me not ten minutes earlier. I'm telling you, that bra must have been viewed by more people than the Oscars.'

'The buttonhole on my uniform is loose,' shouted Tara. 'It just kept popping *undone*.'

'I'm sorry.' Icily, Daisy addressed Dev Tyzack. 'But you aren't helping matters here. In fact you're being downright obnoxious. If we're going to sort this out, you need to calm down and stop throwing wild accusations at my staff. As far as I'm concerned, your friend Dominic is the guilty one around here. Has it even occurred to you to fling any accusations in his direction?'

Oh God, thought Tara, petrified. Daisy was losing it, she was going way over the top now. Her eyes were bright with fury, her fists clenched at her sides and she looked as if she wanted to punch him. She was going to get into the most terrible trouble, the repercussions could be horrendous.

This had evidently occurred to Dev Tyzack as well. A derisory smile twisted the corners of his mouth, the very mouth Tara had earlier thought so attractive. Well, she didn't any more.

'Not a very professional thing for a hotel manager to say, is it?'

'Maybe not,' Daisy shot back, 'but I am being truthful. If you're going to be obnoxious, I'll tell you you're being obnoxious.'

'Not worried that you might end up looking for another job?' Dev Tyzack raised a mocking eyebrow.

'I won't get the sack for this, I can promise you. I have the owner's full backing.'

'Really? Aren't you the lucky one. Who *is* the owner, might I ask?' Having affected surprise, he now allowed his gaze to come to rest on a framed photograph on the desk. It was a group photograph featuring Daisy as a teenager, doubled up with laughter between her parents. Tanned and healthy, the three of them had been celebrating New Year's Eve in the Cayman

Islands and it was Daisy's all-time favourite photo. 'Oh, I *see*,' said Dev Tyzack. 'The owner of this hotel is Hector MacLean and he just happens to be your father. Now I understand how you got the job.'

Tara couldn't bear it. Her stomach was churning like a tumble dryer. She was innocent but she *felt* guilty. And what if she wasn't as innocent as she thought? Maybe she was just making pathetic excuses for herself to avoid having to admit that she should never have gone with Dominic to the summerhouse in the first place.

What's more, Daisy was looking more homicidal by the second. And there was a big brass paperknife on her desk, not to mention a ferocious-looking stapler that fired staples like a Kalashnikov.

Praying that Daisy wouldn't actually start firing it like a Kalashnikov, Tara clapped a hand to her mouth, muttered ''Scuse me, think I'm going to be sick,' and made a bolt for the door.

As she rushed from the office, she caught sight of Dominic. He was in the lounge bar across the hall, standing in front of the fireplace clutching a drink.

Tara's palms were clammy as she made her way towards him. The only other person in the room was Rocky, polishing glasses behind the bar and pulling a 'Rather you than me' face at her when he realised she was approaching Dominic.

'Oh God. What do you want?' Dominic didn't look at all pleased to see her. Gone were the loving tones he'd employed twenty minutes earlier.

That was fine by Tara.

'You've lied to everyone.' She came straight to the point. 'You told them I threw myself at you.'

There was a sheen of perspiration on his upper lip. He was

gripping the tumbler of Scotch in his hand so tightly it was a wonder the glass hadn't shattered.

'Of course I lied. What would you have done in my situation?' He kept his voice low.

OK, thought Tara, fair enough.

'So you didn't mean all those things you said?'

'I didn't mean for this to bloody happen! Christ, I can't believe it, this is my fucking wedding day.'

Tara took a deep breath. 'Do you still want to marry Annabel?'

He turned and looked at her as if she were a bag lady. 'What? Are you *mad*? Of course I want to marry her! But she's upstairs, having a complete head fit and refusing to marry *me* . . . Jesus, what have I done to deserve this? It's *so* fucking unfair.'

Chapter 7

Tara's least favourite person in the world opened the door to the Bellingham Suite. Actually, Tara decided, Dominic was her number one least favourite person. But Jeannie had to be number two.

'Oh God, I don't believe it. What is this, some kind of sick joke?' Jeannie, who was smoking a cigarette, exhaled a long stream of smoke right into Tara's face.

'I'd like to talk to Annabel.' It was a lie, of course; there was no question of liking it, but Tara pressed on regardless. 'Alone. Please.'

'Oh, this is too much. You seriously think my sister would *want* to talk to you?'

'Look, could you just ask her?'

'Don't you think you've done enough damage?' Jeannie snapped.

Tara swallowed, red-faced with shame. 'Yes, I do. That's why I'm here now.'

The door was abruptly slammed shut in her face. Tara heard a lot of furious whispering inside the room. Moments later the door swung open again. Without looking at her, Jeannie and a middle-aged woman in a vast purple mother-of-the-bride outfit marched out.

'Five minutes,' Jeannie hissed as she passed Tara in a rustle of apricot satin. 'Then,' she warned, like Schwarzenneger only scarier, 'we'll be back.'

Annabel, her blonde hair still fastened up in an elaborate chignon, was sitting rigidly on the window seat wrapped in one of the hotel's white towelling robes. Her wedding dress lay in a crumpled heap on the four-poster bed. She looked at Tara as if she were a dentist arriving to rip out all her teeth.

'Well?' Annabel demanded without preamble. 'What happened?'

Tara took a deep shuddering breath. 'I'm sorry. It was all my fault and I'm so ashamed. Seeing Dominic again after all this time was too much for me. I just couldn't cope with the fact that he was marrying someone else and I threw myself at him. It was a mad thing to do and I don't expect you to forgive me but please, you have to forgive him. You can't call off the wedding. He told me how much he loved you. I'm just so sorry I caused all this trouble. You have to marry him. It wasn't his fault, it was mine.' There. Who said she wasn't an actress?

Tara waited miserably for the other girl's reaction.

A single tear rolled down Annabel's cheek. 'Really?' It came out as a whisper. Her fingers were agitatedly winding the belt of her towelling robe around her knuckles, above which glittered a hefty emerald and diamond engagement ring. 'Is that the truth?' There was hope in her eyes.

Tara nodded. 'It was me. All me. I just . . . lost control, I suppose. And I'm sorry.' Pause. 'But he really does want to marry you.'

Another tear slid down Annabel's made-up face. Instinctively Tara ripped a couple of tissues from the box on the coffee table in front of her and crossed the room with them. 'Here, don't wreck your make-up.'

'Thanks. For the tissues, I mean.' Annabel jerkily dabbed

beneath her eyes. 'I'm not going to thank you for telling me you threw yourself at my boyfriend.'

But it's what you wanted to hear, thought Tara, because you thought he might have been the one up to no good. Who knows, maybe Dominic's done this kind of thing before. But you don't completely trust him, do you?

God, was she doing the right thing here? Should she be lying to this girl, persuading her to go ahead and marry someone she so evidently *couldn't* trust? Then again, all hell was going to break loose if she didn't.

'I did a bad thing. I'm sorry,' Tara said again, glancing out of the window and spotting a familiar figure hurrying up the drive. 'The registrar's just arrived. What are you going to do?'

'This was supposed to be the happiest day of my life.' Annabel sounded bewildered. Luckily she didn't seem the punch-your-lights-out kind.

'You have to make your mind up. If the wedding's off, the registrar needs to know.' Steadily Tara said, 'Do you want to marry Dominic?'

'Of course I want to marry Dominic! Of *course* I do.' Annabel's voice trembled with emotion. 'I love him. Everyone says we're the perfect couple. And he loves me.'

Scarcely daring to breathe, Tara said cautiously, 'So the wedding's on again?'

'Yes. Yes, no thanks to you,' Annabel shot back. 'And I don't want to see you here this afternoon either.'

'That won't happen. I'll leave now. Thanks for listening to me, anyway.' Hugely relieved but at the same time stung by Annabel's tone, Tara backed towards the door. On impulse she added, 'If you like, I could iron your dress.'

'What, so you can burn scorch marks down the front? No

thank you, my mother and sister'll be back any minute. I don't need any help from you.'

For a moment Tara was tempted to snipe back that if she was going to be marrying Dominic, she'd be needing all the help she could get. She didn't say it.

'Right, well, I'll go down and let everyone know the wedding's going ahead.'

'And then you'll leave the hotel,' Annabel frostily reminded her.

'And then I'll leave the hotel.' God, there had to be a simpler way to wangle an afternoon off.

'Will you be sacked?'

'I don't know.' Tara crossed her fingers behind her back. 'Probably.'

'Good.' Annabel wasn't brilliant at playing the bitch, but she was giving it her best shot. 'People like you have no shame. I hope you realise how pathetic you are. You deserve to lose your job.'

'It's back on again,' Tara told Daisy, and briefly ran through her stressful encounter with Annabel.

Daisy shook her head. 'You didn't have to do that.'

'I did. They might have sued the hotel.' Tara shrugged. 'My word against theirs. We wouldn't have had a hope.'

This was undoubtedly true.

'Maybe not. So she's going to marry a lying weasel,' sighed Daisy, who knew all about lying weasels. 'Oh well, that's not our problem. You're a star.' She gave Tara, who was looking miserable, a hug. 'And cheer up, for heaven's sake.'

'They want you to sack me.'

'You big wally. Of course I'm not going to sack you.'

'What happened to the best man?' Blinking back tears of relief,

Tara changed the subject. 'I half expected to come in here and find him staple-gunned to the wall.'

'It crossed my mind. What a bastard. He's in the bar with Dominic.' Daisy grimaced, realising that she now faced the delightful prospect of being forced to admit to Dev Tyzack that he had been right and she'd been wrong. She could just picture the supercilious look on his face.

The preparations for the wedding were cranking into overdrive as Tara slipped away from the hotel. The rain had stopped but the grey clouds were as low as her spirits. Why hadn't she taken Daisy's advice in the first place and swapped shifts with one of the other chambermaids? Why couldn't she just have resisted the urge to see Dominic again and stayed away? How, *how* could she have thought that surprising him on the morning of his wedding would be fun?

Disconsolately, Tara kicked her way through a pile of soggy dead leaves. There was no getting away from the truth; basically, she was as guilty as if she had hurled herself at Dominic and ripped his trousers down to his knees.

God, what a disastrous day.

Maggie Donovan stood at her kitchen window, a cheerful smile fixed to her face. As her lover reached the rickety wooden gate at the end of her back garden he turned, as he always did, and waved at her. Maggie, as she always did, waved back and thought how handsome he was, what a gorgeous smile he had, how lucky she was to have such a special man in her life and how—

Oh stop it, *stop* it. Maggie gave herself a mental slap around the face. You're fantasising again, making an idiot of yourself. Get a grip, woman. The very reason he's using the back gate is so that no one will see him leaving your cottage. He's smiling and waving goodbye because he's just completed a satisfactory business transaction. And he isn't your lover, he's your *client*.

Maggie's smile faded as she watched him slip away into the woods beyond her cottage. Very handy, those woods, enabling him to come and go without being observed by the rest of the village. She was under no illusions that if the trees hadn't been there, their arrangement would never have come about.

And that was what it was, Maggie reminded herself. An arrangement, pure and simple. One that suited them both.

To prove it, she moved away from the kitchen window and crossed to the crowded oak dresser. Reaching into the blue and white china teapot on the second shelf, Maggie drew out the small roll of notes. There was no need to count it, she knew he had left her one hundred pounds. Because that was how much he always left.

She would love to be able to describe herself as a one-man woman, but that wasn't true. Let's face it, she was a one-client prostitute.

Maggie sighed. It wasn't what she wanted to be, but what was the alternative? If she refused to take his money, he would no longer sleep with her. And she couldn't bear to give him up. He was the highlight of her week. If she could have afforded it, she would have paid him to sleep with her.

But, Maggie reminded herself, she couldn't afford it, and he knew that. It was why he gave her the money each week. And there was no denying it came in handy.

Tara had left one of her enamelled bracelets on the dresser. Maggie picked it up and headed for the stairs. It was no good wishing things could be different, because they weren't. She had to accept what she had and make the best of it. And since she *was* only a one-client prostitute, she also had plenty of work to be getting on with. Not to mention a bed to make.

Upstairs, Maggie put the bracelet back where it belonged in the jewellery box on Tara's dressing table. The next moment, glancing out of the bedroom window, she let out an involuntary squeak of alarm. Tara was making her way down the High Street towards the cottage.

Oh good grief, what was she doing coming home at this time of day?

Like lightning, Maggie shot across the landing to her own bedroom, ripped off her dressing gown and threw on a black sweater and jeans. In twenty seconds flat she re-made the crumpled bed, flung open the curtains and dragged a brush through her shoulder-length blonde hair. Grabbing the laundry basket, she hauled it downstairs. When the front door opened, she was on her knees in the kitchen frantically shovelling clothes into the washing machine.

Phew, that was close. The closest shave yet, thought Maggie with a shudder of relief. Imagine the horror if Tara had come back to the house ten minutes earlier. Or, worse still, twenty minutes.

It didn't bear thinking about.

'Tara! Heavens, what's the time?' Feigning astonishment, Maggie sat back on her heels. 'I thought you were on duty until six o'clock!'

'Daisy sent me home.' Tara flung herself onto one of the kitchen chairs and groaned loudly, far too wrapped up in her own guilt to notice her aunt's. 'You won't believe what happened. Major disaster. Maggie, why do men do it? Why do we even bother with them? Not that you ever *do* bother with them,' she amended, raking her fingers through her spiked-up hair. 'And let me tell you, you have exactly the right idea. From now on, I swear to God, I'm going to take a leaf out of your book. No more being lied to and cheated on and treated like a puddle of sick. No men, no trouble. That's *it*.' Looking up in despair at her forty-five-year-old aunt, who had been divorced for the last seven years and now lived an idyllic, hassle-free, man-free life, she proclaimed vehemently, 'From now on I'm going to be just like you.'

The wedding ceremony had gone ahead without a hitch. The bride had looked beautiful, the groom had repeated his vows as if he actually meant them. The hotel was wonderful, the best man's speech had been brilliantly witty and the food a triumph.

This was according to Sheila, one of the waitresses, who had been eavesdropping on the guests throughout the reception. Daisy, who had spent most of the afternoon in her office, said, 'So they all seem happy.'

'Couldn't be better.' Sheila gave her a motherly, reassuring smile. 'Why don't you go and see for yourself?'

Because I might stab the bridegroom and the best man with that big silver knife they're using to cut the cake, thought Daisy.

Then again, she had been in charge of making all the arrangements for the wedding. She should at least show her face.

Chapter 8

The wedding party was in full swing as Daisy pushed through the double doors. Outside it had grown dark, but here in the ballroom the chandeliers blazed, candles flickered on the tables around the edge of the room and the dancing had begun.

Unsurprisingly, Hector was already there, swinging the radiant bride around the dance floor and making her laugh with his usual lavish compliments. Watching Annabel's face light up and her elaborate dress swirl around her ankles, Daisy told herself that Tara had done the right thing. If everyone went around calling off weddings willy-nilly, simply because the groom was an untrustworthy little shit, well, there wouldn't be a lot of married people around.

The band began to play 'In The Mood'. Annabel was claimed by some walrus-moustachioed elderly relative and Hector promptly swept Annabel's mother onto the floor. In her vast purple outfit she looked like a hot-air balloon, but a delighted and deeply flattered hot-air balloon. Within seconds she was giggling like an overexcited schoolgirl at Hector's flirtatious remarks, her purple sequinned shoes a glittering blur as she jitterbugged merrily away.

'If you like,' a voice offered in Daisy's ear, 'we could dance together while you're making your grovelling apologies to me.'

It was Dev Tyzack, the expression in his eyes faintly mocking, his tone conversational. No longer sporting jeans and a polo shirt, he now wore a well-cut dark suit. He had loosened his tie and there was a faint peach-tinted lipstick mark on the collar of his white shirt.

Oh well, get it over with, thought Daisy. Being forced to be polite to people who didn't deserve it was all part of the joys of hotel management. At least after today she'd never have to see him again.

'I'm sorry. How could I ever have doubted you? Your friend Dominic did nothing wrong and my chambermaid was entirely to blame for what happened earlier. Please accept my deepest and most sincere apologies,' lied Daisy, shooting him the blandest of smiles.

'Oh dear.' He started to laugh. 'That wasn't very convincing. Surely you can do better than that.'

I could, thought Daisy, but I'm jolly well not going to.

Treating Dev Tyzack to another blatantly insincere smile, she said, 'I meant every word.'

'And I think you could do with a drink.' Effortlessly catching the attention of a passing waitress, he presented Daisy with a flute of champagne.

It was a mocking gesture, clearly designed to tell her that it was time she loosened up.

As if.

'No thanks.' Daisy shook her head. 'I'm on duty.'

'Of course you are. Well, we could still have that dance.'

He was so enjoying having the upper hand.

'I don't think so.' She nodded briefly in the direction of his neck. 'You've got lipstick on your collar, by the way.'

Dev raised an eyebrow. 'Lucky you aren't my wife, then.'

'Very lucky.' Very lucky for *me*, thought Daisy.

'So are you married?' He glanced with some amusement at her ringless left hand.

'No.'

'Incredible. Who'd have thought it? You know, if you relaxed more,' Dev advised, 'I'm sure you could find yourself a husband.'

Luckily, the cake-cutting knife had by this time gone back to the kitchen.

'A husband?' Daisy opened her eyes wide. 'One of my very own, you mean? Or somebody's else's?'

He laughed again. 'Don't worry, I understand. Young girl running her dad's hotel, desperate to prove to him that she's up to the job. It can't be easy having to admit that you made such a big mistake.'

Don't retaliate, *don't* retaliate . . .

'It isn't easy.' Out of the corner of her eye, Daisy saw that both the mother and sister of the bride were watching her. 'You're absolutely right, Mr Tyzack. And as I said before, I can only apologise. Still, at least it's ended well. Everyone seems to be enjoying themselves. I'm sure the bride and groom will be very happy.'

'You don't think any such thing,' Dev Tyzack remarked cheerfully. 'You think Dominic's only marrying Annabel for her money.'

Daisy looked innocent. 'Why, does she have some?'

'Her father was in the underwear business, in quite a major way. When he died last year he left forty million pounds to be shared between his family. That's the three of them – his wife, Jeannie and Annabel.'

Forty million. Phew. That explained a lot. Crikey, forty *million*.

'In that case,' said Daisy, 'it must be true love. What's more,' she went on sweetly, 'I can't imagine what you're doing wasting time talking to me. You really should be over there dancing with Annabel's sister.'

'Come in, come in, look at you, you're soaked through,' Maggie chided, ushering Daisy in out of the driving, icy rain and through to the welcoming warmth of the living room. 'Shift your big bottom, Tara, let the poor girl sit by the fire.' Apologetically she added, 'You'll have to excuse her, Daisy, she's a bit maudlin.'

'I'm not surprised.' Teasingly, because she knew how much Tara hated it, Daisy reached over and ruffled her spiky, peroxide-blonde hair.

'I'm not maudlin,' Tara defended herself, batting Daisy's hands away from her head. 'Just mad. Pissed off with men in general and complete arseholes like Dominic in particular. I've decided to be a spinster all my life, like Maggie. A metaphorical spinster,' she added, wagging her finger as Maggie opened her mouth to object. 'OK, so you were married once, but that doesn't count. I'm talking about now and next year and the next twenty years after that. You know, I used to feel sorry for you,' Tara earnestly informed her aunt. 'I used to think it was dead sad, you leading such a boring lonely life with nothing ever happening in it, but now I realise you have absolutely the right idea. And that's it. From now on, I'm going to model myself on you.'

'Blimey, how much wine has she had?' Daisy seized the bottle of Montepulciano and held it up to the light. 'I think I'd better drink the rest of this.'

'Don't look at me like that, I'm not totally bollocksed,' Tara grumbled. 'Not hog-whimpering drunk. Just . . . just . . . piglet-whimpering.' God, why did whimpering have to be such a hard word to say?

'And you have every right to be.' Daisy gave Tara's arm an

affectionate squeeze. 'But if you want to carry on living here in this cottage, I'd stop calling your brilliant and generous auntie a sad, lonely old spinster if I were you.'

Tara shook her head emphatically, slopping red wine down the front of her sweatshirt. Luckily, being her designated staying-in-and-getting maudlin sweatshirt, it was used to being slopped on.

'No, no, *no*. I meant it in a nice way. It's a compliment! Maggie has the loveliest life of anyone I know, and from now on I want to be just like her. I'm going to start making jam and sewing things and listening to *The Archers* and baking cakes.'

'Fantastic.' Daisy kept a straight face.

'I'm going to give up nightclubs,' Tara was warming to her theme, 'and take up tapestry.'

'Oh, good grief, now I need a drink too,' exclaimed Maggie, disappearing into the kitchen and returning with a chilled bottle of Frascati and two more glasses. 'All this fuss over some silly ex-boyfriend you didn't even care about. Daisy, red or white?'

'But that's the whole point,' Tara argued. 'If someone you don't even care about can cause this much trouble, think what could happen if it was someone you were madly in love with! I'm telling you, I'm better off out of the whole thing. Go on then, I'll try the white now you've opened it.'

'You won't be able to drink like this when you're a professional spinster,' said Daisy. 'You'll end up baking the tapestries and sewing the jam.'

'How did the wedding go?' Maggie sat cross-legged on the rug in front of the fire. 'Everything run smoothly in the end?'

Daisy pulled a face. 'Well, they got married.'

'I don't know why he's bothering,' Tara snorted. 'He'll only cheat on her.'

'I could hazard a guess.' Daisy's tone was dry. 'He's probably bothering because she's just inherited a few million. Her father was big in knickers, apparently.'

'So she's loaded. No wonder he married her. Oh well.' Tara sighed and pulled the sleeves of her black sweatshirt over her knuckles. 'That's something to be grateful for, I suppose. At least nobody's ever going to want to marry me for my money.'

'Speaking of fathers.' Eager to get Tara off the subject of Dominic, Maggie turned to Daisy. 'How's your dad? When I bumped into him outside the shop the other day he told me he'd done something to his knee.'

'It's fine again now.' Daisy rolled her eyes. 'When I left the reception he was still dancing away, charming the slingbacks off all the women there. Do you know, they were actually arguing over who was next in line for a dance? And the bride's mother was foxtrotting around the room with him looking the picture of smugness. Honestly, she was like a whale wrapped up in a shiny purple shower curtain. Oh God,' Daisy groaned at the thought, 'and she's a stinking rich widow, probably on the lookout for husband number two. Poor Dad, what chance does he have? By the time I get back she'll have carted him off to Gretna Green.'

Laughing, Maggie topped up their glasses. 'I'm sure your father can look after himself.'

'She had an awfully determined glint in her eye. And huge long purple nails.'

'Speaking of nails,' Tara raised her head in order to rejoin the conversation, 'why did that best man look familiar? I know I don't know him, but I'm sure I've seen him before.'

'Dev Tyzack,' Daisy explained for Maggie's benefit. 'He used to play rugby for Bath and England. He retired last year. But I don't see what he has to do with nails.'

'He's as hard as nails. As mean as nails. All sharp and pointed and horrible, and I'd love to hit him on the head with a hammer.' At the sight of their blank faces, Tara shrugged and slumped back down on the sofa. 'Oh well, it made sense to me.'

'Dev Tyzack.' Maggie was visibly impressed. 'He is rather gorgeous.'

Tara curled her lip. 'Shame he doesn't have a personality to match.' She looked at Daisy. 'So did you have to apologise to him?'

'I did. But I made sure he knew I didn't mean a word of it.'

'And he was OK about that?' Tara raised her eyebrows. 'I mean, was he nice?'

Daisy thought for a moment.

'How can I put this?' she said finally. 'Uh . . . *no*.'

An hour later Daisy headed back to the hotel. The wedding party was winding up; already two taxis had passed her as she made her way along the High Street. The rain had eased off once more but the road was still wet and the temperature was dropping fast. Lucky old honeymooners, heading off for their three weeks in balmy St Lucia. Then again, Daisy thought, if marrying Dominic Cross-Calvert was the price you had to pay, she'd rather stay here freezing her doo-dahs off in Gloucestershire.

Except . . . was she being too hard on Dominic? What had he done really, other than find himself unexpectedly faced with an ex-girlfriend and, in the heat of the moment, get a bit carried away?

Then lie about it, of course, when he was caught out. Lie until he was blue in the face and swear he'd been the innocent party. Again, being brutally honest here, was there really anything so astonishing about that? About to marry Annabel, he'd simply panicked. And, who knew, maybe he wasn't marrying her for her bank balance, maybe it was her irresistible personality he'd fallen in love with after all.

'Yeeeuurrgh,' Daisy spluttered as a third taxi shot past, careering through a huge puddle and sending a great wave of muddy, ice-cold water over her. Great, just what she needed; the cream wool coat Hector had bought her for Christmas was now a filthy wet brown-stained cream wool coat. Furthermore, the soaking had been so comprehensive that even her face and hair were splashed with mud. What a brilliant end to a truly brilliant day.

Except it wasn't the end. As she was wiping her eyes and face with her equally wet hands, Daisy found herself caught in the glare of yet another set of headlights. As the car reached her at the hotel's gates, it slowed to a halt. The driver's window of the sporty black Mercedes slid open to reveal Dev Tyzack grinning up at her. Next to him in the passenger seat sat Jeannie, looking as if all her birthdays had come at once.

'What?' Daisy was curt, hideously aware of the muddy water trickling down her cheeks.

'You know, when I was little I always wanted to be the Milk Tray man.' Dev acted as though they were continuing a conversation that had been interrupted only moments earlier. 'I had this fantasy about abseiling from tall buildings, swimming through crocodile-infested waters and swinging across ravines to give the lady what she wanted more than anything else.'

Go on then, Daisy was hugely tempted to retort, better get a move on, because we all know what the lady in your passenger seat wants right now.

Aloud, she said, 'Really? How completely fascinating.'

'The bad news is, I'm all out of chocolates,' said Dev Tyzack.

'Gosh. Tragic.'

'Dev.' Next to him, Jeannie sniggered with delight. 'Come on, close the window now. I'm *coooold*.'

'Here. Don't say I never give you anything.' Still grinning, Dev passed a box of Kleenex through the open window.

Then, with a wink, he roared off.

Chapter 9

'This lot always amaze me,' murmured Rocky as Daisy joined him behind the bar to help out. 'I always thought writers were quiet, mousy types who wore tweed and wouldn't say boo to a goose. I just can't believe they make so much noise and drink so much. I'm telling you, these booky people know how to put it away.'

'They're probably excited to have been let out for the day.' Unlike Rocky, Daisy didn't bother lowering her voice. There wasn't a lot of point. The writers' group who met at the hotel for lunch and gossip every three months were networking madly and shrieking with delight at seeing each other again. Being allowed to talk to real-life humans instead of having to write about pretend ones was – along with the pre-lunch gin and tonics – clearly going to their heads.

'Don't forget I've got an hour off at lunchtime,' Daisy reminded him as she emptied bottles of Schweppes into a row of glasses.

'One till two. I know.' Clattering ice cubes into a tumbler, Rocky said hesitantly, 'Are you . . . um . . . looking forward to it?'

Oh God, was that a crass thing to say? He didn't have a clue. It was one of those weird situations not mentioned in the etiquette books. Not that he'd ever read an etiquette book, but he'd bet a year's wages it wasn't covered.

And now Daisy was looking at him as if he'd just asked permission to change into a tutu and pirouette the length of the bar.

'I don't know if I'm actually looking forward to it.' She pulled a face. 'Depends what this chap's like, I suppose. He's the one who was so keen to do this. I just don't want him to be, well, disappointed.'

'Kind of like a blind date,' said Rocky, and immediately wished he hadn't. How did he manage to come out with this stuff?

But Daisy was grinning.

'You know what you are, don't you? A hopeless case. Me meeting this chap at one o'clock is absolutely nothing like a blind date. From now on, Rocky, it's probably better if you stick to doing what you do best. Serving drinks.'

'I know.' Rocky was humble, mentally apologising for all he was worth. 'Sorry.'

'Anyway, apart from that, do I look all right?'

Enough of the apologies. He flicked a practised eye over Daisy as she did a brief twirl next to him.

'You look awful, a complete mess.'

Barney Usher was early. Far too early. The train from Manchester had reached Bristol Parkway bang on time, at eleven o'clock. He had jumped into a taxi and arrived in the village of Colworth at eleven twenty-three precisely.

Which meant he still had an hour and a half to kill. For Barney it felt like waking up at five thirty on Christmas morning, knowing that your parents had warned you on pain of death not to wake them before seven.

The fact that he was also feeling slightly sick had been partly due to the fact that for the last twenty-odd minutes he had been enclosed in a cab with his own aftershave. In his nervous state, he had slapped on far too much Kouros. It was a relief to climb out of the taxi and breathe in lungfuls of much-needed fresh air.

The taxi driver shot him a knowing smirk as Barney, shivering with a mixture of cold and anticipation, paid his fare and added a generous tip.

'Meeting a young lady, are we?'

Barney, who had been waiting for more than a year for this day to arrive, replied emphatically, 'Oh yes.'

But now that he was here at last, he could relax. The village was like no village he had ever seen before, and he couldn't wait to explore every inch of it.

The meandering main street was bordered by dinky Cotswold stone cottages. A river ran through the centre of the village and hills reared up on either side. To Barney, a born-and-bred city boy, everything looked unbelievably picturesque, like something out of a Disney film. It was hard to believe that real people actually lived here. But they did, they truly did. A real person was at this very moment emerging from her cottage a little way up the street, pushing one of those old people's shopping bags on wheels and heading for the village store.

Barney wondered why shopping bags on wheels were always tartan.

Well, why?

But at the same time he marvelled at how relaxed the old person was. Any pensioner hailing from his own neck of the woods in a rough part of Manchester would be scuttling down the road by now, in fear of being mugged and battered senseless by some psychopath or mad drug addict. This one, by contrast, was actually stopping to stroke a fat tortoiseshell cat on her neighbour's stone wall.

It was a complete eye-opener. Barney could hardly believe it.

Imagine stopping to stroke a cat! It genuinely hadn't occurred to this old dear that she might be on the verge of being set upon by thugs.

He took his time exploring the village, enjoying himself every inch of the way. There were three knick-knacky, souvenir-type shops. A village store doubling as a post office. One church. One pub. And an astonishing number of tourists, seeing as it was still only eleven thirty on a Friday morning in a small Cotswold village miles from the nearest town.

Plus, of course, there was the hotel.

Barney had done his homework, he knew that Colworth was famous for being one of the most beautiful villages in England. But he was still knocked out by just how fantastic it managed to be on an icy-cold morning in late January.

Aware of just how over-the-top he had gone with his after-shave, he was glad of the opportunity to walk around the village dispersing some of it into the cold, crisp air. He wanted to make a good impression, after all. Not send Daisy Standish heaving and vomiting into the nearest flower bed.

Checking his watch for the hundredth time, Barney decided to pay a visit to the post office-cum-general store. He would buy a packet of chewing gum and maybe some postcards of the village to take back and show his mum.

As he approached the shop, the door clanged open and a girl manoeuvred a pushchair with some difficulty out onto the pavement. Barney watched her struggle to get the wheels straight, but something was stopping them turning.

'Sorry, I'm in your way,' the girl panted, kicking the brake to make sure it was off. 'Damn, the wheels are locked, I don't know what's going on here.'

She was young and pretty, with wide grey eyes and dark brown shoulder-length hair, cut in a bob. The baby, by contrast, was very blond with dazzling blue eyes that exactly matched his all-in-one snowsuit. Entertained by all the frantic to-ing and fro-ing and jiggling about, he waved his carton of Ribena and shrieked with delight.

'It's OK, I can see what's happened.' Crouching down, Barney followed the plaited length of wool from the baby's discarded mittens and found it wound tightly round the nearside front wheel. 'The wheel's being garrotted. Keep it still . . .'

The plaited string was muddy and oily. Carefully he began to disentangle it. As he bent his head lower to see what he was doing, Barney felt something cold drip onto the back of his neck.

'Oh God, Freddie, stop it! Give me that,' the girl exclaimed, and the baby let out a squeal of outrage. Above Barney's head a swift battle ensued as the baby fought with his mother for custody of the Ribena carton. Barney flinched as a fountain of cold liquid sprayed his left cheek.

'There, all done.' Triumphantly he sat back on his heels and held up the freed length of mangled mitten string. The baby, making a grab for it, dropped the carton, watched the remains of his blackcurrant drink seep out into the gutter and promptly began to howl.

'You twit,' the girl exclaimed, adding hurriedly to Barney, 'Not you, I didn't mean you! Oh no, and now you're covered in Ribena, this is *so* embarrassing.'

She rummaged in the bag dangling from the handles of the pushchair and produced a packet of baby wipes. Barney rubbed one of the wipes over his face and the back of his neck. The baby, his screams doubling in volume, drummed his heels against the pushchair's footrest, pointing in dismay at his upended Ribena carton.

'I'm sorry, I'm really sorry. Once Freddie gets started, there's no stopping him,' the girl apologised profusely. 'All you did was help me out and now look at the state of you. I feel *terrible*.'

'I'm fine, really,' Barney assured her. 'It doesn't matter a bit. And he's only upset because he's lost his drink. Let me buy him another one and he'll soon cheer up.' He waggled his fingers at Freddie as he spoke. He liked children. When he crossed his eyes and pulled a face, Freddie was so entranced he actually stopped crying.

The next moment, remembering his motivation, he started again. Barney laughed.

'God, you are so nice,' the girl marvelled. 'I mean it. You're a seriously nice person.'

'I've got three nephews and four nieces,' said Barney. 'I've had plenty of practice with children. Now wait here, don't go away.'

Two minutes later he emerged from the shop with two cartons of Ribena, a Milky Bar, a box of Black Magic, several postcards of Colworth and three packets of Wrigleys Extra.

'Oh, come on.' The girl held up her hands in protest when she saw the Black Magic. 'I definitely can't let you buy me a box of chocolates.'

'Actually, I didn't get them for you,' said Barney, and grinned when she flushed pink.

'Sorry. Just ignore me, I'm an idiot.'

'There you go. Don't drink it all at once.' Barney stuck the plastic straw through the top of the Ribena carton and placed it carefully between Freddie's chubby hands. This earned him a gurgle of delight followed by a hefty burp.

'He says thank you,' the dark-haired girl solemnly explained.

'I know. His hands are cold.'

'Tell me about it.' She rolled her eyes in good-natured despair. 'He won't keep his mittens on for two minutes.'

'Anyway, he can have these later.' Barney slipped the Milky Bar and the second carton of juice into the bag containing Freddie's nappies and baby wipes.

'Oh God, you've got Ribena on your shirt! It's all soaked into the collar.' She looked appalled.

Barney couldn't see the dampness but he could feel it. He said, 'Maybe we could sponge it out somehow.' It was his best white shirt; he had bought it specially for today, from Next. It crossed his mind that this pretty girl, who must live here in the village, might offer to take him home with her in order to help with the spongeing. 'I'm meeting someone up at the hotel,' he added by way of explanation. 'I really wanted to look my best.'

'I know what we can do.' Mind-reading, sadly, didn't appear to be one of the girl's great strengths. 'The pub at the end of the street will be open by now. We'll go there and sort your shirt out in one of the loos. I'll scrub the collar with hot water and you can dry it under the hot-air thingy.'

Barney forced himself not to be disappointed. Of course she couldn't invite a total stranger into her home; for all she knew, he was an axe-wielding maniac.

Or, *or*, she might be embarrassed because her house was a tip, with washing-up in the sink and crumbs inches deep on the living-room carpet.

Then again, she could be married. Just because practically all the girls he knew back home were single mothers didn't mean there weren't some around who still did things the traditional way.

Stomach lurching, Barney glanced at her left hand. No rings, apart from a big swirly silver one on her thumb. Not married, then. Although she could still have a live-in boyfriend who might not take kindly to her bringing home unknown men in order to scrub purple stains out of their shirts.

Barney hoped she didn't.

The pub, the ludicrously picturesque Hollybush Inn, opened early in order to serve coffee and over-priced croissants to the tourist trade. Thankfully nobody else – no ladies, at least – were in need of the loo. Having stripped off his navy sweater and the brand new Next shirt, Barney watched the dark-haired girl rinse the collar under the hot tap, douse it with liquid soap from the squidgy machine and scrub it for all she was worth. Freddie, in his pushchair, was delighted to discover that by waving his fat little fingers in the air he could make hot air whoosh noisily out of the machine on the wall.

Fifteen minutes later, the shirt was dry.

'We've cost them a fortune in hot air,' said Barney. 'The least we can do is buy a couple of coffees.'

Freddie's mother looked with regret at her watch. 'I can't. We have to go. Dentist's appointment.' She pulled a face, then straightened his shirt collar. 'Still, at least you're sorted. You'll make your good impression.'

She was right. Of course she was. For a few minutes he'd forgotten why he was here.

'Thanks,' said Barney.

Freddie's mother broke into a broad smile. 'My pleasure.'

Tara, halfway through her shift, was polishing tiles on autopilot. Her body might be working away energetically but her mind was elsewhere, going fretfully over and over last night's horrendous discovery.

It had been awful, it really had. One minute she'd been draped across the sofa happily watching some drippy girl in *EastEnders* whining, 'But why's it always *me* wot gets dumped? Woss *wrong* wiv me, eh?' The answer to this one being that whining drippy girls with lank hair and as much personality as a parsnip deserved to be treated appallingly and surely couldn't expect to keep a boyfriend for longer than it took to boil an egg. The next moment, a weird creeping sensation Tara wasn't immediately able to place had made its insidious way up the back of her neck.

With a jolt of horror, she had realised finally that the sensation was one of . . . familiarity.

EastEnders forgotten, Tara had begun mentally counting back on her fingers, running through her list of boyfriends in reverse order.

Oh no, surely not, she wasn't that much of a loser, was she?

But it was looking that way. Still counting, Tara reached the ages of fifteen and sixteen, her earlier dating years.

There was Trevor, who'd had the most extraordinary up-and-down voice – God, he'd practically yodelled when he talked. Then Dave, who'd had funny ears but a cute smile. And Andy Buckingham, who, despite being the star of the school football team, had had skinny legs and a sprouty mole on his cheek. None of them had been what you'd call perfect, yet—

'Hi, it's me.' Daisy stuck her head round the bathroom door. 'Fancy going out tonight? We could hit a couple of clubs in Bath.'

Crikey, it's not as if we're talking Brad Pitt here, Tara thought wildly. I mean, if you went out with Brad Pitt you'd *expect* to be dumped. But these had just been ordinary boys, nice enough, each with their own good and bad points.

'If you polish those tiles any harder,' said Daisy, 'you're going to end up crashing through the wall.'

'Every boy I've ever been out with,' Tara blurted out, 'has finished with me! Every single sodding buggering boyfriend I've had! I can't believe it, I never realised until last night. I even wrote them all down, made a proper list in case I'd accidentally missed anyone out, but I hadn't. Oh God, can you imagine? It's so humiliating. I've never been the one to do the dumping, I've always, *always* been the dumpee.'

'Oh, come on, you're exaggerating.' Daisy attempted to reassure her. 'That can't be true.'

'It is, it is!'

'What about when you were at school?'

'Especially when I was at school! God, I'm a completely pathetic person,' Tara wailed.

'OK, right, we'll sort you out.' Daisy took control. 'This evening we'll go into Bath. You can chat up heaps of men and hand out your phone number to all and sundry. Then, when any of them ring you up to invite you out for a drink, you can say no. Turn them down flat. Would that make you feel better?'

'Tuh. Doesn't count.'

'It's a start.'

'Anyway,' Tara bent down to polish the bath taps, 'I don't fancy giving my number out to a load of idiots.'

'OK, tell them to call you on this one. Write it down for them,' said Daisy, taking a pen from her jacket pocket and reversing out of the bathroom. She returned moments later with a sheet of hotel writing paper upon which she had scrawled:

770 2219

Tara stared at it blankly. 'And what good would that do?'

'Turn the paper over,' said Daisy with a wink, 'and hold it up to the light.'

Chapter 10

The sun came out as Daisy was making her way down the hotel drive. She had arranged to meet Barney Usher at the main gates at exactly one o'clock. Something about the tone of his letters told her Barney would be prompt.

And yes, there he was, waiting for her. She could see him up ahead, leaning against one of the lichened stone pillars, wearing a navy crew neck sweater over a white shirt and dark blue trousers.

And with one of her late husband's kidneys pumping away inside him.

Well, maybe not pumping exactly, but working away doing whatever it was kidneys did.

As she drew closer, Daisy saw that Barney Usher looked younger than twenty-six. The sunlight bounced off his gleaming blond hair. He had a sweet, youthful face, dark hopeful eyebrows and long-lashed big brown eyes like a spaniel puppy.

In view of his prettiness, she couldn't help wondering if he was gay. Ha, that would really piss Steven off.

'Mrs Standish?' he said eagerly, and for a moment Daisy almost looked over her shoulder. Even when she'd been married to Steven she'd had a struggle to remember that, officially, this was her name. It had always made her feel like an impostor. Reverting to MacLean had been such a relief.

'Call me Daisy.' She smiled at him, wondering if he was as nervous as she was. This was definitely a weird situation to be in.

But it didn't appear to have occurred to Barney Usher to feel nervous. He took her hand and shook it, his face lighting up with happiness.

'And I'm Barney – although of course you already know that! Thank you for agreeing to meet me . . . you don't know how much this means . . . giving me the chance to thank you in person . . . it was such a fantastic thing you did and I'm just so grateful—'

'OK, *stop*,' Daisy blurted out and he obediently froze in mid-sentence. 'Look, you thanked me in your first letter. You thanked me in your second letter and in the third and in the fourth. It's done now, you don't have to say it any more.'

'But I *want* to—'

'Stop! I already know how grateful you are. But I haven't done anything heroic here, and it's starting to get embarrassing. So can we give it a rest?' She tilted her head and smiled. 'Please?'

'OK.' Barney nodded, smiling too. 'I'm sorry. Oh, and these are for you.' Opening up his carrier bag, he pulled out a box of Black Magic chocolates. 'It's not much, I know, but I didn't want to carry flowers all the way down on the train in case they wilted or got squashed. I hoped there'd be a flower shop here in the village, but there isn't. So I picked these up in the post office. They didn't have a lot of choice. I wish it could have been something more, but—'

'Black Magic are my favourites,' Daisy lied firmly. 'Thank you. Thank you. Thank you thank you thank you, they're perfect, I'm so grateful, thank you thank you.'

When Barney laughed, he looked like Prince William.

'OK, I get the message. I promise to shut up. I'll never

say thank you again.' His brown eyes danced with mischief. 'I might be thinking it, but I won't say it. You have my word.'

They visited the graveyard first. Barney stood and gazed at Steven's headstone in silence, no doubt mentally thanking him too. Daisy, who had been worried that he might cry, was glad when he didn't.

At last, his voice gentle, Barney said, 'You must have loved him very much.'

It didn't seem an appropriate moment to say, 'Hardly at all, actually. In fact I hated his guts.' Instead Daisy murmured, 'He was my husband,' which was a complete cop-out, of course, but the truth nevertheless.

'Beautiful flowers.' Barney nodded at the fresh roses, evidently thinking she had left them there herself.

'Yes,' agreed Daisy.

'You must miss him terribly.'

'Oh well, you know how it is. Life goes on.' Daisy couldn't bring herself to tell him; she didn't have the heart. This visit was for Barney's benefit, not hers. Spoiling the fairytale for him would be like telling a small child that Cinderella had ended up in a refuge for battered wives.

She shoved her hands into her jacket pockets and shivered.

'You're cold,' said Barney, apparently impervious to the dropping temperature himself. 'I'm sorry, keeping you out here like this.'

'Why don't we go up to the hotel,' Daisy suggested, 'and have a nice drink and a chat?'

They headed together up the drive. Barney was deeply impressed by Colworth Manor.

'Look at this, it's so beautiful.' He shook his head, lost in admiration. 'I've never seen anything like it before. What a fantastic place.'

It was like leading a three-year-old into Santa's grotto. As Daisy took him through the hall and into the bar, he was gazing around in wide-eyed wonder, genuinely knocked out by the oak-panelled walls, the Adam fireplace and the chandeliers.

'Now,' said Daisy. 'Coffee or a proper drink?'

'Oh, coffee would be great. I don't really drink,' Barney explained.

God, no, he probably wasn't allowed to for medical reasons. She mentally kicked herself.

'If you like, I'll show you around the hotel later.'

He looked delighted. 'I'd love to see it, if you're sure you're not too busy.'

'And how about food? If you're hungry, we could have some lunch.'

'This is really kind of you,' said Barney. 'But I don't want to be a nuisance.'

Daisy felt guilty. It wasn't kind of her at all, she was just desperately trying to find things to do to pass the time. When someone had travelled all the way down from Manchester to see you, it hardly seemed fair to give them coffee and a biscuit, chat to them politely for ten minutes and then send them packing. That would be mean.

At least the bar was relatively peaceful now; the writers' convention had piled noisily into the dining room. Having arranged for a pot of coffee to be brought through to them, Daisy settled herself opposite Barney on one of the sofas flanking the open fire and announced brightly, 'So, here we are then, isn't this nice?' and instantly felt ancient. God, of all

81

the patronising, ridiculous things to say. She sounded like some 75-year-old tweed-knickered maiden aunt.

Barney, his tone understanding, said, 'Are you finding this a bit difficult?'

'*Me?* No!' She rattled her head vehemently from side to side, like a big maraca. 'Of course not, why should it be difficult?'

He gave her a sympathetic look. 'It must feel a bit strange. More strange for you than for me.'

'Well,' Daisy conceded, 'a bit strange. But not in a horrid way,' she added quickly, in case he was offended.

'How about if I tell you about myself?' Barney offered. All of a sudden he seemed to be the grown-up, the one in charge. Eagerly, he went on, 'I'll talk about me for a bit, then you can tell me about you. Then you could talk about your husband Steven . . . but only if you want to . . . and then after that I'll go. Does that sound OK?'

He'd clearly spent ages planning this out, Daisy realised. Well, it meant a lot to him, of course he'd planned it.

Grateful that he had, she nodded with relief and said, 'Sounds perfect.'

Together they pored over the photos he had brought along with him.

'That's me when I was seven,' Barney explained, 'with my mum. She sends her love, by the way. And this is us about three years ago. We were out on our balcony and it was a windy day, that's why Mum's hair's gone mad.'

'Balcony,' teased Daisy. 'Now there's posh. And look at the view!'

Barney smiled. 'It's the twenty-seventh floor of a tower block, that's why we've got a view. And no, it isn't what you'd call posh but, you know, it's home. Well, it *was* my home,' he went on, producing the next photo with a flourish.

'But I'm here now, sharing a flat with some friends from work.'

To spare her embarrassment he had moved swiftly on. Pink-cheeked, Daisy studied this new photo of Barney and three other lads laughing together on a sofa.

No danger of calling this living room posh. It was a typical student-type flat, awash with overflowing ashtrays and lager cans, the carpet spectacularly threadbare, the sofa stained and torn.

Since she could hardly say how lovely it was, Daisy said, 'Looks like fun.'

'Well,' Barney's smile was self-deprecating, 'in a grubby, messy kind of way. Mum's really houseproud so she almost had a fit when she first saw it, but the lads are great. And up until last year I never thought I'd be able to do normal stuff like going out to clubs and meeting girls. I'd spent so long in hospital missing out on that kind of thing, it was like a miracle. I'm just so lucky to have this new start.'

A lump sprang into Daisy's throat. The next moment it expanded as he showed her the third photo.

'This is me on my eighteenth birthday. I'd been through a bit of a bad patch, which is why I'm looking a bit feeble,' Barney explained.

Talk about understatement.

The photograph had been taken in his hospital room. Barney, pale and hollow-cheeked, lay in bed attached to some huge machine, but he was smiling and holding up a plastic beaker. Birthday cards were strung up over the bed and friends and family were gathered around self-consciously clutching cups of tea and plates of birthday cake.

'Not the wildest party you ever saw,' Barney said cheerfully. 'Me on dialysis and pumped full of drugs, my auntie bursting into tears every five minutes because she was convinced I was about to die, and my nephews begging to go home because they couldn't stand the hospital smell.'

Daisy wanted to hug him. 'You've got some catching up to do.'

'Don't I know it.' Barney's eyes shone. 'This is the life I never thought I'd have, and I'm not going to waste a day of it.'

Over lunch in the dining room – well away from the shrieking, well-oiled authors – he asked Daisy about Steven and she told him everything he wanted to know. The questions ranged from what had been Steven's favourite food, which sports he had most enjoyed and what kind of music he'd liked, to how he and Daisy had first met. Daisy, who had prepared for this eventuality, took a couple of photographs of Steven out of her handbag and let Barney study them closely for a couple of minutes. Terrified that he might launch into another chorus of 'God, you must miss him terribly', she declared, 'And now I want to hear all about your job!'

Barney worked for the Civil Service. He was a clerical officer in the Department of Transport. It was pretty dull, but he was grateful to be employed and the people in his office were OK. Daisy, interrogating shamelessly, discovered that one of the young secretaries had a bit of a crush on him, but otherwise no, he didn't have a girlfriend right now, he was waiting for the right one to come along.

'My mates think I'm mad,' Barney confided with a shy smile. 'They reckon I should be shagg— um, working my way through all the girls in Manchester, making up for lost time. But that's not what I want to do. The right girl's out there, somewhere. I'd rather wait. That way it's more special, don't you think?'

Bless him! Bless his little heart! I'm sitting here having lunch with the last virgin in Manchester, thought Daisy. Heavens, his mother must be proud.

Brenda, Daisy's secretary, approached their table with an apologetic lift of her eyebrows.

'Daisy? Sorry to interrupt, but I'm off in a minute. Could you just check the ad to go in the local paper, make sure it's OK? Then I can fax it through to them before I leave.'

Daisy took the typed sheet of paper and shooed hard-working Brenda away.

'Don't worry, you can go now. I'll fax the ad through.'

Brenda, desperate not to miss the bus into Bath for her tap class, said gratefully, 'You're an angel.'

Daisy grinned. 'I know, I'm fabulous. Off you go.'

After lunch, she gave Barney a guided tour of the rest of the hotel. He loved every inch of it.

'And don't forget your fax,' he reminded Daisy in his soft Mancunian accent as they left the ballroom.

'Right, I'd better do it now. Oh Lord, just ignore them,' Daisy hissed as they passed the bar where the rumbustious writers' group were now gathering around the piano. 'Especially ignore the embarrassing man with the green bow tie and the loudest voice. After a couple of whiskies he does like to pretend he's Pavarotti.'

Barney, his eyes wide, murmured, 'Is he one of your guests?'

'Much worse than that. He's my dad.'

But it was, of course, impossible to avoid Hector. Having spotted them, he rushed out to the hall and greeted Barney like a long-lost son.

'You must be Barney! How marvellous to see you, and looking so well! Now, tell me, do you sing?'

'I know I've got to kill him,' a female voice fretted, just behind Barney. 'I just don't know how.'

'Carving knife? Shotgun?' suggested a second voice. 'Or how about shoving him off the top of a tall building?'

'D'you know, I thought of that, but I don't want anything too messy. Shattered skulls and intestines splattered all over the place aren't really my scene. What I'm after is something quick and painless – after all, he's not such a bad chap. Quite sweet, really. I'll miss him dreadfully when he's gone.'

His mouth dropping open, Barney swung round to stare at the mousy-looking pair deep in conversation not three feet away. Two women in their fifties, earnestly debating the best way of murdering some poor chap who was . . . good grief . . . quite sweet really.

'Come on,' Hector urged, clapping Barney on the shoulder. 'A fine-looking lad like you must be able to sing! How about "Mac The Knife"?'

'You could always poison him,' suggested the mousier of the two women behind Barney. 'A nice drop of cyanide would do the trick.'

'Oh, excellent idea! D'you know, I think I'll do that! Now, where would I be able to pick up some cyanide?'

'Don't panic,' Daisy told Barney with a grin. 'They write murder mysteries.'

Barney pretended he'd known that all along. *Phew*.

'Maybe a duet?' Hector persisted. '"New York, New York"? You must know the words to that one.'

'I'm not very good at singing.' Barney looked worried.

'No problem,' Hector declared. 'I'm sensational. Maestro, please!' he bellowed across at the thriller writer-cum-guest pianist.

'Dad, don't bully him into singing if he doesn't want to.' Daisy did her best to protect Barney, but it was too late. Hector was already dragging him over to the Bechstein. The pianist promptly launched into an almost accurate rendition of 'New York, New York', Hector and Barney sang their hearts out and the writers' group – by this time well away – joined in with boisterous enthusiasm.

Barney, bright-eyed and flushed with success, was giving it his all and clearly having a whale of a time. Daisy, watching from the doorway, decided with amusement that Steven would be turning in his grave and groaning with disgust if he knew that even one small part of him was involved in one of Hector's infamous impromptu sing-alongs. He had always flatly refused to participate on the grounds that it was, variously, pathetic, undignified and the kind of activity that only a complete moron would enjoy. Joining in for the sheer fun of it was a concept Steven had never been able to understand.

Oh yes, if he was watching now, he'd definitely be loathing every minute of this.

The song ended and the audience applauded wildly, which just went to show how drunk they were. Laughing, Barney made his way back over to Daisy as a vast blonde woman in her late sixties flung her arm round Hector's waist and joyfully announced to the room that, 'Tonight, Matthew, I am going to be Martine McCutcheon.'

'Don't say I didn't warn you,' Daisy told Barney.

He shook his head in wonder. 'What's it like, having a dad like that?'

'Embarrassing.' Daisy paused then added cheerfully, 'But never dull.'

'Don't forget that fax.' Barney nudged the sheet of paper still in her hand.

'God, no, I mustn't. I'll do it now. D'you want to stay here, or come with me?'

The pianist launched into 'Perfect Moment'. The enormous

87

blonde woman, her heavily bejewelled fingers clutched to her chest, opened her mouth and began to sing in a quavering off-key falsetto.

Heroically, Daisy kept a straight face.

'If you don't mind,' said Barney, 'I think I'll come with you.'

Chapter 11

Afterwards, Barney would always be able to recall in technicolour detail the moment he changed the course of his life. He'd been standing in Daisy's chaotic office with his back to the window and his hands in his pockets, watching her sift through the list of phone messages left by Brenda, the tap-dancing secretary. Daisy was perched on one corner of her desk, her long, brown hair swinging over one shoulder and one foot casually propped up on the swivel chair in front of her. She was wearing a peacock-blue silk shirt and a narrow, emerald green skirt that ended above the knee. As she swivelled round to grab a pen, the letter waiting to be faxed through to the newspaper fluttered to the floor.

Eager to help, Barney bent to retrieve it and said, 'Do you want me to deal with this for you?'

Daisy looked up, pleased. 'Could you? That'd be great.'

He didn't mean to be nosey, but Barney couldn't help noticing what was on the sheet of paper before he fed it into the machine.

It wasn't a letter, he realised. The hotel was advertising in the local *Gazette* for a porter.

That was the moment it happened.

Catching his breath as the idea came hurtling up at him, Barney stopped and gazed out of the window at the cedar trees, the sweeping lawns, the rush-fringed river and the rolling hills, now wreathed in mist. Then he looked across at Daisy, busy scribbling something on her calendar. Across the hallway drifted the sounds of a piano being played with rather more enthusiasm than finesse, and twenty or so inebriated writers, led by Hector MacLean, raucously bawling along to 'We'll Meet Again'.

'Problem?' said Daisy. 'Want me to show you how it works?'

Barney took a deep breath. Here goes.

'This, um, job. It doesn't say anything here about qualifications.'

Daisy grinned. 'It's for a porter, not a brain surgeon.'

'The thing is, how would you feel if . . . I mean, I know this might seem a bit weird,' Barney stammered, 'but, well, what I'm getting at is, would you consider me if I applied for the job?' He heard himself blurt the words out in a rush. OK, not the smoothest interview technique in the world, but up until twenty seconds ago none of this had even occurred to him. It was the ultimate spur-of-the-moment decision.

Daisy was looking pretty startled too. 'What? You mean you want to be a porter? But you work for the Civil Service!'

Barney was touched that she made him sound so important, like the head of Nato or something, rather than the lowly pen-pusher he actually was.

'Look, I don't want to sound creepy, like some weirdo or something. I know I came here to meet you today because of . . . you know, what happened to Steven. But that's not why I want the job, I swear.'

'Well, good,' said Daisy. 'Because you're right, that would definitely give me the creeps.'

Barney shook his head vigorously. 'The thing is, the moment I got out of the taxi this morning, I just thought what a fantastic place this was. The village is . . . amazing. And the people were so friendly! Then I met you and you showed me over the hotel and it's like nothing I've ever seen before. Where I live, it's . . . well, pretty rough, to be honest. Lots of drug addicts, violence, flats getting broken into, people getting mugged. It's scary, you don't ever really relax. Unless you've lived there, you can't imagine what it's like. It's the opposite of here. I mean, look at this.' Turning, he gestured out of the window. 'Imagine waking up in the morning and seeing this view, instead of boarded-up shops and burnt-out cars and people dealing hard drugs on the street. Living here would be – God, it would be like a *dream*.'

Daisy's gaze had dropped to the sheet of paper he was still holding. Barney realised that his hands were trembling with excitement.

'What about your job?'

'I hate my job.' He said it with a passion. 'I do, I can't stand it! I loathe being stuck in an office where you can't even open the windows. It's like being back in hospital, it drives me mad. I'd much rather be a porter, I know I would!'

'You'd be a long way from home.' Daisy was concerned. 'And there's your family to consider. How would your mum feel about you moving away?'

'She knows I hate my job. Mum just wants me to be happy,' Barney said eagerly. 'She'd be pleased. If she could see this place, she'd love it as much as I do!'

'This portering business,' Daisy warned. 'It doesn't pay much.'

'I don't care!'

'It's shift work. Days and nights.'

'No problem!'

'Do you know what hotel porters actually *do*?'

Uh . . . no. Not a clue.

'Carry cases?' Barney hazarded. 'I can carry cases,' he added

91

proudly, in case she thought he was some kind of invalid. 'I'm really strong.'

'Carry cases,' Daisy agreed. 'Clean people's shoes. And deliver their papers. Basically, you'd be a gofer. Anything the customer asks for, you sort it out. If they want a prostitute at three o'clock in the morning, you arrange it for them.'

Blimey. Barney's eyes widened.

'I'm joking,' said Daisy.

'Oh. Right.'

'And the staff quarters are pretty basic. You wouldn't be living in a suite like the ones I showed you upstairs.'

'I know that,' Barney said patiently. 'I'm not stupid.'

Daisy smiled. 'Of course you aren't. May I?' She held out her hand for the sheet of paper. Barney passed it over, expecting her to rip it up and say cheerfully, 'Well then, looks like we won't be needing this after all!'

He watched in horror as she promptly fed it into the fax machine.

'Oh, but—'

'No, I'm not going to say yes now.' Daisy was firm. 'You have to go home and think about this. Sleep on it. The advert's going into the paper this weekend because we need a porter and you might change your mind. Talk it over with your family. Think of the friends you'd be leaving behind. Give me a ring on Friday and let me know what you decide. If you want the job, it's yours. If you don't want the job, we'll find someone else. Now, would you like to have a look at the staff quarters before you go?'

'No.' Barney shook his head. 'Because I've already decided, and it doesn't matter what the staff quarters are like. You could show me a wooden rabbit hutch in the back garden and I'd still say yes.'

He meant it, he'd never been so sure of anything in his life.

For a mad moment he thought of asking Daisy if she knew the name of the girl he had met in the village, the one with the straight dark hair and the startlingly blond blue-eyed baby. Daisy would be bound to know her, wouldn't she? Plus, she'd be able to tell him whether the girl was as single as her ringless hands had seemed to suggest . . .

No, no, no, he *couldn't* ask that. What would Daisy think, that he was actually some kind of creepy stalker-type after all? That he only had to be in a new place for five minutes before getting fixated on some innocent young mother?

Barney inwardly shuddered with relief. God, thank goodness he hadn't actually said it; she'd think he was a complete saddo.

'Go home and have a chat about it with your family,' Daisy repeated. 'Give me a ring on Friday.'

'OK.' Barney grinned at her. 'You're the boss.'

Shortly before nine o'clock that evening, Daisy and Tara arrived at the Clifton Wine Bar in Bristol. Tara couldn't wait to hand out her phone number to heaps of men then snub them when they rang her up. She'd been looking forward to it all day.

'So what's this Barney fellow like?' she asked Daisy, once they'd been served at the bar.

'Sweet, young and very innocent.' Daisy gave her a don't-get-your-hopes-up look. 'You'd scare the living daylights out of him.'

'I don't know why.' Tara was fretful, clutching her drink. 'I mean, it's not as if I'm a scary person.'

A group of lads three feet away, having overheard her, promptly threw up their hands in terror and in unison screamed, 'Aaarrgh!'

'Oh ha ha, very droll. But tell me honestly,' Tara pleaded,

turning to them, 'how could anyone look at me and find me frightening?'

The tallest of the boys stepped back and pretended to assess her from head to toe.

'Seriously?'

'Seriously.'

'OK. The make-up, the chest and the jacket.' He paused. 'Especially that jacket.'

'But it's new!' cried Tara, plucking in distress at the fitted, faded denim with the embroidered collar and satin-trimmed facings.

'It's naff,' the boy kindly informed her.

'Oh no, it definitely can't be naff. Nigella Lawson wears embroidered denim jackets and she's a goddess. That's why I bought this one,' Tara earnestly explained. 'So I could look like Nigella.'

'But you don't.' Struggling to be honest, the boy surveyed her short, white-blonde hair, top-heavy curves, skin-tight jeans and pointy-toed boots. 'You look like Dolly Parton with her wig off.'

Daisy felt sorry for Tara. OK, so tonight's outfit wasn't helping, but it didn't seem to matter what Tara wore, she always managed to look faintly . . . wanton. Even in her chambermaid's uniform she exuded an air of availability. This was probably why her love life was so disastrous; any man meeting her for the first time automatically assumed that she was a saucy good-time girl up for a bit of fun.

'Oh, cheer up.' The boy gave Tara a reassuring nudge. 'At least you aren't ugly. Tell you what,' he added generously, 'I've got to go now, but why don't I take you out for a drink some other night?'

This was another thing Tara had come to notice over the years.

If men were genuinely interested in a girl, they invited her out for dinner. In her case it was almost always a drink.

Still, what the hell, she didn't fancy him either. Him or any of his smirking mates.

'Sounds great. Give me a ring.' Pleased with herself, she scribbled her name and number on the back of a beer mat.

'I'll call you tomorrow,' said the boy. 'My name's Jerry, by the way.'

By eleven thirty, thanks to some pretty intensive flirting, Tara had managed to give her real number out to four more men as well as the joke number to a total nerd. As they made their way back to Daisy's car she did a little twirl of satisfaction on the pavement, narrowly missing a lamp-post.

'Now that's what I call a decent night's work. Five men are going to ring me tomorrow and I'm going to tell each and every one of them to get stuffed. God, I can't wait.'

'They might not all ring,' Daisy warned.

'Oh, stop it, you're just jealous, you can't stand it that I'm irresistible and you're not. I really, really enjoyed myself tonight!' This time Tara spotted the lamp-post in the nick of time, grabbed hold of it and swung herself round it like Gene Kelly. 'Ha, and I'm going to enjoy myself even more when those phone calls start rolling in.'

Daisy wished she had six glasses of wine sloshing around inside her like Tara instead of a gallon of Coke.

'Isn't it about time you learned to drive? I thought Maggie was going to teach you.'

'Excuse me, have you *seen* the way that woman drives? No thanks.' Tara hiccuped and shook her head vigorously. 'Get her behind a wheel and she turns into Eddie Irvine. It's terrifying. She'd just be yelling at me to go faster all the time. Anyway, don't change the subject. I've had a brilliant time tonight, tomorrow's my day off and I'm going to dump loads of men. Well, at least three.'

Tara woke up at ten o'clock the next morning, feeling all-powerful and extraordinarily good about herself. When she looked in the bathroom mirror she saw an attractive, desirable person. Her stars in the *Daily Mail* informed her that today was the day to initiate change and prove to the world that she wasn't a pushover.

Which was all excellent news. Tara could hardly wait to get started.

The trouble was, the phone didn't ring. Not even once.

Chapter 12

His name was Otto, but that wasn't his fault. He was six years old and he was sobbing so hard he could barely speak.

The same, sadly, couldn't be said of his mother, who was showing no signs of running out of breath.

New Yorkers. Couldn't you just gag them? That shrill nasal whine like a dentist's drill was reverberating right through Daisy's head.

'Mrs Wilder, I know Otto's upset, I can see he is, but I promise you I *can't* dial nine nine nine. The fire brigade only rescue people or animals. They really wouldn't like it if we called them out to rescue a plastic aeroplane from a tree.'

'But he's cryin' here! Look at his little faaace,' shrieked Mrs Wilder as Otto's sobs doubled in volume. 'And it's not like it's some kinda *cheap* plastic aeroplane. This cost a lotta money, we got it in Harrods, let me tell you. Jeez, Otto baby, willya give it a rest? You're gonna burst Mommie's eardrums with all that racket.'

It was certainly a bit much at nine thirty in the morning.

'I'm really sorry, but we still can't call out the fire brigade,' Daisy repeated patiently.

'But I'd pay 'em!' Mrs Wilder wrenched open her bag and flipped open a wallet bristling with credit cards. 'They'd come then, wouldn't they? If I gave 'em, say, two hundred of your English pounds?'

'P-p-p-please,' sobbed Otto, huge tears rolling down his pale freckled face.

Daisy's heart melted. Mrs Wilder might be a nightmare but Otto was actually a sweet little lad, cheerful as a rule and far nicer than you'd expect. Yesterday he had shyly confided in Daisy that his favourite film was *The Sound Of Music*.

'Come on,' Daisy said, with an inwardly sinking heart. 'Let's go and have a look. Why don't you show me where it is?'

Otto, his eyes lighting up with hope, slipped his small hand trustingly into Daisy's.

'You'll be able to help me, won't you?' His lower lip trembled as he blinked up at her from behind his round, Harry Potter spectacles. 'You'll get my aeroplane back.'

The cedar tree out on the front lawn was sixty or seventy feet high. Bert and Kelvin, the hotel's handymen, had propped an aluminium ladder against one of the lower branches. Otto's red and white aeroplane was lodged thirty or so feet above the top rung of the ladder.

'We gave it our best shot, love.' Bert shook his head apologetically at Daisy. He would address the Queen as love if she rolled up in her royal carriage. 'Kelvin got up as far as the third branch, but then 'e lost 'is nerve.'

'It's dead slippery up there.' Kelvin's tone was defensive. 'Joe and Barry had a go after me, but they couldn't do it neither. We've tried everything now.'

Otto's face crumpled once more. He was still hanging on tightly to Daisy's hand.

'OK, OK.' Daisy realised she had to at least try. As a child she'd always been brilliant at climbing trees. 'Ssh, don't cry, sweetheart. Bert, lend us your boilersuit. I'll give it a go.'

'Wow-ee,' Otto screamed delightedly, jumping up and down. 'You'll be like Wonderwoman!'

Well, maybe.

Three minutes later, feeling absolutely nothing like Wonderwoman, Daisy began to scale the lower branches of the tree. She was wearing Bert's poo-coloured boilersuit over her cream leather trousers and burgundy cashmere sweater. Her feet were bare, for better grip. And every time she moved, droplets of water showered down from the leaves above. Which was unexpected, seeing as it hadn't rained for over a week.

'Why's it so *wet* up here?' Daisy called down to the small gathering below.

'Kelvin's idea,' Bert bellowed back. 'He tried to dislodge the plane wiv an 'igh pressure 'ose.'

Oh, fantasic, Kelvin. Top marks. Daisy blinked as yet another avalanche of water splattered her face. Her feet were icy and her hair was dripping, but she was making progress. As she strained to reach the next branch, a car roared up the drive and swung round into the car park.

'Nearly there, nearly there,' screamed Otto, delirious with excitement.

Daisy's heart lurched into her mouth as she momentarily lost her balance. She grabbed the branch above her head and clung on for dear life, steadying herself before taking a deep breath and searching for the next secure foothold. The brightly painted plane was just a few feet out of reach, she couldn't give up now. Blimey, it was a long way down.

An incredulous voice, drifting up from below, said, 'Rescuing a what? A toy *plane*? What kind of idiot would climb a tree that size to rescue a toy?'

Daisy paused to hear Otto, her hero, reply with passion, 'She isn't an idiot, don't call her that! She's Wonderwoman.'

Gazing down in disbelief, Daisy saw Dev Tyzack peering up at her.

'Daisy, you must be mad.' He had his hands on his hips and his expression was serious. 'Come on now, that's enough. Just get yourself down in one piece.'

Was that his don't-mess-with-me, I'm-the-boss voice? The one he used when he was ordering other people around? Daisy couldn't resist giving the branch she was currently clinging to a quick shake, hoping to catch him before he dodged out of the way.

Damn, he was quick.

'Daisy! This is dangerous,' Dev warned.

'Nearly there,' she sang back, more determined than ever not to give up now. Curling her toes against the rough bark, she climbed higher and higher. At last the aeroplane was within reach.

'Hooray!' screamed Otto, clapping his hands. 'Don't break it!'

Daisy tugged the plane free from the v-shaped branch in which it had become wedged, and sent it sailing down to earth.

Dev Tyzack. Of all the times to bump into him again. It was just typical.

Climbing back down was harder than getting up the tree. Feeling ungainly and less than alluring in her poo-coloured boilersuit, Daisy wished they'd all go away and leave her to it, instead of gathering around like some enthralled circus audience, watching her bottom getting bigger and bigger as it approached them.

Finally reaching the ladder, she looked down and saw that Dev was holding it steady.

'Let go,' she told him crossly. 'I can manage.'

'You've got this far, Wonderwoman,' he drawled back. 'No point breaking your legs at the last minute.'

Daisy's feet were by this time so numb with cold she could barely feel them. Water from the leaves had drenched her hair and was running into her eyes. If Dev Tyzack put his hands on her hips in order to guide her down the last few rungs, she would know he was one of those over-familiar, touchy-feely men and be forced to accidentally kick him in the ging-gangs.

He didn't. Realising that she had been holding her breath waiting for him to make physical contact, Daisy reluctantly conceded the point.

He was laughing at her. 'Nice job, Wonderwoman. Well done.'

Otto, running up and flinging his arms round her legs, cried, 'Gee, thanks, Daisy! I knew you could do it. You're brilliant. I'm gonna go and show my dad!'

'You could have killed yourself,' Dev Tyzack said flatly as Otto raced off across the grass. 'All for the sake of a toy plane.'

'A toy plane from Harrods.'

He nodded gravely, acknowledging the difference. 'I hadn't taken you for the tree-climbing type.'

'It's one of my talents. What are you doing here anyway?' As she spoke, Daisy unzipped the boilersuit and stepped out of it, in case he thought this was the kind of gorgeous thing she normally wore on duty.

'Like Wonderwoman in reverse,' Dev observed. 'Actually, I came to see you.' He paused, quite deliberately, before adding, 'I need to book a conference room.'

'Really? And you'd like me to recommend a hotel? Well, there are several good ones in Bristol and Bath—'

'I thought maybe here.' He watched with amusement as Bert stepped forward to retrieve his boilersuit, handing over Daisy's boots in exchange. 'Do you need a hand getting those on?'

Daisy wished her balled-up purple socks weren't unceremoniously stuffed into the tops of her tan leather ankle boots. Oh, sod it, just head for the hotel and sort the footwear out later. Why was she even worrying about being caught in possession of a pair of dodgy socks?

Back in her office, she sat down and flipped through the bookings diary on her desk.

'Yes, the conference room's free on that day. We can do it. If you're sure you want us to.'

'I like this hotel.' Dev was openly grinning at her now. 'You're handy for the motorway. Although I'd prefer it if your chambermaid didn't seduce my guests.'

'I'll make a special note of it. Nooo sed . . . uct . . . ions,' Daisy slowly repeated as she wrote it down. 'How's your friend Dominic, by the way?' She raised her eyebrows, feigning interest. 'Still married?'

There was a knock at the door. Pam, the receptionist, stuck her head round.

'Daisy, the electrician's on the phone. Is tomorrow afternoon OK for the safety check?'

'It's my day off tomorrow. Could you arrange it with Vince?' Vince was the assistant manager. Daisy watched Pam give Dev Tyzack a swift once-over and waggle her eyebrows in appreciation behind his back. Pam might be forty-three and a grandmother several times over but in her mind she was still twenty-two.

'Would you like me to organise coffee?' Pam was still admiring the view available to her of Dev in faded jeans and a charcoal-grey sweater.

'No thanks, we're fine.'

Pam was despatched back to reception. Asking questions and taking notes, Daisy arranged the conference booking for Dev Tyzack's management development company. Modestly known as Tyzack's. He also owned a video production company, Daisy learned, which made training videos.

'Right. All sorted.' She sat back in her chair finally, ran her fingers through her hair and realised it was still dripping wet.

'You looked like that the last time I saw you,' Dev Tyzack observed with a brief smile. 'Not quite so muddy this time. What are you doing tomorrow?'

Caught off guard, Daisy wondered what he meant.

'Sorry?'

'Tomorrow. Your day off.'

She felt water trickling not very seductively down one temple.

'I don't know. Brush up on my tree climbing, maybe. Get the crampons out and tackle one of the big oaks down by the river. Why?'

'I just thought if you were free . . . well, there's something you could help me out with.'

Stalling for time, Daisy reached down for her boots. Slowly and deliberately, to prove she wasn't embarrassed by her woolly purple socks, she put them on.

'Help you out with what?'

'Something important. A decision I have to make. How about if I pick you up at ten o'clock? We'll drive into Bristol, do what we have to do, then I'll treat you to lunch. Sound good to you?'

The cheek of it. He was already assuming she'd say yes. Just because he was Dev Tyzack, who had once captained the England rugby team and earned himself God only knows how many caps, he was taking it for granted that she'd collapse in a heap of gratitude, clasp her hands together in girlish delight and squeal, 'Oooh, yes please!'

Bloody cheek!

'If you aren't going to tell me what this is about, forget it.'

Infuriatingly, Dev Tyzack smiled. 'Oh, come on. Where's your sense of adventure?'

'Up a tree.' Picking up her left boot, Daisy stuffed her foot into it, willy-nilly. The bad news was, it was her right foot. His smile broadened.

'I thought you of all people would be game on. So that's it, is it? You're turning me down?'

Daisy managed to get the right boots zipped up on the right feet. She gave him her best don't-mess-with-me stare.

'Am I supposed to be overcome with curiosity? Because I'm not. If you won't tell me where we're going, I'm not doing it.'

Even more infuriatingly, Dev Tyzack shrugged. 'OK.'

She waited.

And waited.

And waited some more.

''Bye then,' said Dev.

Bastard.

''Bye.' Daisy flashed him a professional smile as he moved towards the door.

He was leaving, he was actually *leaving*, dammit.

This was outrageous.

'OK,' said Daisy, her fingernails digging into the palms of her hands. God, he was probably loving every second of this.

Dev Tyzack paused in the doorway, as if he'd known she wouldn't be able to resist him. No doubt he'd used this ploy dozens of times – the old magical mystery tour ploy – and it had never failed him yet.

'Good. See you tomorrow then. I'll pick you up at ten thirty.'

'Hang on,' Daisy blurted out as he was about to leave. 'This isn't a date, is it? I'm just checking, making sure it's nothing like that.'

'Good grief, the very idea. I wouldn't dream of it.' Dev Tyzack's wicked dark eyes flashed with triumph. 'No worries, Wonderwoman. It's definitely nothing like a date.'

Chapter 13

Maggie's trysts with Hector MacLean were the highlight of her week. For over eighteen months now, their secret meetings had been what she looked forward to with frantic, almost teenage anticipation – fluttery stomach, feeling sick with excitement, the works. And, thanks to mobile phones and text messaging, nobody else was any the wiser.

Which suited them both, down to the ground.

Hector, of course, had no idea how much he really meant to her, and Maggie worked hard to make sure he never would find out. As far as he was concerned, theirs was a mutually beneficial arrangement. He enjoyed meeting her for pleasurable, uncomplicated sex without the hassle of an emotional relationship. And in return he paid her, enabling her to enjoy a better lifestyle than she would otherwise have been able to afford.

Maggie had agonised endlessly, in the early months, over the money. She would have much preferred not to accept it. But any mention of this had brought a categorical response from Hector. If she refused to accept payment, their arrangement would have to end. It wasn't fair on her, he explained; he couldn't expect any woman to sleep with him when there was no relationship between them. And a relationship – with anyone – was the last thing he needed. Since his beloved wife's death, Hector had become one of Gloucestershire's most sought-after singles. He had been chased and propositioned by startlingly shameless women, both married and single themselves.

It had all happened quite out of the blue, one summer's night at a party in the grounds of the hotel.

'I don't need the hassle,' Hector had confided to Maggie. 'I don't want a new woman in my life and, God help me, I can't imagine anything more horrible than getting into the dating scene again. The only thing I miss is sex.'

There had been a fair amount of alcohol consumed. If Maggie hadn't been tipsy she would never have said what she did. But with several glasses of excellent wine inside her, it had been incredibly easy to rest a hand lightly on his arm and murmur, 'You need someone trustworthy and discreet.'

Then she had paused significantly, and their eyes had met. Well, why not? Hector was a lovely man. She'd always liked him.

Hector had remained motionless for several seconds.

'Are you saying what I think you're saying?'

Touched by the uncertainty in his voice, she had nodded and smiled.

And that was how it had begun. They had slipped away from the party, unnoticed. Falling into bed with Hector had been a revelation.

Afterwards, he had insisted on giving her the money. By this time already half in love with him, Maggie had been forced to agree that it made a certain kind of sense. And now, all these months later, it made more sense than ever. If she were to put her foot down and refuse any more of Hector's money, she knew he would stop seeing her, because he was a *gentleman*, for crying out loud.

A gentleman with *principles*.

She knew what she should do, of course. Find herself another man. Except she didn't want anyone else. Only Hector.

So this had been Maggie's dilemma. Which should she choose? Delicious, illicit sex with a man who meant the world to her *and* paid her for it? Or no sex and no money?

Let's face it, there really was no contest.

'Bloody hell, who's that?' sighed Hector. They had only just reached Maggie's bedroom when the doorbell began to ring downstairs.

'I don't know. I'm not expecting anyone.' The only person Maggie had been expecting was Hector. They stood and stared at each other, willing whoever it was on the doorstep to give in gracefully, slope off and leave them to it.

Rrrrrinnnggg.

'God, I hate this kind of thing,' Maggie whispered. 'It's like being in a Brian Rix farce. Do I just pretend I'm not here, or bundle you into the wardrobe, or what?'

Hector grinned. 'Not wildly keen on the wardrobe idea.'

'OK. Just wait here.' Maggie slid out of the bedroom and crossed the landing avoiding the creaky floorboards. Crouching down as she entered Tara's messy bedroom, she approached the window sniper-style.

Bugger, *bugger*. Maggie gripped the windowsill in frustration when she saw the distinctive red and white van parked outside the cottage.

This was so unfair. When she'd rung Carver's Superstore in Bristol to complain about her washing machine breaking down, they had hummed and haa-ed and finally arranged to send out a repair man on Monday afternoon. They weren't able to specify a time, naturally, but it would definitely be between two and six o'clock.

Maggie checked her watch. Eleven fifty-three. How bloody, bloody typical.

Well, sod it. He was too early and it simply wasn't convenient. In fact it was outrageously inconvenient, and she jolly well wasn't going to let him in.

Except if she told him this, there was always the possibility that the repairman might take umbrage, come over all temperamental and storm off in a big stroppy huff. Far simpler to quietly retreat from the window and pretend to be out.

'Shit!' bawled Maggie, her inconspicuous withdrawal scuppered by the object on the floor behind her. The upturned post of Tara's earring buried itself in her bare foot. Lurching to one side – the pain was *acute* – Maggie grabbed the bookcase next to her and promptly tipped it over. Tara's selection of blockbusters – even gaudier than her earrings – crashed to the floor. She couldn't have made more noise if she'd set off a volley of fireworks.

Gasping with the pain and pulling the earring out of her foot, Maggie hobbled back over to the window.

So much for silent withdrawal.

Oh, what a surprise, and there was the repairman standing back on the pavement in order to be able to peer up at her. Possibly the tallest, skinniest repairman Maggie had ever seen.

Now he was waving enthusiastically and pointing to the identity tag pinned to his chest. As if the red and white Carver's van wasn't giveaway enough.

Maggie sighed and opened the window.

'Mrs Donovan? Phew, that's a relief! For a minute there I thought you were out. Gerald Porter.' He tapped his identity tag with pride. 'I've come to take a look at your washing machine.'

'You're too early,' Maggie called down. 'They told me you'd be here this afternoon, between two and six.'

'No, no, you're booked in for a morning appointment.' Gerald consulted his clipboard. 'Between eight and twelve.'

Maggie clutched the edges of the windowsill. 'The girl said between two and six. She definitely said that.'

'Did she? I can't see how. Still, never mind. I'm here now,' Gerald announced cheerfully. 'And you're here now. So why don't I just come in?'

He looked like Plug from *The Bash Street Kids*.

'Look, I'm sorry, but it's not convenient,' said Maggie. 'In fact it's very . . .' she searched for the perfect word, 'inconvenient.' I mean, for heaven's sake, can't a woman be allowed to entertain her lover in peace?

OK, *client*.

'Oh. Right. Well, never mind.' Gerald shrugged, clearly disappointed. He turned and headed back to the van.

Delighted by her victory, Maggie gaily called out, 'Thanks very much. See you this afternoon then!'

Frowning, Gerald craned his giraffe-like neck around. 'What?'

'This afternoon. Between two and six.' Maggie gave him an encouraging nod. It would probably be two o'clock, thinking about it. He could have his lunch break now and fix her washing machine in . . . ooh, an hour if he liked.

'Oh no, Mrs Donovan, you don't understand. I haven't got you booked in for this afternoon. You'll need to ring Carver's and fix up another appointment.'

What?

'OK, could you come back tomorrow morning?' Maggie thought of all the washing piled up in the cupboard downstairs. The machine had been playing up for over a fortnight now. She'd been banking on getting it fixed today.

'Sorry, Mrs Donovan, you have to phone Carver's. They'll arrange everything . . .'

In their own inefficient fashion, Maggie thought crossly.

'. . . but I have to warn you, shouldn't think you'd get another appointment before next week.'

'Oh, come on, you're not serious. I can't wait that long!'

'Nothing I can do about it, I'm afraid.' Gerald shrugged his gangly shoulders. 'Unless you let me take a look at your machine now.'

God.

Behind her, Maggie heard Hector quietly clearing his throat. 'Maybe I should leave.'

'No!' She turned and shook her head, then had an idea and leaned back out of the window. 'Look, if you do come in, how long will it take to fix it?'

Gerald brightened considerably. 'Well, if it's something simple, five minutes.'

'Go downstairs and let him in,' whispered Hector from the doorway. 'I'll wait up here.'

The operative word, needless to say, had been *if. If* it was something simple. But it wasn't, of course. It was, apparently, something very complicated indeed.

Maggie, hopping from foot to foot in the kitchen, checking and rechecking her watch, silently urged him to hurry up and work *faster*. But Gerald was one of those slow, methodical types who took a genuine interest in their work and prided themselves on their thoroughness. Worse still, he kept trying to explain what he thought the problem might be, and pausing to point out particularly riveting electrical components.

Stop it, stop it, just shut up and get *on* with the job, Maggie longed to yell, I don't *want* to know how a washing machine works, you moron!

She also itched to flick him with a whip, like a jockey

approaching the last fence at the Grand National, just to see if it would speed him up a bit.

Twenty minutes crawled by. Then thirty. Gerald was still on his knees exclaiming with pleasure over an integrated circuit board when Maggie heard a footstep on the stairs.

Sidling out of the kitchen and closing the door firmly behind her, she met Hector in the hall.

'Bloody man's still got the machine in bits. He looks as if he's settling in for the afternoon.'

'And I have an appointment in Bath at two o'clock. I'm going to slip away.'

'I'm so sorry.'

'Don't be. It's not your fault.' He smiled and gave her a reassuring kiss on the cheek. 'We'll arrange something for another day.'

Hector was taking it well but he must have been disappointed. Nearly as disappointed as me, thought Maggie, who had been looking forward to their assignation all week.

Luckily, sneaking Hector out wasn't a problem; Gerald was so engrossed in his work that he didn't even see him cross the kitchen and exit via the back door before vanishing down the path into the woods behind the cottage.

So that was that.

'Oh, you're back.' Emerging from his own little washing machine dreamworld, Gerald raised his long neck and said happily, 'This is fascinating, you know. Completely fascinating. I don't suppose there's any chance of a coffee?'

The other trick Maggie had fallen for was to believe – idiotically – that the washing machine repairman might actually repair her washing machine. When what Gerald had in fact told her was that he had come out to 'take a look' at it.

Oh yes, and he'd certainly done that. By three o'clock he had taken the machine to bits, put it together again and pushed it neatly back into its slot between the oven and the fridge.

'What I'm going to do, Mrs Donovan, is place an order for a new circuit board and see if that does the trick.'

Maggie couldn't believe it. Three whole hours, five cups of coffee, a chicken sandwich, six chocolate digestives and he *still* hadn't even mended the bloody thing.

'How long before the circuit board gets here?'

'Oooh, let me see now. Five or six days?'

'But—'

'Can't be helped, I'm afraid. These things happen. Now, Mrs Donovan, if you'd just sign this form for me, I'll be out of your hair.'

It was a bloody wonder she had any hair left, Maggie thought sourly as she signed on the dotted line.

Chapter 14

Forty-eight hours and *still* none of them had rung. Smarting from this multiple rejection, Tara was finding it hard to concentrate on anything else. Which was irritating, because she'd never regarded herself as one of those sad needy girls who couldn't think of anything but boys.

It wasn't as if she even wanted a boyfriend, for heaven's sake. She was just desperate to dump one. And in order to dump a boyfriend you had to have one in the first place. Had the total nerd tried ringing the joke number she'd given him? If she'd told him her real number, even hearing his reedy voice would have been better than nothing at all.

Cross with herself for being pathetic, Tara threw herself across the sofa and reached for the *Daily Mail*. Flicking through the pages, her attention was caught by a piece about a girl tipped to win a medal at the next Olympics. Modern pentathlon, fancy that, all manner of running and riding and swimming and goodness knows what else. Tara marvelled at the girl's dedication. She trained, evidently, for six or seven hours a day, six days a week.

Modern pentathlon is my life, the attractive brunette had explained to the journalist interviewing her. Winning is my number one priority. I don't have time for a relationship, but that's not what's important to me right now. I'd rather have a gold medal than a boyfriend, any day!

Golly. And she was really pretty too. Tara was both impressed and envious; imagine having that kind of attitude. Maybe she should take up some form of sport and get so involved in it that boys, quite simply, no longer fitted into the equation. Perhaps she could give marathon running a go? Or golf, or tennis, or—

The phone rang.

In a flash, Tara was off the sofa, scattering sheets of newspaper in all directions and trampling them underfoot.

'Hello?'

'Hi, Tara? This is Jerry. From the other night, remember?'

Yay, result!

'Oh yes, of course I remember. How are you doing?'

'Great, great. Listen, so how about this drink then? Fancy coming out with me tomorrow night?'

Tara's heart began to thud. Oh yes, this was it, this was the moment she'd been waiting for. He'd asked her out and now she could turn him down. It would make her feel so much better, boost her morale, allow her to prove to herself that she *could* say no . . .

The trouble was, it was nice of him to ring her, and it must mean he liked her. Which was flattering in itself. Plus, Tara realised, he sounded really nice on the phone, all sort of cheerful and friendly and actually quite sexy now she came to think of it. The others may have let her down, but Jerry hadn't. He was inviting her out for a drink and a chance for them to get to know each other better.

Crikey, you never knew, he could be The One. Jerry might turn out to be the boy she had been waiting for all her life. If she rejected him now, for the sake of some feeble, fleeting morale boost, she could be condemning herself to a lifetime of lonely jam-making spinsterhood.

'Hello?' said Jerry. 'Are you still there?'

'Yes, I'm here! And I'd love to come out with you tomorrow night,' Tara exclaimed joyfully. 'That sounds great. Oh, but I don't drive, so you'll have to pick me up.'

'No problem.' Jerry sounded unperturbed. 'OK, I've got a pen here. Give me your address.'

There was silence after Tara had finished telling him. Finally, he said, 'Colworth? God, I'm sorry, I didn't realise you lived that far out.'

The local dialling code covered a wide area, ranging from just outside Bristol to . . . well, Colworth, Tara remembered. But it couldn't make that much of a difference to him, surely?

'It's nothing,' she hurriedly assured Jerry. 'Twenty minutes on the motorway. You'll be here in no time at all!'

'Look, I'm not sure . . . oh *hell*.' Tara heard him sigh. 'This is awkward . . . maybe we should just leave it. Colworth's bloody miles away.'

'So what you're saying is, I'm outside your radius.' Tara's voice grew unsteady. She couldn't believe it. This was so hurtful. Didn't he know what he could be missing out on here? Hadn't he heard of destiny?

'Sorry. Never mind, maybe I'll see you around in Clifton or something, OK? 'Bye!'

And that was it. The phone went dead in Tara's hand. Jerry had hung up, scarpered, made his speedy getaway. They weren't going to end up living together happily ever after, after all.

Tara hoped he had a minuscule willy.

And that very soon it would turn blue, shrivel up and drop off.

Why am I here? Why? What am I doing here? Oh, this is mad, thought Daisy as the car sped through the back streets of Bristol, I still don't even know where we're *going*.

She sneaked a sideways glance at Dev Tyzack's hands on the steering wheel, the sleeves of his pale grey sweater pushed up slightly to reveal strong brown forearms and a Breitling watch. He seemed to know where they were going, anyway, although she suspected he was the kind of man who always would know. Dev Tyzack simply wasn't the faffing-about indecisive type.

Well, she jolly well wasn't going to ask him again. She was also extremely glad she hadn't dressed up for the occasion. Black jeans and a black long-sleeved T-shirt had been a deliberate decision, to prove to Dev that she didn't want to be taken anywhere glitzy for lunch. When he had turned up in jeans himself, she had been doubly glad.

Besides, she probably wouldn't even bother with lunch. Once they'd done whatever it was they were here to do, she would tell him that she had other things lined up, and ask to be taken home.

God knows where they were headed, anyway. This wasn't the most salubrious area of Bristol. St Philips, Daisy read, peering at a road sign. Brilliant. She just hoped Dev Tyzack hadn't volunteered her for a spot of canal dredging on her day off.

'I don't know, what is it with you and water?' Sounding resigned, Dev passed her a handkerchief. 'Every time I see you, your face is wet.'

But he said it kindly, not in a sarcastic way, and when Daisy had finished trumpeting into the handkerchief like an elephant he gave her shoulder a reassuring pat.

So much for keeping aloof, thought Daisy, wiping her eyes and struggling to control the great shuddery sobs that were making it almost impossible to speak. This wasn't at all how she'd been expecting the day to turn out.

'Is this why you b-brought me here? To see me m-making an

117

idiot of myself?' She scrubbed at her tear-stained cheeks, too embarrassed to meet his gaze.

'Of course not. I didn't know you were going to get emotional, did I?'

Get emotional? Blub like a big baby, more like.

'This is what I call a dirty trick,' Daisy muttered.

'You couldn't be more wrong.' The corners of his mouth betrayed his amusement. 'Think about it. You run a hotel, you shout at your guests, you climb trees like a—'

'I do *not* shout at my guests!'

'You shouted at me,' Dev reminded her. 'Pretty comprehensively, as I recall. And let me tell you, I was scared.'

'Oh, very funny.'

'Anyway, you get my drift. I thought you'd be perfect for a job like this.'

'Thanks, that's fantastic. You mean you thought I was the kind of cold heartless bitch who drowns kittens and steals money from blind orphans in my spare time.' Daisy shook her head. 'You certainly know how to flatter a girl.'

'I didn't mean it like that. It just didn't occur to me that you'd react like this.' Dev indicated his own face. 'See? I'm not crying, am I?'

Hmm, maybe not. Maybe not actually crying, but Daisy was pretty sure she'd spotted a telltale glistening in his dark eyes at one point. He hadn't been as completely unaffected as he liked to make out.

She blinked hard and took a deep breath, mentally bracing herself.

'Right, I've stopped. I'm OK now. Shall we go back in?'

'Sure?' Dev flashed her an unexpectedly warm smile. 'You don't have to if you don't want to.'

'Come on.' Daisy shoved his damp hankie up her sleeve,

squared her shoulders and turned to face the scuffed, blue painted door. 'Let's do it. I'll be fine.'

There were rows of sectioned-off cages along each side of the concrete corridor. Each cage contained a dog.

So many dogs, of all shapes and sizes. Some were recognisable breeds, others weren't. Some lay on the floor, watchful and silent, but most leapt up as their cages were approached. Some barked loudly, others whimpered with delight in their eagerness to socialise. Their tails wagged, their paws scrabbled eagerly against the bars, their eyes were bright . . .

Daisy's own eyes promptly filled up once more. Well, how could anyone not cry? How could any human being fail to be moved by their innocent little faces?

Oh God, here I go again.

'Right, let's be sensible about this,' Dev Tyzack announced. A little brusquely, Daisy felt. 'I brought you here as the voice of reason. You're going to help me choose the right dog for me. I'm after something that's a decent size for a start, maybe a labrador or a setter. I want a dog that's well trained and intelligent. Nothing yappy or delinquent, and definitely not – Daisy, are you listening to me? How about this Great Dane over here, I've always liked Great Danes . . . Daisy, where are you going?'

'This one,' Daisy called from the far end of the corridor. 'This is the one you have to have.'

'What? Which one?' He joined her, stared into the cage and gave a snort of amusement. 'Oh, please. You have to be joking.'

'This is the one.' Daisy sank to her knees in front of the cage and pressed the palms of her hands against the wire.

'Not a chance,' Dev said flatly. 'Daisy, get up, come and have a look at the Great Dane.'

119

'No. I won't.' Daisy shook her head, breaking into a smile as the dog joyfully licked her hands. This was it, she was in love. Her mind was irretrievably made up.

'Daisy, this isn't why I asked you to come along. You haven't been listening to me at all, have you?'

'Sshh, you'll frighten her. Oh, *look*, isn't she just the most adorable thing you ever saw?' Daisy's eyes shone with happiness as she patted the concrete floor beside her. 'Dev, come on, come down here and say hello.'

Dev didn't say hello. He was seriously regretting bringing Daisy along to the rescue centre now. The dog in front of him was small, for a start. It was also a mongrel of the ugly/quirky variety, terrier-sized and female. Everything, in fact, that he didn't want. The little creature was frantically licking Daisy's face – probably because it was nice and salty – and wriggling her daft stumpy tail so ecstatically it looked as if it was about to whirl right off.

Daisy withdrew her face from the bars and grinned at the dog, who appeared to be grinning back.

'This is Dev.' Daisy solemnly introduced them. 'OK, I know he's looking a bit scary right now, but he'll get better, I promise. And guess what?' she whispered confidentially into the animal's whiskery, pricked-up, asymmetric ears. 'He's going to be your new daddy!'

Dev watched the two of them down on the floor, separated by the metal grille fronting the cage but otherwise irredeemably bonded. It seemed that both their minds were made up.

Dev felt as though he'd advertised in the personal columns to meet a willowy Jerry Hall lookalike and had somehow ended up with Mick Jagger instead.

And then he saw it. The final straw. The slim card fastened to the top of the cage.

'Oh no, I'm sorry, there is absolutely *no way* I could own an animal called—'

'Don't be so wet! She's beautiful,' Daisy declared. 'Dev, you know you can't fight this any more, she's the perfect dog for you. So just stop making feeble excuses and come and say hello to Clarissa.'

Chapter 15

They went for lunch at San Carlo, in the centre of Bristol. Daisy was far too ecstatic to refuse his offer. She was also ravenous. Happily, San Carlo was one of those buzzy, glamorous establishments who weren't bothered about their clientele adhering to a formal dress code. So long as you were buzzy and glamorous too, jeans were fine.

Flushed with success, Daisy ordered seared scallops and fettucine Alfredo. Dev chose the mussels, followed by rack of lamb.

'You lied,' he announced, when the waiter had brought their bottle of Barolo. 'You said she was beautiful.'

'She's *more* than beautiful! She's cute and flirty and fun. Clarissa has character.' Daisy couldn't stop grinning. 'Bags of personality and that's what counts. I promise you, you won't regret this.'

'Look at me.' Dev sat back and gestured to himself with an air of despair. 'I'm six foot three, I played rugby for my country, I have an image to maintain. People expect to see me with a certain kind of dog, something sleek and powerful with a name like Brutus or Jet. When they catch sight of me with a scruffy little handbag-sized apology for a mutt called *Clarissa* . . . well, I'm just going to be a laughing stock. I'll never live it down.'

Daisy wasn't worried. She knew he didn't mean it. Even as

he listed Clarissa's many shortcomings he was smiling, despite himself. What's more, he had already paid the rescue centre's fees and filled in all the necessary forms. By two o'clock the rest of the paperwork would be completed and they could go back there and pick up Clarissa.

'You saved her life. Imagine being kept behind bars when you haven't even done anything wrong. And she'd been there for ages,' Daisy reminded him. 'Another week or so and it would have been curtains for Clarissa. She'd have had to be put down.'

'OK, fine, you can stop the emotional blackmail now. You've made the sale. I'm not about to change my mind and send her back to death row.' Dev paused. 'I don't think they do that anyway, you know.'

Daisy didn't either, but it sounded good. And you could never be absolutely sure.

'Let's change the subject.' She stuck her elbows on the table and reached for a marinated olive. 'Tell me about this business of yours. What made you go into management development?'

Their first course arrived and Dev told her how he had set up the company. More recently he had begun producing management training videos. The business was young, but doing well, due in part to his own high profile as the rugby star who had led his country's team to victory in both the Six Nations and the World Cup.

'Then again,' Dev added, 'I've worked bloody hard to build the company up. It didn't happen on its own. You have to put in the hours.'

'And then there's your modelling,' Daisy mischievously reminded him, unable to resist it. There was a range of sportswear endorsed by Dev Tyzack. She imagined him at a photo shoot, having a tantrum because the stylist hadn't got his

123

hair exactly right or maybe going into a strop because his café latte was the wrong temperature.

'Don't knock it.' Sensing her amusement, Dev said bluntly, 'Signing that contract was what enabled me to get my own business up and running in the first place. If they're willing to pay silly money to have my name on their clothes, that's fine by me. Here, try one of these mussels.'

Moments later, Daisy caught a glimpse of her reflection in one of the many gilded mirrors lining the walls of the restaurant. It gave her a jolt to see herself unexpectedly like that, leaning forward with her elbows resting on the table, laughing and tilting her head back as Dev Tyzack deftly tipped the mussel out of its shell and into her mouth.

Anyone looking at us now would think we were a couple. Crikey, from the way we're carrying on they might even think we're a couple of newlyweds!

Shaken, Daisy hastily swallowed the mussel, sat back in her chair and took a hefty gulp of wine.

'How are your scallops?' said Dev with a grin.

For heaven's sake, what was going on here? Was she supposed to feed him one of her scallops now?

Well, she certainly wasn't going to do that. Anyway, there was only one left on her plate. Spearing it with her fork, Daisy stuffed it into her mouth. When she'd chewed and finished swallowing, she licked her lips in appreciation and said, 'Great.'

If he was that desperate to try a scallop he could jolly well order a plate of his own.

Shuddering inwardly, Daisy experienced an unwelcome flashback. At home, at the back of the wardrobe somewhere, lay an album of wedding photos. Among them was an informal shot of her and Steven sitting together at the top table during their reception, her head thrown back with laughter as Steven attempted to feed her the last langoustine from his plate. It had been the happiest day of her life. She had loved Steven and thought he was in love with her. Whereas in all probability he had been secretly congratulating himself on having inveigled himself into her family.

Don't think about it.

Just don't.

'Any word from the happy honeymooners?' said Daisy abruptly.

'Dominic and Annabel? As a matter of fact I had a postcard from them yesterday. They're flying home this weekend, and they've had a fantastic time. Their hotel was right on the beach and they couldn't fault the service, apparently.'

'Hot and cold chambermaids in every room, you mean?' Daisy pleated the edge of the blue tablecloth between her fingers. 'Your friend was the one in the wrong, you have to understand that. He made all the running with Tara. She wasn't to blame for what happened before the wedding.'

Dev was relaxed, his smile playful. 'You're probably right.'

'I *am* right!'

'OK, you win. Anyway, it doesn't matter any more. All forgotten.'

Daisy was astonished. 'Are you serious? Did you always know it was Dominic's fault?'

Dev shrugged easily. 'I didn't know for sure, but I wasn't surprised. It's the kind of thing he'd do, I suppose.'

What?

'But you blamed Tara! You stood in my office and argued with me. You accused her of practically seducing your precious friend! I can't believe this!'

'Come on,' reasoned Dev. 'What else could I do? When you're someone's best man you have to take his side.'

'Even when he's a complete and utter shit?'

'Even then.' He nodded gravely, but with a hint of a smile. 'You defended Tara, didn't you?'

'Tara didn't do anything wrong!'

'OK, maybe not wrong. But definitely stupid. And you still defended her, because she's your friend.'

Daisy sensed she was being backed into a hole. She felt as if she were being cross-examined in court by a rapier-tongued barrister. Of course she had sided with Tara.

Damn, she hated losing an argument.

'It wasn't fair, though. Tara had to take all the blame and apologise to Annabel.'

'And I daresay it's taught her a valuable lesson.' Calmly, Dev added, 'Next time, with a bit of luck, she won't be so gullible.'

Now why did this sound so familiar? Oh yes, thought Daisy, I remember now. I've had to learn that lesson too.

'So how come you and Dominic are such great friends?' she demanded. Or was that a silly question?

'We met at university. Shared a flat for a couple of years.' Dev shrugged. 'Then we went our different ways, but every so often we'd meet up. I was moving around a fair bit, but Dom's always kept in touch.'

So they weren't that close, Daisy guessed. Just old mates from college, one of those casual male friendships that didn't actually mean much at all. And Dominic, no doubt, had made the effort to maintain contact because he enjoyed being able to boast that one of his oldest mates was Dev Tyzack, star of the England rugby team.

Why was she not surprised?

'So will you invite Dominic to be your best man when you get married?'

He looked amused, aware of what she was implying.

'Honestly? Probably not. Then again, who says I'm getting married?' Pause. 'Unless you're about to make me an offer . . .'

Oh, those eyes. He was flirting with her now. That was definitely a flirtatious remark.

'Been there, done that,' Daisy responded lightly. 'No thanks.'

Dev looked interested. 'You were married? What happened?'

'What can I tell you? I have truly terrible taste in men. The marriage was a disaster. It didn't last long.'

She wasn't about to blurt out the whole grisly story. Dev didn't need to know. Daisy didn't want sympathy and she certainly didn't want him thinking she was the kind of pathetic wife who wasn't even aware that her husband was cheating on her. It was none of his business anyway.

'So you got rid of him,' said Dev.

That sounded more like it! Daisy shook back her hair in the manner of a woman not to be messed with.

'Put it this way. He's not around any more.'

Dev smiled his smile as their main courses arrived at the table. 'And now you're playing the field.'

Daisy waited until the waiter had left before saying, 'I think that's your speciality, isn't it?' because the tabloids were for ever coming up with stories about Dev Tyzack and the latest girl in his life. Sometimes it seemed that every time she opened a paper, there he was with someone new on his arm.

'I'm single. It's allowed,' he pointed out reasonably.

'But these girlfriends of yours never seem to last very long.'

'Is there some law that says they have to?'

'No,' said Daisy, 'but isn't it a bit of a shallow existence?'

Unfair, perhaps, but having a dig at Dev, quizzing him about his colourful love life, was a lot easier than discussing her own.

'I'd call it discerning.' Dev shrugged. 'If I meet a girl and like the look of her, I'll take her out because that's how people get to know each other. But if after a week or two I realise she isn't the one for me, I'll end it. If I know it's not going to work out,' he went on easily, 'why should I carry on seeing her? I don't call that shallow, I call it common sense.'

Damn, so much for having a dig. Foiled again.

'But you're in your thirties now.' Daisy's raised eyebrows indicated that he was knocking on a bit. 'And you've never had a long-term relationship. Has it ever occurred to you that maybe you're missing out?'

'You mean am I worried about leading such a sad, empty life?' Dev's dark eyes glittered; he was clearly enjoying himself. 'Oh dear, I know, it's absolutely tragic. Poor me, having to go out with all these beautiful girls. Although to be honest, I have a feeling things are about to change.' He lowered his voice slightly and leaned across the table, causing Daisy's heart to break into a lolloping canter. 'In fact I'm sure of it. You see, I have just met someone who's . . . well, completely different. Not what I'm used to at all. And it looks as if a long-term relationship could be on the cards. It may not work out, but I really think it might. We'll just have to keep our fingers crossed and see how things go.'

Good grief, he was a smooth operator! Nor did he waste much time. Feeling a bit breathless, Daisy wondered if this was a standard Dev Tyzack chat-up line. She wasn't going to fall for it, of course, but there was no denying he had the ability to charm the knickers off a—

The next moment it came to her in a flash. *Thank God* she hadn't blushed and simpered, 'Oh Dev, surely you don't mean me?'

Not that she ever *did* simper, but still. Just blushing would have been bad enough.

Jolted back to reality in the nick of time, Daisy raised her glass of red wine and said cheerfully, 'That's great news. I really hope it works out for the two of you. Now, let's have a toast.' She beamed and clanked her glass against Dev's. 'To the happy couple. You and Clarissa.'

Chapter 16

They drove back to the rescue centre via a pet shop in Henleaze, and stocked up on everything Clarissa would need.

'I feel like a new father,' said Dev, choosing the smartest dog basket, the squishiest beanbag and the squeakiest rubber toys. 'Black lead or red lead?'

'The green one. Oh, and she'll need a ball.' Daisy was having a wonderful time following him round the shop, snatching up anything that caught her eye. 'And dog chews. And a nice blanket – ooh, and a bowl with her name on the side in case she forgets who she is.'

'Nobody could forget their name was Clarissa. Maybe we should change it to Tyson,' Dev mused.

'You can't. You'll give her a complex. How would you like it if I started calling you Doris?'

Dev removed the tartan blanket and king-sized box of dog chews from Daisy's grasp. As he seized them, his hand brushed against hers, sending a zzzap of electricity up her arm.

'Come on, let's pay for this lot and go. She'll be wondering where we've got to.'

Daisy wasn't happy about the zzzap. She didn't need to get involved in any zzzappy-type goings-on. Rubbing her arm to dispel the unnerving sensation, she followed Dev over to the counter and murmured, 'Whatever you say, *Doris*.'

At the rescue centre, Clarissa greeted them as if she hadn't seen them for at least ten years. Daisy, perilously close to tears again at the thought of all the other dogs they were leaving behind, hurried Clarissa out to the car while Dev signed the last of the official papers. By the time he emerged, the pair of them were sprawled on the back seat trying out the various squeaky toys and investigating a packet of dog chocs.

'Right. Let's get going.' Dev started up the car, then glanced at Daisy in the rear-view mirror. 'Are you OK to come back, see Clarissa settled into her new home?'

What, and experience a few more zzzaps? Be given the guided tour of Dev's house in Bath? Take Clarissa for a walk, then be persuaded to stay for dinner, followed by drinks in front of the fire and an invitation to spend the night?

Was that the usual routine? An expert seduction, then maybe a couple more dates, followed by the inevitable waning of interest? And yet another fleeting relationship bites the dust, thought Daisy, wondering how many hearts he had broken in his time. After all, Dev Tyzack was hardly your average, run-of-the-mill man. Had any girl ever dumped him?

'Actually, I won't. If you could just drop me back at the hotel, that'd be great.'

She saw a flicker of disappointment in his eyes.

'Are you sure?'

Ha, so he'd thought she'd be up for a quickie, had he? It hadn't occurred to him that it may have been an offer she *could* refuse.

For a moment Daisy was tempted to say, 'Yes thanks, absolutely sure. You see the thing is, I don't actually want to have sex with you.'

The trouble with that, though, was (a) it wasn't true. The sex would undoubtedly be fantastic, it was the being cast aside bit

131

afterwards that she didn't relish. And (b) if she *did* say it, Dev would only look surprised and say, 'Phew, steady on there, I only asked if you'd like to see how Clarissa settles in.' Which would, in turn, (a) be embarrassing and (b) serve her right.

'I've got some paperwork to catch up on.' Daisy didn't bother to sound too sincere.

'Can't it wait?'

'And I'm seeing someone this evening.' Probably Tara, but never mind.

'Really? Boyfriend?'

Was he laughing at her? In the rear-view mirror, Daisy couldn't see his mouth, only his eyes. It was hard to tell.

'Look, does it matter? I don't bombard you with questions about your social life.'

'Excuse me, but you already have.' Now he was definitely laughing at her. 'You questioned and interrogated *and* lectured me.'

'I was making polite conversation. Otherwise there might have been an awkward silence.'

At that moment Clarissa scrambled off both Daisy's lap and her pristine new tartan blanket. A mixture of delirious joy and an achingly full bladder had taken its toll and the sound of a tumultuous stream of urine hitting the leather-upholstered back seat filled the car.

'On the whole,' Dev sighed, 'I think I'd have preferred the awkward silence.'

Oh no, his scarily expensive Mercedes. And now it was all trickling down behind the leather seats.

Consumed with guilt at having forced him to adopt an incontinent dog, Daisy blurted out, 'God, I'm sorry.'

'That's OK.' This time Dev really was smiling; she could tell from the way his eyes crinkled at the corners. 'When I heard someone weeing on the back seat, to be honest I thought it was Clarissa.'

'Tara Donovan, what's up with you? You look like a bulldog that's just had its wisdom teeth out.'

Tara was taking her break in the staff coffee room. She glanced up at Rocky and said, 'Thanks a lot.'

It was all right for Rocky, he was congenitally cheerful. Nothing ever got him down, not even his frequent appalling *faux pas*.

'Oh, well, no, don't get me wrong,' Rocky hastily amended. 'I didn't mean you *actually* look like a bulldog. I just said it because you look like a bulldog might feel if it *had* just had its wisdom teeth pulled out. Kind of . . . pissed off, you know?'

'Well, it's very clever of you to have noticed.' Tara flicked grumpily through the pages of last month's *Cosmopolitan*, where every face was a cheerful one and the teeth were all startlingly white. 'Because I am pissed off. In fact I'm very pissed off indeed.'

Brandishing the kettle, Rocky sloshed hot water into his mug and showered in Nescafe straight from the jar. Then he threw himself down on the sofa next to Tara, briskly ruffled his peroxide crop with the flat of his hand and said, 'Come on then, tell me what's wrong. Give me all the details.' He paused, pulling a face. 'Just so long as it's nothing gynaecological.'

'It's not, don't worry.' Grateful for the opportunity to have a good moan, Tara chucked *Cosmo* aside and tucked her feet up beneath her. 'Rocky, why am I such a failure with men? Why do they treat me like dirt?'

'Oh, come on, you aren't a failure. You've had loads of boyfriends.' Rocky lit a cigarette and blew a smoke ring. 'Well, a fair few.'

'I know I have. And they always dump me. I was so used to it happening, I didn't even question it,' Tara wailed. 'It didn't occur to me that it was weird, because I'd never known any different. But now I *have* realised, it's making me really miserable. I'm just a hopeless case.'

Vince, the assistant manager, stuck his head round the door. 'Rocky? You're needed downstairs in the bar.'

Rocky heaved a sigh of resignation. 'Ladies and gentlemen, I give you the ninety-second coffee break.' Stubbing out his cigarette and knocking back his toe-curlingly strong black coffee, he turned to Tara, who was looking more rejected than ever. Those pathetically slumped shoulders didn't suit her at all.

Rocky, who had a kind heart, said, 'Look, I'm off at seven. Why don't you and me hit the Hollybush tonight? Have a few drinks, a game of darts and a good old chat. Fancy that?'

Tara was touched. OK, it might not be a date, not a proper date, but it would be a damn sight better than sitting at home moping. Rocky was good company in his own rowdy, laddish way. And she could always tape *Emmerdale*.

She dredged up a smile. That was the great thing about meeting up with someone who lived less than three hundred yards away from you. At least he couldn't complain that you were outside his radius.

'Sounds great,' she told Rocky, feeling chirpier already. 'I'll see you there.'

Tara was in her bedroom trying on different pairs of earrings when she heard the phone start to ring downstairs. So it wasn't a date, but she could still make an effort, couldn't she? No need to turn up at the pub looking like a New Age traveller. Now, the dangly black and gold ones or the sweet little opal studs?

'Tara? It's for you,' Maggie yelled up the stairs.

'Who is it?'

'No idea. Some chap.'

Some chap? Yay, all of a sudden she was Little Miss Popular! Definitely the black and gold dangly ones, Tara instantly decided, admiring her reflection in the dressing-table mirror and smoothing her black velvet top over her hips. Hastily squishing herself with scent – not to impress Rocky, purely to boost her own self-esteem – she clip-clopped down the stairs in her favourite black suede ankle boots.

Well, well, another phone call, this was a turn-up for the books. Maybe her luck was about to change – ooh, and *Emmerdale* was about to start, mustn't forget to switch on the video.

'Tara? Hi, it's me!'

Rocky. Mr Never-Ready-On-Time.

'Oh, don't tell me, let me guess, you're running late and will I head on up there and get the first round in.'

'Well, the thing is, something's come up. This girl I met in Chippenham last week just rang me and invited me over to her place tonight, and I kind of said yes before remembering about our game of darts.'

Tara had been reaching across the coffee table for the video remote control. She stopped in mid-stretch.

'You *kind of* said yes?'

'Well, I said yes, I suppose. But you don't mind, do you? I mean, it was only because we were both at a loose end. I knew you'd understand. She's really pretty. Gorgeous little figure.'

Rocky might be kind-hearted but he was also fickle and monumentally lacking in tact. He didn't even have the grace to sound sheepish. Tara could practically hear him drooling at the prospect of the evening ahead.

The new, improved evening, needless to say.

'OK, fine.' Tara didn't bother to yell at him because what

would be the point? Rocky wasn't going to change his mind. Besides, wasn't this exactly the kind of treatment she was used to?

Annoying about the scent, though. It was a pretty pointless exercise smelling gorgeous in your own living room with no one else around to appreciate it.

'You're a star,' Rocky said cheerfully. 'I'd better be off, then. I don't want her to think I'm standing her up.'

'Gosh, no,' Tara agreed, equally heartily. 'Mustn't do that.'

Maggie had spent the last two hours working her way through a mountain of hand-washing in the kitchen sink. Coming through to the living room to drape wet clothes over the radiators, she said, 'I thought you were meeting Rocky for a drink.'

'That was Rocky on the phone. Can't make it after all.' Tara forced herself to sound casual, as if it hadn't much mattered to her either way.

'Oh, what a shame. Still,' Maggie said chirpily, 'at least now you can watch *Emmerdale*.'

I'm twenty-seven, thought Tara, there has to be more to life.

Sadly, it appeared there was.

'And we need to get the rest of this washing dry,' Maggie went on. 'You couldn't be an angel, could you, and get the old clothes airer out of the loft?'

Chapter 17

'It's pretty small. I did warn you,' said Daisy from the doorway. As the bishop no doubt once said to the actress.

Barney turned and flashed her a dazzling smile. The room was basic but clean, with the walls painted white and a cobalt-blue carpet covering the floor. There was a single bed, a low chest of drawers, a table and two chairs and a narrow wardrobe. He loved every inch of this attic room, with its eccentrically sloping ceiling and diamond-leaded windows.

'It's perfect,' he told Daisy. 'I can't believe I'm really here.'

He had phoned her on Friday, having thought of nothing else all week. When he'd announced, 'I haven't changed my mind,' Daisy had said, 'Somehow I didn't think you would.' Sounding as if she were smiling, she'd added, 'So, when can you start?'

And now, three days later, here he was. Thanks to the amount of annual leave owing to him, he had been able to hand in his resignation and leave that same afternoon. Half the people in his office had thought he was mad, while the rest were deeply envious. Escaping the Civil Service was something they dreamed of doing but could never actually bring themselves to go through with. Gerald, one of the middle-aged clerical officers who still lived at home with his mother *and* wore tank tops she knitted for him, had got quite carried away, exclaiming that Barney was like Steve McQueen in *Papillon*, escaping from that terrible prison on the island – 'Only you have more teeth,' Gerald had concluded reassuringly.

Gerald being Gerald, it was hard to tell if this was an attempt at a joke.

'Thanks,' Barney had said, guessing that it wasn't.

'You take care of yourself now. We'll miss you.'

Gerald had gone a bit misty-eyed at this point. Barney had wondered if he was gay. Lying through his teeth (glad he had enough to lie through), he'd said, 'I'm going to miss all of you too.'

'Or that other film with Steve McQueen in it,' persisted Gerald, who didn't get out much. '*The Great Escape* – remember that one? Where all the prisoners-of-war crawled out through the underground tunnel?' He was getting over-excited now, waving his stubby arms to indicate that this gloomy office block was their very own prison.

'Yes,' Barney had patiently reminded him, 'but most of them ended up getting shot.'

Daisy glanced at her watch. 'I'll leave you to unpack and settle in. You can meet everyone later this afternoon.'

Barney's suitcases were stacked up against the bed; he could hardly wait to get started.

'Thanks for everything,' he said happily. 'You won't regret this. I'm going to be the best hotel porter you've ever had.'

It didn't take Barney long to empty his cases and turn the attic room into something resembling home. Not that it *was* anything like his old home, but at least it now had his own things in it, lots of posters up on the walls and photos of his family on the chest of drawers. He'd brought some books with him too, and his precious CD collection. The radio/CD player just fitted on the deep window seat next to his bed. He hadn't brought his portable TV with him, but Daisy had said there was a television in the communal sitting room.

Barney wandered over to the window and gazed out at the view. His room overlooked the back of the hotel, which meant the scenery was less spectacular, but that didn't matter. He didn't mind. A collection of outbuildings, the staff car park and a wooded hill were still better than he was used to. And he was here, in Colworth, where you could hear the distant sounds of a buzz-saw cutting down trees, and birds singing, and the occasional burst of laughter drifting up from the kitchens below.

What more could anyone want?

Well, a deodorant, actually. He'd accidentally left his can of Arrid Extra-Dry on the bathroom shelf at home.

Oh, and maybe some Rowntree's fruit gums.

The sun came out from behind a cloud as Barney headed down the drive. Even the weather, he decided, was on his side. There were quite a few tourists about, taking photographs and clustering around the windows of the two gift shops in the High Street. The Hollybush Inn had just opened its doors and the smell of freshly ground coffee spilled out. It occurred to Barney that this time last week – *exactly* one week ago – he had set foot in the village for the first time and been completely knocked out by it. And now he lived here.

How perfect was that?

Then again, it would be even more perfect if the door of the village shop-cum-post office happened to swing open just as he reached it, bringing him face to face with a pretty girl having trouble with the wheel of her son's pushchair . . .

But that didn't happen. Feeling a bit ridiculous for having even thought it might, Barney pushed open the door and saw that the shop was empty of customers. Where did he think he was, anyway – Brigadoon?

The good news was that they did sell deodorant here. And fruit gums. And batteries for his Walkman.

'Hi,' he said cheerfully, dumping his purchases on the counter and beaming at the man behind it. 'I've just moved into the village – well, the hotel really. I'm going to be working there. My name's Barney, Barney Usher.'

Christopher, who had had a ferocious argument this morning with his boyfriend Colin and wasn't in the mood for social chit-chat, glanced up from the magazine he'd been reading and said with heavy irony, 'New to the village, eh? We'll have to throw you a party.'

'Really?' The boy looked delighted.

Christopher gazed at him in disbelief. *'No.'*

Emerging from the shop with his carrier bag, Barney wondered whether to call in at the Hollybush Inn for a coffee or a Coke. Maybe the staff there would be a bit friendlier. He paused on the narrow pavement, looking right and left . . .

And that was when he saw her.

Barney felt as if he'd suddenly forgotten how to breathe. It was definitely the same girl, making her way across the bridge with her little boy balanced on one hip. As he watched them, Barney saw her stop and lean over the parapet, pointing something out to her son. Freddie was peering down at something in the water below, laughing and clapping his hands.

Barney headed towards them, thinking that maybe this was Brigadoon after all.

Freddie spotted him first, letting out a high-pitched shriek of delight as he recognised the person whose head he had doused with Ribena the previous week.

'You,' Barney pretended to scold him, 'should be wearing your gloves.' He held up the red and white knitted mittens, dangling by their strings from the sleeves of the boy's jacket, then turned and smiled at his mother. 'Hello. Fancy bumping into you again.' He hoped he wasn't blushing; it wasn't the most dazzling chat-up line.

'Hi.' She looked delighted to see him. 'How did it go last week?'

She'd assumed he was visiting the hotel in order to apply for a job there, Barney realised. His smile broadened.

'Brilliant. I moved in this morning. Start work tomorrow. Nothing grand, just a porter's job, but I'm really excited. The people there seem really nice. I was just in the shop,' he held up his carrier bag, 'stocking up on a few bits and pieces. Fancy a fruit gum?'

He didn't launch into the story of how he had come to be visiting the village in the first place; in Barney's experience, telling girls about his kidney transplant was another less-than-successful chat-up line. They tended to be hopelessly squeamish.

'I'd love a fruit gum, but only if it's a red one. We were watching the ducks.' The girl gestured towards the river.

'I don't even know your name,' said Barney.

'Melanie. Mel.'

'I'm Barney.'

'I know you're Barney.' Her eyes danced. 'You told me that last week.'

'Oh.' This time he was definitely blushing. 'Thought you might have forgotten.'

'I hadn't.'

'So, where d'you live?' As he spoke, Barney waved an arm in the direction of the row of cottages behind her, set slightly back from the road. 'One of these?'

Mel shook her head. 'Oh no, I don't live in the village. I'm just here . . . visiting someone. That's my car over there, the green one.' Brushing her dark hair out of her eyes, she pointed to a small Fiat. 'It's not much, but it gets us from A to B. Actually, we should be making a move now.'

Her eyes were grey, but warm grey, Barney decided. And full of fun. They were beautiful eyes.

'So where *do* you live?' he repeated.

'Bristol. A place called Kingswood, but you wouldn't know it.' Turning, Mel shifted Freddie's position on her hip and began to head towards the little Fiat.

She was going! Leaving! Sheer panic propelled the next question out of Barney's mouth.

'With your husband?'

'No,' said Mel. 'I don't have a husband.' She held up her left hand and waggled her fingers, which were as bare as he remembered. All she wore was the big swirly silver ring on her thumb.

'Boyfriend?'

'I don't have one of those either. It's just Freddie and me.' For a moment she hesitated, then said flatly, 'Freddie's father left before he was born.'

Yesss!

'Look, you can say no if you don't want to,' Barney blurted out, 'but I'd really like to see you again. Could we go out for a drink sometime? Or a meal . . . or maybe the cinema? Whatever you like, really. Your choice.'

They had crossed the road by this time. Mel fumbled in her jacket pocket for her car keys.

'I don't see why not. That sounds really nice. I'd like to, only . . .'

Why was she hesitating? Barney's sky-high hopes began to crumble. Freddie sneezed, in his messy, baby way.

'Bless you,' Barney said absently. 'Only what?'

'Well, babysitting might be a problem.' Mel looked awkward. 'I mean, moneywise, things are a bit . . .'

'But that's not a problem! We can stay in! I'll bring round a video and a takeaway . . . I'd enjoy that just as much.' Oh, the *relief*.

'Are you sure?'

'Absolutely!' Barney nodded vigorously. 'In fact I'd prefer it.'

Mel's face softened as she unlocked the passenger door and fastened Freddie into his baby seat. Straightening up again, she said, 'How about you? Are you married?'

Barney laughed. 'Do I *look* married?'

'You never can tell.'

'Well, I'm not, I promise. Now, give me your phone number.' Luckily he had a pen in his jacket pocket. Uncapping it with a flourish, he said, 'I don't know yet which shifts I'll be working, but I'll give you a ring as soon as I find out.'

Mel told him the number and he wrote it on the back of his hand.

'So,' she smiled up at him from the driver's seat, 'I'll wait to hear from you.'

'You'll definitely hear from me,' Barney promised. He waggled his fingers at Freddie, strapped in next to her like an astronaut. ''Bye then.'

The driver's door was still open. Mel raised her eyebrows and said playfully, 'Aren't you forgetting something?'

Barney hesitated. What hadn't he done that he should have

143

done? Crikey, don't say she was waiting for him to give her a kiss?

At the risk of sounding like the village idiot, he said, 'What?'

'I'm still waiting,' Mel told him, 'for my fruit gum.'

Chapter 18

The phone was ringing as Tara let herself into the cottage. For once, her spirits didn't automatically rise. Having bumped into Maggie outside the shop, she had been told to expect a call from the washing machine repair man to let them know when he would be round with the all-important spare part.

Not bothering to rush, she shrugged off her coat first and kicked her shoes under the coffee table.

'Hello?'

'Tara?' said a male voice. 'Is that you?'

She froze, recognising the voice immediately.

'Tara? Hello, are you there?'

Tara hung up.

Why? Why was he phoning her? More to the point, how *dare* he phone her. What the bloody hell did he think he was playing at?

Except it was too late to ask now, because she'd hung up.

Ten minutes later, despising herself for being such a weed, Tara dialled 1471.

The last call, a computerised voice sneeringly informed her, had come from a network that didn't transmit numbers.

Which was irritating, but probably just as well.

By this time thoroughly rattled, Tara opened a can of tomato soup and stuffed two slices of bread into the toaster. While she waited for the soup to heat up, she ate seven chocolate biscuits and conducted an imaginary conversation in her head, the one she *would* have had on the phone if only she hadn't slammed it down. In this conversation, she was sarcastic, bitingly witty and thrillingly fluent as she told him just what she thought of him.

Fantasy conversations were great, you never got into a muddle or came off worst. You were able to have the last word, and it was always a dazzling one. You invariably emerged triumphant, leaving your opponent in emotional tatters.

The phone shrilled again just as Tara was tasting her first mouthful of soup. The mug jerked in her hand and scalding hot Heinz tomato slopped down the front of her uniform.

Don't be so stupid, it's only going to be the washing machine repair man. No need to race out of the kitchen to answer it, for heaven's sake. A casual saunter will do fine.

'H-hello?' Oh God, why did there have to be that telltale catch in her voice? Why couldn't she be as cool and composed as she always was in her fantasy dialogues?

'Tara, it's me. Don't hang up again. Just give me a couple of minutes, *please*.'

Put the phone down, put the phone down, instructed Tara's conscience, like a kindly but firm agony aunt.

Tara, her mouth as dry as cornflour, said, 'Why?'

Stop this. Her conscience promptly snatched up a megaphone and began bawling through it. *Stop this now.*

'I need to talk to you,' Dominic said urgently. 'Please, Tara, I know you probably hate me, but I don't hate you. I haven't been able to stop thinking about you . . . I can't sleep at night, I can hardly think straight . . . it must have been fate that brought us back together.'

'Hardly fate.' Somehow Tara managed to unglue her tongue from the roof of her mouth. 'More like my non-existent acting skills. If I'd made it in Hollywood by now, I wouldn't have been working down here as a chambermaid at the hotel you happened to be getting married in.'

She was waffling, because waffling was what she did best when in a state of shock. When in doubt, prattle on like an idiot and don't let the other person get another word in edgeways, that was Tara's motto.

It was also a handy way of drowning out the voice of your furious megaphone-wielding conscience.

'I have to see you again,' Dominic said simply. He wasn't the waffly type. 'Please, Tara, I can't do this on the phone. At least give me the chance to explain.'

'Dominic, you're married.'

'I know, I know. But I'm not asking you to have sex with me. I just want to talk.' He paused. 'What are you doing this evening?'

This evening? Tara felt the little hairs on the back of her neck go doinnggg. Aloud, she said, 'Are you serious?'

'Never more so.'

'But . . . but where are you?'

'At home.'

'In *Berkshire*?' She shook her head in disbelief.

'It's hardly Tibet,' Dominic countered with amusement. 'Only sixty or so miles, door to door. Just say the word and I can be there in less than an hour.'

Tara's conscience had by this time given up. It was sitting on a low wall, drumming its heels and smoking a cigarette. Meanwhile, all the disappointments of the last couple of weeks were re-playing themselves on fast forward through Tara's brain. Nonstop rejection, basically, hammering home the fact that she was worthless, physically unattractive and about as much fun to be with as a cup of cold sick.

And now here was Dominic, not only begging to see her, but prepared to make a round trip of over one hundred and twenty miles in order to do so.

When you'd been at such a low ebb confidence-wise, this was seriously flattering stuff. Tara knew it was feeble, but she was grateful to him. And as Dominic had pointed out, it wasn't as if he was asking her to have sex with him. All he wanted was a chat.

'How did you get hold of this number?' God, she hoped he hadn't rung the hotel.

'You said you were living in the village with your aunt. I phoned directory inquiries.'

'OK.' Tara took a deep breath. 'Seven o'clock. I'll meet you outside the pub.'

'It's freezing,' said Dominic. 'You'll be cold. Why don't I pick you up from your place?'

Ridiculously, a lump sprang into Tara's throat. He was worried about her getting cold! But she didn't fancy being lectured to by Maggie. If her aunt knew who she was seeing, she wouldn't approve.

'Thanks, but outside the Hollybush will be fine.'

He was there, bang on time, waiting for her. Feeling like a spy, Tara glanced around, double-checking the coast was clear before sliding into the car.

Ten minutes later they settled themselves at a table in the corner of a quiet pub in Lower Hinton, several miles from Colworth. Dominic, who was very tanned, wore a thick navy roll-neck sweater and Armani jeans. The hairs on his brown forearms had been bleached by the Caribbean sun.

'How was the honeymoon?' Terrified of being overheard, Tara hissed the words out like a spy.

'OK, I suppose. Well, not really OK,' Dominic admitted. He spread his hands and shook his head. 'In fact it was a disaster.'

'Why?'

He looked directly at her. 'Can't you guess? I couldn't stop thinking of you. I found myself *dreaming* about you. Tara, I know I messed up the other week, I panicked when Annabel's sister caught us together in that summerhouse, and it was wrong of me to let you take the blame. But it all happened so fast,' he went on urgently, 'and I was worried sick about Annabel. Imagine how she'd have felt if I'd told her the wedding was off. Can you understand that? I had to go through with it, for her sake. Otherwise who knows what she might have done?'

'You told me you loved her,' said Tara.

Dominic ran his fingers through his fair hair. There was pain in his eyes, and genuine regret.

'Maybe I do. In a way. Annabel's a lovely girl. She's done nothing wrong. But, you know, I think I feel protective towards her more than anything else. Like a big brother taking care of his younger sister.'

'His very wealthy younger sister,' Tara pointedly reminded him.

'Do you think that's why I married her? You couldn't be more wrong.' Dominic shook his head sadly. 'I married Annabel despite her money, rather than because of it. We've always got on well. I genuinely thought we could be happy together. But my feelings for Annabel don't even begin to compare with the way I feel about you.'

Golly. He was serious. It was scary, but at the same time Tara found herself experiencing a small glow of pride. Beneath the table, her knees were trembling like whippets.

'But I'm nothing. Just a chambermaid with a—'

'Wrong, wrong,' Dominic interrupted. 'You're *you*. We

always were fantastic together, weren't we? Like I said, the one thing I couldn't handle was your acting obsession; it just killed me to see what you were doing to yourself. And that's the only reason I ended it,' he said seriously. 'But now I find out you're not doing that any more . . . I swear to God, it's just knocked me for six. You can't imagine how it's made me feel. If only I'd *known*.'

'But you didn't know,' argued Tara, feeling a bit light-headed. 'And it's too late now, you're *married*.' She was starting to sound like a stuck record, but how many other ways were there of saying it?

'As if I needed reminding.' Dominic's expression was wry. 'Oh yes, I'm definitely married.' He paused. 'To the wrong girl.'

They arrived back in Colworth at ten thirty. Dominic pulled up outside the Hollybush, but kept the engine running. Annabel had driven over to spend the evening with her mother, Tara had learned, and would be home around midnight.

'I want to kiss you,' said Dominic, 'but I know I mustn't.'

The lights from the pub were shining into the car. Tara could see his infinitely regretful half-smile. For a mad moment – a mere nano-second – she wished he hadn't said it. If he'd just gone ahead and kissed her – nothing raunchy, just a chaste peck on the cheek – she could have pretended to be taken by surprise.

But he'd asked her permission now and, naturally, there was no way in the world she could say yes. For heaven's sake, he was a married man. Freshly married at that. Only a complete trollop with no morals whatsoever would allow such wickedness to happen.

God, there was probably confetti still in his suitcase.

'No, better not.' Tara's heart was thumping with adrenaline and secret delight. See? She *did* have morals! Dominic wanted to kiss her and she'd told him he couldn't, which was exactly the right thing to say.

'It's been so great, seeing you tonight.' Dominic's voice softened. 'I can't remember when I last enjoyed myself so much.'

Tara realised with a jolt that she couldn't either. He was right; it *had* been a great evening, talking and laughing and catching up on old times. Whilst doing nothing wrong, naturally.

'Or have you absolutely hated every second?' Dominic's tone was playful.

Responding in a similar vein, Tara smiled and raised an eyebrow. 'What do you want me to say?'

'I want you to say you'll meet me again.'

Oh God.

'Well—'

'Please.' Reaching across, Dominic touched her hand. His warm fingers closed around hers. 'You don't know how much it would mean to me.'

'But you're—'

'Tara, will you stop going on about it? I *know* I'm married. But we can still be friends, can't we? Old friends who meet up every now and again for a drink and a chat? Would that be so wrong?'

She exhaled slowly, no longer sure. Would it?

'I don't know,' Tara admitted, hopelessly torn. 'Maybe it wouldn't be such a good idea.'

'OK, fine, forget it.'

The unexpectedness of Dominic's reply made her jump. He sounded sad and resigned, but determined to go along with whatever she decided.

Tara promptly began to wish she hadn't said it.

'The thing is,' she went on hesitantly, 'other people might get the wrong idea.'

'I know. Doesn't seem fair, does it? All we want to do is talk. If you were a bloke or I was a girl, there'd be no problem at all, we could meet up for a drink and a chat as often as we liked. But just because I'm not a girl, you won't see me again. Actually, that makes you sexist. I may have to take you to the Court of Human Rights.'

He was teasing her, doing his best to lighten the mood. Tara smiled, but he was right. It really wasn't fair.

'I'm going now. You have to get back.'

'To my wife.' Dominic grimaced. 'God, married less than a month and already my heart sinks at the thought of it, seeing her and pretending everything's fine.' Sadly, he added, 'Do you realise, you're the only one who knows the truth? There's nobody else I can tell.'

Tara's heart went out to him. That was the trouble with men, they might be able to read maps and change tyres, but they weren't capable of sharing their deepest, innermost feelings with other men. It simply wasn't in their genetic make-up. Sport they could discuss with a passion, but emotions were strictly a no-go area. Being able to gossip and confide in her friends, Tara realised, was one of the best things about being a girl. Along with mascara.

'Look, you've got my number. If you're ever desperate, you know where I am.' Hurriedly, as if blurting out the words at a rate of knots didn't count, she promptly flung open the passenger door and leapt out.

'You're fantastic. You know that, don't you?' Dominic shot her a grateful smile. 'Really, the most amazing woman. You have no idea how much this evening's meant to me.'

Pink-cheeked with the cold, but glowing Ready-Brek-warm

inside, Tara let herself into the cottage. Maggie was in the midst of a cushion-making binge, kneeling on the living-room floor surrounded by swathes of silk and velvet and the paper templates she used to cut out the relevant appliquéd shapes. It never failed to astound both of them that Maggie's customised cushion covers, which she sold through one of the gift shops in the village, should prove to be such a hit with the tourists from overseas. Still, it would be churlish to mock their dodgy taste in home accessories.

'What d'you think?' Maggie held up one of the finished cushion covers, depicting two figures silhouetted on Colworth Bridge overlooking the river. Maggie, a whizz with the sewing machine, was a natural free stylist. Around the simply executed tableau were embroidered the words: Hank 'n' EmmyLou, England, 2002.

'Ain't it just the *cutest thing*?' mimicked Maggie, because making fun of the customers was sometimes impossible to resist. 'Of course, in real life they're much fatter. In fact I'm amazed the bridge didn't collapse. Still, it's what they wanted, so they'll be happy.' Patting the cushion cover with satisfaction, she looked up and said, 'You're looking pretty happy yourself. Where've you been?'

'Oh, just out for a drink. With one of the lads I met in Bristol last week,' Tara fibbed.

Maggie raised an eyebrow. 'And? Will you be seeing him again?'

'Um, not sure. Maybe.' Feeling her skin getting hotter, Tara hastily took off her coat. 'Shall I put the kettle on?'

'Ooh, yes, a cup of tea would be lovely. Well, you look as if you had a good time anyway.'

Maggie began tidying up her cushion-making paraphernalia. Tara hurried into the kitchen and began flinging tea bags into mugs. She couldn't possibly tell the truth; Maggie would be shocked and horrified if she knew who she'd spent the evening with. Nor, Tara realised, could she mention it to Daisy.

Honestly, so much for girls being able to confide in each other. Here she was, every bit as isolated as Dominic.

Tonight would have to remain their secret.

Oh, but she *had* had a good time, being paid all that attention, showered with compliments and told over and over again how special she was. Like stumbling for weeks through a parched desert then finding yourself at the entrance to a vast Coca-Cola factory.

And all she and Dominic had done was talk, for heaven's sake.

How could that be wrong?

Chapter 19

Daisy was on the phone when Pam the receptionist knocked and stuck her head round the door of her office.

'Daisy? Someone to see you in reception.'

'Who?' Daisy frowned; there were no appointments in her diary.

'A Miss Tyzack.' Pam's chins jiggled with suppressed laughter as Daisy's head shot up.

'Who?'

'Miss Clarissa Tyzack.'

'Alone?'

'No. She has a gentleman with her.'

Daisy exhaled slowly, stalling for time. 'Pam, I'm a bit tied up at the moment. Couple of important calls to make. Could you ask them to wait and say I'll be out in five minutes?'

The moment Pam was out of the room, Daisy crashed the phone down, scrabbled furiously in her bag, found a lipstick and a scrunchie and got to work. In her dithery state she almost tied her hair back with lipstick and wrapped the scrunchie around her mouth.

Daisy took a couple of deep breaths. It was completely and utterly ridiculous to get into such a flap just because Dev Tyzack had turned up out of the blue. Anyway, he'd already seen her looking far worse than this. But she couldn't help it, her heart was galloping and she had her pride. This morning she'd been in too much of a rush to wash her hair and it was looking borderline-stringy. Fastening it back would help to disguise this. As for the lipstick, why shouldn't she put some on? A dash of pink was always a confidence booster. Nothing wrong with wanting to look your best.

Aaargh, supper last night! Spaghetti swimming in garlic! Rummaging once more through her bag, Daisy fell on a packet of Wrigley's Extra, shovelled three into her mouth and chewed energetically until her jaw felt as if it was about to drop off.

Well, she'd have done the same for any client. It was only polite.

Out in reception, Pam was making a tremendous fuss of Clarissa, who was in turn making valiant efforts to clamber onto Pam's lap.

Which only proved that Clarissa was no Mastermind candidate, since Pam's ample stomach took up all the available room.

Dev, clearly having spotted this too, was manfully keeping a straight face as Pam cooed delightedly, 'Who's a bootiful girl then? Is it you? Is it you? Oh yes, you're *sooo bootiful*!'

'It's a national conspiracy.' Dev shook his head and looked sorrowful. 'This dog's going to get ideas above her station. Next thing you know, she'll be pestering me to enter her for Miss World.'

'She'd look great in a bikini.' As she said it, Daisy caught the gleam of interest in Pam's eye. Their receptionist, who lived for gossip, had instantly noted the scrunchie and freshly applied lipstick. 'So what's this all about then? Not a problem with the conference booking, I hope?'

'No problems at all. I've brought the seating plan for lunch,' said Dev.

'Thanks.' Daisy took the plan, which he could far more easily have faxed through to her.

'But really I thought I'd just drop by so you can see how Clarissa's getting on.'

Clarissa, her tail rotating furiously, had by this time transferred her attention to Daisy. Yelping with delight she licked Daisy's hands and leapt up, her legs seemingly on springs.

'She's looking brilliant. How's the incontinence?'

Dev gave her a saucy wink. 'Fine thanks. How's yours?'

'I meant is she likely to wee all over our expensive rug? Maybe we should take her outside, let her run around a bit.' This wasn't really what Daisy meant, she was just keen to move away from Pam, who was capable of spreading rumours faster than typhoid. By lunchtime every member of staff and most of the guests would have heard that Daisy was embroiled in a red-hot affair with that gorgeous rugby fellow from Bath, the one who was always in the papers with some new showbizzy girlfriend or other, actresses and models and the like.

'She won't wee on your rug, she's a lady,' said Dev, but he headed over to the door anyway.

'Oh, Daisy, there's someone else to see you,' remembered Pam as they moved away from the desk. 'I sent him through to the bar.' Daisy was too busy being enchanted by Clarissa's ability to bounce backwards – like Tigger on rewind – to care.

'They don't have an appointment. I'll see them in ten minutes.'

Outside, Clarissa tore across the gravelled drive to investigate the fountain. Daisy and Dev watched her from the doorway.

'I also came to say thanks.' Dev turned to look at Daisy. 'For making me choose her. She wasn't what I was after, but I can't imagine being without her now.'

'My pleasure.' Daisy's mouth twitched. 'So you've bonded.'

'Oh, we've bonded. She's even sleeping on my bed. It's going to play havoc with my social life.'

'But she's worth it.' Daisy gazed fondly across at Clarissa, now balancing like a tightrope walker along the narrow stone parapet encircling the fountain. 'How could anyone not love her?'

'Something's been puzzling me. If you're so mad about dogs, why don't you have any of your own?'

'I'd love to, but it wouldn't be fair. I work such long hours. We're a dog-friendly hotel,' Daisy explained, 'but I couldn't trail one around with me all day long. And I wouldn't want to have to beg other people to take it out for a walk because I don't have time myself.'

Dev nodded. 'Fair enough.'

'I'll be Clarissa's doting maiden aunt instead,' Daisy went on cheerfully. 'I'll take her out somewhere glamorous every now and again, feed her exotic food and spoil her rotten.'

'Actually, she's pretty used to exotic food.' Drily, Dev said, 'She learned how to open the fridge the other night. Polished off two fillet steaks and a Marks and Spencer double chocolate cheesecake.'

Two fillet steaks? Who had he been planning to entertain? All the modelly-actressy types she'd ever seen him photographed with in the papers had been awfully skinny; they surely wouldn't be seen dead in the same room as a slice of double chocolate cheesecake.

Oh heck, maybe he was still seeing Annabel Cross-Calvert's sister, the sturdily built bridesmaid he'd driven off with after the wedding. She'd certainly looked as if she could demolish half a cow.

'Both the steaks were for me,' said Dev, seemingly capable of reading her mind.

Which was a bit of a worry.

'Serves you right then.' Daisy shook her head pityingly at him. 'Your selfish single days are behind you now. You have to learn to share.'

'That brings back terrible memories.' Dev looked pained. 'My mother always used to say that when I wouldn't let my cousins play with my Action Men.'

'Well, I can see that would be difficult for you.' Daisy was sympathetic. 'But I really think twenty-five's too old to be playing with Action Men.'

He laughed, and Daisy realised with a little shiver of pleasure that she was enjoying herself. She was almost, but not quite, flirting with him.

'So what are your views on double chocolate cheesecake?' said Dev.

'Couldn't eat a whole one. Well,' Daisy went on happily, 'not in under three minutes.'

Dev kept his gaze fixed on Clarissa as she launched herself into the shallow water around the fountain, discovered the extent of its iciness and promptly leapt out again in disgust.

'When's your next evening off?'

Daisy's stomach muscles contracted in surprise. Crikey, this was a bit sudden, she hadn't been expecting this.

'Why?' Prevaricating, she said, 'Don't tell me, you're off out somewhere and you need someone to dog-sit?'

'No.' Dev smiled and shook his head. 'Actually, what I meant was—'

'Hang on a sec.' Daisy stopped him, aware that they had company. Liza, one of the new waitresses, was hovering just behind them. 'What is it, Liza?'

'Um, sorry to interrupt, but there's someone in the bar waiting to see you.'

'I know. I've already told Pam I'll be there in a minute.'

Liza, who had only started working at the hotel a few days earlier, looked embarrassed.

'The thing is, he says it's urgent, he needs to see you right now.'

Daisy heaved a sigh. Bloody guests, they certainly knew how to pick their moments.

'Who is it? Did you get a name?'

'Well, no.' Liza shifted uncomfortably from one foot to the other. 'Not a name, exactly. He just said he was . . . um, your husband.'

Daisy didn't seriously expect to walk into the bar and find Steven waiting to greet her, but for a split second back there she had experienced the mental equivalent of a punch to the solar plexus. Moments later, it occurred to her to wonder who on earth would have the gall to *say* he was her husband. Basically, they had to be either deeply insensitive, seriously psychotic or . . .

Or someone she hadn't seen for a very long time.

Daisy's mouth dropped open in amazement as the figure over by the window turned to face her.

'Josh?'

The man who most certainly wasn't her husband grinned at her.

'Hi, sweetheart.'

'Josh!' With a shriek of delight she raced the length of the otherwise empty bar and threw her arms round him. 'I don't believe it, what are you doing here? Oh my God, mind the window, put me down!'

Daisy's high heels missed the glass by an inch as Josh Butler, all six foot four of him, swung her up into the air and whirled her round like a rotary washing line in a hurricane. Laughing, he lowered her back to earth and planted a resounding kiss on each cheek. As she clutched his arm, struggling to get her balance back, Daisy saw the back end of Dev Tyzack's car swish past the full-length bay window and head off down the drive. Clarissa was jack-in-the-boxing up and down on the back seat.

Daisy gave Josh Butler a hefty thump on the arm.

'*Ouch*. What was that for?'

'Telling the waitress you were my husband. How could you *do* that?'

He looked pleased with himself. 'I was watching you chatting to that bloke. Correction, *flirting* with him. And he seemed pretty keen too. You still aren't married.' Josh picked up her ring-free left hand as he said it, then broke into another mischievous grin. 'I just thought it would be fun to stir things up a bit, see how he reacted.'

Daisy rolled her eyes. 'See that dust cloud?' She gestured in the direction of the gates at the end of the drive. 'That's how he reacted.'

'You mean he's wimped out.' Josh was unrepentant. 'Just goes to prove you could do better. And it looks like this is your lucky day,' he added teasingly, 'because here I am!'

'Still as shy and modest as ever,' Daisy agreed.

'Look, I was right here, watching you.' From the window there was a clear view of the front step upon which she and Dev had been standing. 'You were doing that flirty thing with your eyes, just like you used to do with me. That's when I had a word with that little waitress – ha, you should have seen your face when she told you your husband was here to see you.'

He'd always been a practical joker.

'I'm not surprised,' said Daisy. 'Seeing as my husband died a year ago.'

Cruel, maybe, but worth it to see the look of utter unmitigated dismay on Josh's big freckly face.

Chapter 20

Daisy had met Josh Butler at university ten years earlier. Every now and again he had popped into a lecture, but ninety-five per cent of Josh's time had been taken up with rowing, rugby, drinking, cricket, partying, rock-climbing and golf.

It was a hectic and exhausting schedule that didn't leave a lot of time for studying. Nobody had been more astounded than Josh when he eventually left with a 2:1.

Daisy vividly remembered the first time she'd clapped eyes on Josh. She'd been in the Serpent's Arms with a group of friends one Saturday lunchtime when he had burst into the pub wearing nothing but huge clip-on glittery earrings and a Tina Turner wig.

Well, you had to look, didn't you?

'What's the matter?' Josh had grinned down at her, unabashed. 'Never seen a fully grown man naked?'

'Come here.' Daisy had beckoned him forward. 'Your dangly bits are all caught up – let me sort them out for you.'

By the time she'd finished disentangling his ornate chandelier-style earring from the bird's nest of nylon hair that was his wig, Josh had decided that she was the girl for him.

'I'm Josh Butler. How about coming out with me tomorrow night?'

He was athletically built and impressively muscly, with untidy reddish-brown hair poking out from beneath his wig, sparkling light-brown eyes and thousands of freckles. Happily, thanks to the amount of time evidently spent outdoors, he had managed to achieve a tan of sorts. Daisy was pretty sure she could never bring herself to go out with a redhead whose skin was the colour of cod.

'I thought you'd never ask.' She had smiled up at him. 'What took you so long?'

Josh Butler winked. 'Just painfully shy.'

Josh's sponsored streak had raised two hundred and thirty pounds for charity and his relationship with Daisy took off the following night. For the next six or seven months they were a couple. Then they broke up. For any number of silly studenty reasons, but mainly because Daisy had come to realise that she needed more. Theirs wasn't a bad relationship, they got on well together and had fun together, but somehow it wasn't enough.

It all came to a head one hot Sunday afternoon while Josh was sculling on the river. Daisy, sunbathing on the riverbank with the girlfriend of one of the other rowers, had brought along a pile of newspapers and was idly flipping through them.

'Ooh, Martin Kemp, he's a nine out of ten,' drooled Megan, sprawled next to her on the grass. 'Bleeurgh, Frank Skinner, two and a half.'

'But he's funny,' Daisy pointed out.

'OK, make it three and a half. But let's face it, he's never going to be a sex god. Unlike this little cutie,' she crooned, stroking a picture of Jon Bon Jovi. 'Now he is my kind of boy. Definitely a nine and a half, that one.' She fanned herself energetically with a rolled-up colour supplement.

'Cary Grant,' said Daisy dreamily. 'He'd be a ten.'

'Oh, get a grip, girl, your marking system's shot to bits. Come on, let's go through this magazine. Give me your scores and I'll tell you where you're going wrong. Hugh Grant.'

'Eight,' Daisy promptly responded.

'Julio Iglesias.'

'Minus eight.'

'Jonathan Ross.'

'Seven and a half.'

'Adam Ant.'

'Nine.' Daisy still had a bit of a weakness for Adam Ant.

'Josh Butler.'

'Seven.' The score was out of her mouth before she could stop it. At that moment Josh rowed past them in his boat.

'Oops,' said Megan. 'You can't say that about your boy-friend.'

Daisy watched Josh speed off down the river and realised that she could say it, because it was true. He was a seven.

'You see, this is where you're going wrong,' Megan earnestly explained. 'The person you're going out with has to be a ten. He just has to be. Otherwise, what's the point of being with him?'

And that was it, in a nutshell. A boyfriend who was a seven simply wasn't good enough. What was she doing, Daisy wondered, settling for less than a ten?

She finished with Josh that evening and he took it pretty well. If he was hurt, he did a good job of hiding it. Daisy just hoped he wasn't feeling too terrible inside. They agreed, heartily, to stay friends and she also hoped this wouldn't mean he'd forever be getting drunk and hopelessly maudlin, begging her to please, oh please, give him jusht one more chance . . .

Josh, she discovered three days later, had been so distraught that he'd gone to a party on Sunday night and hooked up with an exotic beauty called Mira, who was studying for a PhD in physics. They'd had fabulous sex, apparently, and had seen each other the following night and the next night, and the night after that. Daisy knew this because Mira promptly told all her friends how miraculous Josh was in bed. Daisy had kept having to remind herself that jealousy was pointless, she already knew how great Josh was. But it hadn't been enough.

It wasn't easy, but she managed to maintain her resolve. Better still, she and Josh did remain close friends. The Mira thing fizzled out after a couple of months and a stream of girlfriends subsequently came and went. No longer jealous, Daisy teased him about his laddish behaviour and Josh in turn made merciless fun of her own determination to hold out for Mr Pinnacle-of-Perfection.

'You could have had me,' Josh informed her with a shake of his tousled head. 'You had your chance and you blew it. In fifty years' time you'll be one of those mad old spinsters in slippers and a bobble hat,' he went on sorrowfully, 'still waiting for Pierce Brosnan to come along and sweep you off your feet.'

'Ah, but won't you be gutted when he does come along?' Daisy had chirpily retorted. 'You'll just have to read all about it in the papers, because you won't be invited to the wedding.'

By the time she'd married Steven, she couldn't have invited Josh anyway. He had disappeared off to America and they had lost touch.

Leaving Vince the assistant manager in charge downstairs, Daisy took Josh up to her flat on the first floor of the west wing. Wasting no time as usual, he unearthed the biscuit tin and began making great inroads into the Hobnobs. Josh had always eaten more than anyone else she knew.

They had so much catching up to do. Five whole years.

'How did you know I was here?' Daisy kicked off her high heels and busied herself boiling the kettle.

'Pure chance. Since I came back from the States a couple of weeks ago, I've been staying with Tom Pride. You remember Tom, single sculls, played Widow Twankey in our final year panto? He's in merchant banking now.' Having polished off the Hobnobs, Josh began investigating the contents of Daisy's fridge. 'Anyway, he's kept in touch with a couple of the other chaps from college and we all met up one night for a drink. We were chatting about old times, I wondered what you were up to nowadays and Marcus Cartwright said he'd seen a piece in one of the Sunday supplements about your dad buying some country house hotel and you running it. He couldn't remember the name, just that it was in the Cotswolds, but that's the wonder of the internet for you. There was a cybercafé just across the road. Two minutes later we had the web page for this place up on screen, and there was the photo of you with your staff on the front steps of the hotel.' Josh shrugged and went on cheerfully, 'Well, seemed like too good an opportunity to pass up. I just had to see you again. Sweetheart, are you saving these eggs for anything?'

If there was any justice in this world, Josh would be the size of a house. Grinning at the piteous look on his face, Daisy passed him a frying pan.

'Help yourself. So what have you been doing in the States?'

'Golf pro. I've been working at a club out in Texas for the past eighteen months. It's a tough job.' Josh winked and gestured with an egg before cracking it into the pan. 'Out on the course all day. Play a couple of rounds, teach cack-handed Texans how to swing a club . . . and then there's the socialising, of course. All those rich young girls out there eager to learn the game because it's a cool way to meet rich young guys . . .'

'Sounds awful,' said Daisy. 'You poor thing. So this is just a flying visit?'

'No, I was head-hunted a few weeks ago. I've got a new job

now, in Miami, at a place that's still being built. Better course, twice as much money, teaching cack-handed Floridians how to swing a club.' Josh was still deftly breaking eggs into the pan. 'But I don't start there until the beginning of June, so I thought I'd give myself a break and come to England for a few months. I was planning to stay with my mother but she's gone and got herself a new bloke. They spend all their time draped over each other like besotted teenagers.' He pulled a comical face. 'One weekend was enough. I could tell I was in the way. To be honest, it was putting me off my food.'

'Can't have that,' said Daisy as he gave the frying pan an expert shake-and-swirl. 'There's bacon and tomatoes in the fridge if you want them.'

'This is hard to believe. You, running a hotel. Who was that chap you were flirting with outside? One of the guests?'

Quick, weigh up the options. Is that what Dev Tyzack is?

Daisy shrugged. 'Kind of.'

'But you can sort it out.' Josh was seeking reassurance, belatedly. 'You'll explain to him that I'm not really your husband, won't you? Tell him it was just a joke.'

'Don't worry, I'll tell him,' Daisy repeated solemnly. Too right she would.

'Is it serious?' Pausing, Josh glanced across at her. 'I mean, do you really like this bloke?'

Daisy's stomach instantly began to squirm. Of course she liked Dev. She liked him so much she was scared witless.

Panicking inwardly, she said, 'Of course not.'

'Phew, thank goodness for that. I'd hate to think I'd messed things up.' Breaking into a huge grin, Josh added, 'Mind you, you had me going back there, with that dead husband line. I swear to God, for a moment I thought you were serious.'

It really was lovely to see Josh again, and to discover that he was as capable as ever of wedging his big feet in his even bigger mouth. In deference to his fragile appetite, Daisy sat down opposite him at the kitchen table and waited until he'd demolished his Desperate Dan-sized fry-up before saying, 'I was serious.'

Josh froze, his knife and fork suspended in mid-air.

In slow motion, he shook his head. 'Really?'

'Truly.'

'He's actually dead?'

'Actually dead.'

'Oh fuck.'

'It's all right,' said Daisy. 'I was about to divorce him. It was all over between us. I couldn't have chosen a worse man to marry.'

Carefully, Josh put down his knife and fork. 'What happened?'

'Car crash. He had his girlfriend with him at the time, but she wasn't hurt. He was a liar and a cheat and an all-round con merchant,' Daisy sighed. 'Which just goes to show how brilliant my choice is when it comes to men.'

He half smiled. 'That's not true. You used to have excellent taste.'

'Whereas you went for quantity rather than quality.' Daisy couldn't resist teasing him. 'Anyway, never mind all that. How long are you down here for?'

Josh shrugged and ruffled his hair. 'I'm easy.'

'We already know that.'

'I mean I don't have any plans. I came back for a holiday, and to cheer up my lonely old mum, but she isn't lonely any more. Tom's flat in London is hardly big enough for one grown man, let alone two. Marcus did say I could stay with him, but he's got two-year-old twins and a bawling six-week-old baby.

Still, I suppose I could always go and live in a cardboard box somewhere.'

Daisy kept a straight face. A year after she and Josh had broken up, she and her flatmates had been unceremoniously – and completely unfairly – evicted by their landlord for holding one riotous party too many. Josh had taken her in at once and generously allowed her to stay rent-free on his sofa until she scraped together enough money for a deposit on the next flat.

'Better fetch your cases then.'

Josh did his best to look mystified. 'My cases?'

'Those big things you pack your belongings in,' Daisy helpfully explained. 'Sort of rectangular, with handles. I think you'll probably find them in the boot of your car.'

Chapter 21

Daisy had made a point of not fussing over Barney since his arrival. He appeared to be settling well into his job and Vince had told her he was a willing and eager worker, already proving a hit with the guests – particularly the female variety – thanks to his cheerful manner and fresh-faced good looks.

But moving to Colworth from Manchester had to be a huge shock to the system. Worried that he might be lonely or homesick, she cornered Rocky in the bar later that afternoon.

'How's Barney getting on?'

'Fine, I think.'

'You think?' Daisy frowned. 'Don't you *know*?'

'He seems OK.' Bewildered, Rocky said, 'I haven't really seen that much of him outside work.'

'Well, that's not very kind, is it? When a group of you go out to the Hollybush, do you invite him along?' Daisy experienced a surge of indignation on Barney's behalf. She pictured him sitting alone in his little attic room, feeling excluded from the crowd, miserably wondering why nobody wanted to be his friend.

'Of course we've invited him,' Rocky protested. 'You know we try to make the new staff feel welcome. But Barney always says no.'

They obviously weren't trying hard enough, Daisy thought crossly.

'You mean he stays here all on his own?'

'You must be joking,' Rocky exclaimed. 'He's got himself a girlfriend, hasn't he? And I'm telling you, a couple of our waitresses had their eye on him and they were well pissed off when they found out he was already taken.'

Daisy was amazed. 'A girlfriend? What, here? *Already?*'

'The quiet ones are always the worst.' Rocky grinned, relieved that the misunderstanding had been cleared up and that he was off the hook. 'The moment he comes off shift, we don't see Barney for dust. He gets into his car and, zoom, straight off down the M4. She lives in Bristol.'

Well, well, well, who'd have thought it? Maybe this was why he'd been so eager to move down here in the first place.

'Actually, you're wrong,' said Daisy.

'She does! Barney told me she lived in Bristol!'

'I meant about the quiet ones being the worst.' Daisy raised a playful eyebrow. 'From what I hear, you're certainly one of the worst. And nobody could call you quiet.'

Barney was loving every minute of his job. He was currently loving every minute of his life. Finishing his day shift at five o'clock meant he could strip off his porter's uniform, jump into the shower, change into jeans and a sweatshirt and be in Bristol by six. The car he had bought for four hundred pounds in Manchester – a rusty Rover in a distressing shade of mauve – was bearing up so far, intermittently belching out great clouds of black smoke but bravely refusing to do the girly thing and break down on the motorway. It wouldn't last for ever, but it was doing well enough for now.

Barney's absolute favourite moment of the day was when he pulled into Mel's street and drew up outside her flat. Next moment the front door would swing open and there she'd be, with Freddie on her hip, beaming all over her face.

It just felt so . . . special. Barney couldn't get over how great she made him feel. All his life, through no fault of his own, he had been looked after by other people. Now, for the first time, the balance was equal. He knew that Mel looked forward to his arrival just as much as he looked forward to seeing her.

Their first evening together, Barney had turned up as promised with a takeaway from the Chinese around the corner. The next evening Mel had made a lasagne, and the evening after that she'd served up toad-in-the-hole with fried onions and gravy, followed by chocolate mousse.

'You don't have to cook me a meal every time I come round here,' Barney protested. 'It isn't fair on you.'

'Why isn't it fair?' Mel's grey eyes sparkled. 'I like cooking for you. It's just so nice having you here.'

But Barney's conscience was at work. Food cost money, after all. Feeling wonderfully macho (me Tarzan, you Mel), he told her, 'Tomorrow night, we're going to the big supermarket at Emerson's Green. They're open 'till eight.'

That had been yesterday, and now he was outside Mel's flat. Mel, locking the front door behind her, was wearing her red fleece and jeans, and Freddie was bundled up in his navy snowsuit. Jumping out to fasten the child seat into the back of the car, Barney realised he was as excited as if they were setting out on a trip to Disneyland, Paris.

He'd never pressed her for details of Freddie's father. Just once, he'd asked casually if there was a chance he'd ever come back. Mel, shaking her head, had replied firmly, 'No chance at all. He's gone for good.'

This was fine by Barney.

It felt fantastic, trawling up and down the supermarket's busy aisles with Mel at his side and Freddie beaming happily from his seat in the trolley.

We look like a normal family, thought Barney, swelling with pride as an old lady stopped to coo with delight over Freddie.

'Ooh, that's a lovely little boy you've got there,' she complimented Barney. 'Going to be a real heartbreaker when he grows up.'

'He doesn't do so badly now,' Barney told her with a grin.

'We'll go halves with the bill,' Mel said, as the trolley began to fill up. 'I can't let you pay for his nappies.'

'I want to. Please, just let me do it.' Barney was firm. 'I've never been to a supermarket like this before.' Hastily he added, 'I mean, the three of us together.'

Smiling, Mel briefly squeezed his arm. 'Neither have I.'

By seven thirty they were back at her chilly basement flat. Mel, busy unpacking carrier bags and putting everything away in cupboards, watched Barney switch on the gas fire, carefully fasten the fireguard back around it, then help Freddie out of his padded snowsuit. Her heart contracted at the sight of the two of them laughing together. It was almost scary, the difference Barney had made to their lives in such a short time.

For the first time in over a year, Mel realised, she felt normal. OK, maybe it did sound pathetic, but being together in the supermarket, giving the appearance of being a family, had been a real thrill. Since Freddie's birth it had been something she'd yearned to do; each routine shopping trip had been accompanied by a jolt of envy whenever she saw a proper family, the father pushing the trolley, entertaining his child, humping the heavy bags into the car . . .

Exhausted by his evening jaunt, Freddie was fast asleep within minutes. As Mel was tucking him into his cot, Barney appeared behind her in the bedroom and whispered, 'Red wine, or white?'

'White,' Mel whispered back, then jumped as his hand came to rest on her shoulder. Together they gazed down at Freddie with his long eyelashes casting shadows over his flushed cheeks, his little arms flung above his head.

'He's perfect,' said Barney.

So are you, thought Mel.

Back in the living room, she saw that he had laid the table, lit candles and torn open the foil-lined bag containing their spit-roasted, ready-cooked chicken. The salad had been dressed and tipped into a bowl, the garlic baguettes were warm and their pudding – rhubarb crumble and double cream – awaited them on top of the fridge.

Hot tears of gratitude sprang into Mel's eyes. She wasn't a wimp and she was perfectly capable of taking care of herself, but . . . oh, it was *so* nice to be spoilt for a change. Even if Barney had lit the ornamental carved red candles that were far too pretty and expensive to ever actually use.

After dinner, with Macy Gray crooning soulfully away in the background, they played Scrabble. The room was warm now and Barney had pulled off his navy sweater. Inwardly buzzing with anticipation, Mel wondered whether tonight would be the night he made his move. If Freddie stayed asleep and she managed to persuade Barney to drink a second glass of wine, it just might happen. Of course she could take the lead herself, but was determined not to. She didn't want Barney to think of her as some brazen seducer who went around ripping men's trousers off willy-nilly.

Besides, Mel sensed that he would want to be the one who made the decision; she had to leave the first move up to him. It would be awful to scare him off and lose someone she cared for so—

RRRINGG, went the doorbell, startling them both.

'Who's that?' said Barney.

'No idea.' Mel uncurled her feet from beneath her and slid off the sofa; she didn't have any friends likely to drop in unannounced. 'Unless it's that moaning Minnie from the flat upstairs, complaining about the noise again.'

Actually, this was quite likely.

Barney gazed up at the ceiling in bewilderment. 'What noise?'

'God, any kind you can think of. Putting our Scrabble letters down on the board in a clicky way. Taking the wrapper off a bar of soap. Brushing your hair noisily. Anything,' Mel rolled her eyes in despair. 'That bloody woman has ears like a bat.'

To be on the safe side, she turned Macy Gray off before answering the door.

If the old bat upstairs was Mel's least favourite visitor, the skinny woman on the doorstep ran her a close second. Mrs Jefferson, her landlady, was in her late forties, with a face like a hatchet and a manner to match.

Typically, she didn't hang about.

'Here's your written notice to leave.' She thrust the envelope into Mel's hands and glanced icily at Barney, who had appeared behind Mel. 'You've got one month to get out.'

Instantly Mel felt sick. Being booted out of her flat had long been one of those vague fears floating around in her subconscious, but she'd never really expected it to happen.

'Why?'

'I'm selling the building.'

This was a blatant lie.

'I'm not noisy,' Mel insisted.

'You may not be, but your kid is. I've had endless complaints,' Mrs Jefferson snapped back.

'That's not true! Freddie's a *happy* baby.'

'Glad to hear it. If he's so fantastic, you won't have any trouble finding another place to live.'

'But this isn't *fair*,' wailed Mel, so loudly that Freddie promptly woke up and began to bawl. 'It's that bloody boss-eyed old witch upstairs, isn't it? I'm telling you, she's barking mad!'

'Really?' Mrs Jefferson, her voice like permafrost, said, 'How interesting. She's also my mother.'

'I don't care, I don't care. This is a shitty dump anyway.' Mel's voice quavered as she recklessly sloshed wine into her glass, but she wasn't the weepy-waily type. She was damned if she'd cry. Waving a dismissive arm, she said bitterly, 'I mean, look at it. Bosnian refugees would turn their noses up at this place. I'll find somewhere better in no time.'

Barney's heart contracted with love. He'd give anything for Mel to burst into tears now, so he could comfort her properly. Then again, the fact that she was trying so hard not to cry only made him love her more.

Was it love? Really? Barney didn't care, he just knew he'd do anything he could to help Mel.

Anyway, she was right. Despite her best efforts to clean it up, this place was still a dump. The wallpaper was peeling off the walls, the window frames were rotten, the carpets practically worn down to the threads.

'I'll go with you when you go flat-hunting,' he told Mel. 'We'll find somewhere great, you'll see.'

Mel's shoulders slumped in defeat. 'Who are we kidding? We won't find anywhere great at all. If I'm very very lucky I may find somewhere marginally less damp and disgusting, occupied by a slightly better class of cockroach.'

Barney put his arm round her. 'What about the council?'

'You mean go into a hostel? Spend six months in some bed and breakfast place before they offer me something on the sixteenth floor of a drug-infested tower block? Forget it. Anyway,' Mel gave herself a shake and abruptly stood up, 'this isn't your problem, and we're not going to talk about it any more. Help yourself to another drink,' she added over her shoulder. 'I'm just going to the loo.'

Two minutes later, plonking herself back down on the sofa, Mel turned her attention to the Scrabble board and said briskly, 'Now, where were we? Is it your turn next, or mine?'

Then her gaze slid over the letters propped up on her letter stand. Eight of them now, instead of the seven that had been there before.

The letters spelt out: I LOVE YOU.

For a long moment Mel was too choked to speak.

At last she said unsteadily, 'You know I could have sworn I had a J and an X just now.' Then her eyes softened. 'But I much prefer these.'

'I want to make you happy,' Barney told her.

'You do make me happy.' Mel leaned over and kissed him, tentatively, on the corner of his mouth. She pulled away, then kissed him again, her eyelashes trembling against his cheek. Two brief kisses, that was enough. She wasn't a strumpet. The rest was up to Barney.

Barney took the hint. Tilting his head, his mouth found hers. The next moment his arms were round her. Emotion welled up inside him and he drew Mel closer still, feeling the rapid thud of her heart through her thin grey sweatshirt.

Overwhelmed by the effect she was having on him, Barney cradled her head in his hands and wondered if it was possible to feel happier than this.

Then, as Mel's fingers moved tentatively to the front of his jeans, he discovered it *was* possible.

'I love you too,' she whispered in his ear.

This, Barney realised, was why he had never gone in for one-night stands. Why would anyone want to settle for anything less perfect than this?

Freddie remained asleep in his cot in Mel's bedroom. By unspoken mutual consent, they made love in the living room, on the rug in front of the gas fire.

Afterwards, Mel said dreamily, 'I thought he might wake up again.'

'He's on our side.' Barney smiled and stroked her hair, admiring her body in the flickering orange glow of the fire. He loved the fact that she was so unselfconscious about being naked, and the teasing way she ran her hands over his chest. In fact he wished they could stay here like this for ever.

'What's this?' Mel's fingers had moved lower and sideways, towards his back. Gently, she explored the fine, four-inch scar with her fingertips.

'It's a scar.' Barney's mind began to race.

'I know that, stupid. How did you get it?'

'Knife.' Well, scalpel. Same thing.

'Someone attacked you with a knife?' Mel was horrified.

Some surgeon, actually.

But Barney couldn't bring himself to tell her. Not yet. He was still gripped with the fear that finding out about his condition might put Mel off, make her view him in a different light. Just because he was healthy now, didn't mean he would always be well. Like batteries, transplanted kidneys could wear out.

'What can I tell you?' he parried lightly. 'I grew up in a rough part of Manchester. See this here?' Deftly, he drew her attention to the little finger on his left hand, which was bent out of shape. 'I sat on a collapsible chair when I was

179

five. And it collapsed. In Manchester, even the chairs are dangerous.'

He was changing the subject. Mel didn't pursue it. One of the things she liked most about Barney was the way he hadn't bombarded her with questions about her own past.

'It's eleven o'clock.' She glanced in the direction of the bedroom door. 'Can you stay?'

'Are you sure? You'll have to set the alarm for six.'

'You're joking, aren't you? Freddie'll be up by five.' Mel pulled a face. 'God, what did I tell you that for? Now you'll be off like a shot.'

'Don't be daft,' Barney said happily. 'I can't think of anything nicer than staying here with you.'

Chapter 22

Maggie's eyebrows rocketed in disbelief when the phone rang at five past eleven.

'If that's the repairman, you can jolly well tell him to stick his spare part up his bottom! The bloody cheek of that man, he promised *faithfully* he'd be round this afternoon, if he thinks he can phone up now and—'

'Hello?' Having pounced on the phone, Tara pressed it tightly to her ear. The next moment, an idiotic grin spread across her face as she heard the voice she'd been waiting to hear. 'Not your man,' she mouthed at Maggie.

He's my man, my man, *mine* . . .

'Still haven't been able to stop thinking about you.' Dominic's voice, low and intimate, sent ripples of pleasure cascading over her shoulders.

'Me neither,' Tara whispered back.

'How about dinner tomorrow night? I thought we might give Lettonie a whirl.'

Tara was overwhelmed. She counted herself lucky if some chap bought her a packet of smoky bacon crisps to go with her half of lager. Restaurant Lettonie, in Bath, had a stunning reputation *and* two Michelin stars. Dominic must really like her.

A *lot*.

'Sounds fine,' she said casually, as if men whisked her off to Michelin-starred restaurants practically on a daily basis.

'I'll pick you up at eight. Same place as before.'

'OK. 'Bye.' Tara wondered if he was keeping his voice low because he was phoning from home, and determinedly didn't feel guilty. It wasn't her fault he was trapped in a miserable marriage.

'Who was that?' said Maggie when she'd hung up.

'Oh, just Robbie Williams. He's been ringing and ringing for ages, pestering me to go out with him. Poor thing, he can't get a girlfriend to save his life. So I said I'd see him tomorrow night.'

'That is such a kind thing to do,' Maggie exclaimed. 'Giving up your precious spare time to keep some ugly rock star company. Where's he going to take you?'

'Bless his heart, he hasn't got much cash to spare. Probably Burger King,' said Tara.

'You know, you really are a wonderful person.' Maggie shook her head in admiration. 'That Robbie Williams, he's lucky to have you.'

'I know.' Tara beamed modestly at her. 'I'm a saint.'

Daisy couldn't remember when she'd last had such a relaxed and completely enjoyable evening. Stretched across the sofa with her bare feet resting comfortably on Josh's lap and a mug of coffee – made by Josh – in her hands, she said, 'I should be in bed by now. You're turning into a bad influence already.'

'*I'm* the bad influence?' He shot her a look of disbelief. 'You're the one who made me sing "Roll Out The Barrel" downstairs. You forced me to join in with "Underneath The Arches". I thought this was going to be a nice quiet hotel, a genteel little place full of genteel little old ladies playing Canasta.'

'Oh well, that's my father for you,' said Daisy. 'Anyone the least bit genteel is banned from the premises. If they even try to creep up the drive he has them shot on sight.'

Josh grinned. 'Your dad hasn't changed a bit.'

Daisy slurped her black coffee and wriggled her bottom into a more comfortable position on the sofa. Hector had greeted Josh like a long-lost son, declaring to the room at large that Josh had been the best by far of all his daughter's old university friends and the only one he'd ever really liked.

'And you actually told Daisy that at the time?' Josh, joining in like the trouper he was, had clapped his freckled hand to his forehead in mock horror. 'God, no wonder she dumped me – *nothing* puts a girl off a chap more than knowing her parents think he's great.'

Next to them, Daisy had rolled her eyes and said, 'That's not true.'

And it wasn't, she'd thought as Hector had launched into a rousing chorus of 'Daisy, Daisy, give me your answer do'. It was a ridiculous idea.

Wasn't it?

'Go on then,' Josh prompted, dragging her back to the present. 'Tell me about this husband of yours. If he was such a bastard, how come you married him?'

'Ah, well, he did that sneaky man-thing,' Daisy riposted. 'He forgot to mention the fact that he was really a bastard. When we first met, Steven gave a good impression of being pretty much perfect. And I fell for it.'

'Oh, don't tell me, you thought you'd found your ten.' Josh was looking insufferably smug.

'Go on, smirk all you like.' Daisy was seriously beginning to regret the burst of honesty years earlier that had compelled her to admit the whole truth to Josh. 'But yes, if you want to put it like that, I did think I'd found my ten. Steven was funny and charming – *ouch*.'

Josh, pinching her big toe, protested, 'I'm funny and charming.'

'And he was very, very good-looking – ouch, *ouch*,' squealed Daisy as he grabbed her other big toe.

'That's a face-ist remark. You're a face-ist.' Josh shook his head sorrowfully at her. 'Ugly people have feelings too.'

'I know, I know, it's shallow and I'm ashamed of myself, but I'm just being honest. And you aren't ugly,' Daisy told him. 'Anyway, as far as Steven was concerned, I thought he was perfect. And as it turned out, I couldn't have been more wrong. Oh please, *please*,' she begged, wriggling like an eel as he began to tickle her feet mercilessly, 'stop it, I've been punished enough, I promise, I'll never be face-ist again!'

'So have you learned your lesson?'

'Yes, yes!'

'Actually, no, you haven't,' Josh tut-tutted. 'I saw you this afternoon, remember? Flirting with that chap outside the hotel. And you can't tell me he was ugly.'

Daisy looked innocent. 'Wasn't he? I hadn't noticed.'

'Come on, tell me all about him.'

Reluctantly she did. And braced herself for his reaction.

Josh, predictably, roared with laughter. 'Oh, this is priceless. Daisy MacLean, this is your life! Don't you see, you're setting yourself up all over again?'

'I'm not setting myself up,' Daisy said crossly. 'I'm just not, OK? There's absolutely nothing going on between me and Dev Tyzack.'

'Sweetheart, pull the other one.'

Don't tempt me, thought Daisy.

'But there *isn't*.'

He wagged a finger at her. 'I was watching you, remember.'

'And did I throw myself at him?'

'You looked as if you wanted to.'

Oh God, thought Daisy, horrified. I didn't, did I?

'These ladykiller types are all the same,' Josh went on. 'It's a law of nature. They can have any woman they want, so they do. As soon as they make a conquest, they lose interest and move on to the next one. It's a thrill-of-the-chase thing. Fun for them,' he concluded sympathetically, 'but not very relaxing for you, waking up each morning and wondering if today's the day you're going to be given the old heave-ho.'

'And I actually said you could stay here,' Daisy wailed, giving his knee a swipe. 'I offered you a bed out of the sheer goodness of my heart and this is the kind of abuse I have to put up with!'

'Not abuse. Sensible advice. You're free to do whatever you want,' Josh said easily. 'I'm just reminding you what'll happen when it all goes wrong.'

Having planted an affectionate kiss on her cheek, Josh had disappeared into the spare bedroom and been out for the count within seconds. Daisy, lying in her own bed gazing up at the beamed ceiling, heard him begin to snore gently through the adjoining wall.

But this wasn't the reason she couldn't get to sleep. Josh's remarks were rattling round her brain like beans in a jar. Basically, Daisy admitted, because he hadn't told her anything she hadn't already figured out for herself.

High-risk men – men like Dev Tyzack – only ended up making you miserable.

Better not to get involved.

Chapter 23

The board in the front window of the village shop was plastered with a variety of notices. Baby rabbits were advertised, free to a good home. A babysitter was offering her services. Someone was desperate for a cleaner three mornings a week. Somebody else was selling their sunbed, their Spanish guitar and an upright freezer. One of the cottages in the village was being advertised for holiday lets. If anyone had seen a black cat with a white smudge on her nose, missing since the beginning of February, could they please contact Fred and Eileen in Brocket's Lane.

The bell clanged above the door as Barney entered the shop. Christopher and Colin were both in there, busily re-stocking the shelves and bickering amicably with each other. Today they wore matching pink and grey checked shirts, grey trousers and pink knitted waistcoats.

'Hey, it's the boy Barney.' Colin enjoyed teasing him, protesting that anyone as pretty as Barney couldn't be straight. Even Christopher, relieved to discover that Barney wasn't gay, was friendly towards him now. It was hard, being insecure and jealous and terrified that your young boyfriend might be persuaded to stray.

'I was looking at the ads in the window,' Barney began.

'And you want to buy the Spanish guitar? Hallelujah,'

exclaimed Colin. 'I thought we'd still be advertising that bloody thing in ten years' time.'

'No—'

'Don't tell me you've found Smudge.' Christopher looked hopeful.

'Sorry, I haven't,' Barney blurted out, because otherwise they could be here all day. 'It's about the cottage.'

Christopher and Colin looked surprised.

'Hill View Cottage? The holiday let? They're asking four hundred pounds a week for that place.'

'I know,' said Barney, 'and I can't afford anything like that. But I just thought maybe you'd know if there were any other places to rent around here. Something smaller and cheaper. Well,' he amended, 'quite a lot cheaper.'

Christopher pulled a face. 'All the holiday properties cost a bomb, they've been chintzed and ruffled to within an inch of their lives. You wouldn't find anything for less than two hundred a week.'

Terrific. Barney's spirits took a dive. Since being seized by the idea this morning, he'd been counting the minutes until his lunch break, convinced that Christopher and Colin would be able to help.

'What's wrong with the hotel? Have they kicked you out?' Always eager for gossip, Colin had abandoned his shelf-stacking. His eyes widened. 'Were you caught doing something naughty?'

Barney hated to disappoint him. 'I just wanted somewhere with a bit more room.' Shyly, but with some pride he added, 'For me and my girlfriend.'

'Sweet,' sighed Colin.

'Well, if we hear of anything we'll let you know,' Christopher assured him. 'But don't hold your breath.'

'In the meantime,' Colin said brightly, 'you're looking a bit pale. Are you sure you wouldn't be interested in a sunbed?'

News travelled fast in the village. At four o'clock Barney was beckoned outside by Bert Connelly, one of the hotel's handymen.

'Hear you're lookin' for a place to rent.' Bert came straight to the point.

Startled, Barney hoped and prayed Bert wasn't about to offer to squeeze him into his own cottage in the village, which was already full to bursting with his three lumbering farmhand sons and a wife the size of a haystack.

'Um, well, it was just a thought.' Please, no.

'Only I had an idea.' There was a meaningful glint in Bert's eye.

'Oh yes?' By this time Barney was beginning to feel like Hugh Grant in *Mickey Blue Eyes*. Except Bert was somehow scarier than the Mafia.

'Reckon I might be able to help you out, see.'

'The thing is, the money—'

'I know, I know what you young lads get paid.' Bert tapped the side of his huge nose and drawled, 'That's why I thought of it. And don't you worry, I'm sure we can come to some kind of arrangement.'

It was now or never. Summoning up all his courage, Barney blurted out, 'Actually, I've changed my mind. I think I'll stay where I am, but thanks for . . . well, you know, thinking of me.' There, he'd said it. Now he wouldn't have to share a bed with one of Bert's sons and a couple of even more terrifying dogs.

'Oh.' Evidently disappointed, Bert slid a fat hairy hand into the pocket of his overalls. Pulling out a scrap of paper, he scrunched it up in his fist and shrugged. 'Well, just a thought.

Seemed a shame, little place like that standing empty. Still, never mind, eh?'

Completely wrong-footed, Barney repeated idiotically, 'Standing empty?'

'Oi, Bert!' Kelvin yelled across from the van that had just trundled into view. 'Are we goin' to fix that fence or not?'

'Brock Cottage,' Bert explained, turning to go. 'Rose Timpson's old place, at the end of Brocket's Lane. Not that it's much to write home about, but I thought you might've been interested – all right, all right, I'm coming,' he bawled back at Kelvin. 'Keep yer 'air on.'

As Kelvin had only a few functioning follicles, this was probably a joke.

'I might be interested!' Barney's heart leapt with hope. 'Who's Rose Timpson? Is that her phone number?' It took all his self-control not to grab the balled-up scrap of paper from Bert's hand.

'Hardly likely to be.' Bert chuckled at the thought. 'Dead, isn't she? Kicked the bucket a couple of months back. Still, eighty-seven, can't say the old bird didn't have a good innings.'

'Bert, get a move on, will you?' roared Kelvin.

Happily, Bert didn't share Kelvin's eagerness to get the job done. 'Place has been empty since she died, see. Trouble is, it's a complete tip. Rubbish everywhere, needs major work doing on it. Rose's son wants to fix the place up and flog it, but he's stuck out on a twelve-month contract in Dubai. So at the moment it's just sitting there doing bugger all.' Bert shook his head slowly. 'And like I say, it's not as if he can rent the place out, the state it's in. Leastways, not in the normal way, to holidaymakers and the like.'

'Bloody hell, Bert, are you gonna stand there yacking all day?'

'But I reckon Bobby Timpson wouldn't say no to the chance of a bit of extra cash, like, if I told him you might be interested in takin' the cottage on for a few months.'

'That sounds fantastic.' Barney could have hugged Bert. Well, almost.

'Right then, here's the key.' Bert delved into his other pocket. 'What you want to do is take a look around the place after work, then pop in to us and let me know what you think. If you're up for it, we'll give Bobby a ring. I'll vouch for you, tell him you're a good lad, and I reckon we'll have ourselves a deal.'

Rose Timpson evidently hadn't squandered her pension money subscribing to *House Beautiful*. She had, however, been an avid hoarder. Both bedrooms of the tiny cottage were stacked high with teetering piles of old newspapers. Pictures of cats had been cut from magazines and Sellotaped to the walls of the living room. There were dead pot plants lined up along every window ledge, damp patches on the walls and dozens of used light bulbs in a big box in one corner of the kitchen. The wallpaper was awful, there was a chilly damp smell in the air and a huge plastic chandelier coated with grime and dust dominated the minuscule bathroom.

'See what I mean?' Having spotted Barney making his way along Brocket's Lane, Bert had abandoned his vast cooked tea and ambled after him. 'Told you it was in a bit of a state. Well,' he amended, kicking a corner of the ratty living-room carpet, 'quite a lot of a state. Now you've seen it, you might want to change your mind.'

But Barney's eyes were shining. The cottage only smelled damp because it had been left unheated since December. Once Rose's belongings had been moved out, the place would have real potential. During his long stays in hospital he'd watched enough episodes of *Changing Rooms* to know that a few gallons of fresh paint and an electric sander could work wonders. They could chuck out the awful stained carpets, polish up the floorboards, put up new curtains . . .

He'd never actually put up a curtain before, but maybe Mel would know how to do it.

Mel and Freddie . . .

'I haven't changed my mind,' he told Bert.

'Want me to ring Bobby, then?'

'Yes please.'

Barney had been half expecting to follow Bert down to the phone box in the village, but the older man promptly produced the latest Nokia Orange and punched out the numbers.

Seconds later he was greeting Bobby Timpson as easily as if he'd just bumped into him in the pub.

Within a couple of minutes, the deal was done. For thirty pounds a week, Barney was the new tenant of Brock Cottage.

'Thank you, thank you so much,' he babbled when Bert passed the phone over to him.

In Dubai, Bobby Timpson sounded amused. 'No problem. At least now I won't have the job of clearing out all that junk when I get back.'

'I'll decorate it, make it look nice,' Barney fervently promised.

'Don't go too mad. The place is going to need rewiring before I sell it, so don't bother putting up a load of fancy wallpaper.'

'Just paint,' Barney said happily. 'You won't recognise the place when you next see it.'

'Give the rent to Bert each week. He'll keep it for me. By the way, any trouble on that score and you'll have his lads to answer to.' Bobby's tone was light, but the underlying note of warning was there.

'There won't be any trouble, I can promise you that,' Barney said eagerly. 'You don't know how much this means to me. I won't let you down.'

Chapter 24

Lettonie was fabulous. Tara, who was *feeling* fabulous, gazed around the opulent entrance hall with a shiver of delight. Colworth Manor was equally posh, of course, but everyone there knew her as a chambermaid and kept asking her to do depressingly chambermaidy things like fetching more towels or scrubbing out that grate.

Suppressing a smug grin as she glimpsed her reflection in one of the long Georgian mirrors, Tara revelled in her anonymity. The maître d', leading them through to the sitting room for their pre-dinner drinks, had already called her 'madam'. And if she said so herself, she really was looking stunning tonight. Anyone seeing her and Dominic together would take them for an affluent couple, accustomed to frequenting only the best restaurants. Crikey, even her hair – slicked back tonight, instead of sticking up in its usual arrangement of chaotic spikes – looked chic.

'I love this place,' Tara whispered excitedly when they had been served their drinks and left in peace to survey the menu. 'This is so great – oops, sorry!' She clutched at her stomach, which was growling like a cement mixer.

'Don't apologise. You look gorgeous.' Dominic reached for her hand, raised it to his lips and kissed it. He smiled. 'I've been looking forward to this all week.'

Tara's heart overflowed with gratitude. A man being nice

to her was one of her favourite things in the world. A man bringing her to a place like this, gazing lovingly into her eyes and paying her lavish compliments was enough to make her insides go completely squirmy.

On an impulse, she leaned over and kissed him – just briefly, but quite lustfully, on the cheek. Maybe it wasn't what chic, affluent couples did in restaurants ('Oh God, a public display of affection, how naff!'), but she didn't care.

Dominic didn't seem to either.

'You don't know what you do to me.' As he murmured the words, his mouth hovered tantalisingly close to her own. 'God, Tara, you should come with an X rating, you're so – *shit!*'

'Thanks a lot.' Tara spluttered with laughter, but Dominic wasn't listening. Abruptly shoving her off him, he leapt to his feet, straightened his tie, snatched up his drink and shot over to the other side of the room.

What?

Tara stared at him, wondering if this was some kind of joke. When he'd sucked in his breath and sworn like that, she'd thought he had cramp in his leg. But now he wasn't even looking at her. For heaven's sake, he was behaving as if she didn't *exist*.

Mystified, she followed the direction of his panic-stricken gaze. The maître d' had just shown another couple into the sitting room and was busy taking their coats. As the middle-aged woman turned to decide where she'd most like to sit, she spotted Dominic and let out a shriek of delight.

'Oh my goodness, I don't believe it! Gerald, Gerald, will you look who's here?'

Tara didn't believe it either. Dominic, his face suddenly wreathed with smiles, crossed the room and greeted them both with apparent delight.

'Marion, Gerald, how *are* you? This is such a coincidence,

Annabel and I were only talking about you this morning, saying we hadn't seen you since the wedding.'

Wedding. Oh fuck. Sliding down in her seat, Tara grabbed one of the glossy magazines from the low table in front of her, wrenched it open and held it inches from her face.

'Darling boy, of course you haven't seen us! You've not long been back from your honeymoon.' Marion twinkled up at Dominic. 'Oh, but what a wedding that was! Beautiful, just beautiful . . . I wept buckets, didn't I, Gerald?'

You weren't the only one, thought Tara.

'You and Annabel must come over for dinner soon,' Gerald jovially announced. 'You can tell us how you're settling into married life.'

'It's our thirty-second wedding anniversary,' Marion went on, sounding smug. 'That's why we've come out tonight. But what are you doing here, Dominic?'

Sensing the older woman's eyes flickering over her, Tara concentrated violently on the magazine, apparently riveted by a feature on barn conversions.

'Business meeting,' Dominic said easily. 'I've been having dinner with a couple of clients. You've just missed them actually, they had to drive back to Taunton. I'm waiting for my taxi to arrive and take me home.'

Tara swallowed. Inside her shoes, her toes were scrunched up so much they were practically bent double. The feature on barn conversions blurred before her eyes as she listened to Dominic cheerfully telling the couple how well they were looking, how great it was to see them again and how much he was enjoying married life. Finally, announcing that his taxi had to be here by now, he said his goodbyes, kissed Marion on both cheeks, shook Gerald's hand and made his way out to the entrance hall.

Leaving her sitting there with an empty glass, a furiously rumbling stomach and aching, doubled-over toes.

Over by the open fire, Marion and Gerald chatted happily, enjoyed their drinks and slowly – very, *very* slowly – perused their menus.

'Poor thing,' Tara heard Marion whisper in that carrying way so beloved of women in their sixties. 'See her all on her own over there, Gerald? Mark my words, that girl's been stood up.'

Heroically, Tara didn't react. In her head, she thought of all the things she *could* say. As she turned the pages of the magazine – *Country Life*, to add insult to injury – she mentally willed Marion and Gerald to knock back their drinks, race through to the dining room and give her a chance to *get out of here*.

As Tara made her way across the darkened car park she thought for a sickening moment that Dominic *had* disappeared in a taxi.

But he was still there, waiting for her in the car. She found him huddled down in the driver's seat like a refugee in a lorry.

'Jesus,' Dominic hissed, glancing furtively around him before driving out through the gates. 'That was close. That was *way* too bloody close.'

'Where are we going?' Tara wondered why he'd turned left instead of right. Right was the way that led into Bath.

'What?'

'The Red Rose isn't far from here. That's supposed to be really nice.'

Puffing out his cheeks and exhaling noisily, Dominic shook his head. 'No way. Sorry, sweetheart, but I'm not going through that again. Let's face it, restaurants like that are too much of a risk. There's always the chance of bumping into someone who knows you.'

'And your wife,' muttered Tara, not quite under her breath. It didn't seem quite fair, somehow. She *wasn't* 'the other woman', yet she already felt like one. All of the guilt and none of the sex to make up for it. *And* she'd had to settle their drinks bill before scurrying out.

'Sweetheart, I'm just as disappointed as you are.' Briefly, Dominic reached for her hand and gave it a squeeze. 'But we had a bloody lucky escape back there.' With a wry smile he added, 'To be honest, I don't think I could eat a thing now, anyway.'

Tara suppressed the urge to scream. It clearly wasn't such a big deal for Dominic. He ate out at swish restaurants all the time; one more or less gourmet meal didn't bother him.

But Tara's stomach didn't work that way; it wasn't so readily put off. She had read the menu at Lettonie, heard the gentle clinking of cutlery against plates in the dining room, smelled the fabulous cooking smells emanating from the kitchen . . .

Basically, her stomach was ready for food and it wasn't going to be fobbed off.

'I'm hungry. I'm starving.' Her voice wobbled and rose a couple of octaves. 'I want us to go out for a meal *now*.'

Tara kept trying to tell herself it didn't matter, it really didn't matter that Dominic had brought her to possibly *the* most horrible pub in England.

But it did, it just did.

The Brown Cow was one of those ugly, soulless establishments built in the sixties. Apart from a few surly regulars clustered around the bar, the place was empty. Every footstep echoed like a gunshot against the linoleum floor.

Dominic, evidently still not hungry, ordered a meal and ate nothing. Tara forced herself to chew her way grimly through sausage 'n' chips in a basket, apparently the culinary high point of the evening menu at the Brown Cow. The chips had been microwaved, the sausage was tougher than a dog chew and the peas kept getting wedged in the gaps between the woven plastic strips that formed the basket, but she didn't stop eating until every last hideous morsel was gone.

She didn't know if she was punishing Dominic or herself.

'I'm sorry,' he said again. For about the twentieth time.

'Don't be. I'm fine. The tomato ketchup was delicious.' Tara's voice had gone jerky and brittle. Taking a swig of lukewarm white wine – God, was this *really* wine? – she said, 'And did you notice how perfectly it matched my dress?'

She was wearing, needless to say, her very best dress. Crimson velvet and spaghetti-strapped, daringly low-cut but in a way that was elegant rather than tarty, it had been perfect for Lettonie. Whereas here at the Brown Cow, she looked a complete prat. Apart from Tara and Dominic, every other customer in the pub wore mud-encrusted wellies.

'I'd rather be here with you,' Dominic took her hand, 'than in any five-star hotel with Annabel.'

For a moment Tara couldn't speak. Some juvenile part of her longed to yell that it was OK for him, he'd already stayed in plenty of five-star hotels, she'd only scrubbed their toilets.

'I've blown it, haven't I?' said Dominic sadly. 'You won't want to see me again after this.'

Tears sprang into Tara's eyes. Oh God, how could he even think that? It wasn't his fault.

'You can say it,' Dominic went on. 'Go ahead, I know you feel let down. Just tell me it's over.'

'And you'll what?' Her voice was low, her knuckles clenched white.

'Me?' He looked regretful. 'I'll leave you alone, to get on with the rest of your life.'

The rest of her life, ha. That would be her completely shitty, no-fun, man-free life, would it? The one she'd been trudging through like treacle for the last couple of years?

Were the wellie brigade listening to them? It had gone suspiciously quiet up at the bar.

'All this hassle and we're not even having an affair.' Tara managed a wobbly smile. 'Oh God, this is stupid. Of course I still want to see you. Just as a friend,' she added hastily, in case their table was bugged.

There was a collective snort of laughter from the regulars. The one with the muddiest wellies, nudging his neighbour, leered, 'Yeah, and the rest.'

Chapter 25

Once, when Maggie Donovan had been six or seven, she had put her tooth under the pillow and fallen asleep happily dreaming of the tooth fairy.

When she'd woken up the next morning, her tooth had still been there.

It was exactly how she was feeling now, Maggie realised. Except this time it wasn't the tooth fairy who was too busy to visit her. Nor, at forty-five, was she allowed to fling her teddy across the room, stamp her feet and burst into floods of noisy tears.

'Sorry to mess you about.' Hector, on the phone, sounded genuinely apologetic. 'It's all my fault. I thought I was meeting my accountant next week, but it's tomorrow, and I can't really cancel at such short notice.'

'Of course you mustn't cancel.' Who's more important, after all – your fat-cat accountant with his swish offices in Clifton, or your paid tart in her unswish cottage in the High Street?

Maggie didn't say this. To make sure she sounded cheerful and unconcerned, she determinedly fixed a bright smile to her face.

'Are you sure you don't mind?' Hector sounded relieved.

'Me? Heavens, why would I mind?' Gazing out of the living-room window, alarming a couple of locals heading home from the pub, Maggie realised that her smile was making her look deranged. It was also starting to make her cheeks ache. 'I'll be fine, I've got heaps of things to do tomorrow anyway.'

'We'll fix up another meeting,' said Hector.

Go on then, thought Maggie, silently willing him to set a date. But, frustratingly, he didn't.

'I'll give you another ring in a day or two when I know what's happening.' He paused. 'By the way, did you get that washing machine fixed?'

'No.' The washing machine saga was driving Maggie to distraction. 'The bloody repairman was meant to be bringing the spare part this afternoon. He rang and told me he had flu.' It's really been my day for being fobbed off with feeble excuses, she didn't add.

'I wish you'd let me buy you a new one,' said Hector. 'Wouldn't that be simpler all round?'

It wasn't the first time he'd offered, but Maggie was adamant.

'No, it wouldn't. My washing machine *is* new, for heaven's sake. It's six months old, still under warranty, and it's jolly well going to get fixed by the people who are meant to fix it. Why should you let them off the hook?'

'But—'

'It's the principle of the thing,' Maggie said firmly. She might not have many principles but she was determined to hang on to this one.

Hector chuckled. 'Look, what's the time? Only ten thirty. If you're on your own I could pop over for twenty minutes.'

It had evidently just occurred to him. With Tara safely out of the way, he could slip out of the hotel, take the short cut through the woods and arrive at her back door in ninety seconds flat.

A consolation prize, Maggie thought, to make up for ducking out of their original agreement. Even more humiliatingly, there was nothing she'd like more. But Tara hadn't said what time she'd be back. It would be too much of a risk.

Normally Maggie would have come straight out and told him the truth. This time, though, she heard herself say, 'I don't think so. Bit short notice. Actually, I've got a couple of cushions to finish.'

'Oh. Right. Well, I'll be in touch.'

Was Hector put out? Just a tiny bit miffed? Ha, jolly well served him right, thought Maggie. He'd started it.

Carelessly she said, 'OK, fine, 'bye!'

Barney was fast asleep. He didn't stir when Mel slid out of bed at midnight.

Her mind still whirling, she bundled herself up in her ancient blue towelling dressing gown and went through to the icy kitchen to put the kettle on.

Could she really move into a cottage in Colworth? *Dare* she?

Padding back into the marginally warmer living room with her mug of tea, Mel curled up on one corner of the tatty sofa and tried to picture it. Barney had been so thrilled with his news when he'd turned up after work this evening, she hadn't had the heart to spoil it for him. As far as he was concerned, it was the answer to all their problems.

'But . . . but it isn't your problem.' Mel had struggled to hide her shock. 'It's mine.'

'That's rubbish. You know how I feel about you.' Barney had shaken his head vigorously. 'Look, I know this is all a bit sudden, but we're a couple, aren't we? Why take things slowly when we both know what we want? And it's fate, don't you see? Now we can be together properly, the three of us! Mel, I can't think of anything nicer. I want to look after you and Freddie more than anything else in the world.'

His eyes had shone as he'd gone on to describe the cottage to her. Freddie had demanded to be lifted on to his knee and without hesitation Barney had obliged. Mel, watching the pair of them together, had felt sick with fear. Barney *thought* he loved her, but how would he react if he knew the truth? He had mentioned Daisy MacLean several times already and clearly liked and admired her a lot. Daisy had given him the job he'd so desperately wanted, she was by all accounts a great person to work for, all the staff were devoted to her and – Barney's words – she hadn't had an easy time of it either.

'She's a widow, you know. Her husband was killed in a car crash just over a year ago.' His dark eyes had actually filled with tears as he'd related the story to her. 'They were really happy together, then something like that happens. Can you imagine how she must have felt? But she doesn't go on about it. She's just a brilliant person.'

'I'm sure she is.' At the time, Mel had swiftly changed the subject. Happily married – yeah, right.

But now Barney was forcing the issue. Sooner or later she would have to tell him. And face the fact that it might drastically alter his feelings towards her.

Mel wrapped her chilly fingers round the mug of tea in an attempt to warm them up. Barney had moral standards, he might be disgusted and repulsed when he learned she'd had an affair with a married man. How much more badly might he take it when he discovered her particular married man had belonged to none other than his precious boss, the oh-so wonderful Daisy MacLean?

There was Daisy's reaction to consider, too. She might sack Barney on the spot.

And then, of course, there was Freddie . . .

'What are you doing?'

Mel jumped. Barney was standing in the bedroom doorway looking worried. His hair was stuck up on one side of his head and he was wearing just his T-shirt and boxer shorts.

Would he hate her when he found out?

'Nothing.' Guilt made her feel sick. 'Couldn't sleep, that's all.'

'I woke up and you weren't there.' He broke into a crooked smile. 'See? Must be love.'

The smile melted Mel's heart. She said, 'Do you want a cup of tea?'

'No thanks.' Grinning now, he moved towards her and removed the Simpsons mug from her hand. 'I want you to come back to bed with me.'

As he put his arms round her, Mel buried her cheek in the warm, comforting curve between his neck and shoulder.

She had to tell Barney.

She *would* tell him.

Just not yet.

Josh was kissing her, and Daisy was wondering how this had happened.

One minute they'd been roaring at the TV, attempting to drum some sense into the dithering housewife on *Who Wants To Be A Millionaire?* The next minute, Josh had taken her face in both hands and kissed her.

Her, Daisy. Not the dithering housewife from Beckenham who didn't know her flageolets from her haricots.

It was one o'clock in the morning. Daisy always recorded *Millionaire* to watch before she went to bed and Josh had never seen the British version before. There was something wonderfully cosy and reassuring about watching the programme together, just as seeing Josh and her father returning from a round of golf this afternoon had given her a warm, Ready Brek glow in the stomach. Glancing out of her office window at three o'clock, Daisy had seen them pull up outside the hotel entrance in one of the electric buggies, laughing and joking with each other as they unloaded their clubs and headed through to the bar.

That was the thing about Josh, everyone loved him. He was humorous, easy-going and unfailingly good company. For her own sake, Daisy knew, Hector had always made an effort to get on with Steven and had pretended to like him, but in reality he hadn't thought much of his son-in-law. He'd hidden it well because he wanted her to be happy. But, deep down, Daisy had always known how he felt.

Anyway, *anyway*. Back to the present. The nice thing was, she had quite forgotten that kissing was something Josh had always been brilliant at.

'Well.' Daisy realised she was panting a bit. 'I wasn't expecting that to happen.'

'Silly old bag,' said Josh.

Indignantly she pinched his arm. 'That's not fair. How could I know you were going to do something like that?'

'Not you. Her.' Josh nodded at the TV screen. 'Dippy Dora got it wrong, she's just lost fifteen grand. And I just felt like it, OK? I wanted to kiss you. Don't worry, I've stopped now. Won't happen again.'

This instantly made Daisy want it to happen again.

'Why not?' Whoops, steady, those three glasses of wine had gone straight to her head.

'Because we tried it once before, remember? And it didn't work out. I'm not perfect enough for you.' Josh shrugged, apparently unperturbed. 'I'm a seven, maybe an eight. And as far as you're concerned, only a ten will do.'

Was he right? Was he *still* right? Or was this where she'd been going so horribly wrong all these years? Sitting next to him on the sofa, Daisy realised that she was idly stroking his thigh. And she still wanted Josh to kiss her again. Quite badly in fact.

'Maybe it's time you were promoted.'

'I'm not a ten.' Josh's eyes crinkled at the corners. 'I'll never be a ten. What's more, I wouldn't want to be one.'

That was what she liked about him. Josh was supremely comfortable with himself, he always had been. What you saw was what you got, there was absolutely no hidden agenda.

'OK,' Daisy conceded. 'Maybe it's time I sorted myself out. Made up my mind what I really want.'

'You and your search for Mr Perfect.' Josh's smile was playful. 'What you need is a real man.'

'Warts and all?'

'Bloody cheek, I don't have warts!'

'You have faults, though,' Daisy reminded him. 'Leaving tea bags in the sink, for a start.'

'You're not so perfect yourself,' Josh promptly retorted. 'I'm not nearly as untidy as you are.' As he said it he reached over and, with his finger, lightly traced the outline of her mouth.

Lightning streaks of desire darted like fireflies through Daisy's body. Frowning, she said, 'You leave wet footprints on the bathroom carpet when you get out of the shower.'

'God, how dreadful, no wonder I'm only a pathetic seven. You never put the lid of the coffee jar back on properly. *And* you have disgusting knife habits. There was peanut butter in the jam yesterday, and you left Marmite in the butter this morning.' This time, as he spoke, Josh moved slowly towards her. Frustratingly, his mouth stopped short a couple of inches from her own, leaving her craning her neck like a puppy desperate to be tickled.

'You snore,' Daisy whispered.

'Ah, but only when I'm on my own. If I'm in bed with someone else, I never snore.'

'That's not true!'

'What, you don't believe me? You think I'm lying? Come on then, I'll just have to prove it to you.' Pulling her gently to her feet, Josh kicked her discarded shoes out of the way. 'And that's another thing you do, leave your shoes all over the place.'

Reaching for the remote control, Daisy pressed the OFF button.

'And you always leave the TV on.'

'Bloody hell, good job there're some things I'm brilliant at, don't you think?' Mischievously, Josh planted another brief kiss on her mouth. 'Now, your room or mine?'

Chapter 26

Tara, on her knees halfway up the main staircase, was busy polishing the brass stair rods when she saw Barney Usher hovering outside Daisy's office.

Barney was a sweet boy and a huge hit with the residents, but Tara always felt a bit squeamish at the thought of him going around with one of Steven Standish's kidneys tucked away inside him.

Observing Barney check his watch, she called down, 'Problem?'

He looked concerned. 'It's nine o'clock. I wanted a word with Daisy, but there's no answer. She's usually in her office by half past eight.'

Tara's knees were aching. Slowly she straightened up. God, she was twenty-seven and suffering from chambermaid's knee, how glamorous was that?

'I'll pop up to the flat,' she told Barney. 'Maybe her alarm didn't go off. What did you want to see her about?'

'Oh, um, well, it's kind of personal.' Barney flushed and hesitated, his long eyelashes batting like Bambi's.

'You can't tell me that, it's not allowed. Rule of the hotel,' Tara teased, because it was such fun making someone else blush. 'No secrets.'

'OK.' He threw up his hands in defeat. 'I'm moving out of

the hotel. Renting a cottage in the village. I thought I'd better check with Daisy that it's allowed.'

'Blimey, did you win the lottery?' Astounded, Tara said, 'Which cottage?'

'Brock Cottage, at the end of Brocket's Lane.'

So he hadn't suddenly become a millionaire. Tara pulled a face; rather him than her.

'Rose Timpson's old place? Bit manky, isn't it? She was as mad as a hatter, used to wear necklaces made out of conkers and milk-bottle tops. What d'you want to live there for, anyway?'

'So I can be with my girlfriend.' Barney looked proud.

'Has she seen it yet?'

'I'm going to clean the place up first. Make it look fantastic.'

Bless his heart, thought Tara. Must be love.

'I'd better go and see what's happened to Daisy. I'll tell her you'd like a word. Don't worry, she'll be fine about it,' she added cheerfully over her shoulder.

She had almost reached the landing when Barney called up after her. 'Oh, I almost forgot, can you tell Daisy that Mrs Penhaligon's going to be arriving this morning now, instead of this afternoon? Her driver just rang to say they'll be here around eleven, and Pam said Daisy would want to know.'

'Mrs P, eleven o'clock. Got it.'

Barney lowered his voice, forcing Tara to drape herself over the polished mahogany banister rail.

'Is that Paula Penhaligon?' he whispered reverently. 'The one who sings?'

Was there likely to be another one, being chauffeured down the M4 and booked into the hotel's King Suite?

'It is,' Tara told him. 'Good news for Hector; he can't wait to get her kicking up her heels around that piano of his, bellowing out "My Old Man's A Dustman".'

She grinned to herself as she headed towards the private wing, leaving an awestruck Barney wondering if she was having him on. That was the great thing about a character like Hector; you could fabricate almost any story about him and it would probably end up being true.

Having planned to hammer on Daisy's door and yell, 'Quick, get up, Charles and Camilla are here,' Tara discovered she didn't need to. Daisy's key was – carelessly – still in the lock.

Which, if past experience was anything to go by, meant that Daisy had ended up getting hammered last night.

Brilliant! Gleefully, Tara pictured the scene. Daisy would have stumbled up the stairs, struggling and cursing for ages while she attempted to fit her key in the door. Finally staggering into the flat, kicking off her shoes and managing to peel off a few clothes if she was lucky, she would have crashed unceremoniously into bed with her make-up still on and without remembering to set her alarm clock.

Ha, serve her right, Daisy was going to have the hangover from hell! She was also about to get the surprise of her life. Oh yes, this was going to be fun.

Tiptoeing across the darkened living room, Tara wondered how she should go about it for maximum effect. *Launch* herself through the bedroom door? Leap onto the bed and mercilessly tickle her feet? Hide herself in Daisy's wardrobe and start wailing like a ghost? Ooh, or get some ice-cold water from the fridge and drip it onto her from a great height?

Actually, maybe not. Seeing as she was hoping for a lift from Daisy the next time she drove into Bristol, giving her an unpleasant shock might not be the best idea.

Opting instead for the more subtle approach, Tara opened the bedroom door without making a sound and sank down on all fours. With the curtains still tightly drawn, the room was in total darkness but she was just able to make out the lump in the bed that was Daisy buried beneath a mountain of bunched-up duvet.

Slowly Tara crawled across the carpet, reached the end of the bed and slid her hand under the duvet. Within seconds she encountered bare flesh. Daisy's foot. As lightly as she could, she tickled her toes until they twitched.

Oh, this was brilliant, Daisy was completely out for the count! Chuckling silently to herself, Tara waited a few seconds before running her fingertips in a spidery fashion up as far as her ankle. The foot twitched again, more irritably this time. Tara danced her fingers around Daisy's ankle bone and up over the lower part of her shin, enjoying herself hugely but at the same time surprised – and yes, actually quite shocked – by the hairiness of Daisy's ankles. This was something she certainly hadn't expected. These legs clearly hadn't seen a razor in months. OK, so some women didn't bother to depilate during the winter months when their legs weren't on general release, but it hadn't occurred to her for a moment that Daisy would be one of them. God, she really was *incredibly* hairy, like a woolly mammoth! Gross, thought Tara, and *such* a turn-off for the opposite sex. Poor old Daisy was never going to find herself another chap at this rate, didn't she realise how repulsed men were likely to be by the sight of a woman with mohair legs?

Daisy was showing signs of waking up. Tara, flinching as the top end of the duvet moved, began to wish she'd never started this in the first place. The winter-woolly legs were, frankly, something of an embarrassment. Oh well, maybe she could get away with pretending she hadn't noticed how revoltingly neanderthal they were.

Oops, this was it, more movement from the pillow end of the bed. Resisting the temptation to duck down on her hands and knees and scurry backwards out of the room before Daisy saw her, Tara bravely stayed put. For heaven's sake, she and Daisy were best friends, weren't they? They weren't going to let a bit of superfluous leg hair come between them. Even if there was enough of the stuff to fill a small cushion.

Plastering a bright smile to her face, Tara raised her head . . .

And found herself gazing into the eyes of a complete stranger.

'Oooh!' It came out as a stifled, indrawn squeak. Tara, sucking in her breath and still on her knees, almost toppled over backwards in shock. The head that had emerged from the duvet was little more than a tousle-haired silhouette but there was no getting away from it. Those eyes – and those shoulders – definitely didn't belong to Daisy.

As she stared in horror, a hand emerged from the duvet. The stranger in Daisy's bed put a finger to his lips, then pointed to the door.

'She's still asleep,' he murmured, tilting his head to indicate Daisy lying curled up next to him. 'Put the kettle on, will you? I'll be out in two secs.'

Tara, still gaping, scrambled clumsily to her feet and whispered, 'Right.'

'Strong coffee. Black, two sugars,' the stranger murmured as she reached the bedroom door. Sounding as if he might be smiling, he added, 'And I wouldn't say no to some toast.'

By the time he emerged a couple of minutes later, Tara had recovered her equilibrium.

Well, most of it.

'Mm, just right.' The owner of the hairy legs she'd so recently been fondling tasted his coffee and gave a nod of approval. 'And two rounds of toast, I'm impressed. Although,' he added, his tone conversational, 'I'd have preferred blackcurrant jam. I'm not actually that wild about marmalade.'

'Make your own then, Mr Picky.' Tara, perched on a high stool, scooted the loaf of bread along the breakfast counter and helped herself to his toast and marmalade. 'So who are you anyway?'

'Me? I'm the bloke whose toes you tweaked.' He paused in the act of energetically sawing the loaf into doorsteps and solemnly held out his hand. 'My name's Josh. Josh . . . Picky.'

Tara was beginning to enjoy herself. When in doubt about a situation, make the most of it. She swallowed a mouthful of toast and shook his outstretched hand. 'And where did Daisy find you?'

'Daisy? Is that her name?' He winked. 'Only kidding. Actually, right here.'

Her eyes widening, Tara gasped, 'You mean you're a *guest*?'

This was riveting stuff. Daisy made a point of never tangling with hotel guests, it was one of her self-appointed rules. Which meant she'd either been mega-plastered last night, or this one was extra extra special.

'Was she drunk?' Tara bluntly demanded. Well, she needed to know.

'Thanks a lot. You really know how to flatter a bloke.' His smile endearingly crooked, Josh said, 'So as far as you're concerned, it's the only possible explanation. Daisy wouldn't have touched me with a barge pole if she'd been sober.'

'I didn't mean it like that,' Tara blustered. 'It's just you being a guest. Daisy's always said she'd never get involved with a guest, it'd be unprofessional.'

Well, it was half the truth. And barge pole might be putting it a bit strongly, but he did have a point. If Josh stood in a line-up of potential men for Daisy, Tara wouldn't have expected her to pick him out. Being brutally honest here, she wouldn't have thought he was Daisy's type.

Not that he was hideous-looking, but he did have a broken nose, messy reddish hair, baggy eyes and an awful lot of freckles. His eyes were nice, Tara hastily amended, kind of greenish-brown and friendly, and his mouth was cheerful, but there were definitely a couple of crooked teeth in that mouth, and there was no denying his ears were big. What's more, his blue shirt and black trousers were crumpled, although presumably this was due to the fact that they'd been left lying in a heap on Daisy's floor all night; he'd probably looked a lot smarter yesterday evening when he'd begun chatting her up in the bar. Plus, of course, he would have been wearing shoes and socks.

'I get by on personality,' Josh told her, evidently aware that she'd been giving him the critical once-over. He added mildly, 'We can't all be James Bond.'

'That's not fair,' Tara protested. 'I wasn't thinking that.'

'Yes you were.' Reaching for the blackcurrant jam, he began slathering it onto his popped-up toast. Calmly, he went on, 'Looks aren't everything, Tara. I do pretty well for myself. And by the way, Daisy wasn't drunk last night. I seduced her with my dazzling wit, my easy charm and, as I believe I mentioned earlier, my spectacular personality.'

'How do you know my name?' Tara blurted out.

'Hmm?' Affecting surprise, Josh picked up his toast. 'Oh, just a gift I have. Five minutes talking to anyone and it just comes to me. Actually, it's a great way to chat up girls, they love it to bits. Gets them every time. Got me Daisy last night,' he added with a conspiratorial wink. 'Now that's what I call a result.'

Tara raised her eyebrows at him. 'Do I look stupid?'

For a horrid moment she wondered if he'd say yes, to be honest, she did. That was the deeply unfair thing about being blonde, busty and forced to wear a chambermaid's uniform, people tended to assume you were dim.

But Josh was grinning at her. 'Oh well, it was worth a try. You're Tara, you work here in the hotel and you're Daisy's best friend. She's told me all about you. I guessed it was you,' he went on, 'when I woke up and found a chambermaid fondling my feet.'

'Standard service, all part of the job.' Tara shrugged. 'We do that to all our guests.'

'Excellent idea. Better than an alarm call any day. But I'm surprised Daisy hasn't told you about me,' said Josh. 'I'm here as a guest of Daisy's, not the hotel's. We knew each other years ago and I came down to see her on Monday. She invited me to stay.'

Well, well, this was a turn-up for the books. Tara, guilty about meeting up with Dominic again, had made a particular point of avoiding Daisy yesterday.

'I was busy. We haven't spoken to each other since Monday morning. Speaking of which, it's now Wednesday morning,' she tapped her watch, 'and Daisy's meant to be downstairs.'

'Is it desperate? She didn't get a lot of sleep last night. Couldn't you let her have another hour?'

'I—'

The bedroom door flew open and Daisy shot out. Wild-haired and panda-eyed, she screeched to a halt at the sight of Tara and Josh together in the kitchen, enjoying a companionable breakfast.

'It's twenty past nine! What happened to my alarm clock? What are *you* doing here?' she accused Tara.

'I came to wake you up.'

Something shifty happened to Daisy's mascara-logged eyes. Guiltily, they veered towards Josh.

'And you persuaded her to stay for breakfast instead. Honestly, Josh, you could have knocked on my door, you know I hate it when I've overslept.'

Oh, excellent! Tara realised with delight that Daisy was attempting to bluff her way out of this. She was also hugely relieved to see that below the hem of her hastily flung on white towelling robe, Daisy's bare legs were as tanned and smooth as a Chippendale's chest.

'Josh, I'm serious. Did my alarm go off this morning? Because if it did, you must have heard it through your bedroom wall.' Her eyes wide with meaning, Daisy rattled on, 'You should have come in and woken me up, you *knew* I had to be downstairs by—'

'Ahem.' Josh cleared his throat and rubbed his hand over his bristly chin.

Bristly and blond with a hint of ginger, Tara couldn't help noticing.

'What?' Daisy gazed in confusion at the pair of them. *'What?'*

'Tara knows,' Josh said kindly. 'She tried to wake you up by playing "This Little Piggy" with your toes.' He paused, attempting to keep a straight face. 'Trouble is, she did it to my toes instead.'

Realisation dawned.

'Oh, bum,' Daisy wailed. 'Oh, bugger. That's *so* unfair.'

'Hey, watch what you're saying. I hope you weren't planning to keep me a secret,' said Josh. 'Because I'm telling you now, I could take offence.'

'You idiot, I didn't mean that.' Crossing over to him, Daisy slid an arm affectionately round his waist and stole a bit of toast. 'Tara's my best friend. We don't have any secrets,' she explained to Josh. 'She *knows* I haven't had any kind of a sex life for over a year. I'm just saying *I* wanted to be the one to tell her about us.'

Tara flinched a bit at the mention of no secrets. She hadn't been able to sleep last night for thinking about Dominic.

'Don't worry, you can tell me properly later.' Adopting a lascivious Benny Hill leer, she added, 'And I'll want to hear *all* the sleazy details.'

'Honestly, why is it OK for girls to do that?' Josh protested. 'You'd go mental if two men announced they were going to discuss you.'

'I know. But it's fun. And I'll only be saying lovely things, I promise.' Daisy's tone was soothing. 'Now, I need a shower. Anything happening downstairs that I should know about?'

Tara slipped down from her high stool; it was time to get back to work.

'Paula Penhaligon's going to be here at eleven.' She ticked off the things she had to mention to Daisy on her fingers. 'I wondered if you were still going into Bristol tomorrow afternoon, because I'm on the scrounge for a lift—'

'I'm not,' Daisy apologised. 'The meeting's been cancelled.'

Tara's face fell; it was Maggie's birthday on Friday and she hadn't bought her anything yet.

'Oh. OK, never mind.'

'But Josh is here.' Brightening, Daisy clutched his arm. 'You could give Tara a lift, couldn't you?'

'No problem. What's wrong with your car?' Josh asked Tara.

'She doesn't have one,' Daisy announced.

Josh was shocked. 'You're not serious. How can you live out here and not have your own transport?'

'Easy. Because I don't drive.'

'This is mad.' Josh was by this time incredulous, his sunbleached eyebrows shooting up to his hairline. 'Why on earth not?'

Tara sighed; she was used to people having a go at her. 'I just never learned, OK? Not properly, at least. In London it was easier to catch a bus or the tube. Then, when I moved

217

down here, my aunt tried to teach me and that was a disaster.'

Disaster was an understatement. Maggie had kept yelling at her to stop dawdling and put her foot down. Halfway through her second lesson, Tara had driven Maggie's car into a ditch and promptly vowed never to get behind the wheel of a car again.

'What about a proper driving instructor?' Josh was clearly the persistent type.

'They cost a fortune. And my awful boss pays me a pittance.' Tara's tone was mournful.

Her awful boss, currently swigging back lukewarm coffee and checking her watch, said, 'I offered to give her a couple of lessons, but she's lost her nerve.'

'So how *do* you get about?' Josh was still curious.

Tara squirmed, wishing he wouldn't keep going on about it. It was embarrassing, for heaven's sake, like having to admit you couldn't read or write.

'Bums lifts. Like the one she's going to bum off you to get her into Bristol tomorrow afternoon.' Swallowing her last mouthful of coffee, Daisy headed briskly for the bathroom.

'Oh, and Barney wants a word with you,' Tara called after her, remembering the third thing she had to tell Daisy. 'Bless him, he's got some exciting news.'

Chapter 27

'So, Tara tells me you have some news.' When Daisy finally made it downstairs, Barney was still hovering outside her office like a sixth former summoned to see the headmistress. 'Don't tell me, you can't stand this godawful place a minute longer and you've come to hand in your notice.'

Barney, his brown eyes sparkling, said, 'You know I'd never do that. I love working here.'

'What's this about, then?' Perching on the edge of her desk, Daisy reached for the list of messages left for her by Brenda.

'Well, I've met this girl. And we really like each other. The thing is, she has to leave her flat in Bristol and we really want to be together . . .'

'Crikey, I don't know about that.' Daisy, who already knew what he was leading up to, pulled a doubtful face. 'You mean you'd like her to move into your room here? Don't you think it'd be a bit cramped?'

'No, no, that's not what I wanted to ask you,' Barney exclaimed, moments before realising he was being teased. 'Oh, right. Tara's already told you, hasn't she?'

'She may have dropped a couple of subtle hints.' Daisy's mouth twitched, because they both knew Tara was a stranger to discretion. 'The words "Rose Timpson's cottage" might have been mentioned in passing.'

'Is it OK?' Barney was visibly relieved. 'I mean, you're sure you don't mind?'

'Barney, it's absolutely fine with me, why would I mind? I'm just wondering how your girlfriend feels about it. Isn't Brock Cottage a bit grim?'

Actually, grim was an understatement. Marvelling at his optimism, Daisy realised she couldn't imagine how it must feel to love someone so much you wouldn't mind living in a hovel.

'It won't be grim by the time I've finished with it.' Eagerly, Barney said, 'Bert Connelly's brother's coming over this evening with a big van, to clear the place out. And tomorrow's my day off,' he reminded Daisy, 'and Bert's sending one of his sons over to help me with the cleaning up.'

No longer scared of Bert, Barney now thought he was a wonderful generous man with a heart of gold beneath those baggy brown overalls.

Daisy smiled and said, 'I'm glad you've met someone nice. I'm sure the two of you'll be very happy.'

'Actually, there's three of us.' Barney swelled with pride. 'She's got a baby, a little boy. He's fantastic.'

Blimey, a single mother. This would give the village gossips something to whisper about. Daisy, about to ask what their names were, was stopped by the phone ringing on her desk.

It was Pam, putting through a transatlantic call from an American organising a surprise party for his wife at the hotel. Lots of complicated arrangements needed to be finalised. Covering the receiver, Daisy pulled a face and said to Barney, 'Sorry, bit busy.'

'No problem, I'll get back to work. Thanks for everything.' Barney thought again how lovely she was, how lucky Steven had been to have married her.

'Good luck with the cottage,' Daisy whispered. 'I'll have to come and see it when it's finished.'

'Definitely,' Barney told her with a grin. 'You'll be amazed, I promise.'

For the first time in a very long time, Maggie felt her heart flutter with excitement at the sight of someone other than Hector. He was here! At last! Exactly on time and looking reassuringly efficient. Even the way he locked his van and headed up the front path was impressively brisk.

Delighted, Maggie darted away from the living-room window to answer the front door.

'Hi! Fantastic! Have you got the spare part?'

It was a different repairman today, which could only be good news. Balding and squat, rather like a toad, and wearing an identity tag announcing his name to be Owen Jones, he held up a small polythene bag containing something technical-looking swathed in bubble-wrap.

'It's right here, Mrs Donovan, don't you fret. Soon have you sorted. Bet you thought this day'd never come, eh? Well, don't you worry yourself. Never fear, Owen's here!' Proudly he tapped his laminated ID badge. 'That's me, see?'

Maggie, so overcome she could have hugged him, said the only thing applicable under the circumstances.

'Coffee? Or tea?'

'Ah, a lady who talks my language.' Owen beamed as he followed her through to the kitchen. 'Tea please, three sugars. But it's only going to take a minute or two to fit this little beauty here. Chances are, I'll be finished before you've even made it.'

'Owen.' Joyfully Maggie reached for the kettle. 'You're a man who talks *my* language.'

By the time she'd made him his mug of tea Owen was indeed finished. In no time flat he had dismantled the washing machine, attempted to fit the long-awaited spare part and discovered that it was the wrong spare part. Maggie was still piling in sugar when she realised he was closing the machine back up.

'Heavens, that *was* quick!'

'Sorry, Mrs Donovan, bit of a hitch.' Owen shook his head, evidently despairing of the incompetence of others. 'This is the wrong spare part.'

As Maggie stared at him he puffed out his cheeks, looking more toad-like than ever.

'Owen. Please tell me you're joking.'

'Thing is, see, this is the code number that was written on the order form.' Shuffling over to her, he pointed to the battered sheet of paper in his left hand. 'But someone made a mistake somewhere along the line. See that four there? Well, it should have been a seven. I can guess how it happened, it's the way some people have of putting those fancy foreign horizontal lines across 'em, and then the next person copying it out just thinks it's a four.'

'So my machine isn't fixed.' The mug of hot tea trembled ominously in Maggie's hand.

'Look, I've said I'm sorry, but it really isn't anything to do with me. I'll order another part,' Owen assured her. 'And we'll get back to you as soon as it comes in.'

'In a fortnight, you mean? That isn't good enough! I need a washing machine that *works*.' Maggie plonked the mug of tea down on the drainer behind her; she was damned if he was getting it in return for doing sod all. 'I tell you what, you can take this one away with you and wait for the spare part to arrive. In the meantime, your incompetent company can loan me a fully functioning machine. That's only fair, surely?'

Owen sighed and shook his fat bald head once more. 'No can do, I'm afraid.'

'But it's under guarantee!'

'We guarantee to fix any faults, yes.'

'And you haven't!' Frazzled, Maggie banged the flat of her hand against the top of the useless machine. 'You haven't fixed it!'

'The guarantee covers parts and labour.' Owen was no longer chirpy; the smiling woman who had greeted him so joyously at the door had turned into the stroppy customer from hell. 'If you read your policy,' he added stiffly, 'you'll see that we don't provide replacement machines, nor are we required by law to—'

'This is PATHETIC,' Maggie roared before he could finish. 'It's not good enough! You're going to give me the name and number of your boss so I can ring him up and tell him exactly what I think of his rotten lousy *shoddy* little company.'

Owen couldn't scuttle out of the cottage fast enough. When he'd gone, Maggie glared at the scrap of paper upon which she had scrawled his boss's details. She fantasised about what she would say to him and pictured him cowering in his office, apologising profusely and offering her all kinds of extravagant bribes to stop her contacting *Watchdog*.

Then she came back to reality with a bump. Who was she kidding? Customers who made a nuisance of themselves ended up getting treatment that was worse, not better. Just to teach her a lesson, they'd probably keep her waiting two years for the vital spare part.

It was like customers in a restaurant sending their food back to the kitchen with some complaint or other. All the chef did was spit in it before sending it back out, everyone knew that.

Her toes curling with frustration, Maggie ripped up the scrap of paper and chucked the pieces in the bin. Ranting and raving would do no good at all. She may as well bite the bullet and accept – damn and blast – that she'd be washing by hand for a while yet.

Oh Hector, come round and cheer me up. *Please*.

Barney did his best to retain his composure but it was hard not to stare at Paula Penhaligon as she stepped from the car. She smelled fantastic, for a start. Her neat high-heeled shoes were the most expensive-looking he'd ever seen. From the feet up, she was wearing pale stockings, a honey-coloured narrow suede skirt and a chocolate-brown fitted shirt with a kind of creamy stole thing wrapped around her shoulders. Her glossy red hair was worn in the kind of bob shape that looked as though it had been precision cut in a car factory, her make-up was film star flawless and she was wearing dark glasses. Even though the sun wasn't out.

Barney wasn't stupid, he knew he mustn't point out to her the fact that the sky was currently one vast eiderdown of grey. Wearing sunglasses when it wasn't sunny was just one of those things celebrities liked to do, pretending that it meant they could walk around incognito.

Not that Paula Penhaligon could go unnoticed anywhere. She might be knocking on a bit now – nearly fifty, Barney guessed – but she was still pretty stunning for her age.

Daisy had been waylaid on the phone, so Barney smiled his warm smile and said, 'Mrs Penhaligon, welcome to Colworth Manor.'

'Why, thank you.' In return, Paula Penhaligon fluttered her narrow fingers in the direction of the boot. 'My cases are in there, if you wouldn't mind – *oops*.' As she turned, her ivory cashmere wrap slipped from her shoulders. Like lightning, Barney reached out and caught it before it hit the wet gravel.

'I say, well held.' Paula Penhaligon removed her dark glasses in order to gaze at him with admiration. 'I like this hotel already.'

Her eyes were heavily made up, but there was no mistaking the marks beneath them, faint yellowish bruises just visible through the concealer. With a jolt, Barney remembered that she was currently going through a traumatic divorce. By the look of it, she'd been physically assaulted. Shocked, he realised that her husband must have beaten her up.

'And your name is?'

'Um . . . Barney. Barney Usher.'

'Excellent reflexes,' Paula Penhaligon remarked with a playful twitch of her lips. 'Well done.'

Lost for words, Barney wondered how he was supposed to respond to this. Thankfully, Daisy appeared and took over, freeing him to lift the cases out of the boot. Paula Penhaligon had certainly brought a mountain of luggage with her. Then again, if she was fleeing an abusive husband, maybe these cases contained everything she owned.

'Darling Lionel recommended your hotel to me,' Barney heard her telling Daisy. 'Now, I don't want any kind of special treatment, I'm just here to relax and recharge my batteries. Any inquiries from the press are to be referred directly to my agent.'

Barney felt sorry for the poor woman. She didn't want anyone knowing she was a battered wife.

'Don't you worry,' Daisy assured Paula Penhaligon with a grin. 'If you don't want special treatment, you've come to the right place. We're equally horrible to all our guests.'

Chapter 28

'Quick, get downstairs,' Tara bellowed, sticking her head round the door of the staff sitting room and making Barney jump. 'Paula Penhaligon's husband's just turned up with a shotgun, he's going berserk in reception, threatening to blow her brains out!'

Barney leapt instinctively to his feet, his eyes wide with horror. God, this was *terrible*.

'What?' He stared at Tara, bewildered, as she stood there in the doorway barring his exit. How could she even *think* of laughing at a time like this?

Oh.

'Barney, you are so *sweet*.' Tara was by this time doubled up with laughter. 'Just the sweetest thing ever. You really would have gone rushing down to save her, wouldn't you!'

Caught out again. Twice in one day. He'd be the laughing stock of the hotel when this got out.

'Next time you tell me there's a madman with a shotgun downstairs, I'll just stay here and finish my sandwiches,' Barney said mildly. 'And when he shoots you, you'll be sorry.'

'I know, I know. But Rocky told me what you'd told him and I couldn't resist it.' Wiping her eyes, Tara went on, 'I've just been up to Paula Penhaligon's suite. You big dingbat, she hasn't been beaten up.'

'She has.' Barney nodded vigorously. 'I saw her in daylight. Her eyes were all bruised and swollen.'

'But mysteriously wrinkle-free,' Tara finished for him. 'Barney, she's had a face-lift. That's why she's come down here, dummy. To recuperate.'

'A face-lift?' Barney was both shocked and relieved. At least it meant Paula Penhaligon wasn't being beaten up. It still seemed strange to him, though, that anyone would willingly choose to undergo surgery just to improve their looks.

'She's forty-eight and back on the market. It's something to give the old confidence a boost. She's after a new man.' Tara winked. 'You never know, a pretty boy like you could be right up her street.'

'You're not going to catch me out a third time,' said Barney. Abruptly another thought struck him. 'And you won't tell Daisy about the shotgun thing, will you? I don't want her thinking I'm completely stupid.'

Tara watched him silently pleading with her. What a sweetie; he was genuinely worried.

'You were ready to defend one of our guests from a madman with a gun,' she marvelled. 'Daisy would be *impressed*.'

'Please don't say anything.'

Taking pity on him, Tara relented. 'OK, I promise. In exchange for one little thing.'

'What little thing?' Barney was wary of her now, but sadly not wary enough to guard the remains of his lunch.

'Yum, tuna and mayonnaise, my favourite.' Whisking the last sandwich from his plate, she took a huge bite.

Barney pointed to the bottles of anti-rejection medication on the coffee table in front of him. 'I crushed up my tablets and mixed them in with the tuna.'

Oh God, how *awful*. Horrified, Tara began to splutter and

choke. She spat half the mouthful messily into her cupped hand.

'Not really,' said Barney with an angelic grin.

Hector's favourite walk in the hotel's grounds was the wooded path along the riverbank. The snowdrops and crocuses were poking their way through the ground. Soon, the hazel bushes would dance with catkins and the bluebells would be making an appearance. By April they would cover the lower reaches of the hill with a blue haze and creamy white blossom would sprout on the hawthorn bushes overhanging the river. Heaving a sigh of absolute contentment, Hector thought how right he'd been to buy this place. How anyone could choose to live in a filthy city was genuinely beyond him.

In the pocket of his Barbour, his mobile phone rang. Just once.

Looking at the screen, he smiled. This was the system he and Maggie had evolved. If it wasn't a good moment, he would leave it at that and she would understand. If the coast was clear, he'd call her back.

Since the coast couldn't be much clearer than it was now, he pressed out her number. For security reasons, it wasn't even logged in the phone's memory.

'Hi.' Maggie sounded both harassed and relieved. 'You won't believe the rotten morning I've had.'

Hector smiled. 'What's the problem?'

'Let's just say if you turn on the evening news and hear that a big bomb's gone off at the HQ of Carver's Superstore, you'll know who planted it.'

'I've told you already—'

'And I've told you, you're not buying me another one. Anyway, I've just finished a mountain of hand-washing,' Maggie went on, 'and Tara won't be home before five. I just wondered what you were doing.'

Hector hesitated. Maggie was clearly in need of cheering up and he'd like to see her but, being brutally honest here, he wasn't in the mood right now for sex. This morning's round of golf with Josh had left him with a painful twinge in his back. And, their arrangement being as it was, it wouldn't seem right to pay Maggie a visit and not sleep with her. He would feel as if he were short-changing her. She might be offended. Once a business relationship was established, it made sense to keep to the rules.

'Actually, I'm pretty tied up.' Hector spoke with regret, twisting his body from side to side to double-check that twinge. Ouch, still there. 'But tomorrow afternoon should be OK,' he added with confidence. His back would definitely be better by then.

'Tomorrow?' He heard the disappointment in Maggie's voice and for a moment felt emotionally torn. But that was stupid, Hector reminded himself. Theirs wasn't an emotional relationship.

He cleared his throat. 'Say around two o'clock?'

'The thing is, an Australian couple are dropping by at some stage to pick up their cushions. They weren't able to give me an exact time.' Maggie sounded frustrated. 'If they're here at one o'clock, fine. But they might not turn up till four.'

'OK, OK.' Hector's tone was soothing. 'Don't worry about it. Fingers crossed, they'll be early. As soon as the coast's clear, give me a ring.' As he said it, he heard the sound of bushes rustling ahead. 'Look, I have to go. I'll speak to you tomorrow. 'Bye.'

The phone was switched off and back in his pocket in an instant. In a village like Colworth you could never be too careful; one slip and their shameful secret would be out.

Hector knew it shouldn't be shameful, but somehow it was.

The bushes rustled again as whoever it was made their way along the narrow, overgrown path towards him. The next moment, he heard someone gasp and let out a muted cry.

Don't say he'd stumbled across a couple indulging in alfresco sex? Surely not. It was February – far too cold for such foolhardy behaviour.

God, thought Hector, I'm getting old.

Then he heard the words, 'Oh, sod it, get *off* me,' uttered by a female with irritation rather than fear, followed by, 'You bloody, *bloody* thing.'

Rounding the bend in the path, Hector saw an elegant redhead wrestling inelegantly with a blackberry bush. A long spiky tentacle was wrapped round her left leg like a noose and in bending down to free herself, the end of her cream scarf had managed to get itself entangled with another branch further up. Startled by the sight of Hector, the woman eyed him warily for a moment, then heaved a sigh of defeat.

'God, I hope you're not paparazzi. If you've got a camera on you, that's my street cred gone for good.'

'You're in luck.' Hector broke into a grin. 'I'm the world's most useless photographer. Even if I did have a camera, I'd forget to remove the lens cap. Here, lean on my shoulder,' he added, bending down and lifting her left foot off the ground. 'The more you struggle, the tighter it'll get.'

'Now I feel like a horse having its hooves checked,' the woman complained good-naturedly. 'Ouch, mind my ankle.'

It took a while, but at last Hector managed to free her. Once the bramble had been disentangled from her stockinged leg, he released the scarf from the higher branches.

'God.' Paula Penhaligon shook her head. 'It was like being attacked by a triffid. And I thought I came down here to relax.'

She was wearing hopelessly impractical shoes. Her pale stockings were in tatters. 'Jeans and walking boots might be an idea next time,' said Hector.

'There won't be a next time, I can promise you that.'

'Come on now, that's the coward's way out.' Reaching over, he picked a scrap of crispy, freeze-dried bramble leaf out of her hair. 'If you fall off a horse, the first thing you have to do is get back in the saddle.'

'I really don't think the countryside's my thing.' Paula Penhaligon touched her head defensively – removing the leaf from her hair had been a curiously intimate gesture, but seeing as he'd already been grappling around her ankles she could hardly protest now. 'Thanks for helping me out, but I'm just going to head back to the hotel.'

'You've only just got here,' Hector chided. 'You aren't giving the place a chance, and there's so much to see.'

'Such enthusiasm.' Her tone was dry. 'I suppose that's why you stay here, to commune with the wonders of nature.' Eyeing his battered Barbour, thick corduroys and green Hunter wellies, she added, 'You are a guest at the hotel?'

'Actually I'm not. But I do love this place.' He gestured at the view through the tangle of bare branches bordering the river. 'Which is why I can't bear the thought of you rushing back to London to tell all your smart city friends what a hateful time you had here. Did you bring *any* flat shoes with you, by the way?'

Paula hesitated. He seemed charming and he was certainly attractive, but she hadn't the faintest idea who he was.

Prevaricating, she said, 'Why?'

'Because if you did you could change into them. Then I'd take you for a nice easy walk – break you in gently, as it were.' His brown eyes twinkled. 'And maybe after that we could have a spot of afternoon tea.'

231

This was hard. Did he live in the village? Was he someone she could trust? It would have been nice to hook up with a genial fellow guest, but this was another matter altogether. What if he turned out to be one of those over-eager types, the kind who latched on to you, earnestly declaring themselves your greatest fan?

'I don't think so,' Paula announced. 'But thanks for the offer.'

'Fine. No problem.' He smiled easily, taking the rejection in his stride. 'But if you don't mind, I'll walk with you back to the hotel. You might want to put some TCP on that ankle of yours as well.' The bramble scratches on her left leg were bleeding.

Paula said, 'You don't have to walk back with me.'

'Don't worry, I'm not doing you a favour. I was planning to have a drink or two in the bar.'

Maybe he was the village drunk, charming but unemployable, an alcoholic who idled away his days tramping around the countryside between wild drinking bouts. During her years in the theatre, she'd known plenty of people like that. Still, he had rescued her from the clutches of that blackberry bush.

As they made their way back across the stone bridge, Paula said curiously, 'Do you know who I am?'

'You mean apart from the woman who abhors nature?' His eyes crinkled at the corners. 'I may look like a yokel, but my head isn't entirely stuffed with straw.'

By the time they reached the entrance to the hotel, she had learned that he was retired, keen on golf, and fond of playing the piano. When he had bluntly inquired about the faint bruising around her eyes, she'd explained how she had walked straight into a piece of scenery backstage.

'Well, this is where we go our separate ways.' Her genial

rescuer indicated the bar to their left. 'It's been nice meeting you. If you feel like joining me later, don't be shy.'

Paula gave the man her best professional smile. Clearly, he was settling in for a serious afternoon session. As for joining him later when he was three sheets to the wind, well, she'd rather dive head first into a bramble hedge.

And, frankly, she felt the hotel's standards must be slipping pretty drastically if they allowed visitors to wander into the bar in wellingtons. Even the posh green kind.

To her relief, the reception area had been empty when they'd come in. Now, the door to the manager's office swung open.

'Oh, for heaven's sake.' Daisy MacLean stared at the pair of them in dismay, her gaze instantly taking in Paula's shredded stockings and bleeding leg. 'Dad, I can't leave you alone for five minutes. What on earth have you done to our very important guest?'

Upstairs, Paula changed out of her ludicrously inappropriate town clothes. Well, she hadn't known they were ludicrous at the time; when she'd set out on her walk, she had naturally assumed the paths around the hotel would be tarmacked.

Now, wearing narrow leather trousers and an angora sweater and with her make-up carefully re-done, she entered the bar.

Hector MacLean was already there, having more speedily swapped his countryman's outfit for a smart green and black striped shirt, black trousers and highly polished handmade shoes. He was sitting at one of the window tables with a pot of coffee on a tray before him.

'You lied,' Paula announced as he rose to greet her.

'Actually, I didn't. You asked me if I was a guest.'

'OK, you misled me. Why didn't you tell me you owned this hotel?'

233

Hector poured black coffee into her cup. 'You'd have found out soon enough. I just fancied going incognito for a while, seeing if I could get by on personality alone.' He glanced up, his smile rueful. 'Except, sadly, it seems not.'

'That's unfair. I thought you were a drunk. I also thought you seemed a very nice person,' Paula hastily added.

'But I'm a lot nicer now you know I own this place. Or at least you're prepared to join me in the bar,' said Hector. 'And I could still be a hopeless drunk,' he reminded her. 'You don't know me well enough to say I'm not.'

'You invented Dennis the Dachshund, that's good enough for me.' Paula smiled. 'I used to read those books to my nephew when he was small.'

'What I want to know is, can I persuade you to come out for a proper walk with me this afternoon?' Eyeing her boots, with their modest heels, Hector said, 'I'm still determined to convert you to the glories of nature.'

'Are you serious? Do you have any idea how much these boots cost? They're Ferragamos,' Paula patiently explained. 'You aren't meant to walk in them.'

'OK.' He shrugged good-naturedly; two rejections in one day was enough for any man. 'I give up.'

Paula, realising she didn't want him to give up, put down her coffee cup.

'I'm really more of a pavement person.' Her smile flirtatious, she went on, 'I was planning to do some shopping in Bath tomorrow. If you're free, I'd enjoy the company.'

'Shopping?' It was Hector's turn to look less than enthusiastic.

'Not too much, I promise. And we could have lunch,' Paula said lightly, by way of an additional bribe. All of a sudden she badly wanted to spend the next day with this man. He'd been absolutely right, of course; discovering who he was had made him infinitely more attractive. Well, that was life. And it worked both ways. If she worked in a launderette, he wouldn't be nearly so interested in her.

And he was, oh yes, he definitely was. She could tell.

'Great,' said Hector. 'Little spot of shopping, nice long lunch. I think I can handle that. And who knows,' he added with a teasing smile, 'I may even have to buy you a pair of walking boots.'

Chapter 29

Thanks to her clothes-washing marathon, there was no hot water left in the tank. Having been forced to wash her hair in water that was barely lukewarm, Maggie was still cursing under her breath and vigorously rubbing her hair dry when she realised the phone was shrilling downstairs. With the towel over her head, she hadn't heard it begin to ring.

In her rush to reach it in time she missed her footing on the staircase, crashed down the last couple of stairs and banged her elbow painfully against the wall. Red-hot pins and needles zinged up and down her arm in protest. Gritting her teeth, Maggie raced across the living room and –

The phone fell silent.

Air hissed out from between her clenched teeth. It was five o'clock and Tara would be home any minute now, but there was still a chance it could have been Hector.

Dialling 1471, predictably, was no help at all. Number withheld. Which could still mean Hector, but then again might not.

As Maggie dithered, with ice-cold water dribbling down her neck, the front door rattled and Tara catapulted into the living room.

Great, that was that, no chance of phoning Hector now.

Eyeing Maggie in her dressing gown, Tara said brightly, 'Ooh, you look cosy, have you just had a lovely hot bath?'

This was really rubbing salt into the wound.

'No.' Maggie had to force herself not to snap; it wasn't Tara's fault her day had been a disaster. 'The washing machine man couldn't fix the washing machine. I had to do everything by hand, which used up all the hot water. I've just washed my hair in stone-cold water, the phone started ringing while I was upstairs, I tripped and banged my elbow—'

'The phone? Who was it?' Tara's eyes lit up. 'Someone for me?'

Young people today, Maggie thought sourly. They were just so selfish.

'It was no one for anyone.'

'But did you try—'

'*Yes*, I did, and the number was withheld. But my elbow's fine, thank you very much for asking, and before you start wondering if there's anything for tea, there isn't, so if you're hungry you'll just have to knock up an omelette or – *ummph*.'

Overcome with remorse, Tara flung her arms round her aunt. Maggie might be doing her best to hide it, but she was upset. Probably her hormones, Tara decided. Maybe this was the menopause kicking in. Poor Maggie, forty-five and all alone, no wonder she was so miserable . . . oh God, and it was her birthday on Friday. That hardly helped.

'Do you have any idea how much I love you?' As Tara hugged her, Maggie's cold wet hair plastered itself to her cheek. 'Come on now, sit down in front of the fire and relax. I'm going to make you a cup of tea and cook dinner tonight. I'm going to spoil you rotten!'

'Sweetheart, you don't have to.' Touched, Maggie shot her a wan smile. 'I'm fine, really I am.'

'Don't argue. I'm the boss. We'll have pasta and red wine,' Tara went on happily, 'and I'll catch you up on all the latest gossip. You won't believe what's been going on up at the hotel – in fact, after we've eaten, we could head over there.' Actually, that was a great idea, she could blow-dry Maggie's fine blonde hair and smarten her up, maybe even introduce her to the wonders of make-up. Teasingly she added, 'If you're very good, I may even introduce you to Daisy's new live-in lover.'

Ashamed of her earlier outburst, Maggie good-naturedly agreed to give mascara and lipstick a whirl. Having blow-dried her own hair and changed into navy velvet trousers and a loose-fitting lilac shirt – smart for *her* – she was drawn back downstairs by the smell of pasta puttanesca and the even more beguiling sound of a bottle of red wine being uncorked.

Translated from the Italian, puttanesca meant whore's pasta. Which was unfortunate, Maggie thought drily, but couldn't be helped. It wasn't as if Tara had done it on purpose.

She smiled at the sight of the table, laid with a cloth and lit with candles. Bless her heart, Tara was making a real effort, she'd even tidied the living room.

'You look great,' Tara announced as she brought in the bowls of steaming pasta.

'What's going on?' Realising suddenly why the living room was looking so much tidier, Maggie indicated the naked radiators. 'Where are all the wet clothes?'

'Sit down. Have some wine. They're in bin bags in the boot of your car, and we're taking them to the hotel.' Tara had made an executive decision. 'It's just mad you slogging your guts out doing all this washing. I told you before, Daisy said you could use her machine, she doesn't mind a bit. Tonight, while we're downstairs in the bar, our stuff's going to be happily tumble-drying up in Daisy's flat.'

Maggie did as she was told and sat. A brimming glass was thrust into her hand. Tara was right, she'd been cutting off her nose to spite her face. And an evening up at the hotel would be fun.

'Go on then, tell me what's been happening today. I can't believe Daisy's found herself a boyfriend at last.'

The pasta – hooray for Loyd Grossman's bottled sauces – was delicious. As Tara joyfully recounted the details of this morning's foray into Daisy's bedroom, Maggie relaxed further still. Next, she heard about Barney and the sandwich-spitting incident. In lieu of pudding, Maggie brought out the half-empty box of Thornton's truffles Tara had given her for Christmas.

'I don't know how you can keep a box of chocolates for two whole months,' Tara marvelled. 'I'm such a pig I'd finish the lot in one go.' In fact, if she'd known they were hidden up there on the top shelf of the kitchen cupboard, she would have guzzled them weeks ago.

'Ah, but sometimes it's nicer to save things. It means you've still got them to look forward to.' As Maggie said it, she realised it wasn't only true of chocolate truffles. Take the fact that she couldn't see Hector whenever she wanted to; OK, it was frustrating, but didn't it mean she looked forward to their eventual meetings all the more? Like tonight, for example. If he were there in the bar – and the chances were he would be – just the thought of exchanging a glance loaded with hidden meaning would be enough to keep her going until tomorrow afternoon.

Maggie inwardly shivered with pleasure at the prospect. Oh yes, she was definitely going to see Hector tomorrow, she'd made up her mind on that score. If the Australian tourists hadn't turned up here by two o'clock she was jolly well going to leave their cushions on the front doorstep.

'I'd rather eat them,' said Tara piggily, and for a moment Maggie thought she was talking about the cushions. 'I'd just keep going until they were all gone.'

She was eyeing the Thornton's box with longing. Instant gratification versus delicious anticipation, thought Maggie, feeling superior and grown-up.

'Help yourself, I'll save mine for another day. Oh, I'm *so* pleased about Daisy,' she said truthfully. 'It's high time she started having some fun again.'

'She isn't the only MacLean having some fun.' Greedily, Tara bit into a cappuccino truffle and rolled her eyes to convey its gorgeousness. 'You haven't heard the rest of it yet. I told you about Paula Penhaligon turning up today. Well, she and Hector have hit it off big time.'

Something shrivelled in the pit of Maggie's stomach. Hiding her true feelings whenever Hector's name was mentioned was a skill at which she had become adept, yet she lived in constant fear of giving herself away.

'Really? Hector's smitten, is he?' Her tone light, Maggie leaned across and dabbed a fingertip in the pool of wax around the flame of the nearest candle. The melted wax caused a moment of pain before cooling and setting on her finger.

'If you ask me, they're smitten with each other. They spent *hours* together in the bar this afternoon. Daisy says she's never seen him like this before. And she's not exaggerating,' Tara confided with glee. 'I stuck my head round the door a couple of times and they couldn't take their eyes off each other. Well, you'll be able to judge for yourself, they're bound to be there tonight. He might even start serenading her,' she went on, wriggling with delight. 'Can't you just picture it?'

Maggie didn't want to picture it, she was doing her level best to block it out. Why couldn't pain always be as fleeting and bearable as dabbing a finger in hot candle wax?

But this was the deal; this was the kind of hideous experience she had to put up with. Plastering on a bright smile, Maggie said cheerfully, 'Poor woman, imagine being serenaded in public. For her sake, I just hope he doesn't get his bagpipes out.'

'Hell,' mumbled Maggie five minutes later. Surreptitiously, but loudly enough for Tara to hear.

'What?'

'Hmm? Oh, nothing.' Maggie bravely shook her head, then winced and pressed her hand to her left temple. 'Darling, do we have any paracetamols left?'

Tara looked concerned. 'Headache?'

Uncanny! Give that girl a gold star!

'Migraine. Damn, this hasn't happened for years. Must be the red wine and chocolate.' Maggie gingerly massaged her forehead. 'If I can take painkillers quickly enough it might not develop into a full-blown attack. Otherwise I'll be in agony for days.'

'You poor thing!' Belting upstairs, Tara was back in a flash with the painkillers. 'I didn't even know you got migraines. Hang on, you'll need a glass of water.'

'I'll have to lie down,' Maggie apologised, still clutching her head as she rose cautiously to her feet. 'Just go to bed, stay quiet and keep the lights off . . . it's the only way . . . Darling, I'm so sorry, I've completely spoiled your evening.'

'Don't be silly, you can't help being ill. Now up you go,' Tara said solicitously, 'and give me a shout if there's anything you need.'

'Oh darling, you don't have to do that, I'll be fine. There's no reason why you can't still go out.'

'You're sick. Migraine's a horrible thing to have.' Tara was adamant. 'I wouldn't dream of leaving you here on your own.' With a beaming smile aimed at cheering Maggie up, she said, 'I'll be your chief nurse.'

241

Maggie felt terrible, of course she did. Tucked up in bed with Tara checking on her every ten minutes, she felt both guilty and ashamed.

Slightly irritated too, because the silence and no-lights rule meant she wasn't able to watch TV, listen to the radio or even read a magazine.

But being honest here, what else could she have done?

Maintaining a cheery front in the privacy of her own living room was one thing, but being forced to watch Hector up at the hotel getting all touchy-feely with Paula Penhaligon – having to witness him flirt with another woman and actually mean it – was something else altogether.

Maggie knew she couldn't do that.

Chapter 30

The horrible scrunched-up feeling of dread was still there in the pit of Maggie's stomach the next morning, exactly matching the horribly scrunched-up clothes Tara had retrieved from the boot of the car the night before and jammed back over the radiators. Now they were all crispy-dried and would be murder to iron.

Hector phoned at eleven o'clock.

'Poor you,' he sympathised. 'Tara's just been telling me about your migraine attack last night. Are you feeling better yet?'

Maggie closed her eyes briefly. He really didn't have the faintest idea. Well, why would he?

'Much better, thanks.'

'Good, good. Still, you'll need to take things easy, to be on the safe side.'

He was sounding extremely jovial. Wonder why, Maggie thought sourly.

Aloud she said, 'Really, I'm fine.'

'Well, the thing is, I'm going to have to take a rain-check for this afternoon.'

A rain-check. She knew what he was telling her, obviously. But what exactly *was* a rain-check? You could hear these expressions for years, Maggie discovered, and not have a clue what they actually meant.

Then she took a deep breath. 'No problem, these things

happen. Those customers of mine probably won't turn up until five anyway. Some other time, eh?'

'Some other time,' Hector agreed, sounding grateful. Then he hesitated. 'Look, I was wondering. If you're a bit short of money I could easily—'

'I'm not short of money!' Horrified, Maggie realised he was assuming this was why she'd phoned him yesterday. Strapped for cash? Hey, no problem, just get Hector round to the house and have sex with him! With a shiver of mortification she repeated, 'I'm not.'

'OK, if you're sure,' said Hector.

'Absolutely sure. Better go now.' Maggie lowered her voice. 'Someone's coming to the front door. 'Bye.'

Another lie, to add to all the rest.

Typically the Australians arrived to pick up their cushions at twelve o'clock on the dot.

'I like him.' Tara nodded, watching Josh from Daisy's office window. 'I think he's really nice.'

'Well, thank you so much, I'm glad you approve.' Daisy looked up and grinned. 'I like him too.'

'A lot?'

'Of course a lot! I wouldn't be sleeping with him otherwise. I'm not a trollop!'

'I didn't mean that. He just doesn't seem like the kind of bloke I thought you'd go for.' All dressed up for her trip into Bristol, Tara smoothed her red leather jacket over her waist and checked her boots for mud splashes.

'Josh is fun, he's kind, he's great company and he makes me laugh,' Daisy explained. 'That's good enough for me.'

She knew perfectly well what Tara was getting at. Being fun and kind was all very well, but didn't Daisy secretly wish he could be better looking? And the honest answer to that, Daisy had already decided, was no. Because in her experience, if Josh was knock 'em dead gorgeous, the chances were he wouldn't be the genuinely nice person he was. And she was mature enough to appreciate this.

'What's he doing?' Mystified, Tara peered out of the window. 'He's got a load of string.'

'Hmm?' Daisy glanced up from her computer. 'Oh, he's going to give you a driving lesson.'

'With a piece of string? What's he planning to do, tow me along like Noddy?' Belatedly, Tara did a double take. 'God, are you serious? He's going to teach me to drive?' As she said it, she realised Josh was using the string to fasten L plates to his car. 'But we're supposed to be going into Bristol,' she wailed. 'I've got to buy Maggie a birthday present.'

'You can do both,' said Daisy.

'I'm not insured! What if I smash up his car?'

'I gave him all your details this morning. He's sorted it out with his insurance company.'

'Really?' Tara couldn't believe it. She swung round in delight. '*Really?* God, that's fantastic!'

Daisy grinned. 'Told you he was nice.'

'Hi. Tara told me you'd be here. She said you were doing the place up.' Maggie held out a five-litre can of pale yellow matt emulsion. 'I thought you might be on the scrounge for paint.' When in a state of abject misery, do something nice for someone else – there was always an outside chance it might cheer you up.

'Are you sure?' Barney Usher, looking messier and dustier than she'd ever seen him look before, wiped his grubby hands on his jeans and beamed at her. 'Don't you need it for yourself?'

245

'I bought too much. This was left over after we'd finished the landing. It's only cluttering up the place.' Hefting it into his arms like an unwanted baby, Maggie said, 'Anyway, how are you getting on?'

'Doing pretty well. Come and have a look,' said Barney with pride. There was a lot of dust in his hair and he smelt of Dettol as he stepped aside and ushered her past him into the tiny cottage. Maggie had only met him a few times, and briefly at that, but she had been instantly charmed by his friendly, open manner and dazzling smile.

Amazing to think that one of his kidneys had originally been owned by Steven Standish.

'Gosh, you've been busy.' Truly impressed, Maggie gazed around the empty, scrubbed-clean living room.

'I've had help. Bert Connelly's brother brought his lorry round last night and cleared the place in three hours flat. And Donny's giving me a hand today.'

Maggie nodded and smiled. Donny Connelly, Bert's youngest son, was a cheerful, ox-like hulk of a lad with not too many brain cells but an endless capacity for hard work.

'Which is the equivalent of twenty normal people's hands,' Barney marvelled. 'I can't believe we've got so much done. It's going to look so great here when it's finished.'

Such youthful enthusiasm. Maggie wavered for a moment, wondering whether she should offer to pitch in as well. The ancient wallpaper had already been stripped from the walls and dust sheets efficiently laid down. They were ready to start painting and she could help with that.

But she wasn't feeling saintly enough. There were limits. Anyway, she'd already made up her mind, she was driving into Bath to stock up on cushion pads, zips, embroidery silks and other such riveting paraphernalia.

'This colour will be perfect for Freddie's bedroom.' Barney was exclaiming over the paint with genuine pleasure. Shyly he explained, 'Freddie's my girlfriend's son – he's still only a baby really and I know it should be blue for a boy, but his room's north facing, so blue might be a bit cold. Yellow's more cheerful, isn't it?'

'Much.' Maggie wondered if painting herself yellow would make her feel more cheerful. 'Well, I'd better be off, let you get back to work.'

'This is really kind of you,' Barney told her. 'As soon as we've moved in, we're going to have a house-warming party.' How he loved saying *we*, Maggie noted with a smile. 'You must come.'

'Definitely. I can't wait to see Freddie.'

'Oh, he's brilliant, you'll love him.' His brown eyes shining, Barney added happily, 'And Mel.'

'Now ease your left foot off the clutch and press down smoothly with the right . . . well done . . . OK, now shift into second gear and start indicating left . . . that's it, you're doing brilliantly.'

Tara was feeling ridiculously pleased with herself; all the half-remembered manoeuvres had come flooding back to her and Josh's calm manner and encouraging words were having a wondrous effect. Passing the written part of her driving test had been a doddle, but actually putting what she'd learned into practice had proved a terrifying experience. Her last lesson, over a year ago now, had been punctuated by shrieks and groans from Maggie, the world's most wildly unsuitable driving instructor. Getting flustered and panicky as a result was what had caused Tara to lose control and veer into that fateful ditch.

But Josh hadn't yelled at her once, not even when she'd stalled twice, like a prat, on Colworth Hill. And now she was getting her confidence back. This was actually turning out to be fun.

'Who taught you to drive?' Tara was intrigued. Now that they were on a straight bit of road she felt able to speak.

'Ah well, I was seventeen, I was an impressionable youth bursting with hormones. I'd also just seen a film that had a profound effect on me.' Josh heaved a nostalgic sigh. 'You might know it, that great classic of our time – *Confessions Of A Driving Instructor.*'

'Oh yes, marvellous film.' Tara nodded reverently. 'Won a lot of Oscars.'

'That's the one. Into fourth gear now. Anyway, when I rang up the driving school I specifically asked for a female instructor, blonde preferably, under thirty-five and seriously attractive. And the bloke on the other end of the phone said, "Don't you worry, my lad, I've got just the lady for you. A dozen lessons with her and you'll pass *any* test with flying colours."'

'Blimey.' Tara whistled through her teeth and swerved to avoid a squashed hedgehog – OK, so it was already dead, but being run over twice would be adding insult to injury. 'Who did you get, Melinda Messenger?'

'I got Eunice.' Josh's tone was mournful. 'She was sixty and a spinster, with grey hair in a bun and teeth like a shark. She was the scariest woman I'd ever met, but she knew her job. Within six weeks she got me through my test.' Sounding amused, he added, 'So you see, looks aren't always every-thing.'

Tara kept her eyes firmly on the road ahead, but she could feel herself reddening. Was he making fun of her? God, had Daisy told him what she'd said?

Her lesson lasted an hour, by the end of which Tara had gradu-ated to the dizzy heights of three-point turns. Bad three-point turns, but she was as proud of them as a mother with an ugly newborn baby.

And she hadn't driven into a ditch once.

'You're going to be fine,' Josh declared when she had reversed somewhat wonkily into a gateway. 'We'll get you through this test. Eight weeks max.'

Jumping out of the car, he unfastened the L plates, chucked them onto the back seat and took Tara's place behind the wheel. Tara, having shuffled in an ungainly fashion over the central well and gearstick – oh yes, very elegant, very Nigella Lawson – adjusted her jeans and said, 'Will you still be here then?'

'No problem. You won't be getting rid of me that easily.' He winked, ticking the months off on his fingers. 'March, April, May – I don't start the new job until June.'

June. Tara frowned.

'But what happens after that?'

'What happens? Are you mad? You'll be free to go wherever you want! Get yourself a little runabout and there'll be no stopping you.'

'I meant with you and Daisy. This new job of yours is in – where, Miami? Isn't that going to make things a bit tricky?'

Josh grinned as they sped along the narrow lane. 'I only got here a few days ago. It's a bit soon to start worrying about that kind of stuff.'

This was men for you. They never worried about anything.

'OK, maybe, but I'm just saying. And it's not as if you only just *met* Daisy. You liked each other years ago. A *lot*,' Tara emphasised. 'And Daisy isn't the bed-hopping type. Now that you're back together, the chances are it's going to last. Which of course I'm really glad about,' she added hastily, 'but I can't help worrying about this zipping back to America thing. I don't want Daisy to get hurt again.'

Gosh, she felt terribly grown-up all of a sudden! Warning Daisy's new boyfriend that if he didn't treat her well, he'd have her to answer to.

'What's this?' Josh's eyes crinkled with laughter. 'An interrogation? Are you asking me if my intentions towards Daisy are honourable?'

'Don't make fun of me.' Tara ignored the look of mock horror on his face. 'I just can't see it working out, long-term, if she's here and you're over there in the States.'

'OK, now listen to me. I do like Daisy. A *lot*,' Josh mimicked good-naturedly, 'as you so delicately put it. And I wouldn't dream of hurting her, you should already know that. Making girls cry isn't my style.'

'Next left,' Tara instructed as the sign pointing to the motorway loomed ahead.

'I hope it works out for us,' Josh went on. 'I really do. And if it's meant to, it will. My job in America isn't a major problem.'

God, he really was nice. Tara admired the way the muscles on his forearms moved beneath the skin as he indicated left, turned the steering wheel and simultaneously changed gear. Imagine being able to do all that complicated stuff without even thinking about it.

'You mean you'd find something here instead?'

Josh shrugged as they sped down the slip road and overtook a juggernaut.

'Possibly, but the weather's better in Florida. I actually meant that Daisy could always jack in her job and find something over there.'

Chapter 31

A family of tourists strolling around the hotel grounds caught Daisy's eye as she glanced up from her computer screen. The sight of the children eating ice lollies bought from the village shop recalled last night's dream with a jolt.

Good grief, until this moment she hadn't even known she'd dreamt it, but now it came catapulting back to her, clear as day. She and Dev Tyzack had been sitting together on the front steps of the hotel, talking about . . . well, something or other, possibly rugby. And he'd been eating an ice cream – not a glamorous one, just the swirly synthetic whipped-up kind you got from an ice-cream van. It didn't even have a flake in it.

But it was a hot day, and she'd longed for some of the ice cream. She couldn't tear her eyes away from it. The next moment, Dev stopped what he was saying and offered it to her.

'Want some?'

Oh, she did, she did. Overjoyed, she leaned towards him, steadying herself with her hand on his knee. She licked the ice cream and Dev smiled slightly before taking it back. He licked it too, which seemed wonderfully intimate. Seconds earlier, her mouth had been on the ice cream; now his mouth was there at the exact same spot. Almost like kissing by proxy.

And then he'd resumed his conversation, every now and again

pausing to offer her another lick. They'd shared the whole ice cream, even the cone.

That was it. That had been the sum total of the dream. Feeling hot, Daisy reached for the tumbler of water on her desk and hastily glugged it down. Damn, the effects dreams could have on you. And how embarrassing; a psychiatrist would have a field day interpreting this one.

The phone rang and she grabbed it, glad of the diversion. God, and Josh had been lying asleep next to her the whole time! Sharing a bed with one man and inadvertently dreaming of another was almost like being unfaithful, and why on earth would she want to dream about Dev Tyzack anyway? She was perfectly happy with Josh.

Oops, still not concentrating. Realising she'd forgotten to speak, Daisy hurriedly cleared her throat and, to make herself sound more efficient, said, 'Good morning, Colworth Manor Hotel, Daisy MacLean speaking.'

'You're behind the times. It's good afternoon,' a male voice observed, and for a horrible moment Daisy thought it was Dev Tyzack.

Then, even horribler, she realised it *was* him. Oh God, out of her dreams and into her phone. This simply wasn't fair.

'Sorry. Working too hard to notice the time.' Glancing at her watch, she saw that it was one o'clock. 'What can I do for you?'

'Well, I've got this ice cream here, melting faster than I can eat it. I wondered if you'd like to come and help me out.'

Dev didn't actually say this, *obviously*. It was her imagination working on feverish overtime without any help whatsoever from the sensible part of her brain. Wherever that might be.

'Just ringing with an update on the figures for the conference. It's gone up by eight. That won't be a problem, will it?'

They won't be a problem, thought Daisy. You're the problem.

'That's absolutely fine.' Smiling her best professional smile into the phone, she scribbled it down on a pad. 'Eight more guests. Will they all be staying for lunch?'

'Unless they walk out on me during the morning session. Yes, they'll all want lunch.'

'I'll organise that. Anything else?' Flick-flick, went the fountain pen between Daisy's agitated fingers as she waggled it to and fro like a cigar. Flick-flick – oof, royal blue ink all over her shirt cuff *and* in her eye.

'No, that's it. I'll see you on Friday.'

'Friday?' Scrabbling in her trouser pocket for a tissue, Daisy mopped her eye.

'The conference,' said Dev.

'Oh yes . . . yes, of course.' God, he must think her a moron.

'One other thing. How did the meeting go last week?' He paused. 'With your husband.'

'Oh, that.' Despite the ink, Daisy smiled; so it wasn't only women who were incurably nosy. 'He's not my husband.'

'Well, ex. You looked pretty startled when you heard he'd turned up, so I guessed you weren't still together.'

'We were never married. Josh's an ex-boyfriend from college, we haven't seen each other for years.' Ouch, her eye was beginning to smart. 'He just said it as a joke.'

'A joke. Right.' Dev sounded as if he was about to say something else. Then, with a curt, 'OK, see you on Friday,' he hung up.

Daisy dabbed the scrunched-up tissue in the dregs of her water glass and pressed it to her stinging eye. Black mascara and blue ink ran down her cheek. The door swung open and Brenda, her secretary, said, 'OK if I take my lunch break now and – oh my word, whatever's happened?' Shocked, she took a couple of steps into the office. 'Daisy love, is something wrong?'

Daisy shook her head and tried to laugh, but her eye was now streaming for England. Grimacing like Quasimodo, she flapped her free hand to indicate that she was fine, really she was, not crying at all.

'It's just my eye, I got ink in it,' Daisy explained, because Brenda wasn't looking convinced, but her nose had by this time begun to run in sympathy and it came out as 'I god ig iddit.' Brenda, who was the emotional mother-hen type, looked as if she was about to burst into tears too.

'Really, I promise you, I'b OK,' Daisy snuffled insistently. 'I'b dot *crying*.'

When the phone shrilled again she knew at once that it was Dev, ringing back to say whatever it was he'd been about to say earlier.

It was definitely, definitely Dev. And she couldn't speak to him with Brenda in the room.

'Lunch break, yep, off you go.' Sniffing, Daisy flapped her hands energetically in the direction of the door as the phone continued to ring.

Brenda obediently went.

Right. OK. Dev.

Deep breath, *huge* tube-cleaning sniff, followed by another deep breath.

'Good afternoon, Colworth Manor Hotel, Daisy MacLean speaking.' She cooed the words into the phone, cleverly going through the usual spiel to show Dev she didn't know it was him.

'Crikey, you don't half sound posh when you do that,' jeered Tara. 'Now look, you have to help me out here – actually, no, you have to help yourself out. Josh and I are at the Mall. He came over all romantic and decided to buy you some sexy underwear – which is a really nice idea, of course, in *theory* – but we're here in La Senza and Josh is determined to buy this complete monstrosity of a bra and knicker set *with* matching suspender belt. I mean, trust me, it is *hideous*,' Tara bellowed into the phone. 'Shiny red satin, gallons of purple lace – even I wouldn't wear something this tacky – ouch, what was *that* for?'

Daisy heard signs of a frenzied tussle.

'OK, sorry, sorry.' Tara lowered her voice. 'The manageress was right behind me. Josh thinks I was being a bit loud. Look, all I'm saying is this purple and red stuff isn't really you, and there are heaps of other far nicer things here that you'd much prefer. I've been doing my best to explain to Josh but he won't take a blind bit of notice, he's convinced he knows best.'

'Put him on,' said Daisy.

'God, your friend's bossy,' Josh grumbled. 'I just wanted to get you something nice. If I buy it, you'll wear it, won't you?' he pleaded, willing Daisy to be on his side.

Daisy had no intention of being on his side. She was just glad Tara had had the sense to ring her. Josh had bought her presents before.

'Sweetheart, this is really kind of you. Are you holding the bra and knickers?'

'Yes.' Josh spoke with pride. 'And the suspender belt.'

'OK. Now hang them back on the rail. And walk away from them. Choose something else that's just one colour all over, preferably not red, and don't waste your money on a suspender belt,' said Daisy, 'because I've never worn a suspender belt in my life.' She could practically hear the shock waves reverberating down the line.

'But—'

'Remember that lingerie set you bought me for my birthday that time?'

'Of course I do. The yellow and orange satin one with the turquoise lace,' Josh recalled with confidence. 'You loved it! You wore it all the time.'

'I didn't love it,' Daisy gently explained. 'I just pretended to, because I didn't want to hurt your feelings. I wore it once, and lived in fear of being run over by a bus. Sweetheart, it was a horrible lingerie set. Let's be honest here, choosing underwear isn't your forte. Why don't you let Tara help you pick something out?' Tara's sartorial taste might veer towards the dodgy, but compared with Josh she was *Vogue* on legs.

'You lied to me.' Josh sounded shocked.

'I told you, I didn't want to hurt your feelings.'

'What about hurting them now?'

'You're a big boy now. Old enough to cope.'

'I'm not,' said Josh. 'Actually, I'm starting to cry. Tara, do you have a tissue? Daisy's being horrid, she's making me cry.'

'I'm saving you from a lifetime of disastrous present-buying.' Daisy grinned, picturing the scene in La Senza.

'And I'm going to find you something really cheap as a punishment. Big old granny knickers, that's what you're getting,' said Josh. 'What size do you take anyway, eighteen or twenty?'

256

Chapter 32

The sun had unexpectedly come out as Maggie was making her way around Bath. In an effort to brighten her mood, having first got the boring cushion-making essentials out of the way, she toured the shops looking for something to catch her eye – a new jumper, maybe, a framed print or even a piece of jewellery. Nothing expensive, just cheap and cheerful. Well, it was worth a try, wasn't it? Retail therapy always seemed to work for Tara.

And, against all the odds, it seemed to be doing the trick. By three o'clock Maggie had actually bought quite a lot. An olive-green silk shirt and a brass candelabra in Oxfam – six pounds altogether, which was a *bargain* – a Victorian hatbox from a junk shop in Walcot Street, a new pair of jeans from Gap because her old ones had disintegrated to the point of indecency, and a bag of paperbacks from the second-hand bookshop behind the Octagon.

In fact, what with the cushion pads, she was carrying a fair few bags. Glancing at her reflection in a shop window, Maggie was struck by her uncanny resemblance to a packhorse. As the temperature outside had risen, she had removed both her grey fleece and navy jersey and tied them round her hips. Now, in just a black long-sleeved T-shirt and jeans, she was still hot. Her fringe was sticking to her forehead and her cheeks were pink. Definitely time to head back to the car before her arms dropped off.

Turning the corner, she spotted a Burger King ahead. When her stomach emitted a furious growl, Maggie realised for the first time how hungry she was. Crikey, starving in fact. And she hadn't had a burger for months.

Oh, the blissful miracle of fast food. Within two minutes Maggie found herself wandering along Milsom Street biting greedily into a flame-grilled double RodeoBurger with bacon and barbecue sauce and melted cheese. OK, maybe it wasn't haut cuisine, but when you were in the mood, a good RodeoBurger was hard to beat.

The Tante Elise was up ahead, one of Bath's smartest restaurants, with its navy and cream frontage and sweet little bay trees in glossy dark blue pots flanking the entrance. Far too posh and restrained to have its name emblazoned above the restaurant, a small oval brass plaque on the door was all this establishment needed to announce to its discerning clientele that this was, indeed, the Tante Elise.

Maggie wondered how the customers inside would react if she loitered on the pavement peering at them through the darkened glass with her mouth full of RodeoBurger. They'd be horrified, probably, and a waiter would be sent out to shoo her away.

Never mind, her arms were aching too much to hang around a minute longer than necessary. Pausing to adjust her grip on the carrier bag of paperbacks, Maggie estimated that she was less than five hundred metres from the car park in James Street. Three or four minutes of brisk walking and the muscle-wrenching torture would be over.

The door opened as she drew level with the restaurant, and Hector emerged. With Paula Penhaligon.

For a moment Maggie couldn't breathe. Hector hadn't spotted her yet but any second now he would turn around. And there was nowhere to hide, no way she could escape.

Paula Penhaligon was wearing a cream wool dress with a bronze pashmina artistically draped around her shoulders. Bronze high-heeled shoes. Shimmery russet hair. Expensive watch, expensive jewellery, expensive . . . everything. Hector was looking urbane in a dark suit. Maggie briefly considered backing into the road and crouching behind a parked car, but knowing her luck she'd only be hit by a lorry.

'Maggie! Good heavens, this is a surprise,' Hector exclaimed. 'What are you doing here?'

Maggie wondered what he thought she was doing here. Turning up for a spot of lunch at Tante Elise, perhaps? Or, oh God, did he think she was *stalking* him?

She stood there, rooted to the spot, desperately struggling to chew and swallow the mouthful of RodeoBurger that was refusing to go down. What must she look like, with her Oxfam bags, her Tesco carrier bulging with second-hand paperbacks and all the other bags she'd accumulated during the last couple of hours?

'I've been . . . umph, shopping.' Mercifully, she managed to swallow the wodge of burger in her mouth. The rest of it, protruding from its wrapper, was still in her left hand.

'Shopping? *Marvellous*,' Hector declared, with a little too much enthusiasm. 'Migraine all gone?'

Was he feeling guilty? Maggie wondered if it would even occur to him to do so. Lying to your wife or girlfriend, standing them up and then getting caught with another woman, was the kind of thing that might provoke guilt. But cancelling an appointment with the friendly neighbourhood hooker was hardly in the same league. She simply wasn't that important.

Aloud she mumbled, 'Migraine's gone.'

'This is Maggie, she lives in the village.' Hector turned to

Paula Penhaligon. 'Her niece is one of the chambermaids at the hotel.'

Paula's smile was perfunctory; she was clearly more interested in unfastening her neat leather clutch bag and locating her sunglasses. Christian Dior, Maggie noted with a stab of envy. What else?

'We've just had lunch here,' Hector carried on, determined to appear friendly.

Oh really? I thought you'd probably popped in to use their loo.

Maggie kept this retort to herself. She was feeling scruffy and on the defensive. Why couldn't she have elegant hair like Paula Penhaligon, and gorgeous clothes and dinky size three feet in wafer-thin high heels?

'Nice food?' Lame, but what else could she say?

'Pretty good, pretty good.' Hector was rubbing his hands together as if he was cold.

Paula Penhaligon said swiftly, 'Right then, shall we make a move?'

Hector pulled a mock dubious face at Maggie. 'We're going shopping.'

Maggie considered recommending the Oxfam shop. She gave herself a mental shake. 'And I must get back to the car. Enjoy yourselves.'

Paula, her left hand resting on Hector's sleeve, flashed her a be-nice-to-the-bag-lady smile. 'Oh, we will.'

Don't *smile* at me like that, Maggie longed to bellow, I can look better than this if I want to – in fact you should have seen me last night, all dressed up to see Hector! I didn't have a mouth crammed with RodeoBurger then, you know!

Frustrated, she humped the straining Tesco carrier bag up into the crook of her arm to stop the handles cutting into her fingers.

The heavy bag, stretched beyond endurance, promptly split, sending an avalanche of paperbacks crashing to the ground.

Hector was there in a flash, helping her retrieve them. Paula Penhaligon, keeping well back, glanced briefly at the scattered books then, pityingly, at Maggie.

'They're not mine. I bought them for my next-door neighbour.' Maggie was scarlet with shame even though it was the truth. 'Elsie's eighty-three, she doesn't get out much. She's mad about these kind of books. I bought this one for me,' she added in slight desperation, waving a battered John Grisham. 'Legal thrillers, that's what I like.'

Together, she and Hector bundled the paperbacks into the Oxfam bag along with the olive-green shirt and candelabra. Hector and Paula then headed off, arm in arm, in the direction of the exclusive shops. Maggie, making her way back to the car park, wondered why she'd even bothered to try and explain to them that she really didn't sit at home devouring every novel Barbara Cartland had ever written, dreaming hopelessly of sardonic flashing-eyed heroes and spirited young virgins.

Had Barbara ever written one called *The Hotel Owner And His Whore*?

No, thought not.

Solemnly, Josh handed over the gift-wrapped parcel with silver helium balloons bobbing above it.

'They're beautiful. Just what I wanted.' Having torn open the wrapping paper and lifted out the beige thermal pants, Daisy declared, 'This is so romantic. And extra large too.' She kissed him. 'You are thoughtful.'

'To match your extra large bottom,' said Josh, giving her neat backside an affectionate pat. 'Speaking of which, I'm starving. Any doughnuts left?'

'He's bought you a real present as well,' Tara assured Daisy while Josh was out of earshot in the kitchen. 'I chose it. A dark-blue silk camisole top and knickers. You'll love them.'

'I love these.' Grinning, Daisy waggled the thermal pants at her. 'It's such a Josh thing to do. Steven would never have dreamt of buying me something like this, just as a joke.'

She meant it, Tara realised. Josh was good for Daisy. He'd made her laugh again, put the sparkle back into her eyes.

'You make a great couple,' she said honestly. 'I know I had my doubts at first, but I can really see it now. He's brilliant.' God knows she didn't want to see her best friend disappear off to Florida, but if anyone deserved a happy ending, it was Daisy.

'He's exactly, *exactly* what I need.' Daisy looked smug. 'And it looks like Dad's found someone he's interested in too.' She nodded through the window as Hector's car pulled up outside with Paula Penhaligon in the passenger seat. Then she swung back round to face Tara. 'Now all we have to do is get you sorted. George Clooney? Johnny Depp? Name your man and leave it to me. We'll have you fixed up in no time.'

Inwardly Tara flinched. Daisy was her best friend in the world and she hated not being able to tell her everything.

'Either. I'm not fussy.' Tara feigned a yawn.

The only man she wanted to name was Dominic, and not even Daisy could sort that out.

What's more, she would hit the roof.

Chapter 33

Early the next morning, business types in suits began arriving for Dev Tyzack's management training conference. Daisy, greeting them at the door, showed them through to the room where the conference was being held. Dev would be here any minute now and the first presentation was due to begin at nine thirty. At eleven they would break for coffee. At one o'clock lunch would be served in the restaurant. Another break at three thirty, then the remainder of the afternoon session followed by drinks in the bar.

Daisy, welcoming the next group of arrivals, was determined that everything would run smoothly. After the near disaster of the Cross-Calvert wedding, she felt compelled to prove to Dev that she was up to the job. If a stressed businessman had a heart attack, she would resuscitate him promptly and without fuss. Any female clients going into labour, she would deliver their babies for them in a discreet and efficient fashion. The day was going to go without a hint of a hiccup.

Above all, *no* member of her staff was going to flirt with *any* of Dev's clients, male or female. Henceforth, this hotel would be a flirt-free zone.

Well, apart from her father and Paula Penhaligon, Daisy amended as Hector descended the stairs.

Actually, Hector wasn't so much descending the staircase

as dancing down it. He was looking chirpy and disgustingly pleased with himself. Meeting Paula had certainly put a spring in his step.

'Excuse me, I've got a bit of a problem.'

Daisy turned to face the girl who had touched her arm. Just arrived, smartly turned out and clutching a briefcase, she was looking flustered.

'Fire away.' Daisy was instantly up for the challenge. The girl didn't look nine months pregnant, but you could never be sure.

'I did it as I was getting out of the car.' She bent to show Daisy the huge ladder in her sheer, barely black tights. 'God, it looks awful, I caught it on the clasp of my case.'

'No problem.' Glancing up, Daisy checked that Barney was free. 'There's a shop in the village, I can send one of our porters over to pick up a new pair.' See? Easy-peasy.

'I've already been to the shop.' The girl pulled a face. 'No good. All they had was forty denier American Tan. Hideous,' she whispered. 'Like old age pensioners wear.'

'OK. Give me two minutes.' Daisy was reassuring. 'I'll be right back.'

Upstairs she rummaged through her chest of drawers, finally unearthing an unopened pack of ten denier barely blacks. Racing back down to reception, she glimpsed Dev Tyzack's back view just as he disappeared into the conference room.

'You've saved my life,' the girl breathed, taking the packet with relief and waving a ten pound note. 'You're a star, thank you so much.'

'You don't have to do that.' Daisy shook her head at the money, but the girl pressed it into her hand.

'I do. I can't let you just give me a pair of tights, and these aren't cheap. Please, just take it, then I can go and change.'

It was embarrassing, but the girl was in a rush and she was

insistent. Reluctantly Daisy took the ten pound note. She felt like a drug dealer. A fiver, maybe. Ten was too much, but giving the girl change would only heighten the awkwardness.

Anyway, she was right, the tights hadn't been cheap, they were Aristoc. Daisy was pretty certain they'd cost eight pounds fifty.

Daisy's first proper sight of Dev came at eleven o'clock when the delegates broke for coffee. There was a buzz of enthusiasm about them as they animatedly discussed the meeting so far. Dev, surrounded by people asking questions, glanced up and saw Daisy watching him from the doorway. Smiling in recognition at the girl with the tights, Daisy squeezed her way through the throng towards him.

'Just checking everything's OK,' she said when she reached Dev.

'Everything's fine.' His dark eyes flickered over her, taking in the orange silk shirt, black skirt and glossy black high heels. Almost but not quite smiling he added, 'No complaints at all.'

Stop it, stop it, no flirting allowed, Daisy wanted to bark like a sergeant major. I'm not flirting with you and I *don't* want you to flirt with me.

'Right, I'll leave you to it.' Keen to prove how busy and efficient she was, she tapped her watch in an efficient and businesslike fashion. 'Lunch will be served at one o'clock on the dot.'

Dev said, 'Oh, by the way, when we upped the numbers by eight, I forget to tell you three of them were vegetarians.'

Oh, marvellous. Absolutely great. *Bastard*.

'Three? OK. That's fine,' Daisy lied, nodding and smiling brightly as if there was nothing she enjoyed more than being told there were three extra vegetarians for lunch.

'Not really.' Dev winked. 'Just a joke.'

Daisy exhaled noisily. Thank God for that. She shook her head and gave him a rueful smile. 'Nearly got me there.'

'I did get you there.'

'Now I'm definitely going.'

'Better had.' Dev nodded in the direction of the doorway. 'Someone's looking for you.'

It was Josh, observing them with undisguised amusement. Catching Daisy's eye, he blew her a kiss and beckoned her over.

Dev raised an eyebrow. 'Who is he?'

'Someone looking for me,' said Daisy.

Now why hadn't she just said, 'Who, Josh? That's my boyfriend'? For some reason the words hadn't wanted to come out.

'Can you believe it? I've been stood up,' Josh complained. 'Your father doesn't want me any more. We had a round of golf booked and he's blown me out, found a new best friend to play with.' Looking utterly disgusted, he went on, 'And worst of all, she's a *girl*.'

In her late forties? Hardly.

'Get yourself some breast implants,' Daisy suggested helpfully. 'Slap on a ton of make-up. That might do the trick.'

Josh brightened. 'Win him back, you mean? Make him realise he'd rather be with me?' Breaking into song, he spread his arms like Carreras and warbled, 'Torn between two lovers . . .'

Actually, not like Carreras at all.

'Paula Penhaligon sings better than you do,' said Daisy.

'How about you?'

'Me too. In fact anyone sings better than you do, even Ken Dodd.'

'I meant is that what you are? Torn between two lovers?' He wagged his eyebrows playfully in the direction of Dev Tyzack.

'That is him, isn't it? The one you were so busy chatting up the other day?'

'You idiot,' said Daisy. 'I'm not torn, and he isn't my lover.'

Josh was laughing at the look of indignation on her face, not in the least bit worried; he didn't have a jealous bone in his body.

'That's because you had the good sense to choose me instead.' Modestly he added, 'And I have to say, you made exactly the right decision.'

'Oh, really?'

'I've told you before. Men like him just sweep women off their feet, then dump them faster than toxic waste. You don't want that,' said Josh. 'Me? I'll make you laugh and I won't break your heart. Now be honest, which sounds better to you?'

Daisy grinned. He wasn't telling her anything she hadn't already worked out for herself.

'OK, point made. But you've still been stood up by my dad, and I have to get back to work. What are you going to do?'

'What does any self-respecting bloke do when he's been stood up? Head on over to the golf club and find someone new to play with.' His eyes crinkled with amusement. 'You can stay here and flirt with Dev Tyzack.'

'But I don't *want* to flirt with – mmwphh!' Daisy gasped as Josh kissed her, briefly but thoroughly, on the mouth.

Just like Indiana Jones.

'Right, I'm off.' Affectionately he stroked her left ear lobe. 'And you can if you like.'

Flirt, presumably.

'You shouldn't have done that. I'm in charge of this hotel. Getting kissed in public isn't professional,' said Daisy.

'Don't worry, nobody was watching. Well, only one person,' Josh amended with a wink.

Great.

Daisy kept her distance for the rest of the day, only looking in to check that everything was running according to schedule before disappearing once more. But when the conference broke up at five thirty, Dev came and found her.

'We're having a drink in the bar. Will you join us?'

To drink or not to drink? Daisy, due for a break, breathed in the faint remnants of his aftershave. Josh had taken Tara out for her second driving lesson, which meant the flat upstairs would be empty anyway.

In the mood for company, she capped her fountain pen, stood up and said, 'Why not?'

In the crowded bar, Dev bought her a glass of white wine and checked his watch. 'My neighbour's looking after Clarissa today. I told her I'd be back by seven. She'll be missing me.'

'Your neighbour?'

'Her too, I expect.' Dev smiled. 'Clarissa usually comes everywhere with me, but I couldn't leave her stuck in the car all day.'

'I could have helped out,' Daisy protested. 'She could have stayed in my office, I'd have taken her for a run at lunchtime.'

'I didn't want to impose.'

'It wouldn't be imposing. I'm practically her aunt!'

'You might have been busy. Who was that chap you were talking to outside the conference room this afternoon?'

'Josh? He's the one who played the trick on me last week, the old boyfriend from college.' There, she'd told him now. Still, he'd been intrigued enough to ask. Twice.

Dev looked sceptical. 'Does he know he's an old boyfriend?'

'We're giving things another go.' Oh dear, that didn't sound very passionate; Daisy gave herself a mental shake. 'He's brilliant,' she went on, her eyes bright. 'We're very happy. *Very* happy.' God, I sound like a lousy actress and I'm not even acting. It's the *truth*.

The next moment someone touched her arm. Glad of the diversion – any diversion – Daisy exclaimed, 'Oh, hi! Have you had a good day?'

It was the girl from this morning, the one with the laddered tights.

'I came to say thanks.' She beamed at Daisy. 'You saved my life.'

Doctors and surgeons and firemen saved lives.

'Well,' said Daisy, 'I saved you from being forced to wear forty denier American Tans.'

'I'm feeling guilty, though. I don't think I gave you enough.' As she said it, the girl was searching through her bag. Finding her purse, she took out another ten pound note and held it towards Daisy.

Mystified, Dev shook his head. 'What's this about?'

'Oh, I laddered my tights as I arrived this morning. This girl very kindly sold me a pair of hers. But I've been worrying about it all day. When you gave me that funny look, I wondered if it meant ten pounds wasn't enough and I thought maybe you'd expected more . . .'

Dev frowned, turning to Daisy. 'You sold her a pair of your *own* tights? For ten *pounds*?'

Oh, for heaven's sake, what did he take her for?

'Look,' Daisy held up her hands in protest, 'it's not how it sounds. They weren't old tights, for a start.' Did he seriously imagine she'd dragged some bedraggled old pair out of her knicker drawer? 'They were brand new, still in the packet. And I didn't want any money at all, but . . . but . . .'

'Jennifer,' Dev supplied, when it became obvious she was floundering.

'Jennifer, right. She kept insisting I take it,' Daisy earnestly explained, 'and she was in such a hurry, and I really didn't want ten pounds but in the end it just seemed the easiest thing to do.'

'Ten *pounds*?' Dev repeated, shaking his head in disbelief.

That was the thing about men, Daisy remembered. They might have actually grasped that dresses can cost a lot and underwear can cost a lot and shoes can cost, well, a fortune, frankly, but when it came to tights they really didn't have a clue. Steven had been just the same; for some reason he'd been convinced that tights cost, ooh, maybe seventy or eighty pence a pair.

Trying to hide her irritation, Daisy said, 'OK, maybe it sounds a lot to you, but that's what you pay for a decent pair of tights these days.'

'Is it?' Dev turned to Jennifer, who looked embarrassed.

'Crikey, I don't know. I only ever buy cheapies, the posh kind are way out of my league.'

Daisy's irritation promptly doubled. This wasn't fair. Jennifer was acting all innocent but at the same time effectively digging the knife in. This morning she'd seemed perfectly nice. Was the girl doing it on purpose?

Daisy couldn't work it out at all. Dev, meanwhile, was looking at her as if spiders had suddenly started tumbling out of her ears. Humiliating memories came flooding back, of her schooldays, when she'd been unfairly accused of stealing a Crunchie Bar from the local newsagents. OK, so maybe she *had* actually stolen the Crunchie, but only as a dare. Not because she was a thief.

Dev, clearly on Jennifer's side, said, 'So tell me, how much did *you* pay for the tights?'

What kind of question was that? And how did he seriously expect her to reply?

'Ten pounds,' Daisy lied. Well, more or less. Of course, it *had* been less than that, but she was buggered if she was going to tell him that now. Even though she had a horrible feeling he knew.

'We'd better make a move,' Dev abruptly announced. 'I've booked a table for eight o'clock.'

For a moment Daisy thought he was talking to her. Then she realised Jennifer was flushing with triumph, smoothing her skirt and looking incredibly pleased with herself.

Without thinking, Daisy said, 'What about Clarissa? Isn't she expecting you home?'

'Oh, have you met her?' cried Jennifer with enthusiasm. 'Isn't she a little *doll*? I just love Clarissa to bits!'

Excuse me?

Daisy was instantly confused, she'd assumed Jennifer and Dev had only met today. She was also feeling jealous and hugely protective towards Clarissa. Jennifer wasn't allowed to witter on about how fabulous she was. I found her first, Daisy thought crossly, not you.

'If you left a child at home for this long, the social services would be on to you in a flash,' she told Dev.

'We'll pick her up, take her for a walk, keep her in the car while we're in the restaurant.'

Really? Jennifer or Clarissa?

'Give me two minutes to powder my nose, then we'll be off.' Beaming up at Dev, Jennifer laid a proprietorial hand on his wrist.

'Is she one of your clients?' asked Daisy, when the girl had disappeared to the loo.

'No. Jennifer's my secretary.'

Secretary. Of course he had a secretary. He'd just never

mentioned her before. And now they were going out for dinner together, Daisy thought sourly. Jennifer might not be his usual type, but she was evidently the girl Dev took to bed. When there was no one better around.

It was almost dark outside; Josh and Tara would be back soon. Glancing at her watch, Daisy knocked back the rest of her wine in one go.

'I'm off too. Have a nice meal.' Half of her was tempted to reach behind the bar, snatch a tenner from the cash register and give it to Dev to pass on to Jennifer. The other half of her thought, sod it, why should I?

Back in her office with the lights off, Daisy watched Dev leave the hotel and make his way across to the car park. With that long, confident stride and his jacket slung over one shoulder, she was forcefully reminded once again why she was better off steering clear of men like him.

The car roared into view, coming to a gravel-crunching halt by the entrance. The passenger door was pushed open by Dev and Jennifer, waiting on the steps, joyfully climbed in.

Needless to say, her tights were looking great.

I don't need someone like that, Daisy told herself as the car shot off down the drive. Nothing but trouble.

Anyway, dammit, who cares? I've got Josh.

Chapter 34

'Just five more minutes, then I really want to get home.' Tara didn't mean to sound ungrateful but she was seeing Dominic tonight.

'Fine. Turn right by the clump of trees,' instructed Josh, still new to the area and peering at the road sign. 'Up here, that's it, Brock Lane.'

'Watch out for mad dogs.' Tara pulled a face as they passed the cottage where Bert Connelly lived with his wife, hulking great sons and beloved pit bull terriers.

'OK, this'll do,' said Josh as they reached the next gateway. 'Turn round here. Stop, reverse into it and try not to hit the gatepost.'

Thoughts of Dominic were interfering with Tara's co-ordination; she was too excited to avoid making a pig's ear of the manoeuvre.

'It's dark,' she complained as the back wheel sank into a pothole. 'I can't see where I'm going.'

'Try again.'

'Oh, Josh, don't bully me. Haven't I done enough for one day?'

'Who's the lucky chap?'

Startled, Tara saw through the darkness that he was grinning at her.

273

'No one,' she lied. 'It's Maggie's birthday today, that's all.'

'I know it's Maggie's birthday. We went into Bristol yesterday to buy her a present. How did she like her dressing gown, by the way?'

To be honest, Tara wasn't sure. Having thought Maggie would adore a warm, practical woolly dressing gown, she had been disappointed by her aunt's lack of reaction. OK, so it wasn't the slinkiest outfit in the world, but what would Maggie *do* with a dressing gown that was glamorous?

'I think she might take it back – ooh, there's Barney!' Instantly diverted, Tara realised they were facing Brock Cottage, and that lights were blazing in every window. Now that Rose Timpson's awful grubby curtains had been taken down and – well, *incinerated*, hopefully – you could see the amount of work that had been done inside. Every room had been repainted. The drastically overgrown garden piled with old chicken coops and beer crates had been cleared. And there was Barney on the front path, energetically stuffing paint-stained newspapers into a black bin liner, stripping off his equally paint-spattered overalls and eagerly checking his watch.

Tara buzzed the driver's window down.

'Hey, Barney! Looking good!'

Next to her, Josh shook his head in mock despair and murmured, 'Don't tell me you've got your eye on him. Poor lad, he's far too young for you.'

'I meant the cottage.' Tara gave his arm a friendly thump. 'And I'm not after him. Apart from anything else, he's the one with the kidney.'

Barney, who *was* looking good, loped over to them in his jeans and an old purple sweatshirt.

'It's coming on,' he agreed happily. 'Want to take a look inside?'

'Bit of a hurry,' Tara apologised. 'Have to get back. Another time, OK?'

'OK.' Grinning, Barney ran his hands through his shiny hair, smoothing it into some kind of order. 'It's a shame, though. My girlfriend's going to be here in a minute – she hasn't seen the place yet either. I wanted to get it finished first,' he confided, 'but she's too excited. She can't wait.'

'Nobody home,' Josh observed shortly afterwards as they pulled up outside Maggie's cottage. The place was in darkness. Not surprising really, as Maggie had gone over to Chippenham to celebrate her birthday with friends.

'Thanks for the lesson.' Switching off the ignition, Tara belatedly remembered to pull on the handbrake. 'I mean it, I'm really grateful.'

'And I'm still curious.' Josh stayed where he was, making no attempt to move. 'You're off out somewhere, meeting someone you don't want to be late for, and you won't tell me who it is. More to the point, Daisy doesn't know who it is, which seems slightly weird to me.'

'God, you're nosy. This isn't a soap opera,' Tara complained. 'We aren't in *EastEnders*, you know.'

'I just think there's something fishy going on.' Josh spoke lightly. 'I reckon you're feeling guilty about something.' He shrugged. 'If you want to talk about it, I'm a good listener.'

For a moment, Tara wavered. The idea of confessing everything and being able to talk through the whole muddled scenario was hugely tempting. OK, Josh was Daisy's boyfriend, but she really trusted him and sensed he would understand. It would be so lovely to have someone to discuss it with, especially if they weren't going to give her a good shake and call her a disgusting little tart.

On the other hand, she was still in her uniform and desperate for a bath before Dominic turned up.

'It's nothing. Nobody special.' Tara scrambled out of the car. 'The only reason I haven't mentioned him to Daisy is because he isn't worth mentioning.'

'OK, if you say so.' Also climbing out so he could move into the driver's seat, Josh said, 'Same time tomorrow?'

Phew, inquisition over.

'Great,' said Tara. 'If you're sure you still want to.'

'Of course I do.' Josh winked at her. 'You can tell me all about him then.'

The forecast on the radio had warned of dramatically worsening weather. Plunging temperatures and icy roads followed at the weekend by blizzards. Mel, stuffing her gloved hands into the pockets of her padded jacket, stood beside her car and gazed at the cottage. The air was already cold enough to sting her nose and the tips of her ears. The night sky, purply-black, was dotted with bright stars.

Was this really going to be her home? Less than three hundred yards from Colworth Manor? Would all hell break loose when Daisy MacLean found out?

Shuffling from one frozen foot to the other, Mel thought of something else. She was less than three hundred yards from the churchyard where Steven lay buried. Would *he* mind?

As proud as a new father, Barney gave her the guided tour. Most of the windows were open in an effort to dispel the cloying smell of wet paint. The house was icy, empty and echoey underfoot, but Barney was buzzing with plans.

'I've got carpets coming tomorrow, and a new bed,' he rattled on. 'Daisy's giving me some old stuff from the hotel – a sofa and dining table and chairs. Pam on reception says she's got some curtains we can have and Bert Connelly's brother can get his hands on a cheap fridge-freezer.'

Mel looked at him. 'How can you afford to do all this?'

'I borrowed some money from my mum.'

'Have you told her about us?'

Barney hesitated, blushing wildly. 'Not yet. I said my car needed a new engine. Anyway, I'll pay her back.'

Mel glanced down at Freddie, fast asleep in his baby carrier on the floor next to her. She was touched that Barney was prepared to do so much for the two of them, but something else was bothering her.

'Why didn't you just tell her the truth?'

'You don't know my mother.' His smile rueful, Barney said, 'She'd just ask a million questions and worry herself sick. She's the protective type.'

He was holding back, hiding something. Mel, recognising the signs, realised that he looked like she felt.

'Barney, you're twenty-six. If you were sixteen I could under-stand it, but you're old enough now, you can do anything you want.'

'OK, look. There's something I have to tell you.' Barney shook his head, psyching himself up to do it. 'The thing is, I haven't been completely straight with you.'

Mel shivered suddenly; up until now it had all been going so well. 'God, don't tell me you *are* sixteen.'

Barney smiled slightly. 'It's nothing like that. And it isn't anything awful, I promise.'

'You're married?'

'Of course I'm not married!' Pulling the sleeves of his paint-splattered purple sweatshirt down over his forearms, Barney reached for Mel's icy hands. Puffballs of condensation hovered in the air as he took a couple of deep breaths. 'Right, here goes.'

* * *

Mel didn't know what to think. She'd imagined a lot of things, but not this, never this. So many thoughts were careering around inside her head that she was having trouble keeping them under control.

Barney was alive because Steven was dead. The scar on Barney's lower back was from where one of Steven's kidneys had been transplanted into his body.

'I knew I'd have to tell you sooner or later,' Barney had explained. 'I need to take all these different pills, you see, to stop my body rejecting it.' Pausing, he'd added diffidently, 'You look pretty shocked.'

Shocked didn't begin to describe it.

'Give me five minutes.' Mel had pulled her hands free and moved over to the far wall. As she slid slowly down to floor level, gazing at Freddie still asleep in the middle of the room, Barney said quietly, 'The brushes need washing out. I'll go upstairs and clean them.'

He went, and Mel pressed the heels of her hands hard against her closed eyelids. While Barney had been bracing himself to tell her everything, she had been silently welcoming it, whatever it might be. Because then she could forgive him and reveal her own secret, and he in return, in a rush of gratitude, would instantly forgive *her*. It could have been such perfect timing. One revelation in exchange for another.

Mel twisted the heavy silver ring round and round her left thumb like a string of worry beads. Her stomach was churning and it wasn't just a reaction to the overwhelming smell of paint. Oh yes, it could have worked out so well, brought them closer together still. It was a pretty significant connection, after all.

But there was one major problem. Daisy MacLean. The not-so grieving widow, Mel thought with a grimace.

And it wasn't so much Daisy's reaction that bothered her, as Barney's. Because now at last she understood why he idolised the woman, practically worshipped the ground she walked on. As far as Barney was concerned, Daisy had saved his life and he wouldn't dream of doing anything to hurt her.

By this time numb with cold, Mel stood up and shook some feeling back into her fingers. It was no good; if she told Barney now, he could, if he wanted, kick her out and tell her he never wanted to see her again. Which would leave her – if she couldn't persuade him to change his mind – effectively homeless.

Panic crawled through Mel's bones. Gazing across at Freddie, she knew she couldn't take that risk. Not yet, anyway, not until she absolutely had to.

She breathed out. Stick with the original plan. Move in here with Barney. That way, if he tried to get rid of her, she would have rights. And in the meantime, make him realise how truly happy they were together, how lucky they were to have found each other. Even if the way it had happened was, frankly, a bit bizarre.

Freddie stirred, opened his eyes, spotted his thumb and stuck it comfortably into his mouth. The next moment he was asleep again, his cold cheeks as red as the fleecy lining of his coat.

'Barney.' At the top of the stairs, Mel saw him through the open bathroom door rinsing the paint from the brushes under the tap. He turned to look at her, the merest hint of trepidation in his beautiful light-brown eyes.

All this painting, all this hard work, just for her.

'Yes?'

'I love you.' She held out her arms and smiled. The look on Barney's face was a picture, as if he'd just been told he didn't have to face the firing squad after all. The brushes clattered into the sink.

'I'm sorry, I didn't mean to scare you.' Mel hugged his warm body like a hot water bottle. 'It was a shock, I needed time to think. But I love you and that's all that matters. I want us to be together for the rest of our lives.'

Hopefully, Barney would remember this when the time came for her to spring her own little surprise.

He was smiling now, kissing her and stroking her hair. Monumentally relieved.

'I'm healthy. I'm fine. I'm not going to die,' Barney promised.

'Better bloody not.' For a moment, tears welled up in Mel's grey eyes and this time it had nothing to do with paint fumes. It was all true, she'd meant every word, she *did* love him.

If she didn't love him so much, she wouldn't be having to lie, would she?

Chapter 35

Bath, tick. Hair, tick. Make-up, tick. Sapphire-blue velvet stretchy top and skin-tight white trousers, tick tick.

Overall effect, completely gorgeous.

Having arranged to meet Dominic in the car park behind the Hollybush Inn, Tara was all ready to make her way downstairs, throw on her coat and race up the road, when the doorbell went. Mystified, she squirted herself with scent, checked her reflection one last time in the dressing-table mirror and galloped down to answer it.

'Dominic!'

He grinned at her. 'OK to come in?'

'What are you doing here? You're supposed to wait in the pub car park!' Dumbstruck, Tara stared at him. 'Is something wrong?'

'Don't panic, everything's fine. Change of plan, that's all.'

Oh God, please don't stand me up! Please don't dump me!

Her voice tremulous, Tara said, 'Why?'

'You mentioned on the phone that your aunt was out this evening. It seemed like too good an opportunity to pass up.' Feigning curiosity, Dominic peered past her into the living room. 'I've been wondering what this cottage was like on the inside.'

Oh dear. A bit of a tip, frankly. The usual assortment of wet washing was draped over the radiators, Maggie's sewing materials were piled high on one of the armchairs and the coffee table was littered with magazines and empty mugs.

Tara, watching him look around, felt like an unsuspecting householder opening her door to Loyd Grossman and a gaggle of cameramen.

'It's a mess,' she apologised, trying to kick biscuit crumbs under the sofa while Dominic wasn't looking.

'It's cosy. Small. Nice enough,' he said generously.

When you lived in an eight-bedroomed mansion, Tara supposed, practically anything would seem small.

'I like it,' Dominic went on, turning back to face her. 'I especially like the fact that it has you in it.'

Uh-oh, there was a look she'd seen before; she was familiar with that particular playful smile.

'We should go.' Tara began to panic.

'We don't have to.'

'We really should.'

'There's no need.' Dominic moved closer, hooking two fingers through her chain-link belt and gently drawing her towards him. 'I'd like to stay here.'

Of course he would. Tara knew exactly what was going through his mind. The fact that they had nowhere they could meet and be alone together bothered Dominic. This was the chance he'd been waiting for.

And now he was kissing her. Tara closed her eyes but resolved to be strong. When she'd told him Maggie would be out this evening, it had been because Dominic had asked if she was hungry and she'd been explaining why she hadn't eaten. It definitely hadn't been a hint. Seeing Dominic was one thing, but sleeping with him quite another. He was married and that would be a bad thing to do. Her conscience wouldn't allow her to jump into bed with him.

'You are gorgeous,' Dominic murmured against her neck, his hand busily attempting to unfasten the button on her skin-tight jeans. 'Damn, you're difficult to unwrap. It's worse than trying to get the cellophane off a new videotape.'

'We can't do this. It's not fair on Annabel. Oh, please don't, you *mustn't*,' Tara protested, trembling all over as his warm hand gave up on the jeans button and slid slowly up her spine instead. 'Really, I mean it, we can't stay here.'

'That's not fair on me.' Several wet socks and a couple of thermal vests slithered off the radiator behind Tara as Dominic eased her against the wall. 'None of this is my fault, you know,' he breathed, his tongue deftly exploring the hollow at the base of her throat. 'If you weren't so irresistible, I wouldn't be here now, would I? It's all your fault for being . . . you.'

Tara felt like a Beanie Baby, all floppy and bendy. Her knees, always suckers for a compliment, were no longer capable of holding her up. Damn, it was all very well being strong-willed in principle, but it wasn't so easy when you were actually in the throes of being seduced, when you were feeling all lustful and wanton and—

Rrring, trilled the doorbell, causing Dominic to spring off her in alarm.

'Jesus, who's that?'

'I don't know, do I?' Realising she was panting like Muttley, Tara hastily smoothed her hair and tugged down her velvet top. 'Go and hide in the kitchen.'

'You can't just answer the door, it could be any – AARGH!' Dominic let out a bellow of pain as his ankle caught the leg of the wooden clothes airer. Turning green and clutching his foot, he crashed back against the wall.

'Well, I can't pretend we're not in.' Tara rolled her eyes. Tiptoeing over to the window, she pulled the curtain back an inch and peered out. 'Phew, panic over, it's only Elsie from next door. She's ancient.'

Dominic was still cursing under his breath. 'God, what does *she* want?'

'I don't know!'

'Just get rid of her,' he hissed, limping into the kitchen. 'I think I've broken my bloody foot.'

Men, honestly. The fuss they made.

'Elsie, hi!' Beaming broadly, Tara flung open the front door. 'What can I do for you?'

'Hello there, my love, I heard some banging and crashing going on, are you all right?' Elsie might be eighty-three and pretty lame, but there was nothing wrong with her hearing. Leaning heavily on her briarwood walking stick, she surveyed the empty living room. 'On your own, are you? Only it was Maggie I really came to see. Got her a little something for her birthday.'

'Oh, what a shame, Maggie's not here.' Tara, who adored presents of any kind, eagerly eyed the supermarket carrier bag swinging from Elsie's gnarled hand. 'That's really sweet of you. D'you want to give it to her tomorrow, or shall I take it now and tell her you called round?'

'Well, it's kind of a double present,' Elsie confided. 'My way of saying thank you for all the things Maggie does for me. She brought me back a whole load of books the other day, you know. Such a kind girl. Lots of lovely Barbara Cartlands, none of that mucky stuff you get these days – nothing but pornography, half these so-called modern romances – oh no, you can't beat a bit of Barbara Cartland . . .'

'Shall I take it?' prompted Tara, holding her hands out for the carrier bag. Once Elsie got started she could ramble on for weeks.

'I'd better do it myself, love, carry it through to the kitchen for you. She's dripping a bit, see.' Elsie held up the bag to show Tara the underside. 'I know they put holes in to stop young kiddies suffocating themselves, but it's a blasted nuisance, if you ask me.'

'It's OK! I'll do it!' Tara made a reckless grab for the bag, but the older woman whisked it out of reach.

'No, love, you just keep clear, we don't want you getting blood all over those nice white jeans.'

Tara's heart sank. The old woman might be vehemently anti-porn but she wasn't averse to a spot of violence. Elsie had a chopper and she wasn't afraid to use it.

'It's not one of your . . . ?'

'It is, it is.' Elsie beamed with pride, making her way awkwardly across the living room with the help of her stick. Nudging open the kitchen door with her elbow, she discovered Dominic pretending to be busy making a cup of tea and chuckled loudly. 'Well, well, you must be Tara's young fellow. Thought I heard a man's voice when I was on the doorstep just now.'

There had been no hiding place for Dominic in the kitchen. With the back door locked, he had found himself trapped and unable to escape. Still, at least the old woman hadn't the faintest idea who he was. And she seemed harmless enough.

'Elsie's brought something round for Maggie.' Behind the old woman's back, Tara pulled a face.

'A special treat. She deserves it.' Shoving Dominic's cup out of the way, Elsie swung the carrier onto the drainer with a hefty thud.

'Madge,' Elsie announced, beaming at Dominic.

'How do you do, Madge? Nice to meet you.' Confused, Dominic attempted to shake her wrinkled hand.

Oh God, thought Tara. *Madge*.

'Not me.' Elsie cackled with laughter. 'I'm Elsie. This is Madge in here.' She reached inside the crackling plastic carrier bag and lifted out a dead hen.

Dead, and minus her head.

Dominic shrank back in horror. 'Jesus!'

'She's a little beauty, one of my favourites.' Elsie lovingly smoothed the glossy chestnut feathers. Casting a beady eye over Dominic's white face she added sharply, 'You a vegetarian?'

'N-no.'

'Stop looking so disgusted, then. She's had a good life and a quick death, has our Madge. Who could ask for more? Mind you, she put up a fight after I'd done the deed.' Cackling like a maniac, Elsie gave Dominic a boisterous nudge. 'Flapping all round my kitchen, she was, like a headless chicken!'

'Elsie's joking,' Tara put in hurriedly. 'She doesn't mean it.'

'It's OK, I'm fine.' Looking as if he wanted to be sick, Dominic clutched the side of the sink. Tara, feeling faintly squeamish herself, held the bloodied carrier bag open so Elsie could pop Madge back inside head first.

Well, severed neck first.

'She'll make a lovely Sunday dinner,' Elsie boasted. 'Lots of stuffing, that's the secret, and keep her on her back – ooh, and don't forget to boil up those giblets for gravy.'

'God, how can people *do* something like that,' Dominic shuddered the moment Elsie had left.

'This is the countryside. Elsie's lived here all her life. You keep chickens, you kill chickens.' Tara felt obliged to defend her neighbour.

'She gives them *names*.' Dominic shook his head in disgust. 'It's barbaric. Actually, I could do with a drink.'

'Oh well, don't worry, at least you won't have to eat Madge.'

Reaching up into the cupboard, Tara found the half-empty bottle of Glenfiddich that had been there for years because neither she nor Maggie liked it. In a way she was grateful to Elsie; her arrival had certainly put Dominic off the idea of sex.

'Here.' She poured an inch of whisky into a tumbler and handed it to him. 'Shall we go through?'

Dominic led the way, muttering, 'Anything to get away from that decapitated chicken.'

Back in the living room, he slumped down in one of the armchairs, gazing moodily into the fire and clutching his drink. Less than ninety seconds after Elsie had left, the doorbell rang again.

'Oh, for crying out loud, what now?' He heaved a sigh. 'Let me guess, she's found Madge's head and thinks we might like to boil it up and make stock.'

Dominic stayed put in the armchair; he clearly had no intention of moving anywhere. He was being ironic about Elsie's reason for coming back, whereas Tara suspected he might be spot on.

Bursting with flavour, chickens' heads.

Pulling open the front door, Tara gulped and said, 'Oh!'

Elsie had had a lightning sex change.

'You left your jacket in my car,' Josh announced, holding the offending article in front of him. 'I thought you might need it tomorrow morning.'

'Right, yes, thanks, great.' Tara snatched the jacket from him as Josh's eyes flickered over Dominic. He nodded and smiled pleasantly enough, while Tara's stomach performed agitated cartwheels. This was mad, how could he make her feel this guilty? They weren't even doing anything *wrong*.

'I'll be off then.' Josh winked at Tara.

'Yes, great, 'bye.' What a *stirrer*, she thought crossly as she closed the door.

'Who the bloody hell was that?' Dominic wasn't looking amused.

'Nobody. He's just teaching me to drive. Well,' Tara admitted, 'he's Daisy's boyfriend.'

'Shit!'

'It's OK. He doesn't know who you are.'

'God, I'm *so* bloody glad I came here tonight.' Dominic drained his glass and promptly rose to his feet. 'Let's get out of here before bloody Daisy turns up.'

Chapter 36

'Pssst,' hissed Tara, who was down on her knees polishing the legs of a walnut plant stand when Josh appeared in reception the next morning. Outside, the temperature had plummeted to arctic and the grounds were covered in a thick hoarfrost. Josh, dressed for his morning run in three sweatshirts, a grey knitted hat and black jogging pants, swung round in surprise.

'Oh, hi. Good night last night?'

'Did you say anything to Daisy?'

Josh raised his eyebrows beneath the rim of his pulled-down woolly hat. 'About what?'

'About who I was *with*.'

'I don't know who you were with.' He did a couple of warm-up exercises, stretching from side to side from the waist. 'You didn't introduce us, remember?'

Tara breathed out slowly. Of course she hadn't, but it was still a relief to know she was safe. Last night she'd dreamt that the cottage had been kitted out with hidden cameras, Big Brother style, all ready to transmit her every hapless move on national TV. Hardly conducive to a restful night's sleep.

'Watch yourself out there.' Tara nodded in the direction of the frosty landscape. 'The High Street's like a skating rink. Don't want to break a leg.'

* * *

289

It didn't take her long to change her mind about this.

'So. You and Dominic Cross-Calvert. What's this all about?' said Daisy with deceptive innocence as she poured the coffee.

Tara's stomach squirmed. When Daisy had invited her upstairs to the flat she'd expected a bit of gentle teasing about last night's mystery caller. But not this. Certainly not this. And Daisy wasn't guessing either. She *knew*.

Ever the coward, Tara prevaricated. 'What's what all about?'

'That's what I'm asking you. He was there at the cottage last night.'

Feebly, Tara said, 'Dominic? Who says?'

'Josh told me.'

Bloody bastard Josh. Tara hoped he slipped on the icy road and broke both legs *and* both arms. Shattering the bones to smithereens, preferably.

'Josh doesn't know Dominic.' By this time clinging to microscopic straws, Tara adopted the mentality of a three-year-old stubbornly refusing to admit she'd broken something expensive. Daisy might, just *might*, be bluffing.

'He described your visitor. Light-brown hair. Medium height. Medium build. Averagely good-looking.'

'That describes a million men.' Privately Tara was outraged – Dominic was *very* good-looking. Lots handsomer than sodding Josh, that was for sure.

Daisy, pouring milk into the coffees and sliding Tara's cup across the table, said, 'Oh, and he was wearing a socking great Rolex. On his right wrist.'

Bum.

'OK.' Tara held up her hands in defeat. 'OK, it was Dominic.'

'I know it was Dominic! How long have you been seeing him?'

'Three weeks. Please don't be cross, don't shout at me,' Tara begged in desperation.

'You twit, of course I'm not going to shout.' Daisy was shaking her head as she tipped sugar into her coffee, but she looked as if she wished she could be cross. 'But you have to tell me everything. I want to know why.'

No mention of on-the-spot dismissal. Despite everything, Tara was glad Daisy knew. It had been horrible having to keep Dominic a secret from her best friend.

'He got in touch, begging to see me.' The words came tumbling out in a long-overdue rush. 'He said he hadn't been able to stop thinking about me on his honeymoon, that he still loved me and his marriage was a disaster . . . and he actually comes to *see* me,' Tara emphasised again, desperate for Daisy to understand just how much this meant to her. 'He drives all the way down from Berkshire and he doesn't *mind* that it's a hundred-and-twenty-mile round trip, because as far as he's concerned, I'm worth it!'

Daisy sat back on her chair, understanding only too well. Flattery would get you anywhere and Tara had been through a rough time recently on the man front. Her self-confidence had taken a series of knocks. And now here was Dominic, back in her life again, promising her the world and flattering her for all he was worth.

'Why is his marriage such a disaster?'

'Annabel won't sleep with him,' Tara explained. 'She's frigid. He's married someone who refuses to have sex with him. Can you *imagine* how that makes him feel?'

Like a big old liar, probably, thought Daisy. What was the betting that Dominic had told Tara his wife didn't understand him?

'So he's having sex with you instead.'

'No! No, he isn't.' Vehemently, Tara shook her head. 'We just see each other, that's all. We meet up and talk. No sex, I promise.'

'Although he'd like there to be.'

'Well . . . yes. But I won't do it.'

'Why not?'

'Because he's married!'

'But why is he still with Annabel?' Daisy ruthlessly persisted. 'If he knows it's such a total disaster and it's never going to work out, why doesn't Dominic leave her?'

Tara rubbed her forehead as if it ached. It felt as if it *should* ache.

'He feels he has to give the marriage a chance. He can't give up this quickly. But he knows it's hopeless really. He'll leave her sooner or later. It's more to spare Annabel's feelings, you see. She's actually incredibly neurotic. Dominic's worried about the effect it could have on her . . . I mean, they've only been married a few weeks, she'd feel so humiliated – oh, it's you.'

The door was flung open and Josh burst into the flat. Both legs disappointingly intact. Out of breath from his run, he rubbed his hands together, grinned and said, 'Oops, am I interrupting?'

'Yes,' said Daisy, 'but it's OK.'

'Hello, Judas.' Tara attempted a scowl but it didn't quite come off.

'Don't be bitter. These things are better out in the open. Bloody hell, it's cold out there.' Gleefully, he danced up to Tara and pressed his icy hands against the back of her neck, making her squeal. 'Anyway, if you're having an affair with a married man, that's when you need your friends around to pummel some sense into you.'

'I'm not *having* an affair,' Tara wailed, squirming off her chair and out of reach. 'He comes to see me, that's all. We talk. Swear to God, I'm not sleeping with Dominic.'

'Blimey. Poor sod.' Josh looked amused. 'So what's in it for him, then?'

'He loves me!' Tara couldn't help it; she experienced a burst of pride. Being loved, unconditionally, was a heady experience. Not to mention a pretty novel one.

Daisy's heart sank. She checked her watch. 'I've got a meeting. We'll talk later. But you mustn't sleep with Dominic – you know that, don't you? Promise me you won't.'

'God, you're so boring. OK, I promise,' said Josh with a broad grin.

'It isn't funny.' Ignoring him, Daisy gazed at Tara. 'He's married,' she said steadily. 'Don't ever forget that.'

Tara bit back the urge to remind Daisy, crossly, that of course she knew that, hadn't she just explained that the whole reason she hadn't slept with Dominic was *because* he was married?

But of course it was an extra-sensitive subject where Daisy was concerned. She'd been married to Steven Standish, who had been unfaithful to her. It couldn't be much fun being cheated on.

'I won't forget,' Tara dutifully promised.

'Right, let's get back to work.' Reaching across the kitchen table, Daisy gave her hand a reassuring squeeze. 'I can't stop you seeing Dominic, but I'm telling you now, you deserve better.'

Tara smiled. What a completely ridiculous thing to say. She'd spent the last goodness knows how many years deserving better. Didn't Daisy realise that Dominic was *it*?

Josh, heading for the shower, was peeling off layers of sweatshirts.

'Are we still on for five o'clock? Or am I public enemy number one?' He winked at Tara from the bathroom doorway.

293

She couldn't be cross with him. That was the other thing about Daisy, Tara thought; it was OK for her, she had Josh now. They were happy together. She'd forgotten how lonely and horrible it felt to be minus a man. Plus, in a few months, she could be moving to Florida with him.

Anyway, a free driving lesson was a free driving lesson.

Tara gave Josh a look to indicate that she had forgiven him, but only just. For good measure she threw in a sigh.

'I'll see you at five.'

She did see Josh at five o'clock but didn't get her lesson. By midday the first fat snowflakes had come cartwheeling out of a slate-grey sky. By three o'clock the lawns were iced in a layer of white. By five, the snow was a good couple of inches deep. Now, huge snowflakes were hurtling past the window harder and faster than ever. The roads weren't undrivable but they were slippy enough to scare the wits out of Tara.

'If it's any comfort,' said Josh, buying her a drink in the hotel bar as a consolation prize, 'I can't play golf either.'

'Hmm.' Was that meant to cheer her up? If the snow kept up at this rate, she wouldn't be able to see Dominic for days.

'Look, I'm sorry about this morning,' Josh went on, not sounding sorry at all. 'I didn't know I'd be letting the cat out of the bag. I just notice watches, and which hand they're being worn on. When you're a golf pro, you can't help it.'

'OK. Don't keep on about it.' Tara rolled her eyes. 'Daisy knows now.'

'She's just worried about you. Doesn't want you making a big twit of yourself and ending up suicidal.'

Josh was clearly the chap to come to if you were in need of sympathy and understanding.

'Actually,' said Tara, 'I wasn't planning on doing that.'

'Oh, come on, it's pretty dodgy. Admit it,' Josh scoffed, 'he's not going to leave his wife for you.'

'Thanks a lot.'

'Don't get in a strop, I'm not saying you're too ugly for him. We both know you're not. But let's face it, financially you can't compete. He's married to someone with a lot of dosh.'

'The money doesn't matter to Dominic. It means nothing to him.' Tara's cheeks were flaming but she kept her voice low so that Rocky, behind the bar, wouldn't overhear.

'Sweetheart, that's what he tells you.'

'Is that why you're with Daisy? She's not exactly hard up. Steven married her for her money,' Tara shot back. 'Maybe you're doing the same thing.' Below the belt, maybe. But he'd started it.

'Touché.' Josh acknowledged the jibe with a brief smile. 'No, that's not why I came here. But I can't prove that. You just have to make up your own mind. Or rather, Daisy does.'

Tara didn't think for one minute that he was after Daisy's money, but she was damned if she was going to say so.

'I don't know you well enough to judge something like that. And you don't know Dominic. Nor does Daisy. So neither of you has any right to judge him.'

'We just don't want to see you get hurt,' said Josh as she downed her Bacardi in one go.

'So you keep saying. But I *do* know Dominic. And I know he wouldn't do anything to hurt me.' Tara slid down from her bar stool. 'I have to go.'

'Oh dear. On a scale of one to ten, how much do you hate me?'

'Thirty-eight.'

Josh grinned. 'You deserve better. Married men are nothing but grief.'

Trying to loathe him but failing to manage it, Tara said drily, 'Single ones too.'

Chapter 37

Next morning, Josh built a snowman on the lawn in front of the hotel. Daisy smuggled Hector's second-best kilt out of his wardrobe and they fastened it round the snowman's ample waist. An empty champagne bottle was clasped lovingly to the snowman's chest and beneath his other arm was tucked a set of bagpipes fashioned from a tartan cushion and the wooden spindles from a broken chair back.

'I say, who is that fine figure of a man? What a handsome fellow,' Hector declared when he stepped out of the hotel. Roaring with laughter, he beckoned to Paula. 'And such a relief to know we'll be leaving the place in safe hands!'

Paula, smothered in ivory floor-length fake fur, adjusted her dark glasses and checked that the car waiting for them had been fully defrosted.

'What I want to know,' said Hector, 'is what he's wearing under that kilt.'

'Mmm.' Paula thrust her hands into her coat pockets; if the car's engine had been running for a full ten minutes, it would be warm inside.

'I just hope nobody's stuck a carrot under there.' Hector chuckled. 'Especially not a small *wizened* carrot.'

'Who's it supposed to be?' said Paula.

'Ha! Who does it look like?'

'A snowman.' She sensed she was missing something here. 'In a kilt.'

'It's me, woman! That's me in the MacLean tartan! Of course, you couldn't know,' Hector instantly excused her. 'You haven't seen me let loose with my bagpipes.'

Paula shivered dramatically. Her feet were icy already. According to the weather forecast it was seven below zero, the coldest cold snap for years.

'Hector, the Cardews are expecting us at midday.'

Josiah Cardew and his wife lived in Cheltenham. Josiah, a theatre director, was hosting a lunch for them and they were staying the night at the Cardew's Georgian mansion.

'Let me guess. Josh,' said Hector as Daisy joined them on the steps.

'Who else?' Daisy was quietly marvelling at Paula's ability to shiver in the manner of a Broadway star whilst wearing more clothes than an Eskimo.

'But you were the one who stole my kilt.'

'Hector,' Paula hinted. Heavily.

'Yes. We must go. Will you be OK?' He kissed Daisy on the cheek.

'Oh, I'm sure we'll manage. We've got the boss keeping an eye on us.' Daisy nodded at the jaunty, kilted snowman. 'Just so long as he doesn't melt.'

Maggie bumped into Barney in the village shop. Flushed with success, he told her how the cottage was progressing. It was Sunday morning and thanks to the snow, far fewer bargain hunters than usual had turned out for the car boot sale in Castle Combe, enabling him to snap up all manner of brilliant buys.

'I was there at eight,' he explained happily, 'and back by ten. I picked up a toaster for fifty pence, a fantastic sheepskin rug

298

for a pound, a tricycle for Freddie *and* a set of garden chairs for a fiver.' Checking his watch he added, 'I should just have time to finish the skirting boards in the bathroom before starting my shift.'

Barney had come in to buy a bottle of white spirit and a packet of J-cloths. Maggie envied him his busy-ness. Her own empty day stretched interminably ahead as only Sundays could. She was here to pick up a newspaper, a packet of sage and onion Paxo and, oh God, just *something* to cheer her up.

Wine, maybe. Or a bar of chocolate. Valpolicella versus a giant block of Fruit & Nut.

Sod it, she'd have both.

They left the shop together and made their way up the snowy street. As Maggie reached her front door, she slipped on a patch of ice, felt her legs shoot out from beneath her and landed with a bump on the pavement.

Luckily, her thick padded anorak cushioned her bottom. As landings went, it was more undignified than painful.

'Shit!' Maggie wailed as Barney reached down to her.

'Are you hurt?'

'Bloody bottle's broken.' She gazed in dismay at the carrier bag, leaking blood-red Valpolicella into the snow. And she'd managed to drench her *Sunday Times*. Behind her, she heard the sound of a vehicle making its way down the street.

'Come on,' said Barney, 'up you get.' But the spilt wine only made the snow more slippery, and his first attempt to help Maggie to her feet was unsuccessful. As she tried again, this time going for the ultra elegant all fours approach, the gleaming black Land Rover Discovery approached them. Hector's Land Rover Discovery, Maggie realised, unable to stop herself glancing through the green-tinted windscreen at Hector behind the wheel with Paula Penhaligon beside him.

Hector braked and buzzed down the window. 'Are you hurt?'

'No. I'm fine.' Grabbing Barney's outstretched arms with both hands, Maggie hauled herself upright.

'Is that *blood*?' Hector was looking alarmed.

'Red wine. I'm OK.' As she brushed crimson-stained snow from the seat of her anorak, Maggie couldn't help noticing that Paula was wearing a white fur coat and matching hat like something out of *Dr Zhivago*. And expensive-looking sunglasses like nothing out of *Dr Zhivago*.

'Darling, we don't want to be late,' said Paula.

'I'm OK. I just slipped in the snow.' With all her heart Maggie willed him to drive off.

Before the driver's window slid shut once more, she clearly heard Paula drawl, 'Good grief, is the woman *drunk*?'

Barney helped her into the cottage, then went out to retrieve her carrier bag.

'You don't have to do this,' Maggie protested as he returned with the bag. 'I'm not an invalid, you know.'

But she was touched by the gesture. Barney really was a sweet boy. As she watched him fish out the Paxo and chocolate, Maggie thought what a shame it was that he already had a girlfriend. He'd be perfect for Tara.

'I know you aren't an invalid. But it's not very nice, falling over in the street.' Carefully wrapping up the bag containing the sodden newspaper and broken glass, he dropped it into Maggie's kitchen bin. 'Still, it was nice of Hector to stop, wasn't it?'

'Mm.' Maggie would far rather he hadn't. As she peeled off her heavy anorak she saw that the wine had soaked into the bit where her bottom had landed. Fabulous, something else really bulky to wash by hand and struggle to dry.

'He's great,' Barney went on with enthusiasm. 'I mean, he owns the hotel but he still insists I call him Hector. It's just so brilliant working somewhere like that, it makes all the difference.'

Joining him in the kitchen, Maggie peeled the sodden wrapper off the bar of chocolate and ran it under the tap. She offered Barney a piece.

'Thanks, I love fruit and nut. And she's really friendly too,' Barney added. 'Paula Penhaligon. She gave me a signed photo yesterday for my mum. I thought that was so nice of her. They make a great couple, don't they?'

Presumably not Paula and his mum.

Maggie did her best to ignore the stab of pain in her chest. OK, not pain. Jealousy.

'Oh yes. A great couple.'

'He's mad about her, you can tell. Well, they're mad about each other. Imagine, they might end up getting married, wouldn't that be *fantastic*?'

By this time fighting the urge to batter Barney over the head with her family-sized bar of chocolate, Maggie smiled blandly and said, 'Wouldn't it just?'

Barney left to finish painting his skirting boards and Maggie got on with the task of stuffing Madge. Plucked, Madge had weighed four pounds, which meant that after one hour and forty minutes of lying on her back with her legs in the air on a tray of roasting vegetables, she would be cooked to perfection.

Taking her out of the oven at midday, Maggie realised she'd lost her appetite. Madge looked delicious – glistening and golden and enticingly plump, but Maggie hadn't the heart to eat her. Tara would have to do the honours later when she came off duty.

Honourable though it would have been to pretend that the reason she couldn't bring herself to eat Madge was because she knew her – had known her, in fact, since she was a chick

– the truth of the matter was she couldn't stop thinking about the humiliating moment when Hector had driven by while she was scrabbling on all fours on the pavement.

When Hector had driven by with bloody Paula Penhaligon in the passenger seat.

'You really mustn't be embarrassed about falling over,' Barney had said kindly as he was leaving. 'It's slippery out there. I fell over in the snow at the car boot sale this morning.'

Yes, but not in front of the person who pays you to have sex with them, Maggie had been sorely tempted to retort. Or at least *had* paid you to have sex with them up until they'd found themself someone who'd do it for free. Someone infinitely superior at that. Even if, according to Tara, Paula Penhaligon had had a face-lift.

Madge sat in the roasting tin, growing cold. Never mind; Tara would demolish a breast and a leg when she came home. Minus an appetite, and with no wine to console her, Maggie ate a couple of chunks of fruit and nut in an unsuccessful attempt to cheer herself up. She flicked through the TV channels, found nothing remotely watchable and washed her bulky anorak in the sink that was three times too small for the task and imagined the fun Hector and Paula would be having now. Gorgeous, convivial lunch with friends. Bit too much to drink. You wouldn't believe what we saw as we were leaving Colworth this morning – one of the villagers, pissed as a parrot, sprawled across the pavement. Darling, can you *believe* it?

The doorbell went as Maggie was struggling to wring out the sodden anorak. Wiping her hands on her jeans, she answered the door and found a pink-cheeked, jolly-looking couple stamping their cold feet on the doorstep.

'Oh hello, we're staying at the hotel and we saw some of your lovely cushions in the gift shop down the road.' The girl beamed at Maggie. 'I know it's Sunday but the woman in the shop gave us one of your business cards and said she was sure you wouldn't mind us calling round. You see, we'd just love it if you could make us a cushion.'

'No problem.' Their shiny matching wedding rings and the way they were holding hands told Maggie all she needed to know. 'Come on in.'

Their names were Valerie and Alan and, yes, they were on their honeymoon. Together they had already decided on the design they wanted. Val and Al, Together Forever, in curly lettering, the names entwined within a pink heart on a lilac background with butterflies and smaller hearts bordering the cushion like a Victorian Valentine's card.

'Together forever,' Valerie echoed, her eyes shining with joy as she squeezed her husband's pudgy hand. 'That's going to be us, isn't it, darling?'

Until you get divorced, thought Maggie.

Alan, nodding vigorously, said, 'We'll be able to show this cushion to our grandchildren.'

'That's a lovely idea.' Maggie forced a warm smile. Maybe they *would* be happy. Some marriages did last, didn't they? In their thick fleeces, matching knitted sweaters and unromantic hiking boots they seemed besotted enough with each other to make a go of it.

'We're only here for another couple of days,' Valerie explained. 'I'd better give you our address so you can post it on to us.'

'Don't worry, I can do it straightaway.' Seeing as she had an evening stretching emptily ahead, Maggie said, 'Drop by again tomorrow. I'll have it finished for you by then.'

'Really? Oh, that's so *kind* of you!' Valerie's eyes lit up and she wriggled on the sofa with delight. 'We'll be able to show our families when we get home. This cushion will be our memento of the happiest week of our lives.'

As soon as they'd left, Maggie set to work on the cushion. She felt guilty at having inwardly scoffed at their gullibility. Just because her own life was a miserable mess and she couldn't imagine ever being like that herself, she mustn't automatically assume every couple would eventually split up. It wasn't Val and Al's fault that she'd fallen for a man completely beyond her reach.

The truth was, she was jealous of them and their impossibly rosy view of the future.

A tear slid down Maggie's cheek, plopping onto her wrist as she knelt on the carpet cutting out pink silk hearts.

Pathetic. Furious with herself, she brushed the tears away.

Chapter 38

'I said, scrub my back.' Daisy wriggled in the bath, splashing water and bubbles over the side as Josh's hand playfully slid round her ribcage. 'That's not my back.'

'Anatomy never was my strong point. Good job I'm not a surgeon.' He grinned, glancing out of the bathroom window as his mobile began to ring in the living room. 'Starting to snow again. Hang on, let me get that.'

Daisy heard him answer the phone, greeting one of his friends with enthusiasm. As she lazily soaped her arms, Josh came back into the bathroom.

'. . . what? You're where? God, that sounds fantastic. Hang on a sec, she's right here, I'll just ask her. It's Tom Pride,' Josh explained. 'He's in Austria. There's a group of them sharing a chalet in Kitzbühel and one of the other chaps has just been flown home with a smashed-up pelvis. Which is bad news for him, of course, but on the other hand . . .'

'Good news for you?' guessed Daisy. 'Or do we call it a lucky break? Don't tell me, they've got room for one more and they thought of you.' Was that a niggle there in her voice? A little niggly edge?

'Wrong, actually. The other chap's wife flew home with him. They've got room for *two* more and they thought of *us*.' Luckily Josh hadn't taken offence. Sitting on the edge of the bath he added persuasively, 'So what d'you think? Can Vince take care of things here? It's only for a week. Tom says the chalet's fantastic, the skiing's superb, they've got a great crowd out there – and it's mixed, not just a horrible gang of boys, drinking nonstop and throwing up in the jacuzzi. Come on,' he leaned teasingly over the bath, 'we'd have a brilliant time. You could do with a break.'

Daisy knew she could, but she also knew she wasn't going to get one. Vince had already booked a couple of days off in the coming week in order to attend a cousin's wedding in Glasgow.

'I can't.' Regretfully, she shook her head. 'Vince is away.' It was a shame, but it couldn't be helped.

Josh's face fell. 'OK. Never mind. Tom,' he returned to the phone, 'sorry, mate, we can't make it. Daisy has to work.' A pause while he listened to Tom's voice at the other end, then, 'No, no. Thanks, but I wouldn't feel . . . it wouldn't be . . .'

'You could still go,' suggested Daisy, squeezing bubbles out of the sponge.

Josh looked at her. Hesitating. She knew how much he wanted to.

'Hang on again, Tom. Daisy's saying something.' Moving the phone away from his mouth he said, 'Wouldn't you mind?'

'Of course I wouldn't mind. You love skiing. You can't do much here while the weather's like this.' She waved at the snow tumbling like confetti past the window. 'No golf, no driving lessons with Tara. And it's only for a week.'

She meant it. The moment of nigglyness earlier had been a Pavlovian reaction, a hangover from her marriage. Even when she had thought she'd trusted Steven, some inner instinct had never *entirely* trusted him. But that had been then. Things were

different now. This was Josh, whom she knew she could trust.
He was the polar opposite of Steven.

'You know what you are?' Grinning, Josh leaned precariously
over the bath and gave her a huge kiss. 'Gorgeous.' The phone
in his hand began to cackle and he spoke into it. 'No, not you,
you're an ugly sod. I'm talking to this beautiful *gem* of a girl
here . . . *yes*, I mean Daisy. And she's naked. In the bath. Oh
yes. And right now I don't know if I even want to leave her here
on her own, but she says that if I want to come out to Kitzbühel,
it's fine by her.'

Ten minutes later, it was all fixed. Josh had got himself on
a flight from Bristol to Salzburg, leaving tomorrow lunchtime.
By late afternoon he'd arrive at Chalet Sattelkopf in the heart
of Kitzbühel, for seven days of hard skiing and seven nights of
wild après-ski.

'You're sure you don't mind?' Josh brought a bottle of white
burgundy into the bathroom and handed Daisy a glass.

'I really don't mind.' She smiled, because he was looking like
a young boy on Christmas morning.

'You don't have to worry about me. I won't be getting up to
any funny business.'

'I know that too.' She did. It was a great feeling.

'Unless Jennifer Lopez is there,' Josh amended. 'Obviously.'

'Oh well, goes without saying.' Daisy nodded to show she
understood. He had a bit of a thing for Jennifer Lopez.

'And will you miss me?' Josh sat on the edge of the bath.

'Every minute of every hour of every day.' Tilting her face
up for a kiss, she added, 'Well, unless Jude Law books into the
hotel. Obviously.'

Josh nodded. 'I can understand that. I'd sleep with Jude Law
in a flash. But otherwise I can trust you to behave – what are
you doing?'

'I think you need a bath.' Daisy hooked her wet fingers round the front of his rugby shirt and pulled him towards her.

'Right now?'

She tugged harder. 'Right now.'

'Still in my clothes?'

'You can take them off if you want – oops,' Daisy murmured happily as he landed in the water with a splash. 'Too late.'

Tara was having the most fantastic dream. She was sitting in the hot seat on *Who Wants To Be A Millionaire?* with Chris Tarrant giving her his teasing, twinkly-eyed smile. She was up to five hundred thousand pounds with only one more question to go and the audience was agog.

Chris mopped imaginary sweat from his brow. 'So. Tara. Are you ready for this?'

'I'm ready, Chris.'

'For one million pounds,' he announced, skilfully building the drama. 'Here we go. In Greek mythology . . .'

Tara listened to the question, a smile spreading over her face as he read out the four possible answers. She knew nothing about Greek mythology, but luckily she knew a girl who did.

Even more luckily, she still had her phone-a-friend lifeline left.

'Of course she'll be one of your phone-a-friends,' Dominic had assured her yesterday. 'She'd love to help you. Anything you want to know about literature, art or Greek mythology, Annabel's the one to ask. She's a real expert.'

Hooray for that.

'I'd like to phone a friend, please,' Tara told Chris Tarrant. 'Annabel Cross-Calvert.'

As they waited for the phone to be picked up, Tara fantasised about winning the million. Gosh, it was going to be so brilliant . . . if she had that much money, Dominic might even leave Annabel and come and live with her instead. Not at the cottage, of course, oh no. She'd buy a much grander place than that . . .

'Annabel? Hi, this is Chris Tarrant, I've got your friend Tara here and she needs your help.' Pausing, he added significantly, 'To get her up from half a million to *one million pounds*.'

The audience buzzed with excitement.

'Oh gosh, that's *fantastic*.' Annabel sounded thrilled too. 'I just hope I know the answer! Right, go ahead, fire away!'

As Tara read out the question, her heart began to thump with anticipation. Annabel was an expert, she knew *everything* about Greek mythology. She was seconds away from an astounding triumph.

When she'd finished listing the four possible answers, there was a moment of silence.

Then Annabel said, 'Well, I'm so glad you rang, Tara, because I *do* know the right answer.'

Tara waited.

Chris Tarrant was waiting too.

The studio audience collectively held their breath.

The man whose job it was to send sparkly confetti tumbling from the ceiling prepared to pull the sparkly confetti switch.

'But guess what?' Annabel went on gaily. 'I'm not going to tell you what it is!'

Gasps all round.

'You can't do that! It's not *fair*,' Tara wailed. 'Quick, just *tell* me the answer!'

'Nope. Don't want to. 'Bye, Tara.' And Annabel put the phone down with ten seconds still left to go on the clock.

Totally humiliated, Tara hung her head and said, 'I'll take the money, Chris.'

Oh well, half a million, that was still pretty good, wasn't it? Dominic might still leave Annabel . . .

But now it was Chris Tarrant's turn to be unfriendly. That lovely twinkly smile of his had gone.

'I'm sorry, Tara, but the rules have been broken. You named Annabel as a friend and she clearly *wasn't* a friend. That means you're disqualified from the competition. I'm afraid you leave here with nothing at all.'

Tara woke up with a start, just as the studio audience were beginning to boo her and chant, 'Off, off, *off*.'

What a completely horrible dream. And how *mean* of Annabel. No wonder Dominic didn't love her if she was capable of such a spiteful act. Who in the world would want to stay married to a bitch like that?

Untangling herself from the duvet, Tara climbed out of bed. It was ten to eight. Dominic had said he'd give her a ring at eight o'clock and she didn't want to speak to him before she'd brushed her teeth.

Chapter 39

The big thaw arrived two days later. The following morning, so did Dev Tyzack.

Daisy, discussing deliveries with the head chef at the entrance to the restaurant, heard a familiar voice behind her and felt her heart leap like a salmon. Turning, she saw Dev leaning against the reception desk. He spoke again, making Pam laugh. In fact, making Pam laugh *skittishly*, Daisy couldn't help noticing. What was he doing here? Even more to the point, what were those suitcases doing at his feet?

Feeling as if she was walking through treacle, Daisy excused herself and headed down the corridor towards him.

Hearing her high heels tapping across the polished floor, Dev looked over his shoulder and shot her a dry smile.

'What's going on?' She indicated the three – *three* – Samsonite cases. 'Have you run away from home?' Was he actually booking in? *Why?* Why would he be doing this?

'I have.' He sounded amused. 'And you would too, if you could see my home.'

Pam, who was a huge devotee of bad news, gushed, '*Poor* Mr Tyzack, he was just telling me all about it. The pipes froze, then one of them burst in the night up in the loft. The whole house is wrecked, can you imagine? Curtains, carpets, furniture – everything's completely ruined!'

311

If Kate Adie ever needed a stand-in, Pam was the woman for the job.

'But on the plus side,' Dev kept a straight face, 'Clarissa has learned to swim.'

'How could your pipes freeze?' Daisy was puzzled. He had central heating, surely?

'I've been away for a few days. My cleaning woman was keeping an eye on the house for me. She's a frugal lady,' Dev explained with a crooked smile, 'who couldn't bear the thought of all that heat going to waste while I wasn't there to appreciate it. So she turned the heating off. When we got home at four o'clock this morning, we found water pouring through the ceiling. It was like Niagara Falls. Every room in the house is affected. There's nowhere to sit down because all the chairs and beds and sofas are waterlogged. The electricity's off. The wallpaper's hanging off the walls. I had to get out,' he concluded with a shrug. 'So I rang here.'

'Lucky we weren't fully booked,' Pam trilled.

Lucky? Daisy wasn't so sure. Having Dev Tyzack around was going to be a distraction she didn't need right now.

Anyway, who was this person he had arrived home with at four o'clock this morning? He had definitely said *we*.

'How long will you be here?'

'Until the house is sorted out.' Hazarding a guess, Dev raked his fingers through his hair and said, 'Three or four weeks?'

Booking into a four-star hotel for a month was going to cost him a fortune.

'Couldn't you stay with a friend?' Innocently Daisy added, 'Wouldn't Jennifer put you up?'

'Jennifer's my secretary. She isn't my girlfriend. She shares a flat with three other girls in Bath.'

'My mistake,' said Daisy. 'She acted as if she was your

girlfriend. And you were taking her out to dinner.' Maybe she insisted on being fed before she slept with him.

'Dinner can be just dinner, you know.' Dev's dark eyes glittered. 'Jennifer put in a lot of extra work, helping me set up the conference. It was my way of thanking her.'

'Why move into this hotel, anyway?' Daisy persisted. 'I'd have thought it would be simpler to stay in Bath.'

'Daisy, will you stop interrogating the poor man? Heavens,' Pam exclaimed with a little laugh, 'anyone would think you were trying to put him off!'

Dev, unperturbed, replied calmly, 'I like this hotel. It's handy for the M4. And you allow dogs, which most places don't.'

The phone rang on the reception desk. Pam answered it.

'Who was looking after Clarissa while you were away?' Daisy couldn't help it; she knew she sounded like a disapproving social worker. 'Putting her into kennels isn't going to do her any good, you know. She'll just think you're dumping her back in another dogs' home, she'll feel abandoned all over again.'

'I didn't abandon Clarissa. I took her with me. When I said *we* came home and found the house flooded, I was talking about me and Clarissa.'

Daisy's stomach squirmed with a mixture of relief and horror. Horror because she didn't want to feel relieved that 'the other woman' was only Clarissa. And now Dev was smiling at her in that unnerving way of his, as if he knew exactly what had been going through—

'Daisy, it's for you!' Pam held out the phone she had been giggling into for the last thirty seconds. 'It's Josh, ringing from Kitzbühel.'

Pam adored Josh, who teased and flirted with her unmercifully.

'Daisy's boyfriend,' she cosily confided to Dev. 'He's away

at the moment, skiing in Austria. *Such* a card! He just told me he's dangling by one arm from the ski-lift over a huge abyss.'

'It's not true,' Josh told Daisy. 'Actually, I'm sitting on the terrace of a restaurant at the top of a mountain, surrounded by stunning actresses and supermodels.'

'Plenty of food left for you, then,' said Daisy.

'It's not funny. They keep pestering me, telling me how gorgeous I am. I hope you're missing me,' he said. 'Jennifer, stop it, behave yourself . . . Giselle, tell Jennifer to leave me alone.'

'I'm missing you terribly. But I'm going to have to go,' said Daisy. 'Jude's just turned up.'

At this, predictably, Pam's head swivelled round to the doors.

'You go and see to him,' Josh urged. 'In a purely hotel-manageressy kind of way, naturally. I'll speak to you again later.'

'Happy skiing.' Daisy nodded at Pam as she put the phone down. 'It's OK, he's safe. The rescue helicopter came along and winched him up just before he fell.'

'That Josh, he's a one. He has me in stitches.' Pam beamed up at Dev. 'They make such a lovely couple – yes, Mrs Kendall, how can I help you?'

As Pam moved away to deal with Mrs Kendall, one of the porters came down the stairs.

'James.' Daisy beckoned him over. 'Could you take Mr Tyzack's bags and show him up to his room. Room . . . ?'

'Six,' said Dev. 'But I've got Clarissa waiting out in the car.'

Clarissa! She'd forgotten all about Clarissa. Daisy, her eyes lighting up, said, 'It's going to be so great having her here!'

'Nice to know one of us is popular.' With a brief smile, Dev slipped James some money to take his bags upstairs. 'Want to come and say hello?'

Clarissa threw herself against the passenger window, scrabbling at it with her paws and yelping with delight when she saw them. Panting with excitement, she leapt up into Daisy's arms and licked her face.

'So this is how it feels to be Robbie Williams.' Daisy hugged her number one fan in return. 'Hello, sweetheart, guess what, you're coming to stay here for a while, isn't that brilliant?'

'Better than that,' said Dev. 'The carpets are dry. There isn't water dripping out of the TV. And your Bonios won't float across the kitchen floor.' As he spoke, he retrieved Clarissa's sodden blanket from the boot, along with her basket. 'I'm going to have to dry these out.'

'We'll put them in the boiler room. They'll be dry in no time.' Tilting her head, Daisy let Clarissa lick the blusher off her other cheek. May as well be symmetrical about it.

'Just a thought,' said Dev as they picked their way back through the melting snow. 'But if you're not doing anything tonight, and Josh is away, would you like to have dinner with me?'

Daisy concentrated on stepping round a slushy puddle. Her pulse began to race like a teenager's. Would she *like* to have dinner with Dev Tyzack? Probably. OK, *yes*.

Then again, would it be wise to have dinner with him? Not really. Actually, no, it wouldn't. Not wise at all.

I'm with Josh now. I decided it was for the best, and it *is*.

Dammit, vowing to steer clear of men was all very well, but not quite so easy when they moved into your hotel and started having nerve-wracking effects on your body.

'Just dinner.' Dev sounded amused. 'No hidden agenda, all above board. Nothing . . . *lewd*, if that's what's bothering you.'

Feeling irrationally insulted, Daisy climbed the steps to the hotel, lowered Clarissa to the floor and watched her bound off in search of more friendly faces to greet and strip free of make-up.

'Tart,' Dev fondly observed.

'I can't have dinner with you,' said Daisy.

He shook his head. 'I didn't mean you were a tart. I was talking about Clarissa.'

Honestly, did he think she was completely thick?

'I know, but I still can't have dinner with you. I'm doing something else tonight.'

'Oh.' Dev looked as if he didn't believe her. 'OK. Maybe some other time.'

Daisy flashed her professional don't-bank-on-it smile. 'Maybe.'

'That man thinks he's so irresistible,' Tara scoffed that evening when Daisy told her about the dinner invitation. She had her own reasons for not liking Dev Tyzack. 'He really thinks he's God's gift to women. Well, I'm glad you turned him down. Jolly well serves him right. When did this bottle get empty? Daisy, this bottle's empty, quick, emergency, dial nine nine nine.'

'OK, OK, don't panic.' Daisy, back from the fridge with a fresh bottle, uncorked it and sloshed more wine into their glasses. This was nice, being holed up in her apartment with Tara, the two of them just drinking and relaxing and generally getting everything off their respective chests. 'I mean, I'm happy with Josh. You know how happy I am with Josh.'

'I do. I do know that.' Tara nodded vigorously, clonking her glass against her teeth. 'Josh is brilliant.' Even if he did have a big mouth.

'And I don't fancy Dev Tyzack one bit,' Daisy lied, 'but the thing is, he seems to think I *do* fancy him, which is really annoying, especially now that he's going to be here for the next God knows how many weeks. And I have to be polite to him because he's a guest, but he just seems to think this proves how much I secretly like him and I honestly *don't* . . . Am I rambling?'

'No, no, no . . . well, yes.' Beaming, Tara dangled her bare feet over the arm of the sofa and waggled her toes along to Coldplay on the CD player. 'But that's OK, because you let me ramble on about Dominic. 'S'only fair. Did I tell you about the dream I had the other night?'

'Twice,' said Daisy. 'Did I tell you he's not going to leave his wife?'

'About fifty times.' Tara was no longer letting it bother her. 'So many times you wouldn't believe it. But I don't care, because you think you're right and I know you're wrong . . . oops, spilt a bit, lucky it's not red. Anyway, how's Hector getting on with Ms Nip'n'Tuck?'

'Oh, he's enjoying himself.' Daisy wrinkled her nose. 'She's a bit of a townie. You won't sleep with him, will you?'

More wine sloshed down Tara's chin. *'Hector?'*

'Dominic!'

Phew.

'I've already said I won't.' Tara made it sound like a grumble but inwardly she was hugging her latest idea to herself. She wasn't agreeing for Daisy's sake, but for her own. It had come to her in a flash that afternoon. If she and Dominic were secretly seeing each other *and* sleeping together, where was the incentive for him to leave Annabel? If, on the other hand, she refused to have sex with him *until* he had left his wife – well, wasn't that more likely to propel him in the right direction? Tara-wards?

'And keep your options open.' Daisy wagged a finger at her.

317

'If you meet someone nice in the meantime – someone *single* and nice – don't refuse to consider them because of Dominic. Give them a chance. You never know, they might be just what you're looking for.'

'My shoes, that's what I'm looking for.' It was eleven o'clock; time to make her way home. Peering over the edge of the sofa, Tara just managed to stop herself rolling onto the floor. 'Damn, head's gone spinny. Time to go home.'

'You can stay.' Daisy, feeling pretty spinny herself, waved an arm in the general direction of the spare bedroom.

'No, no. Thanks, but I'd rather . . . you know.' Tara managed to grab her shoes. Dominic might phone and she couldn't bear to miss him.

Jumping up, Daisy careered towards the door. 'I'll walk with you.'

'I'm fine.'

'I want to,' Daisy insisted. 'It's slippery out there. You can't go on your own.'

'But if you walk me back, *you'll* have to walk home on your own.' Tara frowned. It was like one of those brain-teasing puzzles with the fox, the chicken and the cabbage having to pair up in a rowing boat to reach the island. Even sober, it had never been something she could work out.

'Got it! I'll walk with you as far as the hotel gates. Then you can go home and I'll come back here and that'll be completely fair.'

Tara was lost in admiration. Daisy had always been so intelligent. Even if she was currently sitting on the floor struggling to put her wellies on the wrong feet.

'God, these things are uncomfortable.' Daisy waddled like a duck over to the door, then turned and put a finger unsteadily to her lips. 'Now sshh, no giggling. And we'll sneak out the back way – don't want any of the guests thinking we're pissed.'

'Your feet are on the wrong way round,' sniggered Tara.

'What?' Daisy peered down at them. 'Nope. Toes at the front, ankles at the back. My feet have always been like that.'

Chapter 40

Oh yes, fresh air, that was better! Lovely cold fresh air, just what she needed to clear her spinning head. Having hugged Tara goodnight – by some miracle neither of them had fallen over – Daisy watched her make her way down the High Street before turning and heading back up the drive. Well, *wavering* back up the drive.

The thaw was still in full flow. Entranced by the sound of snow plopping from the trees, Daisy veered to the right – God, had these wellies shrunk or something? They were playing havoc with her toes – and lifted her face up to the falling dollops of snow.

Plop.

'Plop,' Daisy echoed.

Plop . . . plop.

'Plop . . . plop.' She felt gloriously at one with nature. She was actually having a conversation with the snow.

Plop.

'Plop,' Daisy solemnly replied. Crikey, never mind Dennis the Dachshund, this was like starring in *Bill And Ben The Flowerpot Men.*

Plop, plop, plop, plop . . .

'Flobalobalobalob,' Daisy conversed – quite authentically, she felt – until it dawned on her that the plops had become

320

more rhythmic. And crunchy. In fact less like snow falling
from branches and more like . . . feet trudging through melting snow.

A voice behind her said, 'Daisy, is that you?'

Oh, fuck.

Mortified, Daisy swung round. Her tone accusing, she said,
'What are *you* doing out here?' Oh God, please don't let him
have overheard her talking to the snow.

'Walking Clarissa.' Dev – dammit – was sounding faintly
amused. 'Didn't want her weeing in my room.'

'Where is she?'

He pointed. 'Over there. Investigating your snowman.'

'That's no snowman, that's my dad.' Through the darkness,
Daisy was just about able to make out the melting outline of
Hector, by this time minus his kilt. As his waist had decreased
in girth it had dropped to the ground, though the champagne
bottle – typically – was still clutched to his chest.

Now, as she paid more attention, she detected a small, four-
legged figure snuffling around the incredible shrinking snowman.

But Daisy had other, more important things on her mind.

'Those tights *did* cost ten pounds,' she blurted out. 'I wasn't
trying to rip off your secretary.'

Well, it had been bothering her.

'OK, fine, I believe you.' Was Dev Tyzack laughing at her?
'Your feet look funny, by the way.'

'For heaven's sake, why does everyone keep going on about
my feet?'

'Probably because you've got your wellies on the wrong way
round.' He moved closer, putting out an arm to steady Daisy as
she lifted one leg into the air to examine it. 'Come on, I'll walk
you back. What are you doing out here anyway?'

'Making sure Tara got home safely. We had a couple of drinks.'

'More than a couple, by the look of you.'

He was holding her as if she were some doddery old lady who needed help crossing the road. Irritably shaking him off, Daisy said, 'I can *manage*,' and promptly crashed into a tree trunk.

'Don't be so obstinate.' Clearly entertained, Dev hauled her back on track. 'Is Tara as bad as you?'

'Bad? Me? What did I ever do wrong? Tara's badder than I am, she's lots badder than me. Even though it isn't her fault.' Daisy wagged an accusing finger at him.

'Really?' He nodded, humouring her. 'So whose fault would it be?'

'Dominic Cross-Calvert. Your oh-so wonderful friend. He's big trouble.' As she said it, Daisy dimly wondered whether she should be telling him this. Then again, Dev wasn't really such a great friend of Dominic's, was he? And why shouldn't he know what he'd been up to?

'Trouble in what way?'

'He's pestering Tara. He comes over to see her all the time. For crying out loud, he's only been married a couple of months and he won't leave her alone!'

Their footsteps crunched through the melting snow as they made their way up the drive.

Dev, tilting his head to one side, said, 'Why doesn't Tara tell him she doesn't want to see him?'

God, and this was a supposedly intelligent man.

'Because she *does* want to!' Daisy spread her arms in despair. 'Look, Tara's been through a rough patch lately. She completely lost confidence in herself. And then Dominic came along, laying on the charm, telling her how much he loves her and that he should never have married Annabel . . . and she's flattered! She believes him!'

'Oh, please. How old is this girl? Tara's not sixteen any more, she's hardly Little Miss Innocent. We *both* know she isn't innocent.' Dev shook his head pityingly at Daisy. 'Let's face it, your friend Tara is the original good-time girl. I bet she's loving every minute of it.'

'He's leading her on!' Outraged, Daisy stopped dead in her tracks and yanked her arm free of Dev's grasp. 'I don't believe this. *He's* a complete bastard, and you're *still* blaming Tara!'

They were only forty feet away from the hotel entrance now, and Dev lowered his voice.

'Maybe she's a complete bitch. Have you even stopped to consider that?'

'How dare you!' Daisy was too furious to care about how loud she was being. 'You have a *bloody* nerve.'

'OK, tell me something. If you met a man who'd only been married a few weeks, would you jump into bed with him?'

'Of course I wouldn't!'

'Sure about that?'

'I just wouldn't. But it's not the same thing.'

'It's exactly the same thing. Your friend is a tart and you're trying to excuse her,' Dev shot back. 'You're blaming *every-one* else—'

'Not *everyone* else.'

'Oh yes you are. You're even trying to blame me, and I can't for the life of me understand why.'

Daisy's eyes blazed. She longed to punch him. It wasn't fair, trying to argue with someone when you were drunk and they were stone-cold sober. And when they were disturbingly attractive and you had your wellies on the wrong feet.

'So why don't you tell me?' Dev persisted. 'Explain why you

think it's anything to do with me. And while we're at it, tell me why you made it so obvious earlier that you didn't want me staying here at your hotel.'

Shit. Shit. Shit, shit.

'You're a man. You're Dominic's friend. If you got married, you probably wouldn't think twice about cheating on your wife.' Gesturing wildly, Daisy began to sway. 'You think Tara's a tart but you don't actually think Dominic's done anything wrong—' Whoops, she'd nearly gone over again. Dev's arms shot out in the nick of time, grabbing her none too gently by the elbows and pulling her towards him.

'I still don't understand. Are you saying you don't want me here because I'm a friend of Dominic's? Or because I make you feel uncomfortable?'

Daisy could feel his warm breath on her face. He was teasing her, but not in a friendly way.

'I . . . I . . .' Pathetically, she couldn't think of a smart reply.

'Is that it?' Dev's dark eyes bored into hers as if he could see right through to her useless empty brain. 'Are you bothered about me being here because you feel I'm a threat?'

Daisy swallowed. God, this was awful. 'A threat to who? Tara?' She felt herself begin to tremble.

'I'm not talking about Tara and you know it.' The corners of Dev's mouth curled upwards and she prayed he couldn't hear the frantic galloping of her heart. 'I meant you and this new boyfriend of yours. I could kiss you right now.' He paused, his gaze never wavering from her face. 'So. Do you want me to?'

Silence. Utter silence. Apart from her stupid heart, of course, still carrying on like a herd of stampeding wildebeest.

'No thanks,' Daisy managed to blurt out.

Dev smiled. 'Are you sure?'

God, he was so convinced he was irresistible!

'Quite sure.' Daisy freed her arms and took a step back. 'In fact, I'm *this* sure.' Raising her right hand, she slapped him hard across the face. 'So thanks for the offer, but I'm really not interested. To be honest, I'd prefer it if you'd just *leave me alone.*'

Barney raced down the steps and across the drive. Right, that was it, he'd seen and heard enough.

'Hey, you, you heard her! Leave her alone,' he bellowed at the dark-haired man whose face Daisy had just slapped. For the last few minutes he'd been watching the two of them through the glass-panelled entrance door. Now he rushed up to Daisy – who was clearly in a state of shock – and said urgently, 'It's OK, you're safe. Just get inside, I'll deal with this.'

'Barney, it's—' Daisy began, but he wasn't going to let her try to play the matter down – he'd seen the slap and heard the louder parts of their heated argument. Pumped up with adrenaline, Barney swung her round and pushed her firmly in the direction of the main doors. As she obediently set off, he noticed a small dog racing across the grass to join her. When Daisy bent to greet the dog, Barney also noticed that her feet were looking distinctly odd. Then he turned back to glare at the dark-haired stranger from whose clutches he had rescued Daisy.

'This is private property. If you don't go, I'll call the police.' For a wild moment, he wondered if he would have to punch him.

The stranger smiled and raised his hands. 'Look, I didn't jump out of a hedge and attack her. Daisy and I do know each other.'

'You were holding her against her will. She didn't seem very happy in your company,' Barney persisted, though his heart sank a fraction. 'I think the best thing you can do is just leave.'

'The trouble is, I'm a guest here. My name's Dev Tyzack,' said the man. 'I'm staying in Room Six.'

This time Barney's heart plummeted. This was his first week of night shifts and he'd never seen the man before. But then why should that make any difference?

'I don't care if you're a guest. You were upsetting Daisy and I won't let that happen.' Barney's voice began to tremble with emotion.

'Very commendable. I'm sure she'll be impressed by your loyalty. Who knows,' Dev Tyzack's tone was light, almost teasing, 'this could mean promotion.'

'Do you seriously think that's why I came out here?' A fresh wave of irritation bubbled up inside Barney. How dare this man make fun of him? 'I'd do anything in the world for Daisy,' he went on defiantly. 'I don't *want* promotion, that has nothing to do with it. She's a wonderful person and she saved my life.'

Dev smiled slightly at this overblown announcement, made with such passion and sincerity. It was touching, in a way, that Daisy was able to inspire such devotion in her staff. The young porter standing before him in his white shirt, dark blue waistcoat and smartly pressed trousers looked too fresh and wholesome to even know what drugs were, but Dev guessed that this was what the boy was talking about. Either drink or drugs had blighted his life, until Daisy had helped him through it, given him a second chance.

Curious, Dev said, 'How did she do that?'

Barney hesitated, shivering in the cold night air. Then he told him.

Chapter 41

Oooh, headache. Daisy, at her desk the next morning, scrabbled in the back of the drawers until she found a half-empty packet of paracetamols. Washing a couple down with water, she massaged her temples. The pain was self-inflicted and she was just going to have to ignore it. Vince was off on leave and she had a job to be getting on with, a hotel to run.

Not to mention last night's embarrassing altercation to put behind her. God, that had been awful, she couldn't believe she'd got herself into such a mess. And short of murdering Dev Tyzack in his bed – or preferably hiring a friendly hit-man to do the honours – she didn't have a clue how she was going to get herself out of it.

Oh well, it could have been worse. At least she hadn't kissed him.

Ten minutes later there was a knock at the door. Daisy hastily hid the bacon sandwich she hadn't been able to face eating in her desk drawer, in case it was Brenda returning to take away her empty plate. Brenda could nag for England on the importance of eating a good breakfast.

'Who is it?' Daisy hurriedly switched on her computer in order to look busy and prayed it wouldn't be Dev.

The door swung open a couple of inches, then stopped. Daisy sat and stared at it. She heard something crackle, followed by the sound of determined scratching. As she watched, a small hairy paw slid through the gap, nudging the door open by another inch or two.

More crackling at floor level, then Clarissa's nose appeared. An enthusiastic waggle of her body and she made it through the door, a cellophane-wrapped bouquet of deep pink roses clamped between her teeth.

Having dragged the bouquet halfway across the carpet, Clarissa promptly abandoned the flowers and jumped up onto Daisy's lap. Scooping the dog into her arms, Daisy went to retrieve them. With her free hand, she ripped open the envelope stapled to the cellophane.

It said: My owner is very, *very* sorry. He's waiting outside the door, if you want to see him. If you don't want to, he'll leave the hotel. I know he's an idiot, but I'd be grateful if you'd speak to him. I like it here. Love, Clarissa.

Impressed, Daisy looked at Clarissa. 'Your handwriting is excellent.'

'Woof.' Clearly in agreement, Clarissa licked her ear.

'I want you to know, I'm only doing this for you.'

Clarissa wagged her stumpy tail in appreciation.

'Better come in then,' said Daisy, loudly enough to be heard outside the office.

Well, she hated awkward situations. At least this way they could get it over with. They were both adults, after all. And he had said sorry first.

God, hope he doesn't have a bright red hand-shaped slap mark on his face.

Dev walked into the office and at the sight of him Daisy's stomach promptly launched into a Mexican wave. He was wearing a pale grey cashmere sweater, faded jeans and snow-encrusted Timberlands. His dark hair flopped over his forehead and his face was . . . well, his face. He was definitely far too handsome. Nobody, Daisy thought, should be allowed to be that attractive. More to the point, nobody should be silly enough to get involved with someone that attractive.

'I really am sorry.' Dev came straight to the point. 'I should never have said what I said last night.'

'And I suppose I shouldn't have slapped you.' To Daisy's relief, there was no bright red slap mark.

'It was justified.' He shook his head, clearly intent on taking all the blame – which was fine by her. 'I was out of order.'

'Where did you get the flowers?' Daisy was intrigued despite herself. It was only nine thirty and this definitely wasn't the kind of bouquet you picked up at the nearest petrol station for a fiver.

'They were delivered this morning for Paula Penhaligon. I intercepted them, decided you deserved them more than she did.'

'Oh my God, you didn't!'

'Of course not.' Dev smiled at the look of horror on her face. 'If you must know, I drove into Bath at eight o'clock this morning.'

Daisy was delighted by this gesture – all the way into Bath just for flowers! – until she realised he'd probably had to check on his house anyway.

'By the way, just to get something straight.' She felt compelled to say it. 'Tara didn't jump into bed with Dominic. She hasn't slept with him, and she isn't going to.' Fingers crossed.

'Fine. Whatever. I don't want any more arguments.' Dev held up his hands. 'I especially don't want to argue about Tara and Dominic. Your porter,' he went on, changing the subject, 'the one who came to your rescue last night. It's good to have someone like that working for you.'

'His name's Barney.'

Dev nodded. 'He did well. For a moment there I thought he was going to punch me.'

Daisy, who had been perched on the edge of her desk holding Clarissa, began to relax. Bending down, she put Clarissa on the floor.

'Barney's great. All the guests love him.'

'He told me about your husband,' said Dev.

Oh.

Not that it was a secret or anything, but Daisy still tensed.

'And?' As she said it, she felt the heat rushing to her cheeks. Clarissa, meanwhile, was snuffling feverishly, desperate to get at whatever was inside the desk drawer.

'I'm so sorry. I didn't know.' Dev shook his head. 'I had no idea.'

'Why should you?' Daisy hated it when this happened. The sympathy thing. She felt such a fraud.

'You might have mentioned it.'

'Why?' She raised her eyebrows. 'Does it make a difference? Would you have been nicer to me?'

'I suppose I would.' He smiled slightly at this admission.

'Don't worry about it.' Daisy heaved a sigh. 'We were only technically married. I'd already asked Steven for a divorce when he was killed. So I'm not the grieving tragic widow, if that's what you were thinking. But Barney doesn't know, I didn't want to dash his illusions.' She grimaced. 'It didn't seem right to tell him that the man whose kidney he got was actually a lying, no-good tosspot.'

Bacon sandwich, it smelt like a bacon sandwich. Clarissa frantically pawed at the desk drawer.

Daisy bent down, slid the drawer open, took out the bacon sandwich and gave it to Clarissa.

'Got any mushrooms and fried tomatoes in there?' Amused, Dev peered over the desk at the opened drawer. Then more seriously, said, 'What was he like?'

'Steven? Very confident, totally sure of himself, extremely good-looking. Out for whatever he could get,' Daisy went on, wondering if the description was ringing any bells with Dev. 'Charming. Deceitful. Oh, and he was unfaithful too.'

'Why—'

'Because he was a bastard!'

'I meant why did you marry him?' said Dev.

'Oh well, that's simple. I fell for it, didn't I? The charm, the looks, the whole package. He was very persuasive.' Daisy twisted her fingers together. 'I even believed him when he told me he had a rare kind of cancer that could only be treated in America. He said he needed twenty thousand pounds to pay for it and I *still* believed him, but there you go, that's what it's like being married to a con artist.' She spread her hands in disgust. 'It never even occurred to me that the real reason he wanted twenty grand was so he could take his new girlfriend off to America for a really nice holiday.'

Daisy stopped. That was quite a little outburst. Why hadn't she just let Dev carry on thinking she'd been happily married?

But she hadn't been able to do that. For some reason she needed him to know the truth. Even if it did make her look stupid.

'Well, I'm sorry. Either way, you've been through a lot. And I'm also sorry about last night.' Dev waited, then said, 'Look, I'd like to do something to make up for that. I've been sent a couple of tickets . . .' Pulling them from his back pocket, he handed them over.

'For Saturday. At Twickenham. The Six Nations Cup,' Daisy read aloud. 'VIP seats.'

331

'England are going for the Grand Slam,' Dev explained. 'And there's a big dinner afterwards, I've been invited to that too. Should be good fun. So what d'you think? Could you take the day off?' He was smiling, looking pleased with himself.

Daisy knew exactly what she thought. Rugby. Played outside, in the bitter cold. Lots of mud-covered men grunting and hurling themselves at each other, chasing an oval ball that couldn't even bounce in a straight line. *And* frozen feet, she reminded herself. Sitting on a hard plastic seat surrounded by roaring supporters all singing and swaying out of time with each other.

For heaven's sake, was Dev Tyzack mad? She'd rather drill out her own wisdom teeth with a Black & Decker.

'Thanks.' Daisy smiled, to spare his feelings. 'But I don't think so. Josh might not be very happy—'

'It's a friendly invitation, that's all. Josh doesn't have to worry about my motives. I just thought you might enjoy it.'

Oh yes, about as much as being forced to eat sheep's eye-balls.

'I may have to work anyway,' lied Daisy. 'You'd better take someone else. But thanks for the flowers.'

Clarissa, sensing that it was time to leave, barked twice and trotted over to Dev.

He nodded. 'And Clarissa says thanks for the bacon sandwich.'

Daisy had been right about one thing. When Josh phoned and she told him about Dev's invitation, he wasn't happy. In fact, she'd never known him so furious.

'He invited you *where*?' Josh bawled down the phone from Kitzbühel. 'Bloody hell, I don't believe this! To the Six Nations Cup *and* to the official dinner afterwards? What did you *say* to him?'

'I turned him down.' Pleased with herself, Daisy thought how lovely it was to have a clear conscience. Smugly she added, 'I said I didn't think you'd be very happy about it.'

'Damn right I'm not happy,' roared Josh. 'Good grief, are you out of your mind? Those VIP tickets are like gold dust, you're missing out on the chance of a lifetime. I can't *believe* you were stupid enough to turn him down. Go and find Dev Tyzack this minute,' he ordered, 'and tell him you've changed your mind.'

'I will not,' Daisy said crossly. 'I'm not interested in a boring old rugby game. Anyway, I told him he'd have to invite someone else.'

'On Saturday? We'll be back by then.' Josh brightened. 'If I dress up in a long wig and a short skirt and promise to have sex with him, d'you think he'd take me?'

Chapter 42

Liza, the new young waitress, gave Tara a nudge. 'That chap over by the bar keeps looking over.'

Liza and Tara, having finished their shifts, had called into the Hollybush Inn for an after-work drink. Since Liza was pretty, Tara said, 'He probably fancies you.'

'It's not me he's looking at.'

As Tara glanced over her shoulder, the boy up at the bar gave her a friendly grin. He was in his mid-twenties, drinking Guinness and wearing a suit that looked as if it didn't get out much.

'I saw him earlier, up at the hotel. He's with the wedding anniversary party.'

'He's nice. And he's definitely interested in you.' Liza giggled and drained her half of lager. 'Go on, finish yours and look thirsty. With a bit of luck he'll buy us a drink.'

With a meaningful smirk in the direction of the bar, Liza made a strategic withdrawal to the loo, leaving Tara sitting alone at the table by the window feeling stupid. She was twenty-seven, far too old to be playing these ridiculous games. Anyway, the only male she was interested in was Dominic – who had phoned this morning to tell her he wouldn't be able to see her before Thursday at the earliest.

The boy levered himself off the bar and came over, indicating the spare chair at their table with a twinkle in his eyes.

'Hi. Mind if I join you? I saw you up at the hotel. Andy,' he introduced himself as he pulled out the chair and sat down.

'Tara,' said Tara, smiling despite herself at his confidence. 'I saw you too. And you're still supposed to be at the hotel with the rest of your party. You're playing truant.'

He pulled a conspiratorial face and offered her a cigarette. 'You noticed. I had to get out of there. My mother re-married a year ago. This is their first wedding anniversary. I'm surrounded by fifty of my stepfather's boring friends and relatives. I tell you, it's a fate worse than death. Not my idea of fun. I didn't think they'd miss me if I absconded for an hour. Can I get you a drink? And your friend, of course . . .'

Liza had been gone for ages. Tara wondered what she was doing in the loo. Filing and re-painting her nails, perhaps. Tidying her handbag. Knitting herself a nice sweater.

Nevertheless, Tara was grateful. She had found herself warming to Andy, who was funny and friendly and actually rather attractive in a subversive, naughty-boy-dressed-up-in-a-smart-suit kind of way.

For the first time in a long time, there was a squirly feeling in her stomach that hadn't been put there by Dominic.

'You've been ages,' said Tara, when Liza finally returned from the loo.

'And now I'm off. You'll be OK here, won't you? Ooh, is this for me? Thanks.' Beaming at Andy, she knocked back the half of lager he'd bought her in one impressive go. 'Have fun.'

'I think she was being discreet,' Andy confided when Liza had jauntily exited the pub. 'Leaving us alone together, giving us time to get to know each other better.' He paused. 'Not that I need it. I already know I like you.'

335

It was an awfully long time, too, since anyone other than Dominic had said that to her. Tara attempted to look nonchalant, as if she heard it at least fifty times a day.

'Only because being here is better than being stuck at your mother's boring party.'

'Speaking of which, I suppose I should be heading back.' Andy regretfully checked his watch. 'They'll have my guts for garters if I miss the speeches. Look, are you doing anything later?'

'Um, not really. Why?' Tara made it sound as though she had no idea why he'd be asking such a question.

'Another couple of hours at the hotel, then I'm out of there. I thought maybe we could go somewhere. If you'd like to,' he added with a teasing grin. 'Just dinner or something. Of course you might not want to at all. Don't worry, you can turn me down. I'm used to rejection, I can handle it.'

Not a drink. *Dinner,* Tara thought joyfully. And he was clearly lying about the rejection; she doubted he'd ever been turned down in his life.

'Sounds fun.' She smiled at him, thinking that it *would* be fun. What the hell, it was better than sitting at home knowing Dominic wasn't going to ring. And Daisy would be overjoyed.

'Great. Meet me back here at six o'clock.' Andy finished his Guinness and rose to his feet. 'I think I can cope now, knowing I've got something to look forward to. And get yourself dressed up,' he added with a flirtatious grin. 'We'll be going somewhere decent to eat.'

Daisy, heading across reception, was stopped by a pretty girl in a fuchsia-pink dress.

'I'm sorry, I know I'm horribly late but could you point me in the direction of the Grenfells' party?'

'Down the corridor, second door on the left. It started at one o'clock,' Daisy added, because it was now almost five.

'I was held up at work. Harry Grenfell's my godfather,' the girl explained. 'But I missed his wedding last year so I had to promise I'd get down here today, so he could introduce me to his wife and her family. I've got some serious catching up to do.'

'Oh well, you'll have plenty of time for that.' Daisy's tone was reassuring. 'The party's expected to carry on all evening.' As the girl started along the corridor, she called after her, 'Have fun!'

'Just thought you might like to know,' said Tara, sounding incredibly smug, 'that you told me to keep my options open, and I am. I've been asked out by someone really really nice and I'm seeing him tonight.'

Daisy, answering the phone out in reception where she was covering for Pam during her coffee break, breathed an inward sigh of relief. Someone really really nice? So not Dominic then. This was just the kind of lucky break Tara so badly needed.

'What's his name?'

'Andy. I met him in the Hollybush this afternoon. He's taking me out to dinner,' Tara boasted. 'Somewhere smart. *And* he's not married.'

'I like him already.' As she idly wound the curly telephone flex around her fingers, a flash of fuchsia-pink caught Daisy's eye. Looking up, she saw Harry Grenfell's pretty goddaughter slip out of the ballroom with one of the other party guests, a lithe boy of around her own age wearing a dark grey suit.

As Daisy watched, they headed on up the corridor. The boy veered left into the gents' loo, leaving the girl outside. Moments later, having ascertained that the coast was clear, his arm shot out like an ant-eater's tongue and pulled the girl inside.

337

'I'm going to wear my red dress,' Tara said happily, 'and my red shoes with the silver bits on the sides.'

'Perfect,' said Daisy. 'You'll have a brilliant time. Look, I've got to go.'

It wasn't the first time this had happened. Bursting into the gents, she found the girl in the pink dress locked in a passionate embrace with her fellow guest. Luckily not too passionate – they hadn't had time to get that far.

'Ahem,' coughed Daisy, shaking her head in mock disapproval as they guiltily sprang apart.

'God, sorry!' The girl stifled a giggle. 'We just got a bit, you know . . .'

'Carried away.' Daisy nodded to show she understood. 'I know. But maybe not here. We don't want to go giving our older guests heart attacks.'

'Sorry.' The boy's eyes twinkled at her.

'No harm done.' Holding the door open for them, Daisy winked at the girl. 'Nice to see you're getting on so well with your godfather's relatives.'

The girl replied with a grin, 'Oh yes, we're really hitting it off.'

'What are your plans for the evening? Tara coming over again?' Hector hoped Daisy wasn't working too hard; when he'd knocked at the door and walked into her office, she'd looked jumpy and on edge for a split second before realising it was only him.

'No. I'm going to have a long bath and an alcohol-free night.' Daisy sat back in her revolving chair and stretched her aching back. 'Complete rest, just me and the TV and a packet of chocolate Hobnobs. Anyway, Tara's otherwise engaged this evening, off out on a hot date with some new man. And she's wearing her red shoes with the silver bits on the sides, so he must be pretty special.'

Leaving Daisy to it, Hector made his way through to the bar. Paula was upstairs in her suite preparing for dinner with her visiting agent. Since her arrival at the hotel, the suddenness and intensity of the relationship between them had caught Hector by surprise, but it was evidently par for the course with Paula. She was in show business, and this was the way things happened in show business circles. You met someone, you slept with them, you declared that you were in love with them . . . it was a whirlwind of exaggeration and high drama that bore little relation to real life. Paula hadn't mentioned marriage yet, but he suspected it was already on her mind. Which was ridiculous, of course, but flattering.

Hector, famously easygoing, was taking none of it too seriously. Paula was an enchanting lady and he enjoyed her company a lot, but he wasn't about to be rushed into anything legally binding. Equally, spending so much time together – both in bed and out of it – was fine, but a bit of breathing space was equally welcome. The news that she would be spending the evening with her agent had actually come as something of a relief. He'd planned to head over to the golf club to catch up with all the golfing news he'd missed out on since Paula's arrival at the hotel. Then again . . .

'Hello?' Behind the bar, Rocky waved a hand in front of Hector's face. 'Can you hear me? D'you want a drink? Hector, you're miles away. Blink once for coffee, twice for Scotch.'

Hector blinked – accidentally – and saw Rocky reaching for the cafetière. It was no good, he'd been doing his best to put Daisy's words out of his mind, but they were still there. Like an ex-smoker catching a waft of unexpectedly delicious just-lit cigarette smoke or a dieter rummaging in the glove compartment and discovering a Snickers Bar they hadn't known was there.

Tara had a hot date tonight. Tara had a hot date tonight.

Which meant the coast would be clear at Maggie's cottage. Tara was out of the way. If he wanted to see Maggie, he could.

And now that he had finally allowed himself to think about it, Hector discovered that he did want to see Maggie again. Very much indeed.

A cup of coffee was pushed in front of him. He frowned at it.

'Who's that for?'

'You,' said Rocky.

'I didn't ask for it.'

'Yes you did.' But Rocky moved the coffee away with a sigh. 'So you want a Scotch instead.'

'Bloody stupid question,' said Hector, checking his watch. 'Of course I want a Scotch.'

Chapter 43

Tara couldn't believe it. Six forty-five and *still* no sign of Andy. For the last fifty minutes she'd been stuck here in the Hollybush and he hadn't turned up.

It wasn't just unbelievable – he'd seemed so *keen* earlier – it was unbelievably, toe-curlingly humiliating. She knew practically everyone in the pub and they in turn all knew exactly what she was doing there, done up to the nines in her scarlet satin dress and looking as out of place amongst the casual jeans and sweaters as a Fabergé egg in a chicken shed.

'Another one?' Gerry, the landlord, indicated her empty Coke glass with a sympathetic smile. At least the smile was sympathetic now, but Tara just knew he and all the other regulars would be having a jolly good laugh at her expense the moment she was out of earshot.

Nearly ten to seven. The excuses she'd been conjuring up on Andy's behalf were beginning to sound increasingly feeble. OK, so he was stuck at a family party, the speeches could be dragging on longer than he'd expected. Or he might have been cornered by some ancient old relative reminiscing endlessly about the war. Or his mother had begged – literally *begged* – him to stay longer, just until seven o'clock . . .

Oh God, Gerry was still waiting for her to say something.

'No thanks.' Tara shook her head; the three Cokes she'd

already drunk were straining against her ribcage and it wouldn't do to start burping like a navvy. 'I'll just give it five more minutes, then—'

'Call it a day.' Gerry nodded wisely. 'Poor old thing, you don't have much luck with men, do you?'

Tara forced a tight smile. Kind of you to point it out, Gerry. Swivelling round in her chair she glanced out of the window – for about the five hundredth time – and conjured up a fantasy of Andy screeching to a halt in his car, rushing into the pub and shouting with relief: 'Oh, thank God you're still here! My family wouldn't let me leave, I was going *frantic*, I was so scared you wouldn't wait for me . . .'

In fact there was a car emerging from the hotel car park and making its way towards them now. Craning forward, fingernails curling into the palms of her hands, Tara mentally willed the dark blue Renault to slow down as it reached the pub.

Outside, dusk was falling but it was still possible to see who was driving the car as it raced past without stopping. It was also possible to see the person in the passenger seat.

There was Andy, laughing and smoking, with a pretty girl in a pink dress sitting next to him, her right hand affectionately splayed across his left thigh.

He didn't so much as glance in the direction of the pub. The next moment the car was out of sight.

Tara wondered if it was physically possible to feel more snubbed than this.

Gerry, his eyes lighting up with recognition, exclaimed, 'Bloody hell! That was him, wasn't it?'

Loudly enough to inform the rest of the pub *and* anyone who may have been loitering in the toilets.

'Thank you for that,' sighed Tara, reaching for her bag.

'Looks like he's had a better offer.' Gerry gave her shoulder a clumsy, consoling pat. 'Oh well, that's life, isn't it, love? Another one bites the dust.'

How long had it been since he'd last seen Maggie? Quite a while, Hector thought as he threaded his way along the overgrown path to the right of the churchyard that led from the hotel's grounds to the cottages bordering the High Street. Since he'd seen her properly, at least. Not sprawled in an ungainly heap on the pavement outside her house. That didn't count.

God, it was disgusting out here in the woods. Cold and wet and with snow dripping gently from the branches overhead. And so *dark*. If he tripped over a tree root, he could break a hip and be left lying out here all night.

What was he doing anyway? He hadn't even phoned first to check that she was there. He knew Tara was out for the evening, but Maggie might be too. And why was he suddenly so desperate to see her? It wasn't the prospect of sex that was propelling him through the dank icy blackness. He didn't want to sleep with Maggie, he just needed, for some reason, to talk to her. Then again, maybe it was his conscience that was troubling him. She slept with him and in return he paid her, albeit discreetly, in cash. He knew she needed the money.

As he neared the cottage, Hector heaved a sigh of relief. Through the trees, he could see that the lights were on. Maggie was at home. Alone. He hadn't come all this way in sodden shoes and with snow dripping down the back of his neck for nothing.

With an ease borne of long practice, his hands deftly lifted the latch on the back gate. Soundlessly, he made his way along the narrow path bisecting her back garden. The blue and white gingham kitchen curtains were closed but the light shone through them, and he was able to make out the shadowy movement of Maggie in her kitchen.

Should he be feeling guilty? Was he in some way being unfaithful to Paula?

Too bad.

Experiencing a frisson of pleasure, Hector raised his cold hand and knocked gently on the back door.

Silence. Abrupt cessation of movement within the kitchen.

It occurred to him that Maggie might be terrified he was a burglar.

Finally he heard her voice, taut with fear.

'Who is it? Who's there?'

Smiling to himself, he said reassuringly, 'Maggie, it's OK, it's me.' Then, just in case it had been so long she'd forgotten him completely, he added, 'Hector.'

This time there was no hesitation. He heard the sound of the key being turned in the lock, then the back door was flung open.

Tara stood there, her hands caked in dough and with flour in her hair.

'Hector, this is so weird, we were just talking about you! But what on earth are you *doing* here?'

Never mind me, thought Hector. What are *you* doing here?

Thinking on his feet, he turned and gestured into the darkness. 'I was just taking a walk and I came across a family of badgers. Five of them, playing in the clearing back there. I didn't even realise there was a sett in the woods. It was such a fantastic sight I just had to share it with somebody, and then I saw the lights on in your cottage.'

'Badgers,' Tara exclaimed, her eyes lighting up as she reached for a tea towel and wiped her doughy hands. 'I love badgers! Maggie, did you hear that? We *must* see them!'

Hector could barely bring himself to look at Maggie, who was hovering behind Tara wearing a stunned expression and a pair of oven mitts. Plus jeans and an old sweater, of course. On automatic pilot, she turned and opened the oven door, removing a baking tray of oddly shaped scones.

'Come on, let's go!' Tara was eagerly tugging on the boots she'd dragged out of the coat cupboard. 'We don't want to miss this!'

They were unable to find the family of badgers. Frustratingly, Tara refused to give up. For twenty minutes the three of them trudged around the clearing, investigated the overgrown paths leading off it and searched for the nonexistent sett.

Sorry, Hector mouthed at Maggie as Tara forged intrepidly ahead.

Maggie shrugged, then abruptly stopped in her tracks.

'Tara, this is hopeless, you're crashing around like a baby elephant. The badgers are probably terrified and my feet are frozen solid. Hector and I are going back inside.'

'Feeble,' Tara shouted over her shoulder. 'I'm not giving up yet.'

Inside, the kitchen was blissfully warm. The baked scones smelt wonderful.

'I'm sorry.' Hector shook his head. 'I should have phoned first. Daisy told me Tara was out.'

'She came back.' Keeping her voice low, Maggie peeled off her anorak and ruffled snow out of her hair. Since Tara could be back at any second, she came straight to the point. 'I'm free tomorrow. Would one o'clock suit you?'

Hector immediately felt tawdry. What kind of a situation had he got himself into here? Maggie was assuming he was visiting her purely for the sex. Then again, maybe she was desperate for money. God, it was all such a mess.

'I didn't . . . I just called round because I wanted to . . . um, no, sorry.' Hector shook his head. 'I can't manage that. Maybe the day after. Look, can I give you a ring?'

'Fine.' Maggie abruptly turned away, busying herself with the tray of cooling scones, and he had a sudden overwhelming urge to put his arms round her waist and kiss the back of her neck.

Luckily he didn't.

'Brrrrr, you're right, it's *bloody* cold out there.' Tara burst into the kitchen stamping her feet and rubbing her hands together. Kicking the back door shut, she dragged off her coat and boots and grinned at Hector. 'OK, now brace yourself, because I never thought I'd hear myself saying these words . . .'

Hector braced himself with foreboding; he had no idea what this was likely to be about.

'Hector.' Tara assumed an air of importance. 'Would you care to try one of my *homemade scones*?'

Hector, his tone grave, replied, 'Tara, I'd love to. But Daisy mentioned something about you having a date tonight. Shouldn't you be getting yourself, um, ready?'

Smart move. This way, it didn't look as if he'd called round thinking that Tara would be out of the house.

'My date stood me up.' Unaware that she still had flour in her hair, Tara struck an aren't-I-irresistible pose. 'Can you believe it? The whole of the Hollybush knows, there's no point trying to pretend it didn't happen. So that's it,' she went on, pushing up the sleeves of her khaki sweatshirt and indicating the debris of rolling pin, mixing bowls, spatulas, wooden spoons and bags of flour strewn across the work surfaces. 'I decided it was high time I did something more constructive with my life.'

'She came home,' Maggie interjected with a dry smile, 'and announced that seeing as her life was a disaster and all men are pigs, she may as well learn how to make scones.'

Tara gazed with almost maternal pride at the baking tray

upon which they sat, peculiarly shaped but lovable nonetheless.

'Maggie showed me how. They've even got sultanas in. I'm going to do a Victoria sponge next.'

Hector ate the scone she offered him, remembering to praise it with as much enthusiasm as he recalled being obliged to praise the rock-solid jam tarts Daisy had brought home from her first cookery lesson at the age of ten.

'Fantastic. Perfect. The best scone I've ever had.' Even if it was shaped like Africa. 'So what were you saying about me before I knocked on your door?'

'Oh that! I was just telling Maggie about you and Paula Penhaligon, how well it's going between the two of you.' Tara beamed up at him. 'It's so exciting, we're all thrilled to bits about it.'

Hector resisted the urge to clamp his hand over her big blabbery mouth. 'Well, I'm not—'

'Oh, don't go all coy on us now! You aren't fooling anyone,' Tara blithely chattered on. 'In fact, I probably shouldn't tell you this, but the kitchen staff are taking bets that by Christmas we'll have ourselves a new Lady of the Manor.'

Chapter 44

'Poor old Tara, getting stood up last night.' Christopher tut-tutted over the shop counter as he took Daisy's money.

'Not just stood up,' Colin eagerly chimed in. 'There she was waiting to meet him in the pub and he drove straight past, *woomph*, just like that, with another girl in his car.'

News travelled super-fast in Colworth. Daisy had already heard about the no-show from Hector, who had – bizarrely – persuaded Tara and Maggie to join him on a badger hunt last night. The next moment, as the shop door clanged open behind her, she was struck by a horrible thought.

'The girl in the car with him. Um, what was she like?'

'Not the foggiest.' Colin shrugged and nodded a greeting at Barney, who had just come into the shop. 'Barney might know.'

'I might know what?' Barney, in turn, smiled hello at Daisy.

'The fellow who was supposed to be seeing Tara yesterday until he found himself a better offer. Daisy wants to know what the girl looked like.'

'Liza was talking about it in the staff room last night.' Barney frowned, trying to remember. 'Long blonde hair, I think. And she was wearing a pink dress. Why?'

Oops. The frisky couple she'd turfed out of the gents' loo.

'Oh, no reason.' Hastily Daisy changed the subject. 'So how's the cottage?'

Barney had moved out of the hotel two days earlier. At the mention of it, his eyes lit up with pleasure. 'Brilliant. We're just so happy with it.'

'His girlfriend moved in yesterday,' Christopher announced. 'So sweet. Love's young dream.' Playfully he nudged Colin. 'Remember when we used to be like that?'

'I'd love you to meet her.' Eagerly, Barney turned to Daisy. 'If you're not doing anything, you could come over now.'

With Vince back from Scotland, Daisy was taking a few hours off. She had come out in her jeans and one of Josh's rugby shirts to stock up on Rolos and Parma Violets and glossy magazines.

'I'm free. That sounds great,' she told Barney because it clearly meant so much to him.

Beaming, Barney paid for his milk and sliced loaf. 'Fantastic. You'll be our first proper guest!'

Maggie was making cushions when Hector rang.

'Maggie, just to say I won't be able to make it tomorrow after all. Paula's arranged for some friends to come over for the day. I thought I'd let you know, so you aren't left waiting.'

'That's thoughtful of you. Thanks,' Maggie said hurriedly before he could start apologising. 'And it's fine, don't worry about it, I've got a million cushions to make anyway.'

God, how many times recently had she told him it was fine and he wasn't to worry about it.

In the beginning she'd accepted the situation on the basis that half a loaf was better than none. But the loaf had dwindled dramatically of late; let's face it, she was down to half a slice.

'I do feel I'm letting you down.' Hector hesitated, sounding awkward. 'Look, would you at least let me send you some money?'

'*No.*' Maggie winced with pain as the needle she'd been using jabbed into the palm of her hand. 'No, Hector, I really don't want your money and you have to stop letting this bother you. We had a private arrangement, that's all. Now that you've met someone else, well, you no longer need my . . . services.' Closing her eyes, she forced herself to say the shameful word.

'But—'

'Hector, let's be honest, we both knew something like this would happen sooner or later. You've got Paula now. Why don't we just leave it at that?'

Long silence. Maggie realised she was trembling violently. Still, it had needed to be done. It was the hardest thing she'd ever had to say. She might not have said it very well but at least she'd got the essential message across.

The sewing needle had sunk into her hand. Blood was now welling out like a miniature balloon. As she gazed down at it, tears simultaneously welled up in Maggie's aching eyes.

This was it; she'd just tipped away the last few dried-up crumbs of the loaf.

'I know what you're saying.' To his credit, Hector at least had the grace to sound disappointed. 'I suppose it makes sense, I just can't help—'

'Have to go. Someone's at the door,' Maggie lied. 'Anyway, see you around, best of luck to you and Paula.' She slammed the phone down. There, done it. Dilemma solved.

It hurt to breathe and she felt more miserable than she could ever remember feeling before, but *it was done*. Their affair – business arrangement – was over and Hector had no idea how she felt about him. Which was a good thing, Maggie decided as the tears burned their way down her cheeks.

It might not be much but at least she'd escaped with her dignity intact.

Just so long as no one happened to be peering in at her through the window, wondering what a pathetic middle-aged woman was doing on her knees in the middle of the living room surrounded by cushions and bawling her eyes out like a child.

Freddie was playing contentedly with an assortment of coloured plastic Ikea bowls on the kitchen floor. Mel, finishing the washing-up and remembering that she'd left her coffee mug and his feeding cup on the windowsill in the living room, shook the suds from her hands, wiped them briefly on a tea towel and made her way through to fetch them.

It was when she glanced through the small leaded living-room window to see if Barney was on his way back from the shop yet that her stomach plummeted like a plane hitting an air pocket.

Barney was heading up the lane towards the cottage. And he had Steven's wife with him.

Oh shit, not now, *not yet*. Backing away from the window in dismay, Mel cursed the cruel timing and briefly considered locking herself in the bathroom and refusing to come out. She had been planning to tell Barney everything tonight. Then, once he'd had a day or two to get used to the idea – and forgive her, of course – she'd decided he would go and see Daisy MacLean and explain the situation to her himself in his own gentle, apologetic way. Daisy clearly liked him, so it would be better coming from Barney. And then the deed would be done, all the awkwardness would be out of the way.

Well, that had been her brilliant plan.

There was no time to do anything. As the wooden gate clicked open, Mel tucked her hair behind her ears and braced herself. Anyway, she'd moved in now. She lived here. And Barney loved her. None of this was her fault, she hadn't done it on purpose.

Her heart racing, Mel heard the two of them crunching up the snowy front path.

'Barney, this is amazing, even the outside looks a hundred times better,' Daisy was exclaiming with delight, evidently admiring the freshly painted front door and window frames. 'I can't wait to see what you've done inside – I'm expecting Blenheim Palace at the very least!'

They were both laughing as Barney opened the front door. Three, two, one, thought Mel. Here we go . . .

Daisy stopped laughing first. She stared at the brown-haired girl with wary grey eyes, recognising her at once.

But how could she be *here*?

Barney, closing the door behind them, said cheerfully, 'I've got the milk, and guess who I bumped into in the shop? Mel, this is Daisy!' Eagerly grabbing Mel's arm and propelling her forwards he added with pride, 'Daisy, I want you to meet my girlfriend, Mel.'

Stunned, Daisy nodded and said, 'Hi.' Not what she wanted to say, but it was clear that Barney was oblivious of the connection between them.

Mel, nodding back and mustering a passable imitation of a smile, said, 'Nice to meet you.'

'I wanted to show Daisy what we've done to the cottage.' Barney gestured around the living room, now carpeted and repainted and simply but comfortably furnished with, among other things, the old sofa Daisy had donated from the hotel.

'It's great.' Daisy numbly looked where he was telling her to look. 'You've worked really hard.'

'You haven't seen anything yet.' His eyes dancing like an

excited child's, Barney said, 'I'm just going to put the kettle on. We'll have some tea, then I'll show you the rest. Won't be a minute.'

The moment he was out of the room, Daisy murmured, 'I don't know what's going on here, but you certainly have some explaining to do. What is this, some kind of *joke*?'

Mel shook her head, twisting the swirly silver ring on the thumb of her left hand. 'I swear, I didn't know who he was. When I found out, I was as shocked as you are. And I was going to tell you, I had it all planned,' she rattled on defensively. 'I was going to come and see you tonight, to explain everything so you wouldn't be shocked.'

'Does Barney know?' Daisy got straight to the point; after all, how long did it take to make three mugs of tea?

'Not yet.' The girl sighed. 'I was going to tell him tonight too.'

'Why didn't you do it before?' As if she couldn't guess.

'I was scared. I don't want to upset him. I don't want him to hate me. I kept putting it off . . . then when he asked me to move in with him here, I knew it was all going to come out . . . I've been gearing myself up to telling him.' Mel raised her chin and gazed into Daisy's eyes. 'I do love him. He's made my life worth living again. And Barney loves me.'

Slowly Daisy nodded. The initial shock was beginning to wear off. She could understand why Mel had been worried about telling Barney. And time was running out.

'OK, look, I won't say anything now. You can tell Barney when I've gone, sort it out with him in your own way.' There. Daisy gave the girl an encouraging nod, feeling she was being more than fair. What more could Mel expect, for heaven's sake? And why was she not looking happier about it? Honestly, talk about ungrateful.

'Here we are!' The kitchen door swung open and Barney reappeared, beaming all over his face and clutching not three mugs of tea, as Daisy had been expecting, but a small child with china-blue eyes and silky white-blond hair.

The previous shock simply didn't compare with this one. Daisy felt as if the new carpet had been, literally, wrenched from beneath her feet.

One incredulous glance at Melanie Blake told her all she needed to know. The boy, brandishing a yellow plastic bowl, was a Bonsai version of Steven.

'Couldn't carry everything out in one go,' said Barney with a grin. Swinging the boy round to face Daisy and waggling his tiny hand at her, he added, 'This is Mel's son, Freddie.'

Daisy no longer cared about being nice. Look where being reasonable and kind and fair had got her. Niceness promptly sailed out of the window.

'I have to go.' She couldn't bring herself to look at the boy; she was having trouble breathing.

Barney looked dismayed. 'Go? Why?'

'Ask your girlfriend why.' Mel's face was stricken. *Good.* 'And while you're at it,' Daisy hissed as she marched past him, 'why don't you ask her to tell you the name of her ex-boyfriend?'

'Ex-boyfriend?' Bewildered, Barney said, 'What ex-boyfriend?'

Daisy knew she was upsetting Barney, who was completely innocent. None of this was his fault. But he had to know the truth.

'My husband.' For a moment she experienced a flicker of satisfaction as Mel visibly flinched. 'The one who gave her that baby.'

Slamming the front door behind her, Daisy left them to it.

Her face felt rigid as if she'd left a face pack on all night. She marched back down Brock Lane, provoking a volley of barking from Bert Connelly's excitable dogs as she passed his cottage. Kicking at the snow, she pictured the toddler's face again and experienced a jolt of anguish so acute it took her breath away. Don't think about it, concentrate on something else, just get back home, get back home . . .

Chapter 45

'Daisy, my fax machine's playing up. OK if I borrow yours for—Jesus, are you all right?'

Oh brilliant, *brilliant*, of all the people to bump into at a time like this. Just what she needed.

'I'm fine. Yes, no problem, use my fax.' She attempted, slightly desperately, to dodge past Dev Tyzack and head on up the staircase but he hadn't captained the England rugby team for nothing. Every time she moved to the left or right, he was there blocking her. Unable to meet his gaze Daisy said tightly, 'I'm melting snow into the carpet. Look, I *said* you can use the—'

'Forget the fax. What's wrong?' Moving closer, Dev forced her to look at him. 'Tell me.'

The fact that he was being kind only caused her mouth to start trembling. 'Nothing. I just want to go—'

'Has something happened to Josh? Skiing accident?'

'No, no . . .' God, couldn't he leave her *alone*?

'Daisy. Tell me what it is,' ordered Dev, and this time her shoulders started to shake.

'S-something h-h-horrible.' She shook her head and sagged against the banister rail. The next moment, Dev's hand was pressing into the small of her back, propelling her up the staircase.

'OK, come on. Let's get you out of here.'

Daisy allowed him to lead her up to her flat. She no longer had the energy to argue, and half of her was desperate to talk to someone. Anyone. Even if it was Dev.

He didn't bother with faffing around in the kitchen making the obligatory tea or coffee, just sat her down on the sofa and said, 'I can stay or I can go. It's up to you.'

Quite suddenly Daisy didn't want him to go. Wearily, she sank back against the cushions.

'You must be busy.'

'I don't have to be. It's not a problem. And you don't have to tell me what's upset you,' Dev assured her. 'Not if you don't want to. It's none of my business.'

This was like uncorking a champagne bottle. Daisy blurted out, 'Barney's just introduced me to his girlfriend. And it turns out she used to be my husband's girlfriend too.'

Dev frowned. 'You mean . . . ?'

'Oh yes, I *do* mean. The one he was seeing behind my back. She's moved into the village with Barney, and you'll never guess what else she's brought along with her.' As she said it, Daisy's voice began to quaver. 'Her one-year-old son. Steven's son. Who looks exactly – and I mean *exactly* – like Steven.'

It shouldn't have been easy, crying in front of someone you really didn't want to cry in front of, but somehow it was. Not normally the blubbing kind, Daisy simply gave up and let go, howling into her hands, trumpeting through a succession of tissues and sobbing unrestrainedly against the front of Dev's denim shirt, while he held her and stroked her hair and patiently rubbed her back until the worst of the grief was out of her system.

Much later, Daisy gave her eyes one last wipe – they were by this time so swollen it was actually painful – and said, 'Well, I must look gorgeous. Bet you're glad you came up here now.'

Dev smiled. 'I can handle it.'

'Still, it must make a nice change.' She paused to blow her nose, honking like a goose into a fresh tissue. 'I bet when girls normally blubber all over you, it's because you've just finished with them.'

'You have such a low opinion of me.' Sounding amused, he added, 'When I finish with a girl, I prefer to do it by fax.'

'So that's what you wanted it for. Oh well, at least I wasn't wearing mascara.' Daisy dabbed apologetically at the damp patches on the front of his shirt.

'Anyway. What are you going to do?'

'Wash my face, I suppose. See if I can find any eyedrops.'

'About this girl,' said Dev.

'Oh. Her.' Mel, thought Daisy, gazing at the black suede boots she hadn't got round to removing yet. Bending over, she yanked them off her feet and hurled them one after the other at the living room door. They thudded satisfyingly against the wood and clattered to the floor.

'That's what I'd *like* to do to her. Knock her flying. Oh hell, I don't know, I just don't know.' A fresh wave of misery rose up in Daisy's throat. 'You know what? I met her at the hospital after the accident. She wasn't allowed into the intensive care unit but I persuaded the nurse to let her in to see Steven. Which, quite frankly, I felt was pretty decent of me under the circumstances. And then a year later I saw her here when she came to visit his grave, and I didn't scream or shout or call her horrible names, I was perfectly polite *again*. But this time . . . God, this time I just lost it.' Daisy shook her head. 'I mean, a *baby*. She gave birth to Steven's baby and now she's brought it back to live here in *our* village . . . I was nice to her and in return she does this to me! It makes me feel sick. Steven didn't even like babies,' she exclaimed bitterly. 'He made damn sure

I kept taking my pills . . . he used to check how many were left in the packet.'

'I thought you said your marriage was a disaster.' Dev frowned. 'Why would you want a baby if it was that bad?'

'I didn't,' Daisy said crossly. 'After the wedding I just said I'd like to have children one day – well, most people do, don't they? – and Steven was horrified. Kids weren't his idea of fun and they didn't fit into his lifestyle. Ironic, isn't it? There he was, counting my pills like Scrooge counting money, and at the same time getting his girlfriend pregnant. *God*.'

'What?' said Dev.

'If he was still alive, I'd punch him.'

'If he were alive,' Dev pointed out, 'you'd be divorced by now. And the chances are he wouldn't still be with this other girl either. He'd have dumped her and left her holding the baby, because that's what men like him do.'

Men like him? Daisy wondered sceptically whether he meant 'men like us'.

'Has it ever happened to you?'

He shrugged. 'A couple of times.'

What? Daisy's heart began to thump unpleasantly in her chest. 'You've got two children?'

Dev broke into a grin. 'Sorry, meant to be a joke. Oh dear, you really don't have a very high opinion of me, do you?'

No.

'I was gullible once.' Defensively, she picked a bit of fluff from her pushed-up sleeve. 'When you've been married to someone like Steven . . . well, it teaches you a lesson.'

'Never to trust any man again?' He sounded amused. 'Daisy, you can't do that. It's no way to live.'

'And it's not what I'm doing,' she shot back. 'I'm just a lot choosier these days about who I trust.'

'So you won't get hurt again.' Dev nodded thoughtfully. 'Take no risks, go for the safe option, don't aim too high – that kind of thing?'

'How dare you!' Furiously, Daisy rounded on him. 'That's a terrible thing to say – and that's *not* what I'm doing with Josh!'

Dev raised an eyebrow. 'Keep your hair on, I didn't say it was. I wasn't talking about Josh. I don't even know him.'

Oh. Right. But then again . . . The skin at the back of Daisy's neck prickled with guilt at the realisation that he might not have been talking about Josh but she had been.

And it hadn't escaped Dev's notice.

There was a knock at the door. Oh God, what now?

Without moving, and without enthusiasm, Daisy said, 'Who is it?'

'Me. Um, Barney.' He sounded very subdued.

'Do you want to see him?' said Dev.

Poor Barney. Her heart went out to him. This had come as much of a shock to him as it had to her.

Daisy nodded, hoping her eyes didn't look too froggy, and watched Dev kick her suede boots to one side before opening the door.

Dev showed Barney into the living room and let himself out. For a couple of seconds Daisy and Barney stared at each other without speaking. If there was a Crufts award for most anguished puppy, Barney would surely win it hands down.

'I'm sorry,' he blurted out, his face the picture of misery. 'I'm so sorry. I swear I didn't know.'

Daisy sighed and patted the sofa cushions next to her, still warm from where Dev had been sitting.

'Of course you didn't know. This isn't your fault. Look, come and sit down.'

Barney hesitated, his hands shoved into the pockets of his jeans, then obediently sat.

'I just can't believe it.' He sighed and shook his head. 'An hour ago I was happier than I've ever been before in my life. Then something like this happens . . . and I just don't know what to *think* any more. I can't believe I've done this to you,' he went on. 'I feel terrible. I bet you wish you'd never met me now.'

He was desolate, awash with remorse, his wounded-puppy eyes avoiding hers.

'Don't be stupid.' Discovering that he was taking this harder than she was made Daisy, in an odd way, feel better. All she had to deal with was the shock, whereas Barney was saddled with the additional burden of guilt.

'I mean it.' Barney pressed his hands to his forehead. 'If I'd known who Mel was when I first met her, I'd never have got involved.'

Glancing across the room at her black suede boots, Daisy briefly considered offering them to Barney to hurl against the door.

'But you did. Get involved, I mean. So how do you feel about her now?'

For a moment Barney was unable to speak. Watching him bite his lower lip, Daisy prayed he wasn't about to cry. She'd used up all the tissues in the box.

Finally he whispered, 'I hate her.'

Daisy waited.

'I love her.' Barney closed his eyes, then opened them again. 'I'm sorry, but I do. I love her and I love Freddie, I can't help it. But now this has happened, I just don't know what to do . . .'

'OK, listen to me.' Daisy couldn't bear to see him so torn. 'Mel wasn't straight with you, but neither was I. You assumed Steven and I were happily married and I let you carry on thinking

361

that, basically because I didn't want to upset you. But we weren't happy,' she said slowly. 'Not happy at all. I didn't know he was having an affair but I still wanted a divorce. Barney, he was only interested in my money. He lied, he cheated . . . he even tried emotional blackmail on me before he died. Steven wasn't a very nice person. Obviously Mel wouldn't agree, but he lied to her too, and he was very good at it. What did she have to say after I left the cottage this morning?'

Barney shifted uncomfortably on the sofa. 'Um, that Steven wanted to divorce you but you wouldn't let him go.'

Daisy nodded, unsurprised. After all, why would Mel believe her rather than Steven? He had always been dazzlingly persuasive.

'And what did you say to her?'

'That I was coming here to see you.'

'And now you've seen me what are you going to do?'

'I don't know.' Barney exhaled helplessly and pushed his fingers through his floppy hair. 'Leave, I suppose.'

Chapter 46

'Tara? Oh, there you are! Phone call for you.' Pam burst into the ladies' loo looking harassed. 'I really shouldn't have to chase around the hotel like this,' she went on crossly. 'I told him personal calls were frowned on but he insisted it was an emergency.'

Tara immediately stopped polishing the gilt-framed oval mirror she had been admiring herself in. It was perfectly true that personal calls were frowned on, but only by Pam. Who, incidentally, regarded her as a bit of a trollop.

Huh, chance would be a fine thing.

But who on earth could be phoning her here at the hotel? Even more thrillingly, who had phoned and actually managed to persuade pompous Pam to get off her fat bottom for once and come and find her?

Good grief, it couldn't be Andy, could it? Overcome with remorse and ringing to tell her he'd made the most terrible mistake and if she could possibly forgive him he'd spend the rest of his life making it up to her?

Maybe not. Let's face it, it was far more likely to be her fire-breathing bank manager.

Yuk, she wasn't so sure she wanted to take the call now.

'Did he sound nice?' Tara said warily. 'Or mean?'

Pam huffed and flicked back her heavily lacquered hair – which wasn't going *anywhere* – with irritation.

'It took me long enough to find you.' *You hussy*, Tara mentally inserted at this point. 'Why don't you go and find out for yourself?'

Reaching the reception desk, Tara took the phone Pam was holding out to her like a nun handing over a vibrator.

'*If* he hasn't hung up by now,' Pam commented, not so *sotto voce* and clearly hoping he had.

'Hello?' said Tara.

'About bloody time too,' crackled a voice that made her heart lollop in a rabbity fashion.

'Oh! It's you!' Her fingers convulsively tightened around the receiver. Dominic!

He sounded amused. 'Who were you expecting, the Inland Revenue?'

'Much worse.' Tara heaved a gusty sigh of relief. 'My bank manager.'

This time he laughed, and she realised that when you were married to a multi-millionairess it wasn't a scenario you were likely to be familiar with. Crikey, in Dominic's position your bank manager probably sent you expensive Christmas cards. And signed them with love and kisses.

'Look, sorry to ring you at work, but I've had an idea.' He paused for effect. 'How d'you fancy booking into a hotel for the night and being spoiled rotten? Romantic dinner, candlelight, champagne, the works.'

The rabbit in her chest was running a marathon. Breathlessly, Tara said, 'Sounds . . . interesting. Who with?'

He was smiling, she could tell. 'Me. But only if you want to.'

The whole night together. Spoiled rotten. *The works* . . .

'What about, um . . . ?'

'Annabel's away visiting an old schoolfriend. She's staying

in London, coming back tomorrow afternoon. So,' Dominic's tone was playful, 'how about it?'

There was no contest, even if Pam hadn't been there emitting chilly waves of disapproval and visibly willing her to get off the phone.

'OK,' whispered Tara.

'That's my girl. I'll pick you up at six, usual place. Better go now,' Dominic said cheerfully. ''Bye, sweetheart.'

''Bye.' Tara put the phone down, her thoughts darting help-lessly in all directions. This was it, then. The one thing Daisy had warned her not to do. It was going to happen . . . how could it not happen? Oh my Lord, a night in a hotel! Just like a real couple—

'Oh, there you are, Mr Tyzack,' Pam exclaimed, sending a shiver down Tara's spine. 'That parcel you were waiting for just arrived ten minutes ago!'

Dev crossed the hall and smiled briefly at Tara. As he reached for the package Pam was holding out to him, he said, 'Have you seen Daisy this morning?'

Tara shook her head. She didn't want to see Daisy either. God, she'd do her best to talk her out of meeting Dominic tonight. And as for Dev, what would *he* say if he knew?

'You look a bit flushed,' he commented.

The trick, she decided, was not to appear guilty. She was tarty Tara, flirty but essentially harmless.

'Probably just the excitement,' she smiled sunnily back at him, 'of standing next to you.'

When Barney pushed open the front door of the cottage, he saw the cases in the middle of the living-room floor. Moments later, Mel struggled down the stairs clutching a couple of stuffed carrier bags in one hand and Freddie in the other.

365

'What are you doing?' said Barney.

'What does it look like? Saving you the trouble of telling me to leave.' White-faced but determined, Mel added the carriers to the pile and lowered Freddie gently to the floor next to them. Straightening up, she said, 'This is what you want, isn't it? Us, out of your life. You're ashamed of me, disgusted by what I did, and you don't want anything more to do with us. Well, Barney, that's fine, that's absolutely fine by me, and you don't have to worry about me doing anything embarrassing like begging you to change your mind, because I wouldn't dream of it. I've just got to pack the rest of Freddie's things and we'll be off. If you want to ring a taxi now, that'll save a bit of time. We can be out of here in twenty minutes.'

'Mel—'

'One more thing,' she cut in, her eyes diamond-bright. 'Just let me say this. I'm sorry I hurt you and I'm sorry if I upset Daisy. But don't ever, *ever* expect me to be sorry I had Freddie.'

Helplessly, Barney shook his head. 'I don't expect you to do that. Of course you aren't sorry about Freddie.'

'Good. Thank you. I'm glad we've got that straight.' Mel gazed for several seconds down at her son, who was playing happily with a disposable nappy from one of the carrier bags. Freddie flashed them both a naughty gappy grin and plonked the nappy bonnet-style on his head.

'Just as well it's a clean one,' said Barney.

'I'll just get the rest of his things.' Mel turned to head back up the stairs.

'Don't.' He put out his arm to stop her.

'Why not?'

'I don't want you to go. You don't have to go.' His Adam's apple bobbed in his throat. 'Daisy says it's OK, you can stay.'

'I don't believe you. Daisy hates me. She doesn't want me here.'

Barney hesitated, because this was certainly true. 'Well, she might not *want* you here, but she isn't going to drive you out of the village. She says she'll cope with it, as long as you . . . well, keep out of her way.'

'Jump into a hedge, you mean, if I see her coming down the road towards me?'

'Just be discreet, that's what she means. Don't expect to be invited to any parties up at the hotel. That's fair enough, isn't it?' Barney pleaded, because Mel was looking truculent. 'I think it's brilliant of her. We can cope with that, can't we?'

Mel looked at him, torn. Half of her accepted that it was a decent offer, but the other half violently resented his attitude.

'Oh yes, it's fantastic, Daisy's so wonderful, she says I'm allowed to stay in the village – even though it isn't actually *her* village – but what about *you*?' she demanded bluntly. 'Barney, she doesn't *own* you. If she'd said I had to go, that would have been it for us. I'd leave with Freddie, you'd stay here and you'd never have seen us again. I don't want us to still be together because Daisy MacLean says we can be, and I'm sure as hell not going to spend the rest of my life being *grateful* to her.'

'Sshh.' Barney smiled and shook his head. 'You've got it all wrong. I told Daisy we were leaving Colworth. I said I couldn't give you up. And I meant it. I wouldn't stay here without you and Freddie. And Daisy knew I was serious. That's when she said it seemed a shame to leave the cottage after I'd worked so hard to do it up.'

'Oh.' Mel relaxed, relief washing over her. 'Well, that's true.'

'So we aren't going anywhere,' said Barney. 'We're staying right here.'

367

'OK.' As he wrapped his arms round her, she could hear the frantic thudding of his heart against her cheek.

'I love you,' Barney murmured.

The crisis was over. She hadn't lost him after all.

'I love you too,' whispered Mel.

Tara's stomach was in knots. She was ridiculously excited. This was brilliant. The hotel, small but romantic, was in Clevedon because Dominic didn't know anyone who either lived or worked in Clevedon. He had gone in ahead of her and given the place a quick once-over while she waited in the car, just to be on the safe side.

And – hooray – it had been safe. For once, nothing was going to go wrong. And about time too, Tara thought joyfully as they were shown up to their room.

'At last,' Dominic echoed this sentiment when the porter had gone, leaving them alone together. With a whoop of triumph, he scooped Tara up into his arms, twirled her round the room and deposited her, with a thud, on the huge bed. Jumping on top of her, he covered her face and neck with kisses, scrabbled at the buttons on her shirt and slavered lasciviously at the sight of her beautiful turquoise bra.

'You pillock,' Tara giggled, pushing him off. 'You're going to have to be much more romantic than that. I want to be wined and dined and made a *huge* fuss of, before we get down to any hanky-panky.'

'Of course you do.' Dominic gave her a soulful look. 'And of course I will.' Pause, followed by a grin. 'But how about a quickie first, just to whet our appetites?'

Letting out a shriek as he lunged at the waistband of her skirt, she rolled out of reach and scrambled into a kneeling position.

'I'm too hungry. I'm *starving*.' Tara patted her empty stomach, which obligingly growled. 'I rushed home from work, had a bath, got ready and threw some clothes into a bag. I haven't eaten a thing since lunchtime. We have to have dinner first,' she insisted. 'Otherwise I'll just faint.'

In response. Dominic kissed her very gently on the mouth, caressing her lower lip with his tongue before pulling away with regret.

'You're absolutely right,' he said. 'Whatever you want.'

Tara was filled with triumph and delight. There, she *wasn't* a pushover!

If Daisy could see her now, she'd be so proud.

Chapter 47

Apart from stiffening slightly whenever anyone new entered the dining room – which was only natural, Tara felt, under the circumstances – Dominic had kept his word. There was excellent wine and plenty of it, there was food, ornately presented on hexagonal silver-rimmed plates, and there was candlelight. The mood was romantic, the staff efficient but unobtrusive. Tara was in heaven. The only shame was her loss of appetite; having been absolutely ravenous earlier, she was now so keyed up she could barely eat a thing.

Luckily Dominic wasn't offended. He took it as a compliment.

'Did you manage to get off work tomorrow?'

Tara smiled and nodded. She'd persuaded one of the other girls to switch shifts, which meant they didn't have to check out of the hotel at some unearthly hour.

'You've gone quiet,' Dominic observed.

'I'm fine.' Reaching over, she gave his hand a squeeze. 'It's just . . .'

'Don't tell me, that conscience of yours. Sweetheart, you know how I feel about you. I married the wrong girl.' Dominic kept his voice low, though the tables in the restaurant were widely spaced. 'I made a mistake. We'll sort it out, I promise you.'

Tara had been about to tell him she couldn't manage any more wine, but never mind. It was only right that they should discuss his marriage.

'How's it been with Annabel in the last week?'

Soberly, Dominic shook his head. 'No change. Like sharing the house with a stranger. I do my best, but she just won't . . . well, help herself.'

'Still no . . . ?'

'Sex? You must be joking.' He shrugged. 'Annabel's not interested.'

It was no way for a man to live. Tara felt desperately sorry for Dominic, but it was sad for Annabel too.

'What about counselling? There are these sex therapy people. Couldn't you persuade her to see someone about it?' Oh my, listen to me, discussing my lover's wife's sexual problems. This definitely makes me a generous, caring person.

'She wouldn't do that.' Dominic grimaced at the thought. 'Annabel? No way in the world. She'd refuse outright.'

Tara was secretly relieved. Making helpful grown-up suggestions was all very well, but she'd be miffed if Dominic were to ring her up next week yelling excitedly, 'It worked, it bloody worked! Since she came back from the sex therapist she hasn't been able to keep her hands off me – sweetheart, I'm telling you, she's dynamite!'

God, imagine. That would be downright unfair.

'Oh Dominic, what are you going to do?' It was such a hopeless situation. Tara gave his hand a sympathetic squeeze.

'Stick it out for a few more months.' Dominic looked resigned. 'For appearance's sake. If it was up to me I'd leave tomorrow, but that wouldn't be fair on Annabel. She'd never get over the humiliation.'

He was so kind-hearted, that was what she loved about him. How many men would be that thoughtful?

'Sorry.' Tara smiled up at the waitress who had arrived to clear their plates. 'The food's great – I'm just not hungry.'

'What about pudding?' To tempt her, Dominic nodded at an adjacent table. 'They've got chocolate mousse.'

Chocolate mousse was Tara's great weakness, but her stomach was still all of a squiggle. Nerves were getting the better of her. Regretfully she shook her head. 'I don't think I could.'

Pushing back his chair, Dominic stood up and took Tara's hand. As they made their way out of the dining room he whispered in her ear, 'We've got something far better to look forward to than chocolate mousse.'

Tara, leaning against him, experienced a hot wave of something that felt almost like . . .

Nausea. It was nausea, and no matter how hard she tried, Tara couldn't make it go away. Back in their room, Dominic had started to kiss her and she'd done her best to join in with enthusiasm, but the smell of his aftershave, which she normally loved, was making her feel sicker by the minute. She was hot, too. Breaking out into a sweat in a way that wasn't pleasant.

'God, you're beautiful,' Dominic murmured, unzipping her dress in one smooth movement and sliding the straps from her shoulders. Tara instantly felt cold and clammy, and was forced to take deep breaths to lessen the sick feeling in her stomach. Assuming that the heavy breathing was a sign of rapture, Dominic steered her over to the bed.

He stood back and gazed in admiration at Tara in her peacock-blue bra and (naturally) matching knickers. Instinctively pulling in her stomach, she winced as a jagged pain like a knife being waggled shot through her intestines.

In an instant Tara realised what was about to happen. Oh no, oh please, God, *nooo* . . .

'So beautiful, so sexy,' Dominic whispered, reaching out and tracing his fingers over the lacy plunging cups of her bra. 'I've waited so long for this.'

The knotted stomach and inability to eat hadn't been nerves. The almost-but-not-quite-feeling-sick sensation hadn't been due to guilt. Tara closed her eyes and the room began to spin around her, tilting crazily like some sadistic fairground ride.

'Mmmph,' she spluttered as Dominic's mouth landed on hers while his hands simultaneously moved to unfasten her bra. The nausea rose up like a whirling dervish and she yanked herself free, covering her mouth and racing past an astonished Dominic to the bathroom.

The next five minutes were the very, *very* worst of Tara's life. She retched and vomited, noisily and messily, until there was nothing left to bring up.

Finally, she heard Dominic call through the locked bathroom door: 'Tara? Are you OK?'

Oh, I'm *fine*, darling, never felt better. What I really fancy now is a chocolate fudge milkshake and a ride on Nemesis!

Tara didn't say this, she was too busy dying of embarrassment. If there was anything less sexy and alluring than the sound of a woman being sick, she didn't know what it was.

Within thirty seconds she found out. The knife-like pains in her stomach intensified, her bowels turned to water and she only just made it on to the loo in time.

After goodness knows how long – twenty minutes probably – Tara regained sufficient control of her bodily functions to stumble over to the sink and look in the mirror. Not a pretty sight. She was wearing her bra and knickers. Her eyes were swollen, her face blotchy and her hair stringy with sweat. Ridiculously, she still had her red stilettos on her feet.

Her legs trembling and weak, Tara cleaned her teeth, washed

her face and wrapped a bath towel round her shoulders because she couldn't stop shivering. The ominous cramping in her stomach was still there. The loo must feel as exhausted as she did from being flushed so many times. Oh God, how was she ever going to be able to face Dominic again?

Through the bathroom door – the *flimsy* bathroom door – she could hear the murmur of voices. Hopefully the TV, rather than an impromptu gathering waiting for her to emerge before popping a dozen champagne corks and yelling 'Surprise!'

Oh well, she could hardly spend the night sleeping in the bath. Taking a deep breath, Tara unlocked the door and stepped out.

Dominic was lying on the bed, fully dressed and watching television. He turned his head to look at her.

'Better now?'

Miserably, Tara nodded. Her stomach was still sore. Her eyelids were so swollen she could hardly see. She had never felt less desirable in her life.

Which was just as well, really, seeing as Dominic wasn't looking exactly inflamed with desire himself.

Her green satin dressing gown was in her suitcase. Dragging it out, Tara kicked off the incongruous stilettos and pulled the dressing gown on. Not knowing what to do next, she hesitantly approached the bed.

Maybe if you'd been married to someone for a hundred years, they'd be able to take the situation in their stride. Perhaps even crack a joke about it, laugh it off and give you the kind of reassuring hug that told you they understood and still loved you anyway.

Dominic turned his attention back to the TV, picked up the remote and changed stations.

'I'm sorry.' As Tara sank down on the edge of the bed, she could have sworn he shrank away. So this was how it felt to have leprosy.

After a long pause, Dominic said, 'What caused it?'

Sadly, Tara had already worked this one out for herself.

'I had a tuna sandwich for lunch. I thought it tasted a bit funny, but I hadn't brought anything else into work and I was hungry so I just ate it. I made it last night at home,' she admitted miserably, 'and forgot to put it in the fridge.'

'Jesus,' Dominic muttered, indicating that he thought she was stupid beyond belief.

'I thought it'd be OK. The cottage was quite cold.' Tara was defensive because last night for the first time in ages Maggie hadn't had every radiator going full blast in a frantic attempt to dry a ton of washing.

Bloody washing.

'Well, it obviously wasn't.' Dominic was sounding seriously pissed off, and Tara couldn't blame him. 'So what do we do now?' he went on tetchily. 'Because I'm not really in the mood for—'

'Nor me,' Tara hurriedly cut in, before he could tell her how physically revolted he was by her traitorous body.

'Shall we just go home, then?'

It was what she wanted more than anything, but to Tara's dismay her stomach was starting to churn ominously once more. Even at this time of night, the drive back to Colworth would take an hour and the prospect of an in-car accident was too terrible to contemplate.

'I'm still not feeling . . . I don't know if I could . . . well, cope with the journey.'

Dominic nodded and picked up the bedside phone. He spoke to the receptionist downstairs about booking a second room.

'The hotel's full,' he announced shortly, hanging up. 'Every room's taken.'

This was a nightmare.

'You could go home,' Tara whispered, because it was clearly what he longed to do. 'I'll stay here.'

'Maybe that'd be best.' Dominic looked faintly exasperated as her shoulders began to shake. 'Oh Christ, don't start crying. What's wrong now?'

What's wrong now?

Hot tears streamed down Tara's face and dripped off her chin. 'It's all s-spoiled! I'm sorry I've messed everything up but I d-didn't do it on purpose . . . and I feel so *rotten*,' she wailed, wiping her eyes with the slippery sleeve of her dressing gown. 'I really feel ill and I don't w-want to b-be on my own!'

Pathetic, utterly pathetic, but true. If she was at home, Maggie would be making a huge fuss of her now, tucking her up in bed, sponging her forehead and being generally caring and wonderful.

Keeping his distance, Dominic gingerly patted her heaving shoulder.

'OK,' he sighed. 'I won't go.'

Tara didn't dare turn round and hug him. She sniffed noisily. 'Th-thanks.'

They checked out at eight o'clock the next morning. Tara had never felt emptier in her life. If she weighed herself, she'd probably find she'd lost five stone. Her whole body was as hollow as a cheap Easter egg. She'd spent the night dozing fitfully, then waking up and hurtling to the bathroom. Dominic, needless to say, hadn't got much sleep either.

But at least she felt safe enough to risk the journey home. Dominic seemed relieved too. She'd never known it was possible before for two people to lie that far apart from each other in a double bed.

It had been a night neither of them would ever forget.

They drove back to Colworth in silence. When Dominic dropped her off at the bottom of the High Street, he didn't kiss her. Tara was convinced she still smelled of sick, despite having brushed her teeth so hard she'd splayed all the bristles on her toothbrush.

'I'll give you a ring.' He glanced at his watch as he spoke, indicating that he was in a hurry to get away.

'OK.' Tara wondered if he meant it. Had she put him off her for good, or would the hideousness of last night fade in time, like childbirth? For about the hundredth time she mumbled, 'Sorry.'

Nodding, Dominic managed his first smile of the day. Just a flicker of one. He said, 'So am I.'

Chapter 48

'Now, you're sure you're OK?' Maggie bustled into the living room with a fresh bottle of Perrier from the fridge. She stroked Tara's hair, rattled her car keys and said, 'Poor darling, you still look dreadful. I'll bring home some little treats for when you get your appetite back. D'you want me to pick up a couple of magazines?'

Tara nodded and felt cared-for. It was three in the afternoon and she'd reached the fragile-but-recovering stage. Every muscle in her body still ached, but she had managed to drink, and keep down, two whole glasses of water. Best of all, she no longer felt sick or as though she might have to dash to the loo at a millisecond's notice.

'I'll be back by five,' said Maggie, who was off to the supermarket for a big shop. 'You just take it easy, watch a bit of telly, have a good rest.'

Oh, it was nice to be cossetted. And Maggie had taped *Rain Man* for her last night. Snuggling up under the duvet on the sofa, Tara waved the remote at the video and determinedly didn't think about Dominic. A couple of hours in the company of Dustin Hoffman and Tom Cruise was just what she needed to cheer her up.

The doorbell rang an hour later.

'Jeopardy,' said Dustin Hoffman on the television.

Wrestling her way out of the duvet, Tara hurriedly ran her hands over her sticking-up hair. It might be Dominic, come back to apologise and tell her he still loved her.

Well, it might be.

Though whether he'd still love her in her Madonna T-shirt and baggy jogging bottoms was another matter.

She opened the door anyway.

'Hello,' said Annabel Cross-Calvert.

Oh God. Tara prayed she'd fallen asleep on the sofa and was in fact having a horrible dream. This really couldn't be happening, could it?

'Probably best if you invite me in,' Annabel suggested. 'We need to talk.'

Oh, buggering hell. This was real. Fighting down panic, Tara wondered if she'd be allowed a phone call to her solicitor. If only she had one.

Dry-mouthed and with her heart pummelling her ribcage, she stepped to one side. Annabel swept past her in a mist of Chanel No. 19. She paused to survey the crumpled duvet, the drawn curtains and the flickering TV screen.

'Uh-oh,' Dustin Hoffman bluntly announced. 'Fart.'

'Sorry, I'll turn it off.' Frantically, Tara reached for the remote control, shovelled the duvet out of sight behind the sofa, cleared a mound of Maggie's cushion-making paraphernalia from the armchair and gestured for Annabel to sit down. 'Um . . . cup of tea?'

'No thanks.' Annabel shook her head and remained standing. She was wearing an expensive-looking grey suede coat, a crisp pink shirt and pale grey trousers.

Not knowing what to do with herself, Tara rubbed her perspiring hands together and said in desperation, 'Coffee?'

'No.' Annabel took a deep breath and looked her straight in the eye. 'You're having an affair with my husband.'

'I'm not.' Vigorously Tara shook her own head. 'I'm not, I promise. I haven't slept with him.'

'Don't bother trying to deny it. You spent last night with him at that hotel in Clevedon. He drove you back here this morning. I know all about it.'

Would this be a good moment to faint? Tara, feeling pretty wobbly anyway, sank down with a bump on the sofa.

'Who told you? Dominic?'

Annabel's upper lip curled with derision. 'Of course not. I've been having him tailed.'

'Tailed? You mean *followed*?' Tara felt sweat break out all over her body. 'By a . . . ?'

'Private detective. That's right.'

'But, but . . . he came to pick me up last night. We didn't see anyone following us.' OK, it was an admission of guilt but Annabel was clearly in possession of the facts. Well, most of them.

'That's because he's good at his job,' Annabel patiently replied. 'And he didn't need to drive bumper to bumper behind you all the way to Clevedon. He'd already planted a tracking device in Dominic's car. The wonders of modern technology,' she went on drily. 'Where would we be without them?'

An awful lot safer, Tara thought, that was for sure. Less caught out. She'd never liked modern technology and now she knew why.

She liked it even less when Annabel clicked open her handbag and took out a tiny cassette tape.

'You had dinner together in the hotel restaurant. Remember the middle-aged man sitting on his own at the table next to yours?'

'No.'

'See?' Annabel sounded almost pleased. 'That's another reason why he's such a good private detective. Nobody ever notices him. But he noticed you.' She paused. 'He also recorded every word you said.'

Well, that was it, the game was well and truly up. In fact it couldn't get more up if it tried.

'You were in too much of a hurry to stay for pudding, it seems. Apparently you missed a treat,' Annabel went on. 'He told me the chocolate mousse was out of this world.' She pulled a funny little face and added, 'Who knows, it might even have been better than sex.'

Tara was suddenly struck by a thought at once both horrifying and welcome. If their room had been bugged as well, it meant Annabel knew that nothing physical had gone on between Dominic and herself. Which could only be good news.

On the other hand, it would mean she'd listened to a tape full of violent retching and throwing up.

Fearfully, Tara said, 'Was there a listening thingy planted in our room?'

Annabel moved her shoulders almost imperceptibly, as if to say, 'Might be, might not.' 'You've been seeing my husband.' Her voice was cold. 'Why don't you just tell me what happened and then I'll tell you whether or not there was.'

Tara rubbed her face hard with both hands, no longer caring how sweaty and dishevelled she must look. 'OK, OK. But I can't do it with you standing there like that. You'll have to sit down.'

'So that's it,' she concluded fifteen minutes later. 'The whole truth. Well, if the room was bugged, you'll already know it's the truth.'

'The room wasn't bugged,' said Annabel.

Tara didn't know whether to be relieved or dismayed. 'It's still what happened,' she said wearily.

'But the fact remains, you would have slept with Dominic if you hadn't been ill.'

'I suppose so.' Miserably, Tara nodded. She wasn't proud of herself.

'You *wanted* to have sex with him,' Annabel persisted.

'And Dominic wanted to have sex with me!' Tara blurted out. 'Look, I'm sorry, I know that what we did was wrong . . . well, almost did . . . but it's not all Dominic's fault, is it? You can't marry a man and refuse him any kind of sex life and seriously expect him to just put up with it! That isn't fair on him. It's no way to treat *anyone*,' Tara rushed on passionately, 'and it's just plain *selfish* not to even consider getting some kind of counselling—'

'Yes, yes, I've already heard this on the tape.' Annabel gestured impatiently with her hand. 'I thought it was sweet of you to be so concerned. Something to do with easing your own guilty conscience, I imagine, plus making Dominic think what a thoroughly lovely person you are.'

Tara flushed. 'But you *should* see a counsellor.'

'Actually, can I change my mind?' Coolly, Annabel raised an eyebrow. 'I think I will have that cup of tea now.'

It was probably what she announced to Dominic whenever he dared suggest going to bed together, Tara thought as she made her way through to the kitchen to put the kettle on.

She was pouring the boiling water onto the tea bags when Annabel appeared behind her in the doorway.

'Shall I tell you why I haven't been to a counsellor?' she inquired.

Because you're frigid, thought Tara, and terrified that you might be forced to discuss body parts with a complete stranger

– heavens, he might even start using revolting words like
intercourse and, ugh, *penis*.

'The reason I haven't been to a counsellor,' Annabel went on,
'is because there's absolutely nothing wrong with our sex life.'

Tara splashed too much milk into her own cup. Oh well, didn't
matter, she wasn't up to drinking it anyway.

Was Annabel *serious*?

'But—'

'We have a fabulous time in – and out – of bed,' said Annabel.
'Great sex and plenty of it. What's the matter, do you think I'm
making this up?'

Tara went cold all over. She turned round to look at her. 'I
don't know.'

'I believed you just now,' said Annabel, 'when you told me
what happened last night. Now it's your turn to believe me.'

'But why would he say it if it wasn't true?' In her heart
of hearts, even as her mouth formed the words, Tara knew
exactly why.

'Because Dominic's a liar. And he's greedy. Face facts,'
Annabel went on with a shrug. 'Everywhere you look, there
are men cheating on their wives and telling their mistresses
how miserable they are at home. They do it for fun, because
two women are better than one. It's a hobby. Is that one mine?
Thanks. And of course he's a very good liar, you already know
that. Well, we both do.'

Tara watched her standing there sipping her tea. Annabel was
taking this remarkably calmly, considering.

'I didn't know,' she protested.

'Oh, come on. What about my wedding day?'

Tara flushed and prodded the tea bag still bobbing around in
her own cup.

'Tell me the truth,' said Annabel. 'You were covering up for him, weren't you? That big confession of yours was to save Dominic's skin. He was the one making all the moves and you ended up taking the blame.'

Oh hell.

'I didn't just do it for him. I didn't want to mess up your big day.'

'See? You're not all bad.' Annabel smiled briefly.

'So what are you going to do now? I mean, you've listened to the tape,' said Tara. 'You heard what Dominic said. He wants to leave you.'

'Actually, I'm quite peckish. Got any biscuits? Of course he doesn't want to leave me,' Annabel went on, as Tara pointed numbly at the black and white biscuit tin next to the kettle. Helping herself to a couple of bourbons, she leaned against the worktop. 'I'm rich, aren't I? Dominic loves being married to me and my millions. He can't wait for me to get pregnant.'

This was becoming frankly bizarre.

'And you don't mind that he cheats on you and tells people you're frigid?'

'Oh, don't be so stupid, of course I *mind*,' Annabel exclaimed through a mouthful of biscuit. Swallowing, and shaking her head in apology, she patted her mouth neatly with the back of her hand. 'Sorry, my old etiquette teacher would have a fit if she could see me now. I mean, Dominic was never what you might call the faithful type, but he swore he'd change once we were married. I wasn't so sure, but he turned on the famous charm and . . . Well, you know how charming Dominic can be when he puts his mind to it. He persuaded me to marry him, and my mum thought he was wonderful. In the end I just got caught up in all the preparations, more to keep my mother happy than anything else. But I did think it was a bit much, him getting off with someone else on the morning of our wedding.'

Tara stared at her in disbelief. 'So you knew it wasn't my fault all along?'

'Oh, come on, you weren't completely innocent. You have to take some of the blame,' Annabel declared with a touch of scorn.

'But you were going to call off the wedding until I came up to see you. If you knew I was covering up for Dominic, why did you pretend to believe me?'

'I couldn't do it to my mother. She'd have had a nervous collapse, or a heart attack or something. All the guests were arriving, she'd been planning the wedding for months. She'd never have been able to live with the shame. This is what didn't occur to my big-mouthed sister when she saw you and Dominic disappearing into the summerhouse,' Annabel said drily. 'If it had been me, I'd have kept it to myself.'

'OK. Right. So what happens now?' Tara was confused by Annabel's relaxed, almost jovial manner. 'Are you going to divorce him?'

'I'm not sure. Haven't decided yet. As I said, we do still have good times together. I just don't want to be married to someone who's unfaithful to me.'

'Technically,' Tara hesitated, 'he hasn't been unfaithful.'

'You've been seeing him for weeks!'

'No sex though.'

Annabel snorted with laughter. 'Thanks to a dodgy tuna sandwich. OK, I trust you now. Are you going to see Dominic again?'

'No. *No way*.' Vehemently Tara shook her head. As far as Dominic was concerned, she had well and truly come to her senses. Every word he'd uttered had been a lie.

'Sure? Even when he rings you up and does his charm bit?'

'Definitely sure.' Tara shuddered. 'Although to be honest I

385

can't see him ringing anyway. After last night's performance, I don't think I'll be seeing him again for dust.' She pulled a face. 'If you do end up having a baby, don't expect Dominic to be great at coping with puking and nappies. Something tells me it isn't his strong point.'

Annabel knocked back the rest of her tea, then checked her watch. 'Time I made a move. Dominic's expecting me back from London at five. Thanks for the tea and biscuits, and the chat. You look after yourself,' she added as they reached the front door.

'Thanks. And I am sorry.' Tara meant it. 'About . . . well, everything.'

'Don't worry. By the way, Dominic's the one who's desperate for me to have that baby.' With a glint of amusement in her eyes, Annabel said, 'He doesn't know I'm on the Pill.'

Chapter 49

At the hotel, a school reunion was in riotous progress in the bar. Two hours after dinner in the restaurant, overexcited forty-somethings were still greeting each other like teenagers, shrieking at the tops of their voices as they recognised someone else they hadn't seen for twenty-five years and exclaiming that they hadn't changed a bit.

Which was, obviously, a huge lie.

Escaping from the smoky overheated bar, Daisy headed for the front steps. As she breathed in lungfuls of cold clean air, a familiar sound behind her made her turn round.

Clarissa was making her way jauntily through reception as if she owned the place, her claws clickety-clacking against the flagstones. Still descending the staircase was Dev, wearing an old Barbour over a black sweater and jeans. As she watched, Daisy saw him pause briefly to chat with Barney, who was covering the night shift this week. Determined not to be left out on the socialising front, Clarissa greeted Daisy with joy, winding her body like a hairy scarf around Daisy's legs.

'How's it going?' Dev joined them on the steps.

'Lovely.' Bending to ruffle Clarissa's ears, Daisy said, 'She's keeping my ankles warm.'

'I meant how are you coping?' Dev gave her a be-serious look.

'OK.' Daisy shrugged. 'I'll live.'

'I'm taking Clarissa for a walk. Fancy coming along?'

At that moment a fresh chorus of high-pitched shrieks and whoops spilled out of the bar. Daisy, whose ears were starting to ache from the sheer volume of noise – blimey, she must be getting old – decided that she did.

'Give me two minutes to change out of these stupid shoes.'

Upstairs in her flat, the phone began to ring as she was peeling off her skirt and wriggling into a pair of jeans. Hopping clumsily over to the phone, Daisy saw Josh's mobile number on caller display and left it. Josh would be surrounded by friends, phoning from some noisy bar to tell her about the wild time they were having. Instead, breathing in and zipping up, she pulled on a pair of flat boots, grabbed her purple fleece and was out of the flat before the call even had a chance to switch to answerphone.

Well, mustn't keep Clarissa waiting.

They set off together down the drive, breathing clouds of condensation into the night air. It wasn't as cold as it had been; a thaw had set in during the day and the snow was now almost melted. Daisy took deep breaths, enjoying the rhythmic sound of their feet crunching over the gravel as Clarissa bounced around, goat-like, on the grass.

'She thinks she lives here now,' Dev observed. 'She's going to be gutted when we leave.'

Glad he wasn't pursuing the subject of how she felt about Mel and Freddie, Daisy said, 'How's your house?'

'Like a bomb site. Well, not quite that bad.' Dev steered her round a puddle as they reached the end of the drive. 'The roof's been patched up and the plumbing's more or less sorted. When I went over this afternoon the decorators were making a start on the bedrooms. You're stuck with me for another couple of weeks yet.'

Clarissa raced ahead of them, investigating potential lamp-posts for wee-ability as they made their way down the High Street. Since it was too complicated to work out whether she would be glad or sorry when they moved out, Daisy shoved her hands into her fleece pockets and said, 'It smells like autumn.'

'No, here girl, this way.' Dev whistled at Clarissa, who was now turning right into Brocket Lane. As Clarissa blithely ignored him and he shouted, 'No, come on, *back*,' Daisy realised with amusement that he was still too embarrassed to call her by name.

'You have a go,' said Dev. 'She might take more notice of you.'

'She's your dog.' Daisy shrugged. 'It's your job.'

Dev whistled again. 'Dammit.' He raked his fingers despairingly through his dark hair. 'She's doing it on purpose.'

'Her name's Clarissa.' Daisy gave him an innocent look. 'You could always try using it.'

'Look, I was trying to spare your feelings.' Swinging round, Dev caught her laughing at him. 'I thought you'd prefer to give Brocket Lane a miss.'

'Because it's where Barney lives with my late husband's mistress and my late husband's baby? That's deeply considerate of you,' Daisy patted his arm, 'but I think I can handle it.' Keeping a straight face she added meaningfully, 'I'm not a wimp.'

Unlike some people around here . . .

'I know you're not a wimp.' Dev ignored the implied slur. 'I just don't want you breaking their windows.'

'I promise not to break any windows. Come on.' Daisy gave him a playful push in the direction of the lane. 'Follow that dog.'

As they passed Bert Connelly's cottage, Daisy sniffed the air again.

389

'Someone's had a bonfire. That's why it smelled like autumn before. I said it smelled like autumn, didn't I? What a weird time of year to be having a bonfire.'

Clarissa barked and skittered on up the lane. Following her, Dev frowned. 'I can smell it too. It's getting stronger . . . *oh shit.*'

He had rounded the bend six feet ahead of Daisy. Catching up, she saw what he'd just seen. Smoke was curling from the downstairs windows of Brock Cottage. The whole place was in darkness, apart from a dull orange glow coming from the living room. As Daisy stared, momentarily rooted to the spot, she heard the faint crackle of flames inside the house.

Oh Jesus, oh no.

'Fire brigade.' Dev was speaking urgently into the mobile phone he'd already pulled from his pocket. 'Brock Cottage, Brocket Lane, Colworth, the place is on fire . . . what? Yes, an ambulance too. I don't know, I think so.' As he spoke, he and Daisy raced the last twenty or so yards to the cottage. She knew what was going through his mind – if the place was in absolute darkness, it could be empty. Did this mean Mel and Barney had had a huge row? Had Mel packed her bags, taken Freddie and left? Had she been so distraught and hellbent on revenge that she'd set fire to the place on her way out? Oh God, surely not – yet in one way it was infinitely preferable to the alternative.

'MEL!' bellowed Daisy, racing up the path and hammering frantically on the locked front door. 'MEL, ARE YOU THERE?'

There was silence for several seconds, broken only by the crackle of flames and Daisy's coughing as the smoke seeping through the letter box made its way into her lungs. The next moment her blood ran cold as they heard a shriek of alarm and a child's piteous wail. Mel and Freddie were in there, upstairs, with a fire raging below. It would be fifteen minutes before any fire engines reached the village.

Above them the front bedroom window was flung open, billowing out smoke like ectoplasm. Stepping back, they saw Mel's face appear, white with terror.

'Mel, it's OK, you're going to be fine,' shouted Dev. 'Just throw the baby down to us and I'll catch him, then we'll get you out.'

Despite her terror, Daisy experienced a rush of relief. Far better that Dev – international rugby hero and all-round sporty ball-handling type – did the catching.

'Help me! Help me! Freddie's in the back bedroom,' screamed Mel, beside herself. 'The door's buckled and I can't get to him.'

Oh fuck. Daisy's adrenaline was sky-high. Dev was already racing to the back of the cottage.

'Mel, it's OK, Dev's here, he's coming to get you, you'll be fine, I promise!'

'HELP! HELP!' Mel bellowed.

'Can you jump out of the window?' Daisy yelled up at her.

'I CAN'T LEAVE FREDDIE!'

'OK, just stay by the window. I'm going to find Dev.' Tearing round the side of the cottage, Daisy found him barging the back door which stubbornly refused to give. There was less smoke here. Picking up a brick, she smashed the small kitchen window, unfastened the latch and began to scramble up onto the ledge. Dimly she recalled Dev warning her about breaking windows . . .

'You're not going in,' Dev shouted, 'I won't let you.'

'And you won't fit.' Her heart hammering, Daisy squeezed herself head first through the narrow twelve-inch gap, wriggled

391

down the other side, brushed broken glass from her hands and unlocked the back door for Dev.

'Good girl, now get out. Go and let Mel know I'm on my way.'

Coughing and spluttering, Daisy did as he ordered. Dev disappeared into the cottage and she heard his feet racing up the stairs. Moments later a bedroom door slammed and he yelled, 'I've got him.' Then there was a sharp cracking noise and a whoosh of flame visible deep inside the house.

'AAARRGH,' screamed Mel as another almighty crack convinced her that the whole place was about to explode.

'It's OK,' Daisy shouted, sick with fear.

'I'm in.' Dev's face appeared at the window above her. The cracking sound had been the bedroom door splintering as he battered it open. 'Right, now stand back and hold out your arms. No, over there on the grass.' He pointed and Daisy saw that he had Freddie in his arms. Freddie looked as petrified as she felt and was howling at the top of his lungs.

'She won't catch him,' shrieked Mel, completely hysterical by now. 'She'll drop him, I won't let you do it!'

'Stop it. She won't drop him, I promise.'

Daisy only wished she had Dev's confidence. She might not drop Freddie, but what if she missed him completely?

'Daisy, tell her,' ordered Dev, his voice hoarse with smoke.

'I'll catch him,' she shouted up obediently. 'He'll be fine.' Oh God, let him be fine, please let me catch him.

'Nooo!' screeched Mel.

'One . . . two . . . *three*,' counted Dev, and threw Freddie out of the window.

Daisy caught him. She hadn't even needed to move her feet, so accurate had been Dev's aim. Freddie, having flown through the air in appalled silence, found himself clutched in Daisy's trembling arms and promptly let out an ear-splitting wail. Daisy, tightening her grip on him and still panting, felt her own eyes fill with tears. She kissed Freddie's blond head, hard, until he flailed his fists at her in protest.

'Ouch, my ear,' whispered Daisy.

'WAAAAHH,' Freddie bawled, whacking her again.

'OK, now move out of the way,' Dev shouted. 'We're coming down.'

Daisy could hardly bear to watch. It was a twelve-foot drop – what if he was killed?

But Dev wasn't risking leaving Mel up there refusing to jump. He helped her onto the narrow window ledge and shouted like a parachuting instructor, 'Three-two-one . . . go.' Mel jumped and hit the ground with a sickening thud.

Chapter 50

'It's OK, you're all right, you're all right.' Daisy rushed over to Mel, praying she hadn't broken her back. Crouching over her, she said anxiously, '*Are* you all right?'

'I think so.' Gritting her teeth, Mel levered herself upright on legs that were shaky but thankfully unfractured. Then, taking Freddie in her arms and hugging him, she burst into tears.

'Bloody hell,' puffed Bert Connelly, arriving on the scene with one of his sons. 'We heard shouting. Christ Almighty, love, are you OK? Is the little 'un all right?'

Great billows of pungent black smoke were shooting from the upstairs window as Dev jumped. This time Daisy really couldn't watch.

'Nice landing.' Bert nodded his approval. 'Keeps himself fit, that one. I rang the fire brigade, by the way, when I realised what was goin' on.'

'So did we.' Weak with relief that everyone was safely out, Daisy began to shiver.

'And the hotel. Told Barney to get himself up here, pronto.'

God, poor Barney, his beloved cottage ruined.

The next moment Hector's Land Rover came screeching up the lane. Barney, white-faced, leapt out of the back before it had even reached a standstill.

'Everyone's fine,' Dev said quickly as Barney raced to

394

embrace Mel and Freddie. Hector, wearing a dinner jacket, swung himself down and said, 'Paula and I had just got back when Barney came pelting out of the hotel. I've phoned nine nine nine. God, what a thing to happen . . . sweetheart, look at your face.'

Daisy's eyes were streaming from the smoke. Putting up a hand to wipe them, she realised her face was streaked with black. Dev's was even blacker; he looked like a commando.

'I threw Freddie out of the window,' Dev told Hector. 'Daisy caught him.'

Despite the horror of the occasion, Hector chuckled. 'Daisy did? Good grief, I saw her trying to play netball once at school. Awful. Well done, darling. This has to be a miracle.'

'Hector,' announced Paula, her tone faintly querulous as she shivered in a pale yellow dress and spindly heels. 'Give me your jacket, darling. I'm cold.'

Two fire engines arrived minutes later, closely followed by an ambulance and assorted villagers. Clarissa, who had quailed beneath a blackcurrant bush while the urgent people-saving business had been going on, sensed that the scary bit was over and began greeting people she knew like an It girl at a party.

'I don't know how it happened,' Mel repeated numbly, trembling as the paramedics led her into the ambulance. 'Oh Barney, look at the cottage, we've lost everything.'

'Don't be stupid. I've still got you and Freddie.' Barney was shaking too. They could both have been killed in there. It didn't bear thinking about. Gazing out of the back of the ambulance, he saw Paula Penhaligon leaning, arms folded, against the Land Rover with Hector's dinner jacket draped around her shoulders. As he watched, Clarissa danced up to her and sniffed one of her elegant ankles. With a look of irritation Paula kicked her, hard enough to send Clarissa scuttling backwards. Barney, who at any other time would have been outraged, was distracted by a piercing scream in his left ear. Freddie was objecting to being prodded with an ice-cold stethoscope.

'We don't need to go to the hospital,' Mel protested. 'We're all right.'

'Well, his lungs sound healthy enough.' The paramedic winced as Freddie's protests, abruptly doubling in volume, blasted down the rubber tubing of the stethoscope. 'But we'd better have you both checked over properly, just to be on the safe side.'

Climbing out of the ambulance, Barney found Dev.

'Thanks for everything.' The words were woefully inadequate, but what else could he say? 'I'm just going with them in the ambulance, but the paramedic's pretty sure they won't be kept in.'

'And what happens after that?' As Dev wiped his smoke-blackened forehead, Barney realised with a jolt what he meant. They no longer had anywhere to live.

'The ambulancemen are waiting for you.' Daisy joined them, Hector close behind her. Wondering why he was looking so dumbstruck, she said, 'What's wrong?'

Barney hastily shook his head. 'Nothing.'

'He's wondering where he's going to go once the doctors have given them the all-clear,' said Dev.

Daisy looked at him, her heart sinking like a stone.

'Oh, for crying out loud, I've never heard anything so ridiculous in my life.' Clapping his hand on Barney's shoulder, Hector boomed, 'You're practically family, lad. You'll stay with us.'

Barney hesitated, looking as if he might cry.

'What about . . . ?' His head turned towards the back of the ambulance.

'I meant all three of you,' Hector declared. 'No problem!

Bloody hell, what did you imagine we'd do – lend you a tent?'

Barney was now gazing at Daisy, who forced herself to smile. Hector, of course, hadn't the faintest idea that there was rather more of a family connection than he thought.

'Daisy? Are you sure that's OK?'

What could she say to Barney? Not on your bloody life?

'Of course it's OK.'

In the darkness, she felt Dev squeeze her hand. Touched by his support, Daisy wondered what the next stage would be. Mel had moved into the village with Steven's child. Now, just days later, she was moving into the hotel. At this rate, by next weekend she'd be taking over her bed.

The ambulance disappeared down the lane. The fire crew were making headway with the blaze. It was midnight and more villagers, alerted by the unaccustomed activity, were turning up to find out what all the excitement was about.

Tara, wearing Maggie's anorak and wellies over her pyjamas, arrived as Hector and Paula were leaving. By the time she found Daisy, she'd heard the whole story of what had happened from Bert Connelly.

Well, not quite the whole story.

'Poor Barney,' Tara breathed, stunned by the sight of the blackened, smouldering cottage. 'Poor all of them. Blimey, his girlfriend's only just moved in and now this. Did you really catch the baby or was that just Bert getting carried away?'

'Come on, let's get out of here.' Daisy took Tara's arm and pulled her towards the lane before she could start drooling over the firemen. (Those hats! Those hoses!) 'Wait till you hear whose baby I caught.'

'I don't believe it! *Her*. What a bitch! What a *nerve*,' raged Tara, stomping around her living room in disgust. 'You should have punched her, that's what I'd have done.'

'What, for having an affair with a married man?' It was nice that Tara was being so indignant but the words two-faced and floozy did rather spring to mind. Holding her wine glass out for a refill – desperate to get the acrid taste of smoke and ashes out of her mouth – Daisy said mischievously, 'Couldn't be like that yourself, then?'

It was just as well Maggie had gone upstairs to bed – some conversations simply weren't suitable for chaste, spinsterly ears.

'That's different. I didn't sleep with Dominic and I didn't get pregnant by him and if I *had* – oops, sorry,' Tara splashed in too much wine, 'I certainly wouldn't move into the same village and flaunt our baby under his wife's nose.'

'You don't know that,' Daisy pointed out. 'You might.' In fact it sounded just the kind of thing Tara *would* end up doing.

'Anyway, it's over. I'm not seeing Dominic any more.'

'Right.' Daisy rolled her eyes.

'Seriously. I never want to speak to him again.' Looking pleased with herself, Tara said, 'He's a waste of space and I deserve better.'

'Blimey. What brought this on?' Had Tara been given a talking-to by one of those TV agony aunts?

'Well, his wife came to see me.'

'What?'

'You remember Annabel. She'd been having him followed by a private detective. Actually, she's OK,' said Tara. 'We had a really good chat.'

Daisy glugged her wine. This was the thing about not bumping into your best friend for a day or two, you could end up with an awful lot to catch up on.

398

Over the rest of the wine, they caught up.

Finally, when the bottle was empty, Daisy said, 'I'd better go. They'll be back from the hospital soon. I have to decide which room to put them in.'

'I don't know how you can bear to look at her.' Tara shuddered. 'Or speak to her.'

'Not much choice. It's something I'm going to have to get used to. If they settle in the village they could be here for years. What?' said Daisy, because Tara was giving her an odd look.

'They might be here for years,' Tara agreed. 'But if you're not, it won't matter, will it?'

Daisy was zipping up her smoke-infested fleece. She paused in mid-zip.

'Why wouldn't I be here? Where would I go?'

'Um . . . well, Miami.'

'Um . . . well, why?' mimicked Daisy, mystified.

Tara prayed she wasn't putting her foot in it. 'Josh said you might go. When he starts his new job, he'd take you with him. I was a bit shocked myself,' she added hastily, 'but the way he said it, it kind of makes sense. I mean, if you two are a couple, it definitely helps if you're on the same continent.'

'He wants me to give up the hotel and move to Florida with him?' Daisy was stunned.

'Look, I'm sorry, I thought he'd have mentioned it. I mean, it's not that far away now.'

'It's thousands of miles away!'

'I meant when Josh leaves. He's only here for a few more weeks.' Tara frowned. 'I can't believe you haven't talked about it.'

Me neither, thought Daisy.

Josh arrived back at the hotel early on Saturday morning,

399

swooshing into reception on imaginary skis and wearing a daft three-cornered hat to match his daft grin.

Tara, who was busy attacking the higher reaches of the oak-panelled walls with her feather duster, said, 'You look such a berk in that hat.'

'Looking pretty berkish yourself, feather-dusting away with your skirt hooked up in your knickers. Ha, got you,' said Josh triumphantly as she let out a little shriek and clapped her hands to her bottom.

Tara recovered herself. 'Good holiday?'

'The best. You seem pretty pleased with yourself too.' Pulling off his hat, he aimed it with a flourish at the newel post and missed.

'The date for my driving test came through this morning.' Bursting with pride, Tara whipped the envelope from its resting place, tucked into her flamingo-pink bra. Since arriving at work she'd waved it – the envelope, not her bra – at everyone she'd clapped eyes on, whether they were interested or not. Actually, so far nobody at all *had* been interested, but she wasn't going to let that spoil her excitement. Just wait until she passed her test and they were desperate for a lift home from a party at four o'clock in the morning – ha!

But Josh seemed genuinely delighted. 'Sweetheart, that's fantastic. When?'

'Two weeks.' She showed him the precious slip of paper with the date on and waggled her eyebrows in mock alarm.

'Right, no problem. Intensive instruction. What time d'you finish today?'

'Three.'

Briskly Josh rubbed his hands together. 'We'll get a couple of hours in. Three till five suit you?'

He really was brilliant. Daisy was so lucky to have him.

Guiltily, Tara wondered if she should warn him about her brief foot-in-mouth incident regarding Miami. Then again, she didn't want Josh to be cross with her and cancel the driving lesson.

'Ten past three,' Tara told him with a grateful smile. 'Give me time to get home and change.'

Chapter 51

Upstairs, Daisy was in the bath when she heard the key turn in the lock, signalling that Josh was back. Hurriedly she sloshed more bubble bath into the water and spun the taps with her toes. Sometimes you wanted just that extra bit of coverage.

The bathroom door swung open and Josh stood framed in the doorway with bottles of duty-free clinking in his arms and a giant bar of Toblerone clamped between his teeth.

'Chocolate and booze, what more could any girl want?' The words came out muffled; it wasn't easy to speak with a bar of Toblerone clamped in his jaws. Letting it drop onto a pile of towels, Josh said with pride, 'Be honest, am I irresistible or am I irresistible?'

Daisy smiled. How could she not smile at Josh?

'Well, you *are* irresistible, but—'

'Although I have to say I'm disappointed. And hurt. I thought you might have tied a few yellow ribbons round the old oak tree. As I came up the drive I thought she's bound to have done that.' Josh crossed to the bathroom window and peered out. 'But no, not a yellow ribbon in sight.'

'Josh, you haven't been gone for ten long years,' Daisy patiently explained. 'It's been six days.'

'You're joking! Seemed like ten long years to me.' Bending over the bath, he kissed her on the mouth. 'Blimey, got enough bubbles in there? You look like a decapitated head floating in a sea of foam. Are you sure there's a body under all that?'

'Josh, we have to talk.' Daisy hadn't meant it to come out quite this abruptly, but he was trailing an investigative hand through the water. Wriggling out of reach – no mean feat in an average-sized bathtub – she looked up at him and repeated slowly, 'We have to talk.'

Josh's expression changed. The laughter lines around his greeny-brown eyes faded. Then, with a brief nod, he turned off the gushing taps and perched on the side of the bath.

'OK.'

'It's not working.' Daisy exhaled slowly, lifting the sponge in her left hand and squeezing it. She watched the water pour out, making a well in the foam.

Almost imperceptibly, Josh nodded. 'I know.'

At least it was out in the open. Light-headed with relief, Daisy babbled on, 'I thought we'd be fine. I mean, I suppose in a way we *are* fine. We get on really well, so it's not as if we don't like each other . . . oh shit, how can I say this?'

'You don't have to say it. We both knew it wasn't going to last.'

'But I didn't know that! I thought it *would* last,' Daisy protested. 'God, I *so wanted* it to last.'

'Because I was safe,' Josh interjected with a crooked smile. He sounded remarkably calm. 'Because you wanted someone to protect you from the kind of man who isn't safe at all. Like that husband of yours.'

Steven's wasn't the face that had flashed most immediately into Daisy's mind. But that was beside the point. The principle of avoiding getting involved with anyone who would only end up hurting you was one she still thoroughly believed in.

All that the past few weeks with Josh had taught her was that making do with someone simply because they were good and kind and unthreatening wasn't a viable alternative.

Depressing, but out of her control.

'And now here I am, finishing with you all over again.' With her index finger, Daisy stroked the springy blond hairs on his left wrist, just below his watchstrap. 'Are you mad at me?'

'We've had fun. We've had great sex. And we're still friends.' Playfully, Josh picked up her wet hand and kissed it. 'What's to be mad about?' After a pause he added, 'Unless this means you're kicking me out.'

'Don't be daft, of course you can stay.' Daisy let out a shriek as he pretended to bite her fingers, and splashed water in his face. 'You have to get Tara through her driving test before you go anywhere. And it's only a few weeks before you go back to the States.'

'Ah, but are you sure I won't be in your way? Not got anyone else lined up to take my place in that big old bed of yours?' Josh raised a teasing eyebrow. 'I wouldn't want to cramp your style.'

'Nobody else lined up.' Daisy was firm. Absolutely no one else.

Josh winked and hauled himself to his feet.

'I'll believe you, thousands wouldn't. Fancy some breakfast?'

Daisy's heart did a double back-flip. He was so nice, and he seemed to be taking all this so effortlessly in his stride. But there was still a niggle of doubt in the back of her mind.

'Just a cup of tea.' She hesitated. 'Josh? Did you really think I'd give up the hotel and come with you to Miami?'

His mouth twitched as he gazed fondly down at her. 'Not for one single solitary moment.'

'So why did you tell Tara I might?'

'Oh, that. Just to see the look on her face.' Josh chuckled and shook his head. 'And let me tell you, it was an absolute picture.'

'You mustn't be mean to Tara,' Daisy protested.

'I'm not mean to Tara. She just doesn't realise what a rut she's got herself into. She's twenty-seven years old.' Josh gestured in disbelief. 'She has a hell of a lot going for her and she doesn't even realise it. She's lost her sense of adventure. At the rate Tara's going, she'll end up spending the next fifty years in this village. She lives with her aunt, she works here in the hotel as a chambermaid, you're her best friend . . . When I suggested you might not be here for ever she practically had a panic attack! Tara needs to realise there's more to life than Colworth.'

Blimey. It was all true, Daisy marvelled. And she'd never even noticed it until now. Oh well, maybe with Dominic out of the way . . .

'Sure you just want tea?' Reaching the bathroom door, Josh chucked her a towel. By unspoken common consent, she realised, from this moment he would only see her with her clothes on.

That was it, they were back to being friends. No awkwardness, no hard feelings, just a smidgen of sadness and a monumental sense of relief.

'Seeing as you lugged it all the way back from Austria,' Daisy said loyally, 'I'll have tea and Toblerone.'

Josh pulled a face. 'How about if I picked it up at Bristol airport?'

The weather had taken a miraculous turn for the better over the last couple of days. The temperature outside was up, the sky was spring blue and the sun blazed down. Daisy, her spirits lifting, stood on the steps of the hotel enjoying the scene; now that the snow had disappeared, there were far more tourists around, even at nine thirty on a Saturday morning. Spring was here at last, the cherry trees were fuzzy with pink and white blossom and the lawns were studded with clumps of daffodils. Across the river, the chestnut trees were putting out lime-green candle buds and the woody undergrowth was thick with primroses. Several brave guests were even sitting out optimistically in short-sleeved shirts.

Being England, of course, it was likely to be bitterly cold and pouring with rain by eleven o'clock, and everyone would come scuttling back for their thick coats and umbrellas.

Hearing footsteps on the staircase, Daisy glanced over her shoulder and saw Dev making his way downstairs. Busy inspecting his phone, he didn't spot her as he headed across reception and veered to the right. Moments later he reappeared behind the French windows at the far end of the bar. Daisy, watching him through the glass as he pressed out a number and began to speak, realised that he was standing exactly where Josh must have been standing when he'd first spied on Dev and herself on the front steps.

Except this time she was spying on Dev. Well, not *spying*, of course. Observing, that was a nicer way of putting it. Taking note of the black leather jacket and smart-looking trousers and the way his dark hair kept falling onto his forehead as he nodded into the phone. Acknowledging that he had an unfairly perfect profile for an ex-rugby player. Wondering who he was talking to and where he might be heading.

The rugby, that was it! It all came back to Daisy in a flash. The final of the Six Nations Cup thingy at – where was it? Oh yes, Twickenham. Stuck out in the freezing cold being jostled and shoved about by thousands of fanatical beer-swilling rugby fans.

Except it wasn't freezing cold, it was sunny and warm. And when she'd told Josh about it he'd actually painted quite a different picture.

Then again, he was a man.

Then again, Daisy wavered, Josh *had* made it sound like the not-to-be-missed experience of a lifetime. And there was always the chance that Dev hadn't invited someone else along.

Stop it. This is a stupid, *stupid* idea.

But Daisy, her heart beginning to beat faster, found herself unable to leave it alone.

She wasn't working today. Josh, having been up all night travelling back from Kitzbühel, had finally given in to red-eyed exhaustion and gone to bed for a few hours. When he woke up, he would be taking Tara out for her driving lesson.

Retail therapy was an option, Daisy acknowledged, but she couldn't think of a single thing she wanted to buy.

Rugby might actually be quite interesting when you put your mind to it.

Heaven forbid that she should become boring, never try anything new and end up stuck in a rut like Tara.

Dev still hadn't spotted her. Daisy watched him end the phone call and turn away from the window. Right, easy-peasy, all she had to do was bump into him in reception and chat brightly about the weather for a few seconds before suddenly remembering that today was the day of the Six Nations thingy – no, not thingy, *tournament*. Then, with a bit of luck, Dev would flash her a rueful smile and say, 'You really would enjoy it, you know. Sure I can't persuade you to change your mind?'

And guess what? He could!

The next two minutes were mortifying. Daisy already had her

smile liberally plastered across her face when she bumped into Dev.

And his female companion.

'Oh! *Hello*,' Daisy exclaimed far, *far* too brightly as shock reverberated all the way down to her toes. The girl had been in the bar all along, waiting for Dev to finish making his call.

'Daisy.' Acknowledging her with a relaxed nod and a smile, Dev turned to the girl at his side. 'This is Daisy MacLean, she runs the hotel. Daisy, this is Kate.'

Kate dimpled. To add insult to injury she was tiny, practically pocket-sized, and extremely pretty with huge green eyes and short curly black hair. She was also, ominously, carrying a caramel leather holdall that might or might not be an overnight case.

'We're off to Twickenham,' Kate said happily.

'Oh, right. The rugby thing.' Daisy nodded, then pulled a face. 'Rather you than me.'

'Not Daisy's idea of a good time,' Dev sounded amused.

'Oh, I *love* rugby,' Kate exclaimed, her dinky black curls bouncing with enthusiasm. 'I'm a huge fan!'

Huge fan indeed. She didn't weigh more than seven stone.

'Anyway, we'd better be off,' said Dev.

'Have fun!' The effort of smiling in such a cheery, carefree fashion was starting to make Daisy's teeth ache.

'We will,' trilled Kate.

As they left the hotel, Daisy turned back to the reception desk. She hoped it rained at Twickenham. Really hard.

Who *was* Kate, anyway?

'Problem?' Pam glanced up from the bookings diary.

'Um, that girl who just left with Dev.' Daisy frowned, doing her best to sound efficient and businesslike, rather than like a jealous teenager. 'Did you see her arrive this morning?'

'The one with the dark curly hair? No.' Unlike Kate's, Pam's curls didn't jiggle fetchingly when she shook her head – they were sprayed rigidly into place. 'Why?'

'I just wondered if she stayed here last night.' Swivelling the diary round on the polished desk, Daisy scanned the list of entries. 'See? Nothing down here. But if she was here with Dev, we really should have her name. I mean, if there was a fire . . .'

'Maybe she didn't stay,' Pam put in helpfully. 'She could have turned up this morning while I was in the office – oh look, here comes Clarissa!'

Clarissa skittered down the staircase, her tail rotating like a propeller. In her wake puffed Adam, the overweight teenage son of the Australian family booked into the Bellingham Suite.

'We're off for a run,' Adam announced with pride.

Daisy was privately amazed he knew what a run was. All she'd seen him do so far was play intermittently with his Gameboy and guzzle mountains of cakes.

'You're looking after Clarissa?'

'For the whole day. While Mr Tyzack's away.' Smugly Adam added, 'He's paying me.'

Now Daisy really was miffed. She could have looked after Clarissa today. Why hadn't Dev asked her?

'But you might have had other things to do.' She frowned at Pam. 'I don't think that's very fair of Mr Tyzack – he shouldn't impose on our guests.'

'He didn't impose.' Adam was eager to exonerate Dev. 'I offered. Clarissa's ace – me and her get on really well.'

Wrong, Daisy thought jealously, *me* and Clarissa get on really well. I *found* her. For heaven's sake, I'm practically her adoptive mother!

'Here, girl, c'mon, off we go.' Adam rattled Clarissa's lead and she was off in an instant, bouncing adoringly out of the front door at Adam's heels without so much as a backward glance at Daisy.

Cheers, Clarissa.

'So,' Pam said cosily, 'what are you up to today?'

Having run out of alternatives, Daisy realised there was nothing else for it. She suppressed a sigh.

'Shopping.'

Chapter 52

Tara was having a great time. She hadn't forgotten how to drive (hooray!), Josh had pronounced her reversing-round-a-corner manoeuvre faultless and she was even remembering not to cross her arms over each other – heinous crime – when turning the steering wheel. Plus, the sun was still blazing down and from his jacket pocket Josh had produced a bag of strawberry sherbets, the irresistible kind that made the inside of your mouth shrivel up – but not enough to stop you having another one.

'Did Daisy tell you?' Tara was touched by his thought-fulness.

'Tell me what?'

'That strawberry sherbets are my all-time favourite sweets.'

'No.' Josh shook his head. 'I bought them because they're my all-time favourite sweets.'

'Really?' Tara was delighted.

'Well, joint favourites. I'm mad about those liquorice Catherine wheels,' Josh admitted.

'And liquorice comfits. When I was little I used to wet the red ones and use them as lipstick,' Tara happily reminisced. 'I thought I looked so great. God, even at seven I was a tart.'

'Don't put yourself down. And check your mirror before you signal,' added Josh as they reached a junction.

'So what happened to your friend after he broke his leg?' Tara was dying to hear the rest of the story – going on holiday with Josh was evidently a perilous business.

'Baz? He hung up his skis and took up tobogganing instead. Then three days later we all went out to this nightclub and guess what happened?'

'He broke his other leg?'

'*Wrong*. Far too predictable,' Josh scoffed. 'In fact he bumped into this girl – literally – on his way to the loo. She'd broken her leg as well and their crutches got into a complete tangle. So of course Baz being Baz, he bought her a drink. They spent an hour comparing fractures and boasting about how they'd got them, and the next thing we knew, they'd gone.'

'Gone where?'

'Hobbled back to her chalet together. God knows what they managed to get up to, but we hardly saw Baz for the rest of the week. He reckons it's the best holiday he's ever had.'

Tara giggled. 'That's so sweet. Oh, speaking of sweets . . .' She opened her mouth to show that the strawberry sherbet was gone, and waited for Josh to unwrap another one.

'It's like feeding a baby bird.' He popped it into her mouth. 'Now, take the next left and we'll do a few three-point turns.'

Mirror, signal, manoeuvre. Tara turned left into a cul-de-sac and pulled up – brilliantly – at the side of the road.

'By the way, I hope you didn't pick up any girls out there.' She gave him a stern look.

Josh grinned. 'Of course I didn't.'

Standard male answer.

'But you could just be saying that,' Tara argued. 'How would we know?'

'It's the truth. That's not why I go away on holiday. I'm not interested in getting up to no good with other girls.'

Tara relented. That was the thing about Josh, you could

actually believe him. He wasn't a cheating scumbag like some men she could think of.

Most men, in fact.

'Well, glad to hear it. Right.' She took a couple of noisy deep breaths and waggled her hands like an Olympic athlete going for gold. 'Three-point turn. Silence please, ladies and gentlemen, as Tara Donovan of Great Britain heroically attempts the near-impossible in a *very* narrow cul-de-sac.'

'Daisy hasn't told you, has she?' said Josh. A statement rather than a question.

'Told me what? I haven't seen Daisy today.' Tara wished he wouldn't interrupt when she was on the brink of something this momentous; couldn't he see she was trying to concentrate?

'We've called it a day.'

Called it a day? She paused, puzzling over the expression. Surely he meant that they'd named the day?

'What?'

'It's over,' Josh patiently repeated. 'It wasn't working out. We're no longer a couple.'

Tara's left foot jerked and slid off the clutch. The car, already in gear, kangarood forwards and abruptly stalled.

'Handbrake,' Josh said automatically.

'You mean you finished with Daisy?' Tara's mouth dropped open.

'Technically, Daisy finished with me. But it was basically a mutual decision. We both knew it couldn't go on. You're still in gear,' he added. 'Put it into neutral.'

'But I thought you were so happy together,' Tara wailed. 'You get on so *well*.'

'And we'll carry on getting on well. Probably until we're eighty.'

'I don't believe this. Aren't you upset?'

Josh flashed her a smile. 'Relieved. Well, relieved that Daisy said it first. That way I didn't have to feel guilty.'

Tara's heart began to pound. 'You mean there's someone else?'

He shrugged. 'Kind of.'

'*Who?*' Her voice rose.

Josh shook his head. Finally he sighed and said, 'Bloody hell, Tara, who d'you think?'

And then he kissed her.

His mouth tasted of warm strawberries. Tara couldn't believe this was happening. But all the tumblers were clicking into place now. The secret code had been cracked. It had never occurred to her before to fancy Josh, because he was her best friend's boyfriend. It simply wasn't something you even considered. In your mind, they were mentally neutered, Tara realised. Best friend's boyfriends just weren't an option.

Yet all this time, buried deep inside her, had been the subconscious acknowledgement that if Josh hadn't been involved with Daisy, she might find him very attractive indeed.

And now she was allowed to find him attractive, she found that she did. Giving herself up to the kiss, Tara decided that his mouth actually tasted better than strawberries. As for his hair – his mad, tousled, red-gold tufty hair – she simply couldn't stop running her fingers through it. And his face, with those baggy eyes and that broken nose and those faint golden freckles scattered across his cheekbones – how could she never have realised how perfect he was before now?

Finally, reluctantly, Josh pulled away. Just an inch.

'This is the moment,' he murmured, 'when we find out.'

Tara blinked in confusion. 'Find out what?'

'Whether you're about to slap my face.'

Oh. Phew. She managed a shaky smile. 'No.'

Josh's eyes twinkled with relief. 'Good job I'm not a real driving instructor. I'd probably get struck off for this.'

Wonderingly, Tara murmured, 'I never knew, I never *knew*.'

'I know you didn't.' His smile was rueful. 'That's why doing that just now was so scary.'

'I thought we just got on really well.' Tara shook her head in bewilderment.

'So did I. Well, to begin with,' Josh amended. 'And then it started to creep up on me.'

'When?' She was trembling all over with delight. 'When did it start to creep up on you?'

'A couple of weeks ago. We were doing hill starts in Tetbury. You were telling me about your acting auditions.'

Tara winced; she'd only bared her soul to Josh because he was so completely off limits. It wasn't the kind of stuff you'd ever want to confide to a potential boyfriend.

'The sleazy ones? Where the casting directors wanted more than just an audition?'

'And you told them to take a running jump,' said Josh.

'Oh.' She squirmed guiltily. There were times when it had been a close-run thing.

'When you told me,' he went on, 'I wanted to punch them.'

'Really?' Tara was absurdly touched.

'I wanted to kill them,' Josh declared. Clumsily, he kissed the tip of her nose. 'That was when I realised what was happening.'

'But you didn't drop any hints,' Tara marvelled. 'I mean, *none*.' And let's face it, she was the world's expert when it came to picking up hints.

'I was with Daisy.' He shrugged.

Daisy. Tara was instantly awash with guilt. 'I feel terrible.' So terrible she could barely bring herself to think about it. 'What's she going to *say*?' Worst of all, she knew that from this day forward until the day she died, she would associate the taste of strawberries with kissing Josh.

'Don't worry about Daisy. She's fine about it.'

Slack-jawed, Tara turned her face up to his. 'You mean . . . she *knows*?'

'I told her before she left to go shopping. Well, I told her how I felt about you,' Josh amended. 'I didn't know if you'd feel the same way, of course. You might have told me to take a running jump. But it seemed only fair to let Daisy know. So I did.' He broke into a huge grin. 'She was delighted.'

'Really?' Tara was desperate for reassurance; lots of reassurance. 'Not mad at all? You're sure she doesn't mind?'

'She truly doesn't mind. I told you, we weren't a real couple,' said Josh. 'We were pretending to each other that everything was great, but we both knew it wasn't. When I went to Austria, you were the one I missed,' he explained. 'And when I got back this morning, you were the one I couldn't wait to see. There's one thing we do have to sort out though,' Josh went on seriously. 'You have to promise me you won't have any more to do with Dominic Cross-Calvert.'

Oh, the relief!

'I promise.' Tara nodded vigorously. 'There is *no* chance of that happening. It's all over between me and Dominic, I never want to see him again.'

'That's what you told Daisy.'

'It's the truth!'

'You might change your mind,' said Josh.

'Oh, give me a break.' Tears of happiness sprang into Tara's eyes as she wound her arms round his neck. Her voice cracking, she whispered, 'Why would I want to when I've got you?'

Chapter 53

'. . . the party's carrying on,' Dev shouted down the phone above a babble of background noise, 'and Kate doesn't want to leave, so we're going to book into a hotel up here for the night.'

Daisy gazed across the living room at her mini mountain of shopping bags and thought sourly, I'll bet Kate doesn't want to leave. *Tart.*

You knew your attempt at retail therapy hadn't had the desired mood-lifting effect when every single thing you'd bought was still sitting unopened in glossy carriers at eleven o'clock at night.

'This is all very interesting, but why are you telling me? You're over eighteen,' she reminded Dev. 'You don't need my permission to stay out.'

'It's Clarissa. I told Adam we'd be home around midnight. Look, I'm sorry, but I've just rung his room and there's no reply. Could you find Adam, have a word with him and see if he wouldn't mind keeping an eye on her until tomorrow afternoon?'

While you *gallivant* in London?

'Don't you think you're being the tiniest bit selfish here?' Outraged, Daisy said spikily, 'Adam was planning to go to Longleat tomorrow. Now I suppose he's expected to cancel *his* plans, just because *you* can't be bothered to—'

'OK, stop, I didn't know about Longleat,' Dev cut in.

Not too surprisingly, seeing as even Adam didn't know about Longleat.

'So what are you going to do?' If she got caught out later, Daisy hastily decided, she'd claim to have misheard what Adam had said. With his gruff adolescent Aussie twang, that was feasible, surely? ('Oh, you meant you were going to be *lonely* on Sunday! Silly me, I thought you said you were going to be at Longleat!')

'Looks like I'm stuck.' Dev paused. 'Unless you could look after Clarissa.'

Yes!

'*Me?* I can't do it, I'm busy.' Daisy's voice rose. 'Dev, you can't expect me to drop everything, just to—'

'OK, OK,' Dev said hurriedly. 'It was just a thought. Right then, I'll sort something else out.'

'What does that mean? Phone round everyone you know until you find someone willing to take her?'

'I don't—'

'Someone who's never even *met* Clarissa? Oh, for heaven's sake.' Daisy heaved a hurricane-force sigh. 'I'll look after her.'

'No. Absolutely not. I'll drive back,' Dev said firmly.

'Don't be stupid. I'll do it.'

'But you're busy.'

'I know I'm busy, but somebody has to take care of Clarissa.'

'Now I feel terrible,' said Dev.

'Good.' Triumphantly, Daisy hung up.

She found Adam and Clarissa downstairs in the bar, listening to Hector murder 'Mac The Knife'. Well, listening to Hector and half a dozen guests from Chicago *all* singing 'Mac The Knife'.

Very badly indeed. It was clearly going to be one of those noisy Saturday nights.

In response to Daisy's beckoning, Adam tipped Clarissa off his knee and they both ambled over.

'Dev's been held up. He's staying overnight in London,' Daisy explained, 'so I'll take over looking after Clarissa.'

Adam's face fell. 'I don't mind. We've had such a great time. She can stay with me.'

'Yes, but Dev won't be back until tomorrow . . . night,' Daisy improvised.

Eagerly Adam said, 'I'm not doing anything tomorrow either. Honestly, I'd be happy to keep her for another day.'

'That's very sweet of you, but I told Dev I'd look after Clarissa.' She gave him her most businesslike look, the one that signalled: I'm the manager of this hotel and I get the dog.

'Oh. Well, OK.' Adam took a slurp of Coke and gave Clarissa a regretful pat on the head. 'See ya then, girl. Be good now.'

Clarissa wagged her tail then licked his hand. It was all very Disney.

'Come on sweetheart, it's past your bedtime.' Daisy felt like Cruella de Vil, luring Clarissa away under false pretences. Although obviously she wasn't planning to turn her into a coat.

Thankfully Clarissa didn't whimper and wrap her paws round Adam's ankle. She trotted happily after Daisy as together they left the bar.

Paula Penhaligon was in reception, sticking stamps onto letters and posting them into the wooden collection box. Despite Hector's urging, he had never persuaded her to join in with his impromptu sing-along sessions. She claimed to be resting her voice but Daisy suspected she felt it was beneath her. Crikey, one quick chorus of 'Roll Out The Barrel' – how much damage could that do? Paula just didn't want to perform for free.

Still, she was Hector's lady friend. Be polite.

'Hi, Paula . . . oops.' As she called out the friendly greeting, Clarissa darted between her legs. Ears flattened, she cowered at Daisy's feet.

'Oh. Hello.' Paula Penhaligon smiled briefly back at Daisy.

But how weird. Why was Clarissa trembling?

'Dad's in full flow in there.' Daisy indicated the bar. 'Are you joining him?'

'Oh no, I don't think so. Those awful Americans keep pestering me to have my photograph taken with them.' Paula pulled a genteel face. 'I wouldn't mind, but they keep telling me about their last trip to Graceland. As far as they're concerned, the only music worth listening to is 'fifties rock'n'roll.'

Daisy heard low-pitched growling coming from around her feet. How completely embarrassing – Clarissa was actually baring her teeth at Paula Penhaligon! Appalled, she swept the dog up and said, 'Sssh, what do you think you're doing?'

'Hrrrrrrhr,' Clarissa growled ominously, quivering in her arms.

'God, I'm really sorry.' Mortified, Daisy shook her head at Paula. 'She's never done anything like this before.'

'That's the trouble with animals. They're unpredictable. You can't let a dangerous dog just run around the hotel,' said Paula. 'You really should put it on a lead.'

'What made you *do* that?' Daisy chided when they were safely inside her apartment. 'Of all the people to get funny with.'

'Woof,' agreed Clarissa, leaping unrepentantly onto the bed.

'That woman could end up being my stepmother, you know. And that's your bed over there,' Daisy added, pointing to the basket she had taken from Dev's room. 'Your basket, your blanket, your lovely squeaky ball . . . oh well, never mind.

Come here.' Collapsing onto the bed, she let Clarissa jump onto her lap and gave her a cuddle. 'Oh, it's so lovely to have you here. Shall we get ourselves some biscuits and watch a video?'

Clarissa wriggled ecstatically and thumped her tail.

As she flicked on the TV, Daisy said, 'I wonder what Dev's doing now.' Then she stopped, because she didn't want to wonder what Dev might be up to. 'Anyway, never mind him. What d'you fancy, custard creams or chocolate digestives?'

Clarissa yapped and lovingly nuzzled her neck.

'Fabulous idea.' Daisy nodded with approval. 'Let's have both.'

It had knocked her for six at the time, but the idea that Freddie was actually Steven's son was one that Daisy was getting used to.

Now, on Sunday morning, she and Clarissa watched from her bedroom window as Mel, kneeling on the hotel lawn with her arms outstretched, encouraged Freddie to take a few tottering steps towards her.

Three tottering steps, in fact, before he lost his balance and landed with a bump on the grass.

He really was an angelic-looking boy. It wasn't his fault Steven was his father.

Leaping down from the window seat, Clarissa raced across to the door and whimpered in a ladylike fashion.

'OK, OK.' Hastily dragging a brush through her hair, Daisy followed her. Clarissa had her legs metaphorically crossed and was desperate to relieve herself. 'We'll go out the back way.'

But if Clarissa understood, she chose to ignore this instruction. As far as she was concerned the front staircase was quicker. Suppressing a sigh, Daisy followed her. Oh well, she couldn't spend the next goodness knows how long avoiding Mel and pretending she didn't exist.

Clarissa decorously emptied her bladder behind a yew tree before speeding across the grass like a bullet to join Mel and Freddie. Belatedly remembering why she'd brought the lead downstairs with her, Daisy yelled, 'Clarissa, *stop*, come *here*.'

Nightmare newspaper headlines flashed before her eyes: small mongrel with ridiculous name mauls angelic toddler. But all Clarissa did was greet Mel like an old friend and nuzzle joyfully up to Freddie before turning and sauntering back, her tail still wagging like a metronome.

Daisy clipped the lead to her collar with relief.

Scooping Freddie up, Mel made her way over.

'I haven't had a chance yet to thank you properly.' With her free hand, she pushed her fringe out of her eyes. 'For saving Freddie . . . letting us stay here . . . well, everything.' Another pause. 'I know it's feeble, but what else can I say? Thank you.'

Didn't have a lot of choice, thought Daisy. When someone was throwing a baby out of a burning house you felt morally obliged to catch it. Otherwise people were going to call you a butterfingers for the rest of your life.

Awkwardly she muttered, 'That's OK.'

'I never meant to hurt you,' Mel went on bluntly. 'I swear I didn't. If I hadn't met Barney, you'd never have found out about Freddie.'

'I know.' Daisy had already worked this out for herself. Plus, of course, if she hadn't given Barney a job he'd never have got involved with Mel. This whole mess was practically her own fault.

'Sometimes these things just happen,' said Mel. 'I'm really not a horrible person. And I do love Barney.'

'Everyone loves Barney. Where is he, by the way?'

'Up at the cottage. We're off to see him now. The accident investigators have confirmed it was an electrical fault. All that ancient wiring,' Mel shuddered. 'It doesn't bear thinking about.'

Daisy shook her head, guiltily recalling the moment when she'd thought Mel might have started the fire herself.

'But you're insured?'

'Yes, thank God. The claims man came out yesterday. We'll be able to get the place fixed up. Why are you keeping her on that thing?' Changing the subject, Mel gestured at Clarissa. 'I've never seen her on a lead before.'

'Oh. One of the guests wasn't too happy about her running around.'

'But Clarissa isn't dangerous!'

'She growled at someone,' Daisy admitted. 'It's not like her at all, but better safe than sorry.'

'And you're looking after her while Dev's away. You know, I did wonder . . .'

'Wonder what?' prompted Daisy when Mel's voice trailed away.

'Well, the other night when you found the cottage on fire. You and Dev were together—'

'There's nothing going on between us, if that's what you think,' Daisy interrupted. 'Nothing at all.' She felt herself getting hot. 'God, he's the last person I'd want to be involved with.'

'Why on earth not?' Mel raised her eyebrows in disbelief. 'He's attractive, he's successful – and *brave*. Now that's what I call a catch.'

'He's what I call a womaniser,' Daisy shot back, because the last thing she needed, frankly, was a lecture from Mel on the subject of bedworthy men. 'And I've already been married to one of those, thanks very much.'

Mel ignored the jibe. 'I just asked,' she said calmly.

'So you did. And now I've told you.'

'I just don't think you should let it mess up the rest of your life.'

Chapter 54

Daisy was draped across the sofa watching *The Great Escape* when there was a knock at the door.

Clarissa, lying on her stomach equally engrossed in the film, pricked up her shabby ears and looked inquiringly at Daisy.

It was six o'clock. Not having bothered to get dressed again after her bath, Daisy tightened the belt of her dressing-gown and called out, 'Who is it?'

'Me.'

Clarissa slithered off her like an eel and bounded over to the door.

Double-checking that she was decent, Daisy followed her and opened it. It would have been nice, at this point, if Clarissa could have retained some dignity and played it cool. Some chance. Whimpering with delight, she hurled herself besottedly into Dev's arms. Like an over-eager girl welcoming back the love-rat boyfriend who endlessly dumps her for other women.

'Thanks for looking after her,' Dev said with a grin, as Clarissa frantically licked his hands. 'I owe you one.'

Daisy stuck her hands into her dressing-gown pockets. 'She thought you'd abandoned her for good.'

'Sweetheart!' Dev held the dog's face up to his. 'I'd *never* do that to you.'

'Woof!' Clarissa agreed, her back legs cycling ecstatically against the crook of his arm.

'Has she behaved herself?'

'She snarled at Paula Penhaligon. I had to keep her on a lead today.'

'*Snarled?*' Dev was taken aback. 'Are you sure?'

'I was there. I know a snarl when I see one.' Daisy was tempted to give him a demonstration – she felt quite like snarling herself.

'Maybe I should take her to the vet, get her checked out. Anyway, thanks again for looking after her. Shall I take her basket with me?' He indicated Clarissa's un-slept in basket on the floor by the window.

As she handed it over, Daisy once again felt bereft, the foster mother returning her much-loved charge to its real family. She had to force herself not to kiss Clarissa goodbye.

'We're down in the bar,' Dev offered, 'if you'd like to join us.'

Us? As in Kate and me? *That* kind of us?

'I'm not dressed.'

He raised a playful eyebrow. 'You could always try – oh, I don't know, putting some clothes on?'

Daisy shook her head. 'No thanks.'

'Are you OK?' Dev gave her one of his you-can-trust-me looks.

'Fine. Never better.' She *definitely* wasn't going to tell him it was all over between her and Josh. 'Just tired.'

Smiling to herself, Daisy observed the difference in Josh when he arrived back at ten o'clock. He was deliriously happy, but doing his level best to hide it in case she was offended.

'I can't believe I never realised before how well-matched you two are.'

'I know.' He grinned, relieved to be able to talk about Tara

426

and ruffling his hair in disbelief. 'We just seem to get on so brilliantly, and the weird thing is, we have nothing in common! She hates all the films I love. I can't stand her taste in music. She's refusing to learn to play golf, and she thinks Roger Moore was a better James Bond than Sean Connery. I mean, let's face it, how tragic is that?'

Daisy hugged her knees with delight, as thrilled as if she'd engineered the entire situation herself. Upon meeting some potential new boyfriend, Tara had always automatically turned herself into the kind of girl she thought he'd like her to be. Out went her own views and opinions, and in came an 'Ooh, me too!' version of his. If she was involved with a man who was mad about motocross, Tara was instantly mad about it too. If she met one who played in a heavy metal band, she'd buy a heap of heavy metal CDs and actually convince herself that she loved them. Despite the fact that her favourite singer was Mariah Carey.

'And she told me she didn't like my shirt.' Josh was shaking his head, clearly appalled by her lack of taste. To be fair, the shirt was yellow and patterned with swirly purple squid. He'd picked it up in Hawaii. Daisy was with Tara on this one.

'You might wear dodgy shirts,' she said soothingly, 'but at least you don't have a secret stash of Starsky and Hutch videos hidden under your bed.'

Oh yes, Tara was a closet Paul-Michael Glaser fan. She'd kill her for this.

But Josh let out a whoop and exclaimed, 'I'm mad about Starsky and Hutch, they're the best!'

'So that's one thing you have in common. You sad, sad couple.'

Except they weren't, of course. Tara and Josh were a happy, happy couple. Apart from one slight awkward dilemma . . .

She waited until he'd brought her a cup of coffee and the biscuit tin before broaching it.

'Josh?'

He pulled a face. 'What? You hate my shirt too?'

'Your shirt is great,' Daisy assured him. 'Especially for cleaning windows.'

He pinched her elbow. 'What did I ever see in you?'

'I'm lovely, just an all-round kind and caring person. Which is why I'm concerned about your sex life.'

Josh choked on his Garabaldi. 'What sex life?'

'Exactly my point!' Daisy spread her hands in despair. 'It's been bothering me all day. You're staying in my flat, Tara's living down the road with Maggie . . . it strikes me you have a bit of a privacy problem.'

'God, Daisy, do we have to talk about this?' He gave her a pained look; for the first time since she'd known him, Josh was embarrassed. 'It's not your concern.'

'Well, I know that, but I'm just asking.' Relaxed though she was about her two best friends getting together, Daisy knew that Josh wouldn't dream of bringing Tara back to his room here. With the best will in the world, it would be too awkward. For all three of them.

'You mean you're nosy,' said Josh.

'I prefer curious.' Daisy helped herself to another biscuit.

'OK.' He sighed, because she clearly wasn't going to give up without a fight. 'You don't have to worry because it isn't a problem. Tara doesn't want to sleep with me anyway.'

This time it was Daisy's turn to splutter and spray crumbs across the coffee table.

'Are you *serious*?'

'Absolutely. No sex. Not for a while at least,' Josh added. Hopefully.

'But why?' Daisy was appalled. Tara had never done anything like this before.

'When I started giving her driving lessons, we talked. For hours,' said Josh. 'About anything and everything. I heard all about her disastrous love life and how she'd slept with too many men for all the wrong reasons. She was able to tell me about it because we were just friends then,' he explained. 'Now, of course, she's mortified and determined to prove she's not some tarty trollop who'll jump into bed with just any old bloke.'

Daisy snorted with laughter; she couldn't help it. 'This is great. Good for Tara.'

'I know, I know.' Ruefully, Josh rubbed his stubbly chin. 'In theory it's all very well. Commendable, in fact. But it's bloody frustrating when "any old bloke" turns out to be you.'

Tuesday was warm and sunny, another beautiful spring day. Inside her cottage, Maggie diligently sewed zips into a pile of completed cushion covers and did her best to ignore the sense of excitement bubbling in the pit of her stomach.

It was idiotic, but she couldn't help it. She felt like a woman previously jilted half a dozen times at the altar, convinced that this time her bridegroom was actually going to show.

Except instead of a bridegroom, she was waiting for her washing machine repair man. Which was almost more thrilling. For not only had Dino – that was his name – promised faithfully to be here by two o'clock, he'd assured her that he'd have with him *exactly* the right replacement part to fix her machine.

He'd sounded so confident that Maggie had forgotten to be sceptical. Her long ordeal was finally over, she was convinced of it. As from today she would be able to effortlessly wash and tumble-dry once more.

In the distance, the church clock chimed twice and Maggie

experienced a qualm of doubt. The next moment she heard the blissful squeak of brakes outside and leapt to her feet, scattering pins and cotton reels in her eagerness to check that – yes, hallelujah, it was Dino, he was here!

Crikey, not bad either. They'd actually sent a half-decent one for a change. Not that it made a bit of difference. The important thing was whether he could fit replacement parts.

'You must be Maggie,' Dino cheerfully announced when she flung open the door to greet him.

Oh dear, she'd spent so long ranting and raving on the phone to his company that they were already on first-name terms. The entire workforce probably referred to her behind her back as Mad Maggie.

'Come in. I'm so glad to see you.' Maggie vowed to show him she was a nice person really, not always a screeching harridan. 'Tea or coffee?'

'Tea, please.' He grinned at her. 'Black, no sugar.'

No sugar? How completely extraordinary. Maggie had always assumed that every repairman had to take three sugars at the very least.

Terrified that he might be an imposter, she said, 'Have you brought the part?'

'Didn't I tell you I would?' In the kitchen, Dino opened his case and held up the polythene bag containing the precious part. Light-brown eyes twinkling, he pretended to tut-tut at her. 'Oh ye of little faith.'

'Don't make fun of me,' protested Maggie. 'I've been disappointed before.'

'No more disappointment. I'm here now. OK, let's get started.' With a commendable lack of grunting he slid the washing machine out from under the worktop and immediately got busy with his screwdriver. Reassured, Maggie put the kettle on and reached for the cups. It was ten past two. By two thirty she could be joyfully bundling armfuls of washing into the machine, pressing the button and watching her clothes sloshing around.

As a special treat she left Dino a Penguin to have with his tea.

At two twenty, he appeared in the living-room doorway. With an expression on his face reminiscent of the one doctors on TV use when they're about to tell you it's malignant.

'Bit of a hitch.' Dino wiped his forehead with the back of his hand.

Maggie, still sewing zips into cushions, slowly looked up at him. 'What kind of hitch?'

'The part we thought was causing the problem . . . well, it wasn't.'

This was not what Maggie wanted to hear. She felt her jaw tighten. 'And?'

'I'm really sorry. We need to order another part.'

He was clearly mortified. Maggie didn't care. 'And how long will that take?' It was a rhetorical question; she already knew the answer. '*Another* two weeks?'

'Maybe ten days. I'd mark it urgent. Look, I know you're disappointed—'

'Disappointed?' Maggie heard her voice unwittingly go soprano. 'Disappointed doesn't even *begin* to describe how I feel. You *promised* you'd have it fixed this afternoon!'

'I know I did, but all I had to go on was what the last engineer told me. He thought he'd located the fault, but he hadn't.'

'Right. Well, in that case, we'll just have to sort it out some other way.' Rising to her feet, Maggie wiped her sweating hands on her jeans before snatching up the phone. 'So what you're going to do is ring your boss *this minute* and tell him I've had enough. I want a new machine, one that actually works. He can arrange to put one into a van and have it delivered here this afternoon. Then you can plumb it in for me before taking away the broken one. Does that sound reasonable to you?'

Dino shrugged. 'Sounds reasonable to me, but I don't know if they'll go along with it. You see, it's not company policy to—'

'Just do it,' Maggie interrupted, shoving the phone into his hand.

And to give Dino his due, he gave it his best shot. She stood in front of him and watched him doing his utmost to persuade someone called Mr Ellison that after all she'd been through, it was surely the least they could do for her.

It soon became apparent, however, that Mr Ellison had no intention of fostering customer relations and was determined not to give in.

Something snapped inside Maggie. For a split second she wondered if steam was actually gushing from her ears. About to wrench the phone from Dino and give Mr Ellison a coruscating piece of her mind, she recalled how effective it had been in the past – basically, not effective at all – and marched to the front door instead.

A desperate situation called for desperate measures. Without even pausing to consider whether what she was doing was wise – or if it would even work – Maggie locked the door from the inside. Having dropped the key into her bra, she moved to the windows and locked them too.

'What are you doing?' hissed Dino, covering the phone.

'Just keep talking,' Maggie ordered. 'Tell him I'll speak to him in a minute.'

She locked the kitchen door and secured the window in there as well. By this time her bra was jangling with keys.

'Right,' Maggie announced, snatching the phone from Dino and deliberately not meeting his eye. 'Mr Ellison? Hello, how are you, this is Maggie Donovan here. I just wondered if you had my replacement washing machine loaded into the van yet? No? Oh dear, I'm so sorry to hear that. Well, just to let you know, I have your repairman here and he's not leaving until my new washing machine arrives. Yes, absolutely serious. I'm holding him as a hostage, Mr Ellison. He can't escape, I've made quite sure of that. I'm sorry? You're asking me to be *reasonable*?' Sorrowfully, Maggie shook her head. 'Mr Ellison, I've spent the last two months being reasonable and it really hasn't got me very far. Yes, fine, you go ahead and call the police. I'm just about to phone the news desk at BBC Bristol. Tell you what, why don't we have a wager and see which of them gets here first?'

Chapter 55

Clink-clank went the keys in Maggie's bra as she replaced the phone on the coffee table.

'Imagine that. He hung up on me.' When she looked over at Dino, he was smiling.

'Are you serious about this?'

'Absolutely.'

'You're kidnapping me?'

'Yes. Well, taking you hostage.' Maggie pulled a face. 'Sorry.'

'It's just that my wife's nine months pregnant,' said Dino. 'She was due to give birth yesterday. What if she goes into labour?'

Horrified, Maggie squawked, 'Are you serious?'

Damn, damn, *damn*.

'No.' He broke into a grin. 'I'm not married.'

'Oh, for heaven's sake!' She clutched her chest in relief. 'For a minute there I believed you.'

'Don't worry. No babies on the way.' He paused, his dark head tilted to one side. 'I do have a squash court booked for this evening, but I suppose I could cancel it.'

'Are you sure?' Maggie wavered. 'I mean, you really don't mind?'

'Being held hostage? Not at all.' Cheerfully, Dino said, 'Fine by me.'

She was lost for words. It hadn't occurred to her for a moment that he'd actually be happy to go along with her mad plan.

'Well, thanks,' Maggie managed finally.

'No problem. I think you deserve a new washing machine. So, how about another cup of tea?'

'Oh yes, of course. I'll just—'

'Whoa, calm down.' Dino put out his arm to stop her bustling past him. 'Why don't I make it? And you can phone the BBC.'

It had evidently been a slow news day. The BBC news desk, very, *very* interested in her story, promised to send a reporter out to Colworth within the hour. Emboldened by such enthusiasm on their part, Maggie followed up the call with another, to the *Bristol Evening Post*. She drank the tea Dino had made and peered out of the window for a while, listening out for police sirens and wondering whether anyone would actually turn up.

'Maybe you should do your hair,' Dino helpfully suggested.

'What?'

'It's looking a bit . . .' His messed-up gestures indicated that it could do with a brush. In her agitation, Maggie had been pushing her hands through her hair like Ken Dodd. 'If they bring TV cameras, you'll want to look your best.'

This made sense. She went upstairs, restored order to her fine blonde hair and inexpertly slicked on a bit of lipstick. Returning to the living room, she found her hostage stretched on the sofa flicking through the TV channels.

'Nothing much on,' Dino reported. 'Not until *Countdown* at four thirty.' He glanced up at Maggie, who was looking preoccupied. 'Problem?'

'I'm just wondering how long this is likely to last. You'll be hungry soon and I don't have much in the house.' He was taking this incredibly well, and Maggie felt the least she could do was provide a decent meal.

'Don't fuss. Let's have a look.' Switching off the TV, Dino headed through to the kitchen. The next thing she knew, he was exploring the contents of the larder, handing her a bag of flour and a carton of eggs.

'Pasta,' he announced with authority.

'Oh . . . um, I think I've got half a packet of spaghetti . . .'

'I'm talking about fresh pasta. Haven't you ever made it?'

'Well, no.' Maggie was stung; surely only Jamie Oliver and people in glossy magazines actually made their own pasta?

'It's easy. I'll show you. Got a rolling pin?' As he spoke, Dino was already pushing up his sleeves and washing his hands at the sink.

Maggie began to chuckle.

'What?' said Dino.

'If nothing else comes of this afternoon, at least I'll have learned to make pasta.'

They chatted easily while they worked. Dino Marinelli was thirty-seven and amicably divorced. He lived in a flat in north Bristol and kept himself fit by playing squash and running marathons. His Italian father had taught him to cook from an early age and he had inherited a pretty good singing voice from his English mother. Enthralled, Maggie learned that Dino had sung in various bands around Bristol until a few years ago. He had even appeared on *Stars In Their Eyes* as a Frank Sinatra soundalike.

'But that's brilliant! Did you win?'

He rolled his eyes in disgust. 'Nah, got beaten by Bonnie Langford. Now, we want a gutsy sauce to go with this. D'you like olives?'

'I do like olives,' said Maggie, 'but I don't have any.'

'Didn't I pass a shop further up the High Street?' Dino shook flour onto the rolled-out sheet of pasta and deftly flipped it over. 'I'll pop up and get some.'

'You can't go to the shop to buy olives!' For heaven's sake, was he stupid? 'You're supposed to be a *hostage*.'

Dino broke into a grin. 'Sorry. Forgot.'

Maggie was beginning to wonder if everyone else had forgotten too. It was three o'clock and so far nobody at all had turned up. At this rate her siege was in danger of turning into an embarrassing damp squib.

The next moment she almost jumped out of her skin as the doorbell rang.

'Oh!' *Help*.

'Here we go.' Dino gave her an encouraging nod. 'Could be Dermot Murnaghan, reporting for *News at Ten*. Or the SAS come to rescue me – don't let them throw smoke bombs through the letter box. By the way, you've got flour on your nose,' he called after Maggie as she went to see who it really was.

A police car was parked outside the cottage. The muscles in Maggie's neck relaxed when she saw that it was only Barry Foster, their local policeman. She wasn't frightened of Barry – in fact, he was probably far more scared of her.

Fishing in her bra, she unlocked the window and opened it a few inches.

'Hello there, Maggie. We've had a call from a Mr Ellison at Carver's Electricals in Bristol. Now then, what's all this about?'

The voice was bluff but he was clearly ill-at-ease. Last year, Barry's wife Yvonne had commissioned her to make two white satin pillowcases with the words 'Snugglebum' and 'Wiggly Wabbit' embroidered across them in pink, as a Valentine's surprise for her husband. Heroically, Maggie had kept this information to herself, but Barry had had trouble looking her in the eye ever since. Now that he was being forced to do so, his cheeks glowed with embarrassment.

'I'm sure Mr Ellison gave you the gist of it.' Maggie remained calm. 'The repairman doesn't leave until I get a new washing machine.'

'Maggie, you can't do this.'

'I am doing it.'

'But it won't work. You'll end up making a fool of yourself.'

'Oh well, we all make fools of ourselves at some stage, don't we?' Not quite under her breath Maggie murmured, 'Snugglebum.'

Barney's neck turned brick-red. 'I'm not Snugglebum.'

So now she knew. She'd always wondered. Barry's pet name was Wiggly Wabbit and Snugglebum was Yvonne.

'Sorry. I won't say it again.' Maggie felt mean. 'But the repairman stays here.'

Barry frowned. 'Have you got him tied up?'

'No, I'm being perfectly nice to him. He's fine.'

'Could I just have a word with him, Maggie?'

'Actually, he's busy right now.'

'Please.'

Over her shoulder, Maggie called, 'Dino? The policeman would like to speak to you.'

'I'm cutting the papardelle.'

'He says please.'

Dino joined her at the window, floury-handed and clutching a knife.

'Look, sir, couldn't we just put a stop to this?' said Barry.

'She's got all the keys.' Gravely, Dino added, 'In her bra.'

'You could climb out through this window,' Barry pleaded.

'*This* window?' Dino cast a horrified glance at the narrow frame, less than twelve inches wide. 'Who d'you think I am, Kylie Minogue?'

'Here comes the BBC,' said Maggie, adrenaline beginning to swoosh through her veins as she spotted the distinctive van trundling down the High Street towards them with two more cars in its wake.

'Phone,' prompted Dino, because the telephone was trilling behind them.

'Maggie Donovan?' said the voice at the other end when she picked up the receiver. 'Hi, this is Tammie Houston, I'm calling from Radio 5 Live . . .'

Pam, who was devoted to gossip, intercepted Daisy as she emerged from a meeting at four o'clock.

'Have you heard about what's going on in the High Street? Some of the guests have just told me there are reporters and TV vans outside one of the cottages. *And* the police are there.'

Any mention of police brought the memory of Steven's accident flooding back. Daisy shivered. 'Did they say what it was about?'

Tara, coming off duty and sauntering through reception with her denim jacket slung over one shoulder, said jauntily, 'What's what about?'

'Something about someone being held hostage.' Pam looked important. 'Imagine, right here in the High Street!'

'Which cottage?' Daisy found it hard to believe. This was Colworth after all, not the Bronx.

'They didn't say. Just that it had a blue front door.'

Daisy and Tara looked at each other. Pam didn't live in the village. The only blue front door in the High Street was Maggie's.

'Come on.' Daisy's heart was thumping. 'Let's go.'

'I don't believe it,' Tara groaned. 'God, this is so embarrassing. My own *aunt* . . .'

Quite a crowd had gathered by this time, milling around in the street along with the assembled press. Maggie, it transpired, was currently on the phone conducting a live radio interview. A TV crew was waiting for her to finish so they could film her for the six o'clock news. Meanwhile, Christopher and Colin from the shop – in matching technicolour waistcoats – were telling a reporter about the months of hassle she'd endured at the hands of the company that had failed to fix her washing machine.

'It's not embarrassing,' Daisy exclaimed, 'it's completely brilliant! Ooh, look, here she is now.'

Maggie appeared at the bedroom window, bright-eyed and confident, facing the cameras like a pro.

'Maggie! Any word yet from Carver's? Are they sending another washing machine?'

'I've just heard from them,' Maggie called down to the journalist from the *Bath Echo*. 'They're consulting their solicitors.' Her mouth twitching, she added, 'I'm sooo scared.'

'Good on ya, girl!' hooted an American tourist, clapping and whistling his approval. 'Way to go!'

'Maggie, could we have a picture of the two of you?'

Tara was still mortified. This simply wasn't the kind of behaviour you expected of a sedate, middle-class, cushion-making aunt. The next moment, Maggie was joined at the upstairs window by her hostage and the cameras began to flash.

'Blimey,' said Daisy, impressed.

Hector, on his way back from the bank, pulled up in his Land Rover and buzzed down the window.

'What's happening?'

'Maggie's kidnapped her repairman. She's not letting him go until she gets a new washing machine.' Daisy was loving every minute of this. 'That's him up there with her now. Isn't it fantastic?'

Hector, looking up at the window, wasn't so sure. Of course he admired Maggie for taking a stand, but the way she and the repairman were laughing together was making him feel distinctly uneasy.

One of the TV crews was currently roaming the street in search of a fresh voice to interview. Since it was the kind of thing Hector was great at, Daisy said, 'Go on, Dad, you speak to them. Tell them we're all behind Maggie.'

'I don't know . . .' Hector hesitated as one of the reporters shouted up.

'Hey, Dino, how's she treating you?'

'Dino,' Tara murmured in appreciation. 'Italian. That explains the eyes.'

'She's treating me very well. Couldn't have been kidnapped by a nicer woman.' Dino's smile broadened to reveal even white teeth. 'No complaints at all.'

Hector's hands tightened convulsively on the steering wheel.

'Tara!' exclaimed Maggie, spotting them for the first time. 'Darling, so sorry about this. You don't mind if I don't let you in, do you?'

Tara was taken aback. 'But—'

'You can stay with Daisy until this is sorted out, can't she, Daisy?'

'No problem. You're doing a great job there, Maggie,' Daisy replied cheerfully.

'In fact, you could do us a huge favour.' Digging in the pocket of her jeans, Maggie unearthed a crumpled twenty-pound note. Beckoning Daisy forward, she dropped it down to her. 'There's just a couple of things you could get us from the shop. A jar of green olives, one of those little tins of anchovies and a bottle of wine.' She turned to Dino. 'Red or white?'

'Red,' said Dino.

'In fact, make it two bottles.' Maggie winked at Daisy. 'After all, we may be here for some time.'

Hector had heard enough. He rammed the Land Rover into gear. 'I have to get back. Paula's waiting for me.'

'But how long is this going to last?' Tara was bewildered. 'I need a change of clothes. I mean, she'll have her new machine by tonight, won't she?'

'That's up to the company,' one of the journalists explained. 'If they refuse to give in, this could carry on for days. Not that he seems too bothered,' he went on, jerking his thumb in Dino's direction. 'Then again, if I was being held hostage by a woman like that, I'd make the most of it too.'

Stunned, Tara exclaimed, 'That's my aunt you're talking about!'

'So?' The journalist glanced up at Maggie in admiration. 'I'm telling you, he's a lucky bloke.'

Slamming his foot down on the accelerator, Hector roared off.

Doesn't want to keep Paula waiting, thought Daisy with a touch of annoyance. Since the incident with Clarissa, she had gone right off Paula. She was also disappointed that Hector hadn't stayed to voice his support for Maggie. Oh well.

'We've got shopping to get.' She waved the twenty-pound note at Tara, then shouted up, 'What kind of red? Merlot? Claret?'

Without hesitation, Dino called back, 'Montepulciano.'

Tara raised an eyebrow. Montepulciano was Maggie's favourite.

Chapter 56

'You're a star,' said Maggie, keeping the safety chain on while Tara fed the olives, the anchovies and the two bottles of wine one by one through the four-inch opening in the door. Having taken possession of everything, she returned the favour by squeezing a supermarket carrier through the gap.

Tara opened the bag. As well as a pair of jeans and a sweatshirt, it contained her toothbrush, Robbie Williams T-shirt-cum-nightie, battered pink towelling slippers (so uncool) and make-up bag.

'So he's staying the night.' She still couldn't believe Maggie was actually doing this.

'Looks like he'll have to.' Maggie shrugged. 'No sign so far of my new washing machine.'

Tara noted with disapproval that she wasn't exactly sounding distraught.

'Never mind her,' said Daisy, indicating Tara's pursed mouth. 'Are you having fun?'

Maggie grinned, instantly looking ten years younger. 'Daisy, the most fun I've had in my life.'

'Daisy. Can I have a quick word?'

Daisy's heart sank as Mel approached her in reception. She had another meeting lined up. She could handle being civil to Mel but she really didn't want to be her friend.

443

'I'm a bit busy.'

'Sorry, I know. It won't take long.' Mel was clearly determined to have her say. 'Barney's just told me something I think
you should know.'

Barney. Brilliant. Had he had an affair with Steven too?

'What?' Daisy glanced at her watch.

'The night of the fire. He saw Paula Penhaligon kicking
Clarissa.'

Now Mel had her undivided attention.

'*What?*'

'He was too embarrassed to tell you. I mean, she is pretty
famous, isn't she? But I said you'd want to know. That night,
she turned up with Hector in her high heels. Barney saw Clarissa
dancing around her and Paula just kicked her away. Really hard,
according to Barney.'

Daisy didn't know whether to feel sickened or elated.

'*Really* hard?'

Mel nodded.

'Like a football.'

Well.

'Thanks,' said Daisy.

She couldn't bring herself to admit it to Dino – too embarrassing
for words – but Maggie had never eaten homemade fresh pasta
before. The difference between homemade fresh and supermarket dried was unbelievable. The two bottles of Montepulciano
had been jolly nice too.

'That was delicious,' Maggie sighed, pushing her empty
plate away.

The great thing about the word delicious was that you could
be a bit tipsy and still pronounce it.

'It was.' Dino nodded in agreement, his elbows resting

comfortably on the table. His dark eyes bright with mischief, he said, 'Are they still outside?'

Maggie raised herself slightly unsteadily from her seat, just enough to see through the living-room window.

'Some of them. I wonder what they're thinking.'

'Doesn't take a tabloid journalist to work it out.' Dino grinned at her. 'You can't really blame them. It's a nice little angle.' He paused, then said gently, 'We could, you know, if you wanted to. I've really enjoyed this evening. I think you're great.'

Gosh. Maggie was flattered but taken aback. It just went to show how hopelessly out of practice she was. These days, clearly, if a man found you attractive and fancied sleeping with you – well, he just came right out and said it. No shilly-shallying around.

'We're both adults,' Dino went on easily. Moving their wine glasses out of the way, he reached for her hand. 'So, what d'you think?'

Maggie was lost for words. Talk about upfront. Then again, why shouldn't he be?

Flushing slightly, she realised she was tempted. Why not? After the misery of the last few weeks, didn't she deserve a bit of cheering up?

'Decisions decisions,' Dino teased. Crossing over to the window he waved to the loitering journalists, flashed them a cheeky grin and drew the curtains.

A ragged cheer went up outside.

Under the table, Maggie felt her knees begin to knock.

'No pressure,' Dino promised, drawing her to her feet. Then he put his arms round her and kissed her.

It was a really nice kiss. Warm and skilful and just the right pressure, not too hard and not too soft. All in all, as kisses went, practically perfect.

Sadly, it came from the wrong mouth.

The moment his lips brushed against hers, Maggie knew she couldn't go through with it. Dino was attractive and single and thoroughly good company, all the things you could ask for in a man, but he simply wasn't Hector.

Gently, she extricated herself and gave him a rueful smile. 'I'm sorry. I can't.'

'Are you sure?'

Maggie nodded.

'Damn,' said Dino good-naturedly. 'I hate it when that happens.'

Maggie laughed; she couldn't imagine it happened often. 'Shall I make some coffee?'

He nodded. 'Coffee would be great.'

While she was boiling the kettle, the phone began to ring in the living room. Dino, who was nearest, answered it.

'Who was that?' said Maggie when he appeared in the kitchen doorway.

He shrugged. 'No one. The line just went dead.'

Two minutes later, the phone rang again. This time Maggie picked it up.

'Jealous lover?' Dino whispered as he put her cup of coffee on the table in front of her.

Some hope.

Maggie briefly covered the receiver. 'Not quite. Sky News.'

'Where have you been?' demanded Paula when Hector came downstairs.

'Fixing up a round of golf for tomorrow.'

'I've been waiting down here for ages,' she complained. 'They're expecting us in the restaurant at ten o'clock, so we've time for a drink in the bar before going through.'

The hotel bar was full of press, but Paula no longer minded. The last faint signs of bruising had faded from her face and neck. That plastic surgeon had certainly known what he was doing. Modesty aside, she knew she looked great.

That was the funny thing about the press – you complained about them when they pestered you nonstop, but after a few weeks without them you found you kind of missed having them around.

Hector glanced in the direction of the smoky bar and shook his head. The hotel was buzzing with talk of Maggie and her handsome hostage; everywhere he went, people were discussing them and speculating on the likely outcome.

'It's too noisy in there. Anyway, I'd rather eat out tonight.'

'Dad! Can I talk to you?' Daisy shot out of the bar to the accompaniment of several wolf whistles, the journalists noisily demonstrating their appreciation of her black-stockinged legs and above-the-knee leather skirt.

'Sorry, we're running late.' Hector, who just wanted to get out of the hotel, abruptly took Paula's arm. 'Some other time.'

'Oh bum,' said Daisy, when they'd gone.

'That's a coincidence.' One of the journalists winked at her. 'We were just remarking on yours.'

Maggie was woken the next morning by the sound of tapping on her door. Her first thought was: bleeugh, red wine hangover. The second was to be fervently grateful that she hadn't slept with Dino last night.

'Are you decent?' called Dino through the door.

'Yes.' *Completely decent.* Hooray!

He came in, carrying a mug of tea and a newspaper. 'Thought you might like to see this.'

Wriggling into a sitting position, Maggie thirstily gulped

down the hot tea and opened the paper. Unbelievably, there they were, on page 14 of the *Daily Mail*. A surprisingly flattering photograph of her leaning out of the bedroom window with Dino beside her. The tone of the accompanying piece – the consumer strikes back – was upbeat and supportive, and for good measure there was a second smaller photo of Dino dressed as Frank Sinatra for his appearance in *Stars In Their Eyes*.

I could have slept with Frank Sinatra last night, thought Maggie with a smile.

The irony that this was Hector's all-time favourite singer didn't escape her.

'I've put some toast in downstairs. And we'll have to switch the phone back on,' said Dino, sounding efficient. Tossing Maggie's dressing gown over to her, he went to pull back the curtains.

'Don't!' squeaked Maggie, but it was too late. Sunlight poured into the room.

'Look at that. They're outside waiting for us,' Dino marvelled.

'And now they've seen you opening my bedroom curtains! What are they going to think?'

Battling frantically to get into her dressing gown, she stopped to listen to herself. 'Oh sod it, who cares? We already know what they think.'

Joining Dino at the window, Maggie exclaimed with delight at the sight of the reporters gathered outside, and flung open the window to hear what they were shouting up at her.

'Morning, Maggie! Did you have a good night?'

'Marvellous, thanks.' She broke into a broad grin. 'I'm feeling very . . . rested.'

'Are you letting him go?'

'Not until I get my new washing machine.'

'Any word yet from Carver's?'

'Nothing so far. Then again, we've still got the phone switched off.'

'Any chance of a cup of tea?' one of the reporters shouted up hopefully.

'What?' Maggie was distracted by the sight of Hector at the back of the group. Until that moment she hadn't realised he was there.

'Cup of tea?' The reporter blew on his hands and rubbed them together; the sun might be shining but it was still nippy outside.

'Of course. I'll put the kettle on,' Maggie promised.

Dino placed a reassuring hand on her shoulder. 'You get yourself dressed. I'll make the tea.'

The reporters chuckled.

'Reckon you'll miss him when he's gone, Maggie. You've struck gold there!'

Hector, not chuckling, turned and headed back up the road.

Chapter 57

The phone rang less than a minute after Maggie had switched it back on.

'Oh! Mr Ellison!' Hurriedly swallowing her mouthful of toast, she waggled her eyebrows at Dino, who was busy piling sugar into an assortment of mugs.

'*Ms* Donovan, you've caused more than enough trouble for Carver's.' Gilbert Ellison, his tone distinctly frosty, didn't add that his company chairman, having been shown this morning's papers, had given him a right bollocking for not getting the matter sorted out before now. 'I'm ringing to inform you that a replacement machine will be delivered to you by eleven o'clock this morning.'

'And fitted,' Maggie prompted. 'Free of charge. And it has to be a washer-dryer,' she reminded him.

'One of our most exclusive models.' Gilbert Ellison sounded as if he hated her. 'Naturally. As a gesture of goodwill from Carver's.'

'Well, thanks. That's very sweet of you,' lied Maggie.

When she'd hung up the phone she looked at Dino, then punched the air in most un-Maggie-like fashion and said, 'Yesss!'

The van duly arrived at ten to eleven. A roar of approval went

450

up from the assembled crowd as the top-of-the-range machine was ceremoniously unloaded and carried into the cottage. Gilbert Ellison had turned up too, clearly determined to prove to the press that Carver's were good sports really. Posing for the cameras, he flashed an oily smile and presented Maggie with a bottle of cheap champagne. Addressing the journalists, he explained how much Carver's valued their customers, and how sorry he was that on this occasion, despite their *very* best efforts, Maggie had been let down.

By eleven thirty the new machine had been installed by Dino and was whirling happily away, washing the first of many grubby loads.

Gilbert maintained a perma-grin for the benefit of the assembled press but spoke through gritted teeth.

'You've caused us so much trouble,' he hissed at Maggie. 'We could still sue, you know. Or have you arrested and charged with false imprisonment.'

'Except Dino wasn't held here against his will.' Maggie smiled blandly at him.

'I enjoyed every minute,' Dino put in cheerfully.

Maggie hoped he wouldn't find himself sacked by midday.

'Never try anything like this again,' Gilbert muttered as he swept past her out of the cottage. 'Right, let's get out of here. Back to civilisation.'

The girl from Radio Bristol touched Maggie's arm. 'Are you ready?'

A car was waiting to whisk her away to the BBC studios for the first in a series of live link-ups.

'Just a second.' Maggie paused, then turned and gave Dino a hug. 'Thanks for everything.'

His eyes crinkling, he murmured, 'Thanks for *almost* every-thing. Maybe I'll bump into you again some time.'

'Who knows?' Maggie smiled and wiped a streak of sticky pink from his cheek. She'd never get used to wearing lipstick.

'I install dishwashers as well,' said Dino.

'Now that's a coincidence,' Maggie said gravely, 'because I was thinking of getting myself one of those.'

Brenda, Daisy's secretary, brought a pile of correspondence into the office for signing.

'I've just been talking to Pam, out on reception.' She frowned as she put the letters on Daisy's desk. 'And she said the oddest thing.'

'Hmm?' Daisy had just remembered she hadn't yet told Hector about the Clarissa-kicking incident. Absently, she looked up. As far as she was aware, Pam quite often said odd things.

'I bumped into Mr Tyzack this morning,' Brenda explained. 'And I asked him how the decorators were getting on with his house. He said they'd nearly finished and that they were doing a great job.'

'And?' Daisy was yet to be enthralled.

'Well, my daughter's looking for a decorator to do her dining room, so I asked Mr Tyzack which company he was using, and he didn't know! I mean, he said he couldn't remember the name offhand, but don't you think that's a bit strange?' Brenda looked perplexed. 'A man like him, you'd think he'd know who was decorating his house.'

Daisy nodded cautiously, wondering where this was heading. 'So then what?'

'Well, his phone rang and he had to rush off. But when I mentioned it just now to Pam, she came up with this strange idea. She said maybe Mr Tyzack couldn't think of the name of the decorators because there *are* no decorators!'

Daisy rubbed her forehead; she had spent the last three hours embroiled in paperwork. 'I don't get it. You mean Dev's doing up the house himself?'

Brenda shook her head vigorously. 'No, no, goodness me no!' Clearly this was a preposterous suggestion. '*Pam* reckons there isn't anything needing to be done to the house because it was never flooded in the first place. She thinks he just used that as an excuse to move in here for a few weeks. D'you think that could really be true?'

Daisy thought it was the maddest idea she'd ever heard. Having read far too many spy thrillers under the reception desk, Pam evidently now fancied herself as Miss Moneypenny.

Aloud she said, 'Why would he want to do that?'

'Well, *Pam* thinks it's because he's after something. Or someone. And I bet you could find out, if you asked him nicely.' Brenda gave her a significant look, the kind that was practically a nudge and a wink and a dig in the ribs. 'Pam and I've both noticed.'

'Noticed what?' Daisy's throat was suddenly dry.

'Dev Tyzack,' Brenda twinkled. 'Don't tell me you hadn't noticed. He's definitely got a soft spot for you.'

Lust, great foaming waves of the stuff, had Tara in its grip. Her hormones were being driven wild. It was all very well boldly declaring that no, you *weren't* going to have sex with someone, but not so easy to follow through when you found yourself subjected to this degree of provocation.

Two hours of hill starts, reversing round corners and adrenaline-pumping emergency stops had resulted in something of a biological emergency of her own. It was entirely Josh's fault – she'd never realised before now that being given a driving lesson could be so erotic. The husky way he said 'Easy on the throttle now' had become an incredible turn-on. The rip in the knee of his jeans was provoking her too; blonde hairs were poking outrageously through the frayed gap and his leg was only inches from her left hand. Oh God, she so badly wanted to tear off those jeans and—

'Hey, look who's on the radio!' Josh, who had been fiddling with the dial, stopped as he recognised Maggie's voice.

'. . . all I can say is, it worked for me!'

'And I have to tell our listeners, you're looking wonderful for it,' Maggie's interviewer said warmly. 'This is Penny Macey, on Radio Bristol, and we have Maggie Donovan, positively glowing with triumph, here in our studios.'

'Next right,' ordered Josh as they approached a junction. 'We'll head into Chippenham. Why's Maggie sounding so posh all of a sudden?'

'It's her telephone voice. She always does that when she's nervous.'

'She doesn't sound nervous – hey, I said *right*.'

'I know you did.' Smiling to herself, Tara turned left.

The High Street was noticeably quieter now than when they'd left it.

'Everyone's gone,' Tara observed as she drove slowly past her home. Leaving Josh's car in the hotel car park, they walked back down to the cottage.

In the kitchen, the new washing machine had ended its cycle.

'I don't know why we're here,' said Josh. 'We could have got an extra couple of hours' practice in.'

'I've done enough driving.' Tara was feeling deliciously wanton and subversive. 'I want to practice something else now.'

'Like what? Golf?'

'Something much more fun than golf.' Her eyes danced as she moved towards him.

'Wash your mouth out. There aren't many things more fun than golf. In fact,' Josh hesitated, pretending to concentrate, 'I can only think of one.'

'What a coincidence. That's the very same one I'm thinking of.'

'Skiing?' Josh raised his eyebrows. 'I say, excuse me, what *do* you think you're doing?'

'It's a complicated technical manoeuvre. Called unbuttoning your jeans.'

'But—'

'We're all alone,' said Tara. 'Maggie's out of the way, broadcasting live from Radio Bristol.' She paused. 'And we're going upstairs.'

'Now steady on. I thought you were meant to be proving to me that you weren't a trollopy, knicker-dropping tart.'

As he spoke, Josh was lightly outlining the white star on the front of her pink top. Tara quivered with longing; who was seducing who here?

Or was it *whom*?

'Let's face it, we both know I'm a big trollopy tart. I've told you all about my dodgy past and it hasn't put you off me. So basically, I think we've waited long enough.'

'Phew, hooray for that.' With a wicked grin, Josh hooked his thumbs through the belt loops of her white jeans and pulled her against him. 'I think I like this idea a lot.'

Tara gave a little wiggle against his hips. 'Guess what? I can tell.'

'I'm very much looking forward to seeing your room.'

'I can't wait to show it to you.'

455

Josh exhaled slowly. 'How long, d'you think, before Maggie gets back?'

As she kissed him, Tara skilfully unfastened the final button on his jeans – oh yes, there were definite advantages to being a trollop.

'Don't worry about Maggie. She'll be gone for hours.'

Chapter 58

Hector had been loitering at the far end of the High Street for some time. The moment the taxi came into view, he knew it was Maggie and his shoulders involuntarily straightened. Right, this was it. The moment of truth. He was either about to make the most monumental pillock of himself, or . . .

Never mind that. She was back and he had to see her. The taxi pulled up outside the cottage, Maggie stepped out and Hector's heart turned over. If he was honest, he'd spent the last two years being a pillock – it had just taken him until now to figure it out.

'Maggie,' he shouted as she searched in her bag for the front door key. The taxi drove off and she looked up at him, sunglasses perched on her head keeping her tousled blonde hair off her face. Not tousled as in artfully-arranged-for-a-glossy-magazine. Maggie's hair was naturally tousled because she never remembered to brush it.

'Hector.' Her manner was guarded; she was wondering why he was rushing over like this, accosting her in broad daylight in the street.

'I need to see you.' Hector ground to a halt six feet away from her. 'I've been waiting for you to get back. We have to talk.'

'About what?'

Unable to stop himself, Hector blurted out, 'Did you sleep with him?'

Silence. Maggie stared at him, then at the small gaggle of camera-wielding tourists making their way past on the opposite side of the street.

'Why?' she managed at last. 'What's it got to do with you?'

'It's got everything to do with me! It *matters*.'

'Sshh. Will you keep your voice down?'

'I will not,' Hector practically bawled. 'I don't care if the whole village hears me.'

Startled, Maggie turned and jammed her key into the front door. Hector might not care, but she certainly did. And how dare he insinuate that while it was fine for him to sleep with someone else, she shouldn't be allowed to do the same?

'You'd better come in.' Pointedly she added, 'Where's Paula?'

'I don't know. Getting her nails done . . . I don't *care*.' Hector waved a dismissive arm in the direction of the hotel. When he'd last seen her, Paula had been awaiting a visit from some manicurist. As far as she was concerned, he was playing golf this afternoon. 'Where are you going?' he demanded now. 'I said we need to talk.'

'Just checking the machine.' Maggie had headed on through to the kitchen. He watched as she opened the front of the washer-dryer, pulled out a white lambswool sweater and lovingly ran her hands over its pristine softness.

'Look at that,' she marvelled.

'Put it down.' Hector was on the verge of losing his patience. 'None of this would ever have happened if you'd let me buy you a new machine when I offered.'

Maggie carefully hung the sweater over the back of a chair. 'Why are you being like this?'

'Because I love you,' Hector bellowed in exasperation. 'I

love you, and I can't stand to think of you being with that man!'

Maggie stared at him. 'Is this a joke?'

'Do I look as if I'm joking? Maggie, you have to know the truth. For some time now, this arrangement of ours . . . God, I've *hated* it. Not the sex,' Hector hastily amended. 'Of course I didn't hate the sex. But paying for it . . . well, it just made me feel . . .'

'Hector—'

'No, let me finish. I wanted more,' he said urgently. 'I realised I had feelings for you, but I also knew you were only doing it for the money. If I didn't pay you, you wouldn't sleep with me any more. And I couldn't give you up, I just *couldn't*.' Hector shook his head. 'I looked forward to seeing you more than you'll ever know. I used to count the hours—'

'Until Paula came along,' Maggie said unsteadily. Had he really counted the hours?

'I wanted a proper relationship, one that was open and above board. Is that too much to ask?' Hector's eyes registered despair. 'It's no good, though. I realise that now. Paula isn't the one for me. She's not my kind of woman.' He waited, then said flatly, 'You are.'

'Is this really happening?' Maggie was in a daze.

'It's really happening. I'm telling you how I feel,' said Hector. 'Of course the rest's up to you. I'm putting myself well and truly on the line here. All I know is that you like me enough to sleep with me for money. But I don't want to be your . . . client any more. I want to see you properly. So, do you think you could handle that, or am I making a complete idiot of myself here?' He shuddered and straightened his shirt collar. 'If I am, just tell me. I can handle it.'

'Oh!' For the first time in a long time, Maggie was lost for words. She knew she should be interrupting by now, putting him out of his misery, but she couldn't quite bring herself to do it. What if she'd somehow misunderstood him? What if her brain was sneakily *willing* her to believe he was saying what she thought he'd just said?

'Right,' Hector announced, quite masterfully under the circumstances. 'I've said my piece. Now it's your turn.'

'I-I . . .' God, I'm hopeless.

'Yes? Or no?' His tone was terse.

Panicked, Maggie squeaked, 'Yes!' before he could walk out on her. Then, clutching her sunglasses, she stammered, 'Wh-what have I just agreed to?'

'You and me.' Hector risked a half-smile. 'Giving it a go. Without money changing hands. Are you sure you're OK with that?'

Maggie swallowed. 'Yes.' It came out less frantically this time.

Encouraged, Hector took a step towards her. 'Really?'

'Yes.'

'And I'm finishing with Paula tonight. Is that OK with you?'

What a question.

'Yes,' whispered Maggie.

'I've already told you I love you. But this thing with whatsisname, the repairman. Will you promise me you won't see him again?'

'There is no thing. There never was any *thing*.' Unbelievably touched by the fact that he had been jealous, Maggie had to clear her throat at this point. Reaching out to him she reiterated, 'Nothing happened. He slept on the sofa.'

Relief was etched on Hector's lined face as clearly as if she'd scribbled all over it with felt-tip.

'Honestly?'

'Honestly.'

'I bet he wanted to.'

Maggie surveyed him with amusement. 'Oh well, goes without saying, of course he wanted to.' Under the circumstances, she felt a trace of smugness was allowed.

'Who wouldn't?' Hector's voice softened, his hand moving up to stroke her hair. 'You're a beautiful woman.'

'But I turned him down,' said Maggie.

'Why?'

'Because he wasn't you.'

Hector's arms folded round her. His kiss felt like coming home. Finally Maggie pulled away, just a fraction.

'I never wanted your money.' She blinked back tears of joy. 'I only took it so you'd carry on coming to see me.'

Hector kissed her again, hard. Gruffly he said, 'We've been a couple of idiots.'

'Look on the bright side.' Maggie broke into a smile. 'We've got some catching up to do.'

'Excellent thought. And no time like the present,' murmured Hector.

'But what about Tara? She could be back any time now.'

Hector shook his head and grinned at her. 'Who cares?'

'Oh shit,' Tara hissed, torn between horror and delight. 'They're coming upstairs!'

'This is fantastic,' whispered Josh, behind her in the bedroom doorway. 'It's going to be like *This Is Your Life*.'

He was shaking with silent laughter. Typical man. Tara turned and gave him a thump. In return, he shoved her out onto the tiny landing.

'Oof,' gasped Tara, bouncing off the opposite wall.

'Oh, good grief,' she heard Maggie shriek from halfway up the stairs. 'What was *that*?'

Ah well, here goes . . .

'Don't panic,' Tara hastily assured them. 'It's only me. Well,' she amended, grabbing Josh's arm and yanking him out onto the landing with her, 'it's only *us*.'

The next moment Maggie, closely followed by Hector, came into view.

'I don't believe this.' Maggie's hands flew to her mouth in horror. 'Have you two been up here *all this time*?'

'Well, I'm not Peter Pan.' Tara gave her a pitying look. 'I didn't fly in through the bedroom window.'

'And I'm not Tinkerbell,' added Josh.

Maggie was cyclamen-pink. Mortified, she gasped, 'Were you . . . um, listening to us?'

'I wasn't,' said Josh. 'I had my fingers in my ears. But Tara was,' he went on helpfully, wincing as she whacked him again.

'We weren't *trying* to listen,' Tara protested. 'It was impossible not to. You weren't exactly keeping your voices down.'

Maggie said faintly, 'So you heard everything.'

'Pretty much.' Tara was still having a hard time believing what they *had* heard. She was stunned. Imagine, Maggie and Hector . . .

Maggie and *Hector*, for crying out loud!

But amazingly, whereas the thought of Maggie and Dino spending last night together and getting intimate had outraged her, this even more astounding scenario wasn't unsettling her at all. Despite the fact that she was obviously still in shock, Tara realised she could handle this quite easily. There was even a touch of admiration in there somewhere.

Looking helpless, Maggie said, 'I'm sorry.'

'Bloody hell, what is going on here?' Hector exploded. 'You are *not* sorry, OK? Neither of us is sorry. In fact we're very, very happy, and nothing you or anyone else says is going to change that.'

All this time, Tara marvelled. Honestly, it just went to show you couldn't trust anyone, not even a spinsterish middle-aged cushion-making aunt.

'*How* long did you say this has been going on?' Maggie hadn't said it at all, but Tara was longing to know.

Proudly, Hector put his arm round Maggie's shoulders. 'Two years. *Over* two years.'

Maggie had finally stopped blushing; even her throat was back to its normal colour. Hector's confidence was catching.

'Two years and four months,' she told Tara.

'By the way,' Hector counter-attacked, 'what were you two doing upstairs?'

'Tara was telling me she's thinking of redecorating her room.' Innocently Josh indicated his lime-green sweater. 'She wanted to see how this colour would look on the walls.'

Biting her lip hard, Tara struggled to keep a straight face.

'Two years and four months. And all this time he was paying you? Actually *paying* you?'

'Let me tell you, she was worth every penny.' Lovingly, Hector squeezed Maggie's arm.

'I hope you're not going to give me a lecture,' Maggie said bravely.

'Bugger the lecture, I think it's a fantastic idea! In fact,' Tara gave Josh a nudge, 'I think I might give it a go myself.'

'Dad, I need to see you.' Daisy darted out of her office, catching Hector as he was heading up to his apartment.

Hector, giving up with good grace, turned and said, 'Thought you might.'

Daisy wished his eyes didn't have to be so twinkly. She really wasn't looking forward to doing this. What if he thought she was embroidering the truth simply because she didn't like Paula?

And she wasn't, she honestly wasn't. More than anything else in the world she wanted Hector to be happy.

'So Tara rang you,' he announced as she closed the office door behind him.

'Tara? Why would Tara ring me?' Oh, stop it, stop looking so *cheerful*.

'Never mind,' said Hector. 'Now, what's this about?'

Here we go, thought Daisy. Whatever Hector decided, she wasn't going to argue with him. He just deserved to know he was involved with the kind of woman who would kick a small dog like a football.

Feeling terrible, she told him about the night of the fire, and Clarissa's run-in with Paula.

Hector listened patiently. When she had finished, he said, 'You never did like her much, did you?'

Daisy squirmed. 'Well, no. But that's not why I'm telling you.'

'I know.' He nodded, looking thoughtful for a moment. 'D'you like Maggie?'

'Who?' Completely wrong-footed, Daisy said in bewilderment, 'You mean Tara's Maggie?'

'That's the one.'

What in heaven's name was he on about? What kind of question was that? Indignantly Daisy said, 'Of course I like Maggie!'

Rising from his seat to leave, Hector replied with a smile of satisfaction, 'Good.'

Chapter 59

'Excuse me, *what* did you just say?'

Paula stared at Hector in disbelief. One minute she'd been happily chatting on the phone to her agent whilst admiring her just-manicured apricot-pink fingernails. Then, in the space of less than thirty seconds, Hector had burst into her suite and announced that their relationship was over.

For a few moments she'd actually waited for him to deliver the punchline and start laughing, so convinced was she that it was a joke.

But Hector was showing no sign of amusement, and there didn't appear to be a punchline in sight.

'No hard feelings,' Hector said calmly. 'It was fun while it lasted.' Although, now he came to think about it, this wasn't altogether true. Paula never had been much of a one for fun. Still, it sounded good.

'You're *finishing* with me?' Paula's mouth narrowed to a hard line. This had never happened to her before. Throughout her life, she had always been the one who did the finishing. For Christ's sake, she was Paula Penhaligon!

'I think it's run its course, don't you?' Hector's hands were in his trouser pockets, his stance casual. As if they were discussing a restaurant that had turned out to be a bit of a disappointment.

'This is outrageous,' Paula exploded. 'You must be out of your mind!'

'You kicked Clarissa.'

'What?'

'Dev Tyzack's dog. The night of the fire.'

Now she knew he was deranged. 'You're saying it's over between us because I kicked a *dog*?'

Hector said, 'Isn't that reason enough?' Then he hesitated. The sooner this was over, the better for all concerned. 'OK, it's not the main reason. There is someone else.'

'You're lying.' Paula's glossy apricot nails dug into her palms. 'How *can* there be someone else? We're always together – you haven't had time to see someone else!'

Hector shook his head. 'She's someone I've known for a long time. A lovely lady. She lives here in the village.'

'I don't believe this.' He was actually finishing with her for some other woman? The nerve of it! Her eyes like shards of steel, Paula hissed, 'Who is she?'

Relax. No more secrets. Everything out in the open.

'Her name's Maggie. She's Tara's aunt.'

Oh no, *no*, this was too much. Not half an hour ago Paula had been flicking through the newspaper, reading the story of the repairman held hostage and studying the accompanying photograph. It was, she'd discovered, the same woman whom she'd last seen bedraggled and sprawled on all fours in the snow with a smashed bottle of wine at her feet.

'She wears an anorak!'

'So do I,' said Hector.

Enraged, Paula picked up a glass ashtray and hurled it at him. Even more infuriatingly, it missed and bounced off the wall.

'You bastard,' she screeched at Hector. 'Just fucking *get out*.'

*   *   *

Almost there, almost there. Feeling like a private detective, Daisy double-checked the name of the road and took a deep breath. Yesterday, looking up the address on the computer in her office, she had jumped a mile when the door had been flung open by Pam. Prickling with guilt and convinced she'd been found out, Daisy had sent the mouse scooting across her desk and yelped, 'What d'you want?'

Of course that had been Pam's cue to exclaim, 'You'll never guess what's just happened. Paula Penhaligon's gone!'

Which had been a double relief.

Paula, it transpired, had called Barney up to her suite to collect her packed bags. She had then stormed out of the hotel and into a waiting car without so much as a goodbye. Nor had she left Barney a tip.

Daisy was just glad Pam hadn't come bursting into the office to accuse her of looking up Dev's address because she fancied him rotten.

But like a song you hear on the radio and can't get out of your head, Daisy had been haunted by Pam and Brenda's remarks. If Dev was only pretending that his house had been wrecked in order to move into the hotel, could it be possible that he was doing it because he did have, as Brenda put it, a soft spot for her? It sounded completely mad, but Daisy couldn't rest until she knew. She also knew she couldn't ask Dev.

Which was why she was here now, turning into Garrick Avenue. And since it was a simple enough mission, there was absolutely no need to be nervous. Dev lived at number 15, further down on the left. All she had to do was drive past the house and see if there were any decorators' vans parked outside. Painters and decorators invariably used vans advertising their company name. One little van, that was all she needed to put Brenda's ridiculously far-fetched theory out of her mind for good.

Slowly Daisy drove the entire length of the broad, tree-lined street.

She turned at the end and drove back again.

Apart from a smart green and white one delivering food from a delicatessen to number 38, there were no vans.

Oh shit. Daisy's mouth was dry, her stomach squirming like a nest of snakes. She'd kind of guessed, of course, that Dev found her attractive – he'd never made an effort to hide it. But for an apparently normal man to lie through his teeth and move into a hotel that quite frankly wasn't cheap, purely in order to be near someone he liked – well, wasn't that the tiniest bit sinister? Dev didn't seem like an obsessed stalker but he might just be brilliant at hiding it.

Unsettled by this creepy thought, Daisy stopped the car. It was only four o'clock, the decorators should still be here. She'd been so sure she'd find a van in the road.

OK, be sensible now. Maybe Dev was using a decorator who for some reason didn't own a van. She'd come this far, she may as well take a closer look. If she wandered casually past the house she might catch a glimpse of a strange man in paint-splashed overalls through one of the windows. Since she'd left Dev back at the hotel it would even be safe to ring the doorbell and see if a painter type answered it.

And then? Well, pretend to be a Jehovah's Witness, obviously, and pray he'd slam the door in her face.

But when she rang the bell, there was no response. Nobody, painterly or otherwise, came to answer the door. Daisy tried again.

Still nothing.

She moved to one of the front windows. With the sun

bouncing off the glass it was hard to see inside, but there certainly didn't appear to be any stepladders and paint pots cluttering the place up. By cupping her hands around her eyes and pressing her nose to the window she was able to make out a Georgian dining table and chairs in the centre of the room, a rather grand marble fireplace and several nicely framed paintings hung on walls papered with—

'Daisy?'

So engrossed in the act of snooping that she hadn't even heard the car pulling up, Daisy banged her nose painfully against the glass and jack-knifed round.

Bottle-green, that was the colour of Dev's dining room wall-paper.

Feeling pretty white-with-a-hint-of-green herself, Daisy waved feebly at Dev in the driver's seat.

This was, officially, An Embarrassing Moment.

'Um . . . hi.'

He raised an eyebrow. 'What are you doing here?'

Daisy winced. She'd been so hoping he wouldn't ask that question. Her brain, scrambling hamster-style for some kind of answer, was spectacularly failing to come up with one. Unless she could manage to convince Dev that in her spare time she actually *was* a door-knocking Jehovah's Witness.

While she dithered, Dev reversed into a tight space. Annoy-ingly, he did it in about two seconds flat without even hitting the kerb or the car behind.

'Well?' he said, when he reached Daisy.

Mentally she psyched herself up. Sometimes, when you couldn't think of a single convincing lie, you just had to resort to the truth.

OK, Mr Expert-Reverser, let's see you get out of this one.

'I wondered how your decorating was coming along.'

'You asked me that the other day.' Dev waited. 'I told you, it's almost finished.'

Despite the fact that he clearly didn't believe her, Daisy persisted brightly, 'Can I see the house?'

'Why?'

Oh sod it, may as well come clean. 'Because someone recently told me that they didn't think your house was being redecorated. In fact, they thought there'd probably never been any burst pipes and flooding in the first place.'

'Really?' The corners of his mouth flickered for a moment. 'And am I allowed to ask what made them think that?'

Not wanting to implicate Pam and Brenda, Daisy waved an arm at the parked cars lining the street. 'Where are your decorators?'

'Finished early today,' said Dev. 'They're off to some stag do in Cheltenham.'

Was this a lie?

'So can I see what they've been doing?'

He hesitated.

He *was* lying!

'OK,' Dev said at last. 'If it'll make you happy.'

Daisy watched him fit the key into the lock. Her heart began to beat faster.

As the front door swung open she was instantly struck by . . .

Chapter 60

. . . the smell of fresh paint.

Slowly, very slowly, Daisy breathed out again. Fresh paint and lots of it. And newly replastered ceilings. Following Dev through to the kitchen she saw rolls of wallpaper stacked up in readiness against the wall. Pots of eggshell emulsion were piled neatly in one corner along with folded-up dustsheets, a pasting table and an assortment of brushes.

'This is the last room,' said Dev. 'They've finished the rest of the house. Unless you think all this stuff's only here to impress visitors.' Drily he added, 'Maybe you'd like to speak to them yourself, just to prove they exist.'

'No thanks.' Daisy shook her head vigorously as he took out his mobile and punched in a number. She backed away in alarm as Dev tried to make her take the phone.

Grinning, he said, 'Jeff, hi, it's Dev Tyzack. Yes, I've just arrived. Now listen, I'm up in London tomorrow so I'll leave the money here for you to pick up in the morning, is that OK? Good. And you'll be finished by Friday? Brilliant. Jeff, before I go, could you just do me a favour and have a word with a friend of mine? Thanks.'

Refusing to be intimidated any longer, Daisy grasped the nettle. Well, the phone.

'Hi, Jeff, I understand you're a painter and decorator. Could you tell me the name of your firm please?'

At the other end of the phone, a bewildered-sounding Jeff said, 'Um, Phoenix Services.'

'Thanks very much.' Daisy nodded efficiently. 'Goodbye.'

'Happy now?' inquired Dev.

'Phoenix Services.'

'Right.'

Since there was no longer any need to protect her staff, Daisy said, 'When my secretary asked you what they were called, you didn't know.'

'Ah, I *see*.' Dev nodded, understanding at last. 'Well, that's because until recently Jeff was trading as JR Services. His surname's Richardson,' he explained, as if Daisy had learning difficulties. 'But a couple of weeks ago, a man called John Rowlands contacted him. He's another decorator from Melksham and guess what his company name is?'

Irritably, Daisy said, 'OK, OK, I'm not *six*.'

'You were the one who wanted to know this,' Dev pointed out. 'So anyway, John Rowlands is branching out, moving to Bath, and he offered Jeff money to change the name of his business. When your secretary asked me what it was called, I couldn't remember offhand what they'd decided on.'

'Well, that's that sorted out.' Daisy wanted him to stop now; she had the nasty feeling he was laughing at her.

'Oh, come on, cheer up.' Dev flashed her a dazzling smile. 'Seeing as you've come all this way, you may as well have a look at what's been done.'

She let him give her the guided tour. It was a stunning house. Jeff had done a good job. Daisy dutifully admired the decor in every room and wondered how soon she could decently leave.

Dev waited until they were back in the kitchen before asking the killer question; the one she'd spent the last twenty minutes dreading.

'What I don't understand is, why would anyone pretend their house was wrecked if it wasn't?' He shook his head at Daisy, seemingly perplexed. 'More to the point, why on earth would they want to move into a hotel when they already had a perfectly good home?'

Oh help, mustn't go red, mustn't go red . . .

'Well, *quite*.' Daisy looked equally puzzled. 'That's exactly what I was wondering! I mean, it doesn't make any sense at all, but when Brenda said—'

'But what I really, *really* don't understand,' Dev interrupted, 'is why, if you were that mystified, you didn't do the obvious thing and just ask me.'

His gaze was impenetrable. Bugger. The ferocious blush Daisy had been so heroically keeping at bay was suddenly rampaging out of control. She felt it swoosh up her neck, all the way to her hairline. In fact the top of her head was probably blushing too.

'I don't know. I didn't want to . . . um, embarrass you.'

Dev smiled. 'Actually, I think I've got it. You thought I'd made up the flood story and moved into the hotel because I liked you so much I was prepared to do anything to be near you. Am I right?'

'Oh, for heaven's sake!' Daisy forced out a laugh that bordered on the hysterical. 'What a thing to suggest! Of *course* I didn't think that!'

Bloody Brenda, this was all her fault. She definitely deserved the sack.

'Sure?' murmured Dev.

'Absolutely! God, that's the most ridiculous thing I ever heard!'

'Only you're blushing.' He moved towards her. 'Quite a lot, in fact.'

That was the really annoying thing about paper bags, they were never around when you needed them.

'I have to go,' Daisy blustered, trying to get past him. Thank God he was moving out of the hotel the day after tomorrow.

'Not yet.' Putting out an arm, Dev said, 'Actually, you were half right.'

Confused, Daisy stopped struggling. 'Half right about what?'

'I liked you a lot. Maybe not enough to run up to the loft and drill holes in the water tank,' Dev amended, 'but enough to choose to move into your hotel rather than any of the others.'

Daisy's heart was beating very fast now; she could feel it leaping in her throat. Hadn't she always known this, really? And why was it having such a paralysing effect now?

But it was all very well knowing it in theory. It wasn't quite so easy to stay calm when the person in question was standing right in front of you, calmly telling you how they felt.

'I've said this before,' Dev went on, 'and I know you don't like it, but you and Josh aren't right for each other. You're with him because he makes you feel safe.' He paused. 'And that isn't good enough. It's a shitty way to live – it's such a *waste*. You deserve more than that. I saw you talking to Josh yesterday and it's obvious you don't love him. It was like watching two friends.'

Daisy realised she was holding her breath. He didn't know that she and Josh were no longer a couple. He didn't know about Josh and Tara . . .

'I don't want to talk about Josh,' she whispered.

'I tried to kiss you once before.' Dev's dark eyes never wavered from hers. 'And you slapped my face.'

He *knew*.

The corners of Daisy's mouth pulled up, just slightly. 'Well, you could always try again.'

The doors were locked. Clarissa was back at the hotel being looked after by Rocky. They were all alone in the house. Daisy wondered when, subconsciously, she had made up her mind to do this. Just once, to satisfy her curiosity and see what Dev Tyzack was really like.

He didn't disappoint. In slow motion, she found herself being led back up the stairs. They barely made it to the top. Magical kissing was followed by frenzied removal of clothes. Daisy, running her hands greedily over Dev's hard athlete's body, could scarcely bring herself to tear her mouth from his in order to breathe. She wanted him so badly she could have made love right then and there on the staircase. It was only thanks to Dev exerting a little self-control that they managed to reach the bedroom. Leaving behind a trail of abandoned clothes, they finally made it to the king-sized bed.

'What are you thinking?' Dev, leaning up on one elbow, pushed a tangle of hair out of her half-closed eyes.

Daisy lay on her back, one hand flung above her head, listening to her breathing slowly return to normal.

'Just wondering how many other women have looked up at this ceiling.'

'You're the first.'

'Of course I am.'

'You are,' Dev insisted, before breaking into a grin. 'This ceiling was only replastered last week.'

Daisy smiled. 'You certainly know how to make a girl feel special.'

'You are special.'

'Oh, please!'

'I mean it,' said Dev, suddenly serious. 'I've waited a long time for this.'

He sounded so convincing, Daisy marvelled. As if he truly meant it.

Then again, this was undoubtedly how he bowled over his numerous conquests in the first place. An expert like Dev knew just how to flatter a girl, how to make her feel important and desirable. It was an elemental part of his seduction technique, one he would have used countless times.

The only difference with her, of course, was that she hadn't jumped into bed with him months ago; she had done the unthinkable and actually kept him waiting. But the wait was over now. He'd got what he wanted. All that remained was for Dev to see her a few more times, make her fall head over heels in love with him, get bored with her in true serial seducer fashion and finally dump her, just as he had dumped all the rest. Pausing only to add her poor broken heart to a pile the size of a coal tip.

Oh yes, Daisy thought. That was exactly the way it would happen.

'This is it,' said Dev, his fingertips trailing down her arm. 'You don't know how much you mean to me.'

Yeah, yeah, heard it all before. From Steven, actually.

But it wasn't so easy to ignore the physical sensations he was arousing with those philanderer's fingers of his. Trembling with renewed longing, Daisy arched towards him. An hour ago she'd told herself, just this once.

Oh well, what the heck. Just once more.

'Six o'clock,' Daisy lazily observed, having reached for Dev's arm and glanced at his watch. Their second lovemaking session had been slower, less frenetic and more sensuous than the first. Dev was indeed proving himself an expert. It had been glorious.

'You don't really have to get back, do you?' He kissed her neck, his warm tongue teasing her hypersensitive skin.

'Oh, I do.' God, I definitely do. If I don't leave now . . .

'I'll come back with you,' said Dev. 'You have to tell Josh.'

Daisy closed her eyes. 'Tell Josh what?'

'You know. That it's over. This is it now.' Beneath the tangled duvet, he ran a warm hand over her stomach. 'You're with me.'

Listen to him, just *listen* to him. As far as Dev was concerned, it was a foregone conclusion. It simply hadn't crossed his mind that she might not want her heart broken and tossed onto the coal tip along with all the rest.

'No I'm not.' Daisy removed his wandering hand and slid out of bed. 'This is just something that happened this afternoon. You kept dropping hints that I was missing out on a treat – and I admit it, I was curious.' She shrugged casually as she reached for her bra and – where were they? Oh yes, dangling from the door handle – knickers. 'But just because we've been to bed doesn't turn us into an instant couple. I'm still with Josh and I'm going to stay with him.'

Dev's face was expressionless, almost mask-like. 'Are you joking?'

'Never been more serious.' Bra fastened, knickers on, Daisy opened the bedroom door and saw her skirt and shoes strewn across the landing. 'Now I don't need to be curious any more.'

'But—'

'This is never, ever going to happen again,' Daisy went on. 'And Josh is never *ever* going to find out. You're leaving the hotel, you and I will never see each other again and we'll all live happily ever after.'

Dev lay there, very still, propped up on one elbow. 'Is that what you want?'

'Absolutely.' She flashed him a bright, must-dash smile. 'And it's what I'm going to get.'

Chapter 61

So much had happened in the past fortnight. First Paula Penhaligon had left the hotel, then Dev and Clarissa had abruptly departed. Within days, Maggie had pretty much moved in with Hector. Next, the rewiring and repairs having been completed, Barney and Mel had moved out of the hotel and back into Brock Cottage.

Tara smiled to herself, having saved until last the most important move of all. Josh was, needless to say, now staying with her at Maggie's cottage. As Josh had remarked in bed only this morning, it was like a complicated game of musical chairs.

And now this.

The man sitting next to her finished writing on his clipboard and turned to speak.

Tara braced herself.

'Congratulations, Miss Donovan,' said the examiner who'd looked so scary earlier. 'I'm delighted to tell you that you have passed your test.'

Tara promptly burst into tears.

'I thought you'd blown it.' Josh enveloped her in a bear hug. 'When I saw you crying I thought you'd failed.'

'I was just so happy. That poor man looked so confused. God,

479

I can't believe it!' Doing a little jig for joy on the pavement, she grabbed Josh's hand and dragged him across the road. 'I'm not a learner any more! He said I did really well! You'll have to drive us home by the way.'

'Why?'

Tara pushed him through the swing doors of the wine bar opposite the test centre.

'Because, you wally, I'm going to celebrate with a great big drink.'

At the bar, Tara was so busy feeling fantastic, she missed the first part of the sentence. All she managed to catch was '. . . with me.'

'What was that? Whoo, sorry.' She rubbed spilt Frascati into the denim stretched across Josh's gorgeous thigh, then waggled her finger playfully through the frayed bit on his knee. 'Did you know you have the most feelable knees I've ever seen?'

'You're not paying attention,' said Josh.

Tara beamed. The alcohol – on an empty stomach because she'd been too nervous to eat breakfast this morning – was fizzing like sherbet through her veins. She was feeling fantastic, fabulous and . . . frisky.

'I don't just like your knees, you know. There are other bits I'm very fond of too.' Tipping forward at a precarious angle on her bar stool she whispered lasciviously, 'I really love your . . . tummy button.'

'Never mind my adorable body parts.' Josh rolled his eyes. 'I'm trying to talk about Miami.'

'Oh.' That was a coincidence; she'd spent the last couple of weeks trying not to talk about Miami. Or to even think about it.

'I want you to come with me,' said Josh.

Oh.

'With you where?' To the airport, did he mean? To wave him off?

'To Miami. I love you.' Josh's big hands closed round hers. 'It's a great place, you'd have the time of your life. And we'd be together.' He paused, his eyes searching her face. 'So, what d'you think?'

Tara thought it was a good job he was holding her hands. Otherwise she was in danger of toppling off her stool.

Moving to America. With a man who adored her. What an offer.

The old Tara would have leapt at the chance. Riddled with insecurity, the most casual boyfriend could have suggested practically anything – living with him in a wooden hut in Siberia, setting up home in a manky tent on the hard shoulder of the M25 – and she'd have been there like a shot, not caring how horrible it might be, just pathetically grateful that someone actually wanted her to wash their socks for them.

But the last few weeks had been a revelation, a truly exhil-arating experience. Like a scratchy old jumper introduced for the first time to ~~the~~ Lenor, she felt silky and cared-for, desirable and ~~re~~-born . . . And confident enough to say no if she wanted to.

'You're going to turn me down, aren't you?' The hope faded from Josh's speckled greeny-brown eyes.

'I love you.' As she wrapped her arms round his neck and kissed him, Tara thought how much she owed him for having made her feel this good about herself. Josh was her very own human fabric conditioner.

'You love me *but*,' he prompted.

'I love you and I'll come out to Miami.'

'I can still hear that *but*.'

481

Tara kissed him again, then smiled. 'But not straightaway.'

'It's all over. I've left him. Well, that's not true – I kicked him out.'

'No! Oh my God. How do you feel?'

'Truthfully? Fantastic.'

Tara had been wary at first when Annabel had rung up and asked to see her. But Annabel had stressed that everything was fine, she just wanted to update her on the Dominic situation. She'd sounded so cheerful that privately Tara had guessed she was going to hear that Annabel was pregnant, Dominic had vowed to turn over a new leaf and the two of them were going to put the past behind them and embrace parenthood with a vengeance. She'd even pictured them, hand in hand, attending ante-natal classes together.

Just as well she'd never been tempted to set up in business as a clairvoyant.

'Tell me what happened,' Tara urged. 'I want to hear everything.'

It was a sunny Sunday afternoon, warm enough to sit outside. Josh had tactfully removed himself from the cottage and was playing a round of golf with Hector. There were, appropriately, birds and bees darting around the back garden, and even a few butterflies investigating the lush delights of the flowering magnolias.

'I came to my senses, basically.' Annabel, sipping her tea, seemed remarkably sanguine. 'Dominic's a liar and he'll always be a liar. When I confronted him, he tried to persuade me I'd made a huge mistake. When I showed him the photos the private detective had taken, he instantly switched to grovel mode and swore he'd never *ever* look at another woman. Well, that's like—'

'A fox promising not to eat a chicken,' said Tara. 'So, let me guess. You caught him out again?'

Vigorously, Annabel shook her head. 'Not at all. Oh no, Dominic was on his *very* best behaviour. It was me. I just realised I'd never be able to trust him again. All of a sudden I knew I couldn't spend the rest of my life being married to someone like that. So I told him to go.' She pushed up the sleeves of her pale blue sweater and rested her elbows on the arms of the wrought-iron garden chair, her manicured fingers loosely laced together. 'Dominic didn't take it well. He begged me to change my mind. When that didn't work, he shouted and called me a fat cow. I told him to leave and he called me a lot more names. Then he left. That was two weeks ago. I haven't seen him since, but I know where he is.'

Riveted, Tara said, 'Living in a cardboard box somewhere?'

Annabel giggled. 'Oh, please. This is Dominic we're talking about. Can you seriously see him roughing it?'

Fair point.

'OK, a mink-lined cardboard box with en suite bathrooms and jacuzzi.'

'Getting warmer. Jeannie does have two en suites and a jacuzzi.'

Jeannie? Who was Jeannie? Belatedly, Tara's eyes widened in recognition. 'Your sister? She's letting him stay with *her*?' Heavens, that was a bit much – surely everyone had the right to expect a show of solidarity from their own sister!

Annabel smiled at the look of indignation on her face. 'He's doing more than just staying with her. It turns out Jeannie's had a massive crush on him for years.'

'Nooo! You can't mean it!' But since Annabel clearly did, Tara shrieked, 'That is bizarre.'

Annabel's blue eyes twinkled. 'Not really. After all, she inherited just as much money as I did.'

'But how can she do that to you! My God, she was mad as a snake when she caught me and Dominic in the summerhouse, she went *mental*.'

'Exactly,' said Annabel. 'Of course we all thought she was going mental on my behalf. But it turns out she was just furiously jealous of you.'

'And now he's moved on to her.' Tara shook her head in disbelief. 'Doesn't that make *you* mad?'

Annabel smiled. 'She's my little sister. She always used to want to play with my toys when we were kids. If I fell for Dominic's lies, how can I blame Jeannie for doing the same? Anyway, I don't suppose it'll last long. She'll see through him in the end.'

Crikey, talk about tolerant.

'You're taking it so well,' Tara marvelled. 'You're so *calm*.'

Annabel shrugged. 'I've stopped kidding myself. I made a mistake and now I've sorted it out. To be honest, it's a relief. I feel great. My mother keeps telling me I'll meet someone else one day, but I'm really not interested. I just want to enjoy myself for a while, do all the stuff I've always wanted to do.' As she flipped back her blonde hair, Tara noted the confidently ringless left hand. 'Anyway, enough about me. How have *you* been?'

Oh dear. Tara hesitated for a moment; was this going to be like telling a bankrupt you'd just won the National Lottery? Still, at least Annabel appeared to be a cheerful bankrupt.

'Well, I have met someone else.' She couldn't not tell her; in her smitten state it was so hard not to talk about Josh. 'And I've never been happier in my life. He's everything I've ever wanted.'

'Married?' Annabel grinned to show she was joking.

'Not even married. It's like a miracle. I love him to bits. And he loves me.'

'Good grief, this sounds serious. Can I be bridesmaid?'

'He's off to Florida in a fortnight to start a new job.'

Annabel's fair eyebrows shot up. 'And you're going with him?'

'He wants me to, but I said no.' As she spoke, Tara swelled with pride. Thanks to Josh, she now had the confidence *not* to scurry after him, petrified that the moment she was out of his sight he'd be up to no good with any number of bronzed blonde beach babes. He was the one who had made her feel secure enough, for the first time in her life, to turn him down.

'But Florida – wouldn't that be a great place to live?' Annabel was clearly confused. 'Are you saying you'd really rather stay here and carry on working in the hotel?'

More pride welled up in Tara's chest. Any minute now she'd pop like a helium balloon. 'I've handed in my notice. Florida's fantastic, but so are loads of other places in America. Ever since I was little, I've wanted to see New York, California, the Grand Canyon – do the whole sightseeing bit. I knew I'd never really see them because I've never had the guts to actually do anything about it.'

Cottoning on, Annabel said, 'Until now?'

'Until now.' Tara hugged her knees with delight. 'I just realised there was nothing to stop me. I'd been saving up for a car, but now I'm going to buy a ticket for a Greyhound bus instead, and see as much of the country as I can. Wyoming,' she said dreamily. 'Seattle. Boston. Los Angeles. And when I've done all that, well, then I'll go to Miami.'

'Where your wonderful man will be waiting for you.' Annabel looked thoughtful.

485

Tara instantly felt mean and tactless. 'I'm sorry, this isn't what you need to hear.'

'Don't be daft, it's brilliant. I was just thinking how much I envy you.' Twirling a strand of long blonde hair meditatively around her finger, Annabel said, 'In fact, if you fancied some company on the trip, I'd be there like a shot.'

Tara's mouth dropped open. 'Are you serious?'

'Why not? I could do with a change of scenery. It sounds fantastic. Two girls travelling together is safer than one. And I wouldn't throw myself into your boyfriend's arms when we reached Miami,' Annabel promised with a grin. 'You can do that bit.'

'Are you *seriously* serious?'

'I'd love to come with you. By the time I got back, Dominic will have been dumped by Jeannie. A couple of months out of the country is just what I need . . . My God, if we're going to Wyoming, I could meet a *cowboy* out there . . .'

'Not for any kind of meaningful relationship,' Tara put in sternly. 'Just sex.'

'Oh, goes without saying. Definitely just sex. So,' Annabel leaned forward, her eyes dancing, 'what d'you think?'

Blimey. Tara glanced at their empty cups, then over at Annabel, who was looking eager and excited.

'I think it's time we opened a bottle of wine. I definitely need a drink.'

Chapter 62

Since he wasn't one of life's great readers, it was ironic that it was Rocky who'd spotted the item in the newspaper one of the guests had left lying in the bar.

Now, turning to the gossip column, he showed it to Daisy.

'Don't let Hector see.' Rocky lowered his voice as Daisy started to laugh. 'He'll go bananas.'

'Don't let Hector see what?' Hector demanded, breezing into the bar and making Rocky jump.

Daisy grinned and patted his arm. 'A day without a faux pas is a day wasted. Go on, Rocky, show him.'

Maggie joined them and read the piece over Hector's shoulder.

'Paula Penhaligon, star of the London stage, is back with a bang from her sojourn in the sticks with Dennis the Dachshund creator Hector MacLean,' Maggie read aloud. 'Of her dalliance with the flamboyant hotel owner, she said, "It was pleasant enough, but I have a low boredom threshold. As I frequently told Hector, it was never going to last." The new man in Paula's life is rumoured to be billionaire financier Alfred Swick who blah blah blah . . .'

'The bloody cheek of that woman,' Hector exclaimed in outrage. 'Making out she was the one who ended it! I've a good mind to ring and let them know what really happened.'

'You will not.' Maggie crumpled up the paper and lobbed it smartly into the bin. 'Because that would be undignified. Anyway, it doesn't matter any more. So what if she's got herself a billionaire financier?' She planted a teasing kiss on Hector's cheek. 'You've got yourself a cushion-maker.'

'What more could any man want?' Hector agreed, sliding his arm round her waist.

'And Alfred Swick's bald,' Daisy put in helpfully. 'At least Maggie has hair.'

'Damn right she does. She's perfect in every way! In fact . . .' Hector banged his fist on the bar. 'Rocky, fetch me my accordion. I feel a serenade coming on!'

Spot the odd one out, thought Daisy a couple of hours later as she watched Josh drop to his knees in front of Tara, spread his arms wide and launch into a boisterous, off-key version of 'If you were the only girl in the world'. Tara blew him extravagant kisses and the assembled guests cheered. Tonight was Tara and Josh's leaving party. Tomorrow they were meeting up with Annabel Cross-Calvert at Heathrow. At midday, Tara and Annabel would wave Josh off on his flight to Miami before setting off themselves for New York on the first leg of their own big adventure.

It was going to be strange without them.

Josh and Tara.

Hector and the radiant Maggie.

Even Barney and Mel were here, at Tara's insistence.

All the couples, Daisy thought with a brief pang. And me.

Oh dear, mustn't get maudlin.

Turning back to the bar, she caught Rocky's eye.

'Another vodka.' Daisy winked at him. 'And will you marry me?'

Rocky sloshed vodka into her glass and gave the proposal some thought.

'I'd like to,' he said at last, 'but I just couldn't.'

'Spoilsport,' said Daisy.

Hector, banging a heavy ashtray on one of the tables, called the room to attention.

'Ladies and gentlemen,' he announced when everyone was finally listening. 'We're here this evening to say goodbye to Tara and Josh. Now Josh, as most of you know, originally came here to renew his acquaintance with my darling daughter Daisy. While Tara, who by the way wears jolly nice bras and frequently flashes them to all and sundry, was having a fairly diabolical time on the man front . . .'

'See?' Rocky shrugged at Daisy as the rest of the room rocked with laughter. 'There's your problem. I mean, you're really pretty and nice and everything, but imagine having Hector as a father-in-law.'

The shudder said it all. It said that Hector was a liability and Rocky a prize wimp.

Just as well she hadn't wanted to marry him anyway.

'I see what you mean.' Knocking back her vodka in one, Daisy licked her lips. 'Ah well, better get another.'

Barney and Mel were walking through Victoria Park in Bath when Freddie, riding on Barney's shoulders, began to jiggle and yell excitedly, 'Car! Car!'

Barney swelled with pride and gave Freddie's ankles a squeeze. The road running alongside the park was choked with traffic.

'Good boy, that's right, *lots* of cars.'

'CAR! CAR! CAR!' bellowed Freddie, clutching handfuls of Barney's hair as he bounced up and down.

'He's a genius.' Barney grinned at Mel.

'Actually, he isn't,' said Mel. 'Motor cars are brrm-brmms. Car was his name for Clarissa.'

But Freddie was right. Having in turn spotted him from afar, Clarissa now raced across the grass to greet Freddie. Lowering him to the ground, Barney watched them clumsily hugging each other. If Freddie had owned a tail, it would be wagging every bit as frantically as Clarissa's.

It was like one of those reunion programmes on television.

Dev, wearing an ancient navy polo shirt and jeans, strolled over to join them. He took off his sunglasses and smiled at the sight of Freddie and Clarissa rolling joyfully together on the grass.

'Look at them. You'd think they hadn't seen each other for years.'

'We're taking Freddie to the children's playground,' said Barney, every inch the proud father. 'He loves the slide.'

'He's grown.' Dev nodded at Freddie, with his shock of white-blond hair and dazzling blue eyes. It had been a month since he'd moved out of the hotel. 'You're back in the cottage now?'

'Oh, for ages,' said Mel. 'Since just after you left. Everything's great,' she added. 'Thanks to you.'

Dev shoved his hands in his back pockets; he didn't want to get into another round of we're so gratefuls. If he was honest, he wished he hadn't bumped into Barney and Mel today. The last few weeks had been hard enough without this. But now that they were here, he may as well ask the question that had been occupying practically his every waking thought for the past month.

'So, how is everyone? Busy at the hotel?'

Actually, that wasn't the question. He was being subtle, leading up to it.

'Really busy.' Barney nodded vigorously. 'You wouldn't believe it. Five major functions in the last week alone. Every room's booked. We're rushed off our feet.'

'Daisy must be pleased.' Dev took an imperceptible breath and said, 'How are they, by the way? Daisy and Josh?'

That was the question.

Barney looked puzzled for a moment, then light dawned.

'I'd forgotten, you left before it all happened. Josh has gone. He and Tara left a fortnight ago.'

Now it was Dev's turn to frown. 'Josh and *Tara*? Where have they gone?'

'America. Together. Well, not exactly together. After Josh and Daisy split up, he and Tara hooked up. It was around the time Maggie was holding the washing machine man hostage. Then when Josh had to leave to start his new job in Florida, he wanted Tara to go with him,' Barney explained. 'But she's decided to travel around the States for a few months first, with some friend of hers called Arabella.'

'Annabel,' Mel corrected. 'Her name's Annabel Cross-Calvert. But after their trip, Tara's going to join Josh.'

This was too much information in too short a space of time. Dev was still struggling to take in something Barney had said earlier.

'Hang on, I'm not with you. Are you telling me Josh and Daisy had split up *before* Maggie kidnapped the washing machine man?'

Barney turned to Mel. 'That's right, isn't it? Or have I made a mistake?'

'No, you're right.' Mel nodded, more interested in the expression on Dev's face. She wasn't sure quite what, but something was definitely going on here.

'And you'll never guess what else,' exclaimed Barney, his

491

eyes bright. 'Tara passed her driving test! Isn't that fant-astic?'

Dev echoed vaguely, 'Fantastic.'

'No, darling, Clarissa can't come with us.' Mel grabbed Freddie back by his dungaree straps as the two of them attempted to slope off down the hill. 'Dogs aren't allowed in the play-ground.'

'I mean, none of us thought she'd do it,' Barney chattered on.

Dev looked up, alarmed. 'Do what?'

'Pass her test!'

'Oh, right.' For a moment there he'd thought Barney was telling him Daisy had done something extraordinary.

Except she already had.

Chapter 63

Daisy checked her watch; five minutes before her next appointment.

Make-up, maybe that would help.

Delving into her desk drawer, she pulled out a small mirror, a worn down Guerlain lipstick in matte pink and her trusty powder compact. She could almost slap it on without resorting to a mirror – and the moment she glimpsed her reflection, she wished she had.

Weeugh, what a sight. Carry on like this and she'd end up giving Olive from *On The Buses* a run for her money. To amuse herself, Daisy pulled an Edvard Munch scream-face at her reflection, but it was actually too true to be funny. She'd lost weight, especially from her face, and it didn't suit her. The sparkle she'd always taken for granted had gone from her eyes. She was looking tired and drawn and no amount of matte-pink lipstick was going to help. Even her hair looked droopy and depressed, as if it could simply no longer be bothered.

Heaving a sigh, Daisy went through the slapping-it-on routine anyway, then dragged a comb through her hair for politeness' sake. Her three o'clock appointment – a late booking pencilled in yesterday by Pam – was with a Mr Smith, who would doubtless turn out to be as thrilling as he sounded.

Oh dear, she definitely needed to drum up more enthusiasm than this. But how, when she just felt so dead inside?

There was a knock at the door as Daisy checked the box under her desk. Hastily she swept her beautifying agents – ha! – back into the open drawer. Rising to her feet in order to greet Mr Smith, she called out, 'Come in.'

The next moment all the breath was knocked out of her lungs. It was Dev.

Oh no, this isn't fair, this *really* isn't fair . . .

'What are you doing here?' Shock had the unfortunate effect of making her voice wobbly. 'You should have phoned, I've got an appointment with—'

'Mr Smith. I know.' Gravely, Dev said, 'I changed my name by deed poll.'

Daisy discovered she no longer had blood in her veins, she had treacle. It wasn't moving round her body properly and her heart was banging like a drum.

'Dev. What's going on?'

He shrugged. 'We weren't exactly on the best of terms when I left. I didn't want you refusing to see me.'

'Sit down.' Waving at the chair on the other side of the desk, Daisy sat too. Rather suddenly. Why, oh why hadn't she washed her hair this morning? What on earth had possessed her to put on a *grey cardigan*?

Dev stayed standing, which put her at even more of a disadvantage. He was wearing a dark suit and a deep-blue shirt and there were certainly no bags under *his* eyes. Basically, he'd never looked more desirable in his life.

'I'd like to book one of the function rooms.' He paused. 'If that's all right with you.'

Daisy exhaled slowly. So it wasn't a social visit after all. Well, she could be businesslike.

'Another conference?'

'Wedding reception.'

Bonnggg. Oh God. Her hands began to tremble. All the colour drained from her face like milk through a sieve.

'You're getting married?' The words somehow stumbled out. If he'd told her he was about to have a sex change she couldn't have been more shocked.

'When you arrange a wedding reception, that's the general idea.' Dev waited, his dark eyes never leaving her face. 'Aren't you going to congratulate me?'

Daisy felt sick. It just went to show what an idiot she was. While she'd spent the last month not eating and pining miserably for him, Dev had been out enjoying himself so much with some gorgeous young thing that he'd realised he wanted to marry her.

Well, let's face it, she was hardly likely to be some ugly old thing.

'Congratulations.' It was hard to get the word out. Why did it have to be so long?

'Thanks. How's Josh, by the way?'

Small talk, how civilised. Just what she needed right now.

'He's great.' Daisy forced a smile. By chance, she'd had a postcard from Josh this morning telling her just how great everything was. The newly built golf complex was, apparently, out of this world.

'Where is he?'

'Playing golf.' A guess, but undeniably a good guess.

Dev nodded. Finally he said, 'You forgot to mention he's in Florida.'

Oh shit.

Daisy clicked and unclicked the ballpoint pen she was twisting between her fingers. Click. Unclick. Click.

'I bumped into Barney and Mel yesterday, in Bath,' Dev went on.

Terrific.

'Really.'

'Why didn't you tell me it was all over between you and Josh?'

It was horribly reminiscent of being asked by the head teacher why you hadn't done your homework. Attempting to stare past him – and feeling like a caught-out fourteen-year-old – Daisy muttered, 'I just didn't.'

'You lied to me.' Dev shook his head. 'You used Josh as an excuse not to see me again. Since Barney told me, I've been trying to figure it out.' He paused. 'And now I think I have.'

Not liking the sound of this at all, Daisy resorted to flippancy. 'Maybe you're just a lousy lay.'

The look he gave her made her stomach squirm with lust.

'Except we both know that isn't true.'

Getting desperate now, Daisy blurted out, 'So who are you marrying?'

'You idiot.' A flicker of amusement crossed Dev's face. 'I'm not getting married.'

Not getting married. Daisy was beginning to feel light-headed.

'No? So why are you here?'

'I told you.' He moved closer to the desk. 'I've finally worked it out.'

'And?'

His voice softened. 'Daisy, listen to me. I'm not Steven.'

Her heart was by this time leaping erratically, like a dancer with absolutely no sense of rhythm.

'What's that supposed to mean?'

'Come on. You *know*. What happened between us the other week wasn't a casual fling. It meant as much to you as it did to me. And it scared you witless,' Dev carried on remorselessly, 'because you'd made some kind of pact with yourself never to get involved with anyone who could end up hurting you. Like Steven did.'

All true. He was so right. Helplessly, Daisy shrugged. 'Doesn't that make sense?'

'Sense? It's been driving me bloody insane! *You've* been driving me insane,' Dev exclaimed, 'ever since the first day I met you. Can you even begin to understand how frustrating it's been, having to stand back and do nothing, knowing you were with someone who didn't make you as happy as I knew I could?'

Daisy bit her lip, unable to speak. She'd certainly learned her lesson there. Having deluded herself that she and Josh could be happy together, she now knew better. Relationships – proper relationships – didn't work like that. It had to be all or nothing.

Dev was *all*, and that was scary. But nothing was utterly pointless.

'I've never felt like this about anyone in my life.' A muscle flickered in Dev's jaw. 'I love you, and I've never said that to anyone before. This last month has been . . . well, I can't tell you how bad. Not seeing you has been worse than seeing you with Josh.' He pulled a face. 'Which is saying something.'

Silence. Finally Daisy whispered, 'Me too.'

He looked down at her. 'Me too what?'

'All of it. Everything you just said. *Me too*.' Daisy couldn't believe she was doing this. She couldn't help it. Unsteadily, she pushed back her chair.

Dev's arms came round her and she clung to him, hot tears of relief threatening to spill over. Because basically, if not being with Dev had made her this miserable, what did she have to lose?

She may as well take the plunge and risk it. Heavens, she might even end up happy!

And he really was . . . *mmm* . . . an exceedingly good kisser.

It was some time before he pulled away.

'So is that a yes?' murmured Dev. 'We'll give it a go?'

Daisy smiled and wiped her eyes. 'What the hell. Why not?'

He really wasn't Steven.

'You won't regret this.' Dev sounded relieved. 'You have no idea how scary it was, coming here today.'

Scared? *Dev?*

'But you said you'd worked it out!'

'In theory, yes. But it wasn't until I mentioned the wedding reception that I knew for sure.' Clearly entertained, he said, 'You should have seen your face.'

'Very clever. Anyway,' Daisy retaliated, 'I didn't believe you for a second.'

'I tell you what. You don't lie to me any more and I won't lie to you.'

Belatedly remembering something else she had to tell him, Daisy said, 'How's Clarissa?'

Dev looked amused. 'Just the same. Bossy as ever. I left her in the car, in case you paid more attention to her than you did me.' He waited. 'She's missed you terribly, you know.'

'I've missed her. Still, she'll have someone else to boss around now.' As she spoke, Daisy was reaching beneath the desk, sliding out the cardboard box she had checked on earlier.

'Someone else? Don't tell me you're pregnant – oh my God.' Dev's expression changed as she folded back a corner of blue and white striped blanket.

A pair of coal-black eyes blinked bemusedly up at him. Beneath the rest of the blanket, a tail cautiously began to wag.

Daisy, scooping the little dog into her arms, kissed the top of his head before proudly presenting him to Dev.

'This is how much I missed Clarissa. I found him at the same rescue centre. His name's Clive.'

Having been woken up, Clive squirmed and licked Dev's hand with enthusiasm. With his sleek black coat and chunky wriggling body, he resembled a fat baby seal.

'Any particular breed?' Dev only said it to be polite; the puppy was clearly a hybrid through and through. Although the length of the body suggested a touch of dachshund.

'He's just Clive.' Lovingly, Daisy kissed the dog's funny pointy nose. 'He's unique.'

'And you keep him in a cardboard box,' Dev observed. 'A battered Ambrosia Creamed Rice box at that. Classy.'

'I bought him a proper basket, but he won't stay in it. He likes this one best.'

'Clive and Clarissa,' Dev mused, then turned as they both heard frantic scratching on the other side of the office door.

When he opened it, Clarissa catapulted into the room. Pam, looking flustered and wringing her plump hands, said, 'I'm sorry, she just came charging through reception . . .'

'I left the car window open. She must have squeezed through. No problem,' said Dev.

Quivering with interest, Pam peered past him at Daisy. 'Everything OK in here?'

'Absolutely fine.' Dev smiled and firmly closed the door.

Spotting the alien creature in Daisy's arms, Clarissa briskly shot into reverse.

'I bet everyone's taking bets out in reception,' Dev remarked drily, 'wondering how we're getting on.'

'Never mind us. How are these two going to get along?'

With a joyous bark, Clive thumped his tail and wriggled to get

499

down. Quivering with alarm, Clarissa flattened herself against the far wall.

'She's not sure yet,' said Daisy with a grin. 'She thinks she likes him, but she hasn't quite made up her mind.'

'Woof,' barked Clive, desperate to win Clarissa over.

'She just needs a bit of time,' Daisy explained.

'Woof woof *woof*.' Clive writhed frantically in her arms.

'It's OK, sweetheart,' Daisy spoke in soothing tones as Clarissa eyed him warily, 'he's not going to hurt you.'

'Now who do they remind me of?' said Dev.

JILL MANSELL

Falling for You

NHS specs, unfortunate hair and wonky teeth were the curse of Maddy Harvey's teenage years. Thankfully she's blossomed since then.

But when she meets Kerr McKinnon one starry summer's night . . . well, that's when the problems really start. Because everyone in Ashcombe knows what happened eleven years ago and her mother, Marcella, would rather tear that family to pieces with her bare hands than see Maddy with a McKinnon.

And, OK, maybe Marcella isn't her real mother, but Maddy owes her so much. How can she possibly go against Marcella's wishes? It's Romeo and Juliet all over again. Quick, hide those sharp knives and that little bottle of poison . . .

Acclaim for Jill Mansell's novels:

'A romantic romp full of larger than life characters' *Express*

'A sure-fire bestseller from the queen of chicklit' *Heat*

'An exciting read about love, friendship and sweet revenge – fabulously fun' *Home & Life*

0 7553 0485 3 (A format)
0 7553 3626 8 (B format)

headline
review

JILL MANSELL

The One You Really Want

Nancy can't quite believe it when her Christmas present from her husband turns out to be a lawnmower. She knows for a fact that Jonathan's been spending a *lot* of money on jewellery. So who's got the diamonds?

Nancy's best friend, Carmen, gave up on romance when she lost her adored husband. What Carmen really needs is a man to wake her up – but choosing the right one isn't going to be easy.

Mia's just arrived in London to live with her dad. Once she's met the potential stepmother-from-hell he's dating, she's determined to play Cupid – but her wayward arrows are just as likely to cause chaos as to ease the path of true love . . .

Acclaim for Jill Mansell's novels:

'Delightfully scurrilous, unpredictable and utterly entertaining' *Daily Record*

'A delightful reworking of the Romeo and Juliet story set in the English countryside. An ideal Valentine's read' *Daily Express*

'A sure-fire bestseller from the queen of chicklit' *Heat*

0 7553 0488 8 (A format)
0 7553 3250 4 (B format)

headline
review

JILL MANSELL

Making Your Mind Up

Lottie can't quite believe what's happened.

When you're a teenager in love with a wildly unsuitable boy, you expect your parents to object. But Lottie's thirty now, a fully fledged grown-up, and she never imagined her children doing the same when she met Tyler Klein. He isn't wildly unsuitable either, he's a catch. But as far as Nat and Ruby are concerned, he's the devil incarnate.

What's a girl to do? Is she only allowed to associate with men who meet with their approval? And doesn't she already have enough to worry about, what with errant ex-husband Mario up to his old tricks, beloved boss Freddie determined to catch up with old friends before life catches up with him, and best friend Cressida brazenly propositioning strangers in shops?

Everyone else needs sorting out. Well, that's fine – it's what Lottie's best at. Until the day she discovers that an attack of the hiccups can have the power – just possibly – to change your life . . .

Acclaim for Jill Mansell's novels:

'A delightful re-working of the Romeo and Juliet story . . . An ideal Valentine's read' *Daily Express*

'Three women with three very different experiences of love make for a fantastic chick-lit novel' *Sun*

'A sure-fire bestseller from the queen of chick-lit' *Heat*

0 7553 3109 5 (A format)

0 7553 0491 8 (B format)

headline
review